The Cast Of A Stone

A Novel

Published at last.

This book is a work of fiction. Names, characters, places and incidents are the product of the author's imagination, or used fictitiously. Any resemblance to events, locales or persons, living or dead, is coincidental.

Copyright 2013 Avril Borthiry
All rights reserved

avrilborthiry.com

This book contains strong language and adult situations.

Chapter 1

Norfolk, England, 1247AD

"I've come for the child, Alicia."

The words, like Alexander's swallowed pride, tasted bitter.

"I've come for her," he repeated, needing assurance. Alicia did not give it, nor could she. Her grave was more recent than the others in the churchyard, but just as silent.

Why, in God's holy name, had he acquiesced? Alexander knew nothing of raising children - a female child at that. Worse yet, this was a fragile bairn, unweaned and not thriving, anchored to the mortal world by a frail thread. He'd been told she'd likely not see autumn, and the summer solstice had already passed a fortnight since. It might not be long, then, till her wretched little soul succumbed.

A blessing, perhaps, for all involved.

His gut tightened with shame at the merciless thought. *Christ.*

Bile, sour as vinegar, burned Alexander's throat as he followed the well-trodden path to the hospital. Twelve stone apostles looked down from their niches above the arched entrance, their saintly expressions unchanged from his previous visit two days before. At that time he had merely peered into the crib, curious to see Alicia's 'miracle' child.

He saw no miracle; only a sickly little girl in need of one.

Oh, he wouldn't deny the sight of the hapless bairn had affected him. He was not, after all, without a heart.

Yet he'd chosen to leave her and walk away, closing his ears to her pitiful cries. So what had brought him back?

He slowed his step as a fresh wave of doubt, unbidden and thick as tidal fog, crept into his troubled mind.

Curse his conscience and damn his honour. It was foolish to think he could do this. His consent to Alicia's dying request had been a simple act of solace - words spoken to ease the pain of her final moments. Nothing more.

Torn by fresh indecision, he paused beneath the archway, straddling the line between daylight and shadow. He looked back toward the main church and beyond to the graveyard, where Alicia lay. Then he turned and peered into the obscure recesses of the infirmary, his eyes seeking out the door to the child's humble cell. It stood slightly ajar, he noticed. He wrinkled his nose. Sickness had an odour. So, he mused, did hopelessness.

Both could be found in abundance within these sacred walls.

A chant escaped from the sanctified confines of the church. The harmonized voices of the monks carried heavenward, filling the air with their stunning clarity. Alexander sighed, and allowed baseless reasoning to stifle his inner voice. The bairn could do worse than to die in such a place, cradled by godliness and piety. If he left her there, at least she'd be close to her mother at the end, may God rest both their souls.

"Forgive me, child," he muttered, the pendulum in his mind swinging to dissent, "but you're not my responsibility." He ignored a sharp stab of guilt and took a determined step back the way he came.

One step only. The sudden and desperate cry of a baby girl stopped him from taking another. He closed his eyes and bit down. Hard.

Afternoon shadows danced on Alicia's grave, which lay beneath the outstretched branches of an ancient oak. Alexander took a deep breath, savouring the sound of wind in the leaves; a soft accompaniment to the continued chant of the monks. He focused inward, trying to unravel a tangled knot of emotions.

At least all his doubts had disappeared and the bairn no longer cried. To Alexander's surprise, she had ceased her wailing the moment he lifted her from the crib. In that same moment, his commitment to her became as steadfast as the northern mountains. True, he had set out on an unknown road, but there would be no turning back. Not now.

He was already lost, heart and soul, to the little bundle resting safely in his arms. Her dark eyes, not yet bestowed with God's chosen colour, stared up at him. She hiccupped and lifted one corner of her lips in the semblance of a smile. Captivated, Alexander stroked a knuckle across her cheek. Instinctively, her face turned toward his touch, her eager mouth seeking a source of sustenance. A hopeful sign, he thought, considering he'd been told the bairn showed little interest in feeding.

"Nay, you'll find no milk in there, lass." He chuckled. "Nor anywhere else on my person. I'll find you some though, don't fret."

She pouted, and thrust a tiny hand skyward as if reaching for him. He put his forefinger in her palm and her fingers closed around it. The grip was feeble, but determined. Alexander hoped it represented the child's hold on life.

"A miracle child..."

"Your daughter's a scrawny wee bairn, Alicia." He drew back the swaddling and eyed the fragile little body with a frown. "Like a skinned rabbit."

A ray of sunlight tumbled into the child's face, making her flinch. Alexander turned to shade her, but not before a glint against the child's chest caught his eye.

"What's this now?" he murmured, easing the fine gold chain from the folds of her blankets. He looked to see what it held. A crucifix, perhaps? Nay, not that. A ring. A small gold ring.

Alicia's wedding band.

He fingered it, trying to make sense of its significance, tears stinging the back of his eyes. He looked down at the freshly turned earth, his chest heavy with a sudden wave of anguish. A question formed on his tongue, one that had lingered in his mind since Alicia's death. He knew he would never know the answer, but he asked it anyway. He would likely be asking it forever.

"Why, Alicia?"

A loud caw came from the branches above him, a rude interruption that served to straighten Alexander's spine. He pocketed the ring and turned his attention back to the child.

"So," he said, tucking the swaddling around the child's body. "Where shall we make our home, little lass? I'm not of a mind to stay in Norfolk."

Another caw cut through the air, followed by a flutter of wings. Alexander lifted his gaze to watch a crow circling overhead, an austere black shape against the placid blue sky. The bird turned and soared upwards, higher and higher, before disappearing over the church roof.

Heading north.

Alexander nodded. "North it is, then. Does that meet with your approval, child?"

"Her name is Emma..."

"Emma," he murmured, stroking the soft honey-coloured fuzz on her scalp. "And you shall call me *Cùra*. It means 'guardian', for that is what I am."

Chapter 2

Cumbria, England. Sixteen years later.

"Stay...right...there." Emma drew the bowstring and took careful aim. The rabbit, bright-eyed, appeared to obey and settled into a vigilant crouch. A fine fat fellow he was; sitting in a patch of sunlight next to his bramble-bush home. He would make a fine stew for them that evening. His ears twitched as did his nose. "By all the saints," he said, "I'm not yet ready to die."

Emma's shot went wide, the arrow plunging into the forest. The startled rabbit skittered back into his thorny fortress.

"What in God's name...?" She froze, her heart all but leaping into her throat. Rabbits didn't speak. Who, then, had spoken? The hair on her neck lifted as she spun around, seeking the source of the voice.

Sunlight pirouetted through the trees and danced on the forest floor, obscuring detail. Emma held her breath, closed her eyes and tilted her head to listen, seeking direction. Moments later, her lids flicked open and she looked to the right.

There. A mutter. A groan. A cough, strained and weak.

Emma slid another arrow from the quiver and readied her bow. With a hunter's stealth, she edged forward, heart racing, nerves sharp. She pressed her spine against the trunk of a large oak and drew the bowstring again. Arrow primed and lungs locked with a fresh gulp of air, Emma peered around the tree into the clearing beyond.

A young man sat propped up against a decaying log. With a quick sweep of her eyes, Emma assessed him. His clothing bore the indisputable mark of wealth and nobility as did the finely forged sword resting in his right hand. His chin rested on his chest, his eyes were closed, and damp tendrils of chestnut hair clung to the sides of his face and forehead.

His left hand was splayed across a large and ominous stain on the front of his shirt. Blood, glistening in the sun, trickled between his fingers, carving a slick trail across his belly and thigh before seeping into the forest floor.

Emma released a slow breath and glanced around the clearing. Whoever this man was, he appeared to be alone.

And bleeding to death.

She relaxed the bowstring and stepped out from behind the tree. At the sound of her footfall, the man lifted his head to fix her with a dark-eyed stare. To her surprise, he offered her a weak smile.

"I might have known it would be you," he mumbled.

Confused, she shook her head. "Me? Ah...you know me?"

"Aye." He managed a wobbly grin. "My mother told me stories about you when I was a child."

"Your mother...?" She frowned. The man was obviously delirious. "Throw your sword away from your side, sir, or I shall not approach."

He looked puzzled. "As you wish. Although I can't imagine why you would consider my blade a threat. 'Tis help I need, not the bleeding corpse of a forest faerie at my feet."

"I'm no forest faerie," she said. "Your sword, if you please."

Pain twisted his features as he tossed the weapon aside. With another careful glance around the clearing, Emma approached and knelt by him, placing her bow within easy reach. She lifted his hand from the wound, snatching her fingers away when he tried to grasp them. Yet his expression held no malice; only curiosity and a good measure of relief.

"You're real," he mumbled. "Praise be."

"Aye, I'm real enough. Keep still."

He flinched as she peeled the fabric from the large gash across his ribs.

"The wound isn't too deep," she said, noting the unnatural pallor of his skin, "but you've lost much blood. Sit forward if you can. We must remove your shirt."

"By all the saints, 'tis a royal shame." He leaned forward with a groan as she peeled his shirt from his arms. "Disrobed by a rare beauty and not enough blood left for an arousal."

Emma bit back a smile. "If I don't attend to your wound, you'll have no blood left at all."

She glanced around the clearing and leapt to her feet when her eyes found what they sought.

"What are they?" he asked, eyeing the leaves in her hands as she knelt beside him.

"They'll help staunch the bleeding." She rubbed the leaves between her palms until they leaked a rich dark juice. "Forgive me if I cause you further pain."

"You're forgiven, little faerie," he whispered, drawing a sharp breath as the leaves met the raw gash in his skin.

Aware of his eyes upon her, she folded his shirt and tied it around his ribs, knotting the sleeves to hold it in place. She, in turn, inspected him, curious about the identity of this injured man she had found. The fine condition of his body, as well as several old scars on his skin, pointed to military training. Emma had little doubt she knelt beside a knight. A small flutter arose in her belly - an unfamiliar, but not unpleasant, sensation.

"Who did this to you?" she asked. "Where's your horse? Your squire?"

His eyes sought a spot somewhere off in the trees. "I have no squire. My horse's body lies yonder. He took a slash to his neck during an attack upon me, yet carried me a good distance more before he dropped."

Emma sat back on her heels, her mind disturbed by the image he'd painted. "Who attacked you? Outlaws?"

"I think not, for they had swords." A bead of sweat trickled over his temple. "Outlaws use bows and arrows, as do green-eyed forest faeries, it seems."

How pale he looked. Emma knew he was fading. "Well, if you believe in faeries, you must also believe in magic. And we'll likely need some to get you back to my house. 'Tis not far, but you're very weak. Can you walk?"

"I think so." He grimaced. "But I would prefer my sword at my side, now you know I've no intent to harm you."

"Even with intent, I doubt you've the strength to use it." She passed it to him, grabbed her bow, and looped his arm around her shoulders. With a groan, he struggled to his feet.

"Take a moment to catch your breath," she said, aware of his pain. "Lean on me."

How small she felt beside him. The top of her head barely reached his shoulders.

"What is your name, sweet faerie?" he whispered through pale lips.

"Emma," she replied. "And yours?"

"Stephen." His weak voice scarcely carried to her ear. "Stephen de Montfort."

Other questions hovered on Emma's tongue, but she held them back. Speaking required the use of energy and she knew the man had precious little to spare. The questions would have to wait, assuming he lived through this. Emma pushed the alternative from her mind.

They set out, Emma's fingers clasping the large hand draped over her shoulder. She wondered who had attacked him and for what reason. Were they still searching for him? Perhaps he was a wanted man, a fugitive who had committed some despicable crime.

Yet she doubted it. Something about the mysterious stranger engendered a trust within her. His eyes were honest and his voice carried only an undercurrent of pain, not deceit.

After a while they reached a stream, one of several that ran away from the nearby river. The small beck bounced along its gravel path, bubbling with silver and gold lights. A good stride could easily carry a healthy man – or woman – from one boggy bank to the other.

"Wet feet." She raised her brows and looked up at him. "Unless you can stride over."

"Thought you might unfold your wings and fly me across," he murmured, his breath brushing her hair.

"Wet feet it is, then. Careful. The stones are slippery."

"Is it... much...farther?"

The obvious effort to speak and the tremble in his body spoke of the man's increasing weakness. Emma's legs trembled also, and her shoulders burned with the effort of supporting him.

"Nay, just over the next wee rise." Under the circumstances, it might as well have been a mile. " Do you wish to stop for a moment?"

"I'll stop when you do."

"A bit farther yet, then. I'm stronger than I look."

She felt his chest shudder as he took in a breath. "Aye, little one." He squeezed her hand again. "That you are. I owe you my life."

Tears came to Emma's eyes, for she knew the man might not yet live. Her resolve to carry him remained as hard as granite, but her physical strength gave out within sight of her house. She cursed as her legs buckled, and her charge dropped to his knees with a soft groan.

"Have no fear," she said. "I'll fetch help."

He grabbed her wrist. "Who?"

"My guardian."

She resisted the urge to struggle against the bloodied hand holding her in place. "Alexander is a good man. He'll help you. Please let me go, Stephen de Montfort."

Bright with fever, his eyes burned into hers. "Swear you'll return, little faerie." His fingers released their grip, leaving his blood upon her skin. "Swear it."

Emma shouldered her bow and paused in the doorway of the barn, squinting into the dark interior, breathless lungs sucking greedily at the air. A man sat just inside on a low stool, his head bent over a harness, his large hands surprisingly nimble as they cleaned the soft brown leather. Thick dark hair curled with abandon around his face as he focused on his task. When Emma's shadow fell across his lap, he lifted his head and studied her through slate-grey eyes.

"What's wrong, *a ghràidh?*" He frowned. "Why are you out of breath?"

"I need you, *Cùra*. 'Tis a matter of urgency." Emma gestured to the sword leaning against the wall. "Bring Darius."

"Urgency?" Alex dropped the harness and shot to his feet, snatching at her bloodstained wrist. "What's this? Are you hurt?"

"Nay, 'tis not my blood. I'll explain on the way, but we must hurry."

Alex knelt by the unconscious body of the knight and rested his fingertips on the man's neck.

"The pulse is steady." He moved his hand to Stephen's forehead. "But he's beset by fever. Here, take his sword."

Emma took the weapon while Alex heaved the man's limp form across his shoulders.

"What you did was foolish, Emma." Alex's anger hardened his voice. "You should never have approached him."

"But I had my bow and I made him throw his sword aside."

"Even so, you should have fetched me. The man is a stranger, for God's sake. He might have hurt you. I thought I did teach you better."

"But he's a knight," she argued, "and badly wounded. He would not have hurt me."

"How do you know he's a knight? Is there a mark on him proclaiming knighthood? Besides, having title does not prevent a man from committing acts of evil. Nor is it wise to approach a wounded animal unprepared, be it man or beast. It was careless of you." Alex paused in front of the house, his breath harsh from exertion. "Open the door for me, child."

His words stung, and Emma pushed the door open with not a little resentment.

"I'm very sorry, *Cùra*." She gave an indignant sniff as Alex lowered Stephen's body onto the bed. "I believed I was doing the right thing."

Alex turned to her, his expression softening.

"You told me you were going to hunt rabbit for supper. Instead, you return with a wounded stranger. When I saw fear in your eyes and blood on your wrist, it shocked me, child. If anything should happen to you...." With a sigh, he shifted his gaze back to the man on the bed. "Prepare a poultice and find a needle and thread. Let's see if we can bring your mysterious knight back from death's door."

Chapter 3

Rain fell in abundance from the night sky, purring like a contented cat as it landed on the thatched roof. Alex welcomed the soft sound. It functioned as a cushion for the thoughts that discomforted his mind. He lay still as stone on the rough straw pallet that served as his bed. The wounded knight had taken Alex's bed, where he struggled against the clutches of a rampant fever, mumbling incoherent words through cracked lips.

Earlier, Alex had watched Emma push the needle into the man's torn skin, inserting twenty-three stitches neatly across the wound. It surprised him to see her aura brighten in intensity as she worked. It appeared this enigmatic stranger had reached out from his unconscious mind and touched her soul.

Second sight was not one of Alex's skills, but he didn't need it to know that fate had shifted its path since the previous day's dawn. Where this new path would lead he had yet to discover, but the calm waters of their existence rippled as if disturbed by the cast of a stone.

The darkness of night wrapped around him, but his sight adjusted to the shadows with little difficulty. His ears also picked up the slightest sound, which was why he had no trouble seeing or hearing Emma as she tiptoed from her room. She stumbled over a chair, making her presence all the more obvious. He smiled at the soft curse that drifted out of the shadows.

"Where are you going, *a ghràidh*?" He pushed himself onto one elbow, hearing Emma's breath snag in surprise.

"God save me, *Cùra*! I thought you slept."

"'Tis difficult to do so when I share a house with such a restless spirit. You're concerned for your patient?"

"Aye, I am. I want to check on him. I'm worried he might die."

"I've been listening to him all the while." Alex got to

his feet, arching his back into a stretch. "He still speaks from his dreams, but his breathing is less laboured than before."

"Still, if you have no objection, I should like to sit with him in case he awakens and has need of me."

"If he should awaken and I'm not at your side, you'll fetch me immediately. I'll have your word on this, child."

"You have it, *Cùra*."

Satisfied with her response, Alex lit a candle. "Fetch some cool water and cloths," he bade her. "I'll watch while you tend him."

Absorbed in her task, Emma whispered soft words of comfort to her unconscious patient, her slender form well hidden beneath her ankle-length nightshirt and the woollen shawl draped across her shoulders. A long thick braid, the colour of dark honey, hung down her back, a few stray tendrils softening the outline of her face and neck.

Alex bit back a sigh. Emma was no longer the little girl who would cling to his neck like a monkey, or fall asleep in his lap as he told her stories of faerie-folk and hidden treasure. A sudden twinge of possessiveness caught him by surprise. He sensed this stranger had affected her young heart.

Alex had instilled in her a healthy respect for the human form. Emma well understood the value and fragility of her virtue, and was not ignorant of the lustful ways of men. Yet, in contrast, Alex had also explained about the pleasure of love that God had bestowed upon man and woman. Such a gift, he told her, was not meant to be squandered.

The knight's sallow face tensed as Emma lifted the dressing from his wound. By the flicker of candle flame, Alex saw that the redness did not extend too far beyond the stitches.

"It looks well," he murmured. " I see no sign of infection."

"Yet he still has fever."

"Aye, but he's strong of form. With God's good grace, he'll rally."

"I pray for it."

Alex heard the longing in her voice and understood what it meant. "Emma, we know so little of him. He may not be what you believe him to be. Keep your mind open, child."

"But he had such honest eyes. I felt no fear in his presence."

"Aye, and he did you no harm, yet I'll reserve judgement until I've spoken with him myself." Alex glanced at the small window where the crude wooden shutters were cradled by the gentle light of dawn. "Are you hungry, *a ghràidh?*"

"Aye, I'm always hungry." She grinned at him, all at once a child again.

He grinned back at her over the candle flame, wondering if she had any idea how much he loved her. "I'll go and warm some bread. Finish here, then join me–"

A sudden prickle ran across the back of his neck. He drew a sharp breath and blew out the candle, his heart quickening.

"*Cùra?*" Emma blinked up at him. "What is it?"

"Riders approaching. Several of them."

"Do you think they're searching for him?"

"I fear so." Alex looked at Emma, her eyes wide in the twilight, and sensed her fear. His mind searched for a solution. *A ruse.* They needed a ruse.

A carved wooden box sat on a table by the window. He opened it and pulled out a small gold ring. "Put this on," he said. "Your third finger. Aye, like a wedding band."

He reached around her and lifted her shawl over her head. "And keep your hair hidden."

"Why?"

"Trust me. Stay behind me and let me speak. If you should have need to address me, do not call me cùra. As far as they're concerned, I'm your father. Do you understand?"

She nodded, her eyes still wide. Outside, the ground rumbled with the sound of many hooves and the air rattled with the voices of men. Alex reached over and cupped his hand to her cheek.

"Have no fear, child. I'll not let any harm come to you." He glanced at the figure on the bed. "Or him."

A thick curtain of rain subdued the jingle of harness and murmur of voices. The voices ceased, and Alex felt Emma's body flinch as a fist pounded against solid oak.

"Come with me." He lifted a corner of her shawl up to her chin. "Hold this across your mouth as you might a mask. I would have them believe we have sickness in the house."

The fist pounded again, a grim sound that found its way into every dark corner. This time it had a voice attached to it.

"Open the door in the name of the king!"

Alex raised a brow and gave Emma a wry smile. "In the name of the king, is it?"

He took his sword and leant it against the wall, hidden from the visitors yet well within his reach. Then he grabbed a cloth from the table and lifted the locking-bar from its wooden cradle. Blessing Emma with a wink, he opened the door with a confident tug.

The speed of the action apparently surprised the man standing there, who cursed, took a step back, and pulled his sword. His dark brows drew together in a menacing frown over a pair of equally dark eyes as rain dripped from the ends of his long black hair.

"We seek an escaped fugitive and would search your house and barn." The man peered past them into the room beyond. "Stand aside that we may enter."

Alex's eyes raked over the group of men, five in total and all armoured. He saw no identifying banner.

"A fugitive?" He lifted the cloth to cover his mouth. "God save us. I thought you had come to warn us of the sickness, but I fear you're too late for that. I know nothing of any fugitive. Is he dangerous? Please, good sirs, search as you will. I would not harbour such a man, intentionally or otherwise."

He stood aside as if to allow them access. Behind him, Emma sneezed into her shawl. The man hesitated.

"Who is that?" he asked. "And of what sickness do you speak?"

Alex glanced briefly at Emma before turning back to meet the man's gaze. "This is my daughter. 'Tis her husband who has been sorely afflicted these past two days."

"Step forward, girl," said the man to Emma. "I would see your face."

She stepped forward, the thin plaid shawl covering her mouth.

"What is this illness?" the man asked. "Let me see this husband of yours."

"As you wish, my lord." Emma coughed. "I believe he suffers from naught more than a wicked ague and a bad attack of boils. He sleeps, but you may certainly look in on him."

"Boils?"

A murmur ran through the men.

Emma nodded. "Aye. Ugly things, they are, with a nasty odour. I've never seen the like before. But he's a strong man, and will rally. Will he not, father?"

She coughed again with feigned breathlessness.

Alex put his arm around Emma's shoulders and kissed her forehead. "With God's good grace, aye." He turned back to the men. "I beg you, gentlemen, complete your search and leave us be. We've been up most of the night and are in need of some rest."

The man hesitated. "We'll leave you in peace," he said finally. "But be warned, peasant. The man we seek is wounded, dangerous and not to be trusted. Should he come to your door, show him no mercy."

"May I know what this man has done?" asked Alex.

"He's a murderer and a thief."

"Indeed? Then I hope you catch him quickly. Is there someone I may inform should I see a wounded stranger hereabouts?"

"Aye." The man turned and clambered onto his horse. "You may send word to Lowland Chase. Bring us his lifeless body and you'll be rewarded."

Alex felt Emma tense at his side and gave her shoulder a soft squeeze. They both watched as the horses rode off into the damp grey light of dawn.

"You did well, *a ghràidh*." His lips twitched with a smile. "'Tis strange I should commend you for lying, but...boils?"

Emma grinned. "I thought it sounded plague-like"

He chuckled, steered her into the house, and closed the door. "You were most convincing. So, your knight is a thief and a murderer. What do you say to that?"

"I say they lie." Emma's tone was adamant. "He is no murderer."

"Then I wonder," Alex mused, "what he has stolen."

Chapter 4

The aroma of warm bread caressed the damp morning air in the house. It eased Emma's solemn mood with a touch of comfort.

Despite her relief at fooling the men, their visit had frightened her. She stood at Stephen's bedside and watched the slow rise and fall of his chest. Questions about him still burdened her mind as she reached over and touched his hand. His skin felt cooler, yet he showed no sign of returning from the dark realm of unconsciousness.

"He's a mystery yet to be solved." Alex's quiet voice spoke from the doorway. "Come away, little one. There's naught else you can do for him at the moment."

Emma sighed and followed Alex into the kitchen. She flopped down on a chair and watched as he pulled a golden-crusted loaf of bread from the small stone oven.

"You must be very tired," he said, setting the bread on the table. "It's been a long night."

His selfless concern wrenched harshly on her weary emotions.

"I'm sorry, *Cùra*."

A frown replaced his smile. "For what, pray?"

"I fear my action has brought danger to you. To us."

"Possibly. You should have come to me first, although I'd have still brought him back here." He pushed the bread toward her. "If you must know, I'm proud of you. Eat, then rest. I'm going out for a while."

"Where?"

"Back to where you found your knight."

"Why?"

"Because if he did steal something, he no longer has it with him. Perhaps he hid it close to where he fell."

"But how do you know what you're looking for?"

"I'm probably looking for something that has no place in a forest."

Alex raised an eyebrow. "Do you doubt I could find such an item, if it exists?"

Emma grinned at his indignant expression. "Nay, Cùra. I would never doubt your abilities."

"I'm pleased to hear it. Bar the door as soon as I leave and do not open it for anyone." With a tilt of his head, he gestured toward the bedroom. "And be wary around him, should he awaken."

"I do not fear him." She watched Alex settle his sword belt around his hips. "Danger might be his companion, but he's not dangerous himself."

He slid his sword into the scabbard. "Perhaps not." He kissed the top of her head. "But be careful. I'll return soon."

Emma dropped the lock-bar securely into its cradle. Anxiety had subdued her appetite, but she nibbled at the warm bread and sipped some hot mint tea. Afterwards, she returned to Stephen's side, dragging a chair to the bed so she could sit and watch him.

He rested peacefully. Emma took the time to study him, frowning at the scars of battle marking his skin. His jaw was dark with stubble, his hair dull from the fever.

"Stephen de Montfort." She leaned toward him. "Can you hear me?" But he did not respond.

Emma yawned and folded her fingers around his. She dropped her head onto the bed and listened to the rain playing a gentle lullaby on the roof. Moments later, sleep dragged her into uncharted dreams.

When she awoke, it was to the sensation of something touching her hair. With a small cry of surprise, she sat up and looked into a pair of soft hazel eyes.

"So." Stephen's fingertips trailed lightly across her cheek. "You were not a dream. Thank God. When I saw you in the forest, I thought you were an invention of my feverish mind."

"You're awake." Emma rubbed the sleep from her eyes. "At last."

He smiled at her. "Aye, my little faerie, so it would seem. Where am I? Have I been ill a while?"

"You're in my house and you have been asleep less than a day. We have taken care of you. Your wound is clean."

"We?"

"My guardian and I."

"Then I owe you both my life. Where's this guardian of yours?"

"He's right here."

Emma jumped at the sound of Alex's voice. She leapt to her feet and whirled around to see him standing in the doorway.

"*Cùra*! But the door is still barred. How did you –?"

Alex interrupted her with a raised hand. He moved to her side and scrutinized the man on the bed.

"My name is Alexander Mathanach." His chin lifted. "Before I welcome you to our home, there are things I would know about you. I trust you'll respect me with honest answers to my questions, since our safety has already been threatened by your presence."

"*Cùra*, please," Emma pleaded, tugging at Alex's sleeve. "He's still weak."

"Threatened?" Stephen winced as he tried to sit up. "Who has threatened you?"

Alex offered his hand to the wounded man. "That's what I would have you tell me."

Stephen leaned forward, his breath ragged, while Emma arranged the pillows at his back.

"There." Emma placed a gentle hand on his shoulder. "You can lie back now."

"My thanks." Stephen's raspy voice was followed by an attack of coughing.

He cursed, his face twisting with obvious pain. "A drink, I beg you."

Emma scurried from the room, returning moments later with a goblet of ale. He drank with vigour and thanked her again, this time with a smile.

"I'm sorry you've been threatened, little faerie." He handed her the empty goblet. "I would not want anyone to harm you."

"I shall not let anyone harm her," Alex said, his eyes narrowing. "You will tell me who might wish to do so and why."

Stephen met Alex's gaze. "You're a Scot," he observed. "I hear hints of the Highlands in your voice."

Alex ignored the statement. "Five armed men came here this morning. They sought the whereabouts of a wounded man – a thief and a murderer. Are you that man?"

"I'm likely the man they seek, but I'm no murderer." Stephen glanced down at his wound. "I killed two of them, but only in self defence. They did this to me and struck a death blow to my horse."

"Aye, I found the animal's carcass, but naught else. What did you steal?"

"There's naught else to find." Stephen pressed a finger to his temple. "What I took from them is in here. I merely obtained information. I act in the name of the king."

"Indeed? How interesting. The men this morning also claimed to act in the name of the king."

Stephen chuckled and looked down at the goblet with a gentle shake of his head. "The bastard has balls," he murmured.

Alex raised a brow. "Which bastard would that be?"

"The one who has leased Lowland Chase."

"You will give me his name."

A flash of resentment ran across Stephen's face.

"You neither speak nor act like a peasant, Alexander. Why demand his name? 'Tis of no consequence to you."

Alex curled his lips into a thin smile. "You have yet to convince me of your worth, young knight, and there will be consequences to you if you do not answer my questions."

"You threaten me?" Stephen asked, his eyes wide with surprise.

"This is my house," Alex replied. "Do not give me cause to remove you from it."

Emma gasped. "*Cùra*! You would not do such a thing. He's wounded."

"Nay, don't fret, little one." Stephen smiled at her. "I've no desire to leave your sweet attention. It matters not if I tell you my pursuer's identity. 'Tis a mercenary knight by the name of Argante. Richard Argante."

Emma heard the breath catch in Alex's throat and looked at him. His face had paled and a small muscle twitched in his jaw. She laid her hand on his arm.

"Are you alright, *Cùra*?"

"Christ help us," he whispered.

"You know him? How?" Stephen leaned forward, the sudden movement causing him to grunt in pain. "'Tis becoming clear to me you're no peasant, Alexander Mathanach. So, then, who are you?"

"'Tis I who ask the questions," Alex replied, "and I would know what information you have stolen from this mercenary knight."

Stephen shook his head. "I'm sworn to secrecy."

Alex gave a grim smile. "Is that so? Then let me tell you, Stephen de Montfort, that apart from defenceless young virgins, Richard Argante only ever pursued one other thing with ill-met obsession. I suspect he still pursues it, which is why he's wandering around these northern hills. Am I right?"

"I know not of what you speak." Stephen sank back into his pillows, his voice barely a whisper.

"Oh, I think you do. I speak of a magical object which fell from the sky many centuries ago, a stone about the size of a pigeon's egg, as green as an emerald, and laced with blood-red veins." Alex leaned against the wall and folded his arms. "How am I doing so far?"

Stephen grew pale and wide-eyed, while his breathing turned rapid and shallow.

Emma, bristling with an inexplicable desire to protect the wounded knight, cast a pleading glance at Alex. "Please stop this. He's not yet well enough."

Stephen's voice finally escaped. "Who the hell are you, Alexander?"

Alex shrugged. "No one you need fear, lad. Argante, however, is a dangerous man. I don't like to think of him living within a day's ride of here. Indeed, I don't like to think of him living at all."

He turned to Emma and for a brief moment she saw a dark shadow in the depths of his eyes. She shuddered inwardly. Who was Richard Argante? Why had she never heard Alex mention him before?

"*A ghràidh.*" A smile softened his face as he placed a gentle hand on her cheek. "Heat some broth and warm some bread. I'm sure our guest is hungry. I'll be outside for the next while. There's something I must do. Call for me if you need me."

"But, *Cùra –*"

"I know you have questions, child. I'll speak with you later." He looked at Stephen. "And I'll speak with you too, young knight. You must decide to trust me and tell me what you've learned from Argante. Your presence here puts us at great risk. Since it will be a few days yet before you're fit to leave, the least you can do is to honour us by speaking the truth."

Chapter 5

A pretty song wandered through the bed-chamber doorway, each note rich and pure. At first, Stephen thought he dreamt it, so angelic was the voice. Only when he opened his eyes did he understand it to be mortal. The hair on his arms and chest lifted in a shameless and exquisite arousal.

Ignoring a twinge of pain, he sat up and swung his legs over the side of the bed. An image of Emma sponging down his body lit up his thoughts and brought about another exquisite response. He glanced down at himself, his lips curving into a smile.

Apparently, his blood loss had been replenished.

Emma's sweet singing beckoned, but Stephen hesitated. To step into the kitchen stark-naked, with his desire jutting out like a jousting pole would, he knew, not be wise. In truth, he had no wish to startle the little maid, nor did he relish the thought of meeting a sword again should Alex appear and misinterpret his intentions. So he grabbed the only thing available to protect his modesty - the bed sheet.

Gritting his teeth against the pain, he rose to his feet. His idle legs trembled at the unaccustomed weight, yet it felt good to stand, to feel his strength returning. With slow steady steps he moved forward, grasping the sheet around him with one hand while reaching for the door frame with the other. At his touch the door drifted open, a noisy hinge betraying his presence. The singing stopped.

Emma turned to face him, her lips still parted by the unsung word, her eyes widening in surprise. Steam from the broth she stirred had bestowed a soft pink glow upon her cheeks and dampened the honey curls framing her face. She wiped a hand down the front of her apron, an innocent gesture ripe with guileless sensuality.

Sweet Heaven. What a glorious vision she is.

Stephen's legs buckled, but not from weakness. Emma apparently thought otherwise.

"Oh, nay!" she cried. "You should be abed, sir. You're not yet strong enough to leave it."

An easy smile slid across his face as he leaned against the door frame.

"I was brought to my feet by your sweet voice and now the sight of you threatens to bring me to my knees. 'Tis not my wound, but a very pleasant ache which makes my legs tremble, little faerie."

Emma cocked her head and smiled back at him. "Your tongue ails not at all, it seems. Likely because of all the honey which coats it." She gestured to the table. "Sit then, if you wish. The soup is warmed through."

Stephen glanced down at himself. "I would prefer to share your food dressed in something other than a bed sheet."

"Your clothes were bloodied beyond any hope. I'm sure my *cùra* will let you have some of his when he returns." She shrugged. "For now, the sheet will have to suffice. If you feel sickly, please tell me. I would not have you collapsing at the table."

"What does it mean, this '*cùra*'?" Stephen settled himself on a chair, tucking the sheet around him, his stomach growling with a sudden hunger.

"'Tis Gàidhlig, the language of the Scots. It means guardian or protector."

"And what is 'a gry'?"

"*A ghràidh* simply means 'my child'." Emma set a bowl of soup before him. Stephen curled his hands around it and raised it to his lips, taking a slow gulp of the rich broth.

He smiled at her. "Thank you. It's delicious."

She nodded and sat across from him, cradling a steaming bowl of her own.

"There's plenty more. Eat your fill."

Curiosity produced another question. "Who is he, Emma? Who is this '*cùra*' of yours?"

"Alexander is my guardian. He has cared for me since I was but a few weeks old." She took a sip of her soup. "Few men, I think, would be willing to do such a thing."

"So why did he do it? What happened to your parents?"

"My father was my *cùra's* good friend. He died in battle before my birth and my mother died right after it. Alexander made a vow to my mother that he would take care of me."

"Who were they? Your parents?"

She shifted in her chair. "You ask many questions, my lord. My father was a knight, my mother the daughter of a baron."

Stephen glanced around the humble cottage, her answer raising more questions in his mind. "So you're of noble blood?"

Emma sighed. "Who birthed me is not important. The blood of a beggar is as red as mine and just as warm."

Her words stirred his heart. "Aye, true enough."

The mystery of this beautiful girl fascinated him. Why would such a creature be hidden away in a Cumbrian forest? He reached for her hand, pleased when she didn't pull away.

"Have you always lived here, little one?"

She chewed on her bottom lip, a gesture both charming and disarming, that caused Stephen to shift in his seat.

"You overflow with questions, sir. Let me see if I can calm your rampant curiosity."

Aye, and curiosity was not the only rampant thing at that table.

Seemingly oblivious to his discomfort, Emma

continued. "I've seen sixteen summers in this forest. I'm skilled in archery and can handle a horse and a sword. I speak English, French, some Latin and some Gàidhlig. I read and write and I hate needlework with a passion." She smiled and pulled her hand away. "Any other questions must wait until my *cùra* returns. I expect he'll have questions for you, too. Please tell him the truth. Alex is an honourable and wise man. You have nothing to fear by confiding in him."

A soft gust of wind filled the room, allowed entry by the opening of the outer door. Alex stood on the threshold, a dark silhouette against the daylight.

"Thank you, Emma." He gave her a smile and cast a sweeping glance over Stephen. "And you're obviously feeling better, young knight. It pleases me to see it."

Stephen nodded. "My thanks to you. I've given your words some consideration and I have a proposition for you, Alexander."

Alex raised his eyebrows. "Indeed? And what might that be?"

"Give me some clothes." Stephen looked down at the sheet. "In exchange, I shall tell you what you wish to know."

Alex gestured to the bedroom door. "There are clothes in the wooden chest that sits at the foot of the bed. Please take what you need. But before you do, let Emma change your bandages. The wound is not yet fully closed against infection. 'Twould be a pity to use the grave I just dug for you."

Emma leapt to her feet with a cry. "What do you mean? What grave?"

Stephen said nothing, for he had noticed a smile nudging the corners of Alex's mouth.

"Calm yourself, child," said Alex. "'Tis only in case Argante's men return. If we're still here, the fresh mound of earth might help support our earlier ruse." His smile became a grin. "You gave our guest the plague, remember? Few survive it."

"Wait." Stephen frowned. "What do you mean 'if we're still here'? Are you going somewhere?"

Emma echoed Stephen's question. "*Cùra?*"

The smile disappeared from Alex's face. He closed the door behind him and unbuckled his sword belt. "Your arrival here, my young friend, has likely shifted the direction of the winds. If so, we may have to shift with them." A sigh escaped him as he leaned his sword against the wall. "Finish your food, bathe and dress. Then we'll talk."

~o~

Stephen sat on the bed, his attention focused on Emma's face while she tended to his wound. A slight frown marred the otherwise flawless skin on her brow. Her silence, he thought, marred the air between them. "Forgive me." His whispered breath stirred a soft amber curl that graced her temple. "I never intended to bring trouble to you or Alex."

Her frown deepened as she tightened a fresh bandage around his chest. "You aren't to blame. It was I who brought you here."

"And now you regret it." He hoped he was wrong.

"Nay, I don't regret it." Her task finished, she sat back on her heels and lifted her gaze to his. "'Tis just..."

"What?" Something twisted inside him when he saw tears in her eyes. "Please tell me."

She lowered her voice to a whisper as a tear escaped down her cheek. "Alex is all I have in this world, Stephen, and today I sensed a change in him. He's no longer...at peace.

He speaks of leaving this place, a place he loves as much as I. I've never heard such talk from him before. 'Tis as if a stone has been cast on calm waters."

Stephen ran his thumb along her jaw and caught the errant tear, his words soft when he spoke. "You're mistaken, Emma."

She gave her head a gentle shake. "Nay, I'm not. You don't know Alex as I do. He hides it well, but he's troubled. I know it."

"Nay, I meant Alex is not all you have in this world." Stephen cradled her face in his hands, captivated by the colour of her eyes. Surely this was no mortal creature kneeling in sad reflection at his feet. "It seems that a forest faerie did capture a wounded knight's heart in the woods yesterday."

A soft blush arose in her cheeks. "'Tis the honey on your tongue which speaks, sir."

He smiled and bent his head to hers. "Nay. 'Tis an honourable knight who speaks, little one. I do not jest with you."

His mouth covered hers in a fateful kiss for he realized, in a single heartbeat, his future had changed. Or had it? Perhaps, he thought, finding her had always been his fate, his destiny. He had never felt so consumed, and he did not even know by what. Pleasure? Aye, but far more than that.

Her lips yielded beneath his and in her moment of surrender she captured him completely. Her sweet taste also sent a surge of blood to his groin. He groaned and pulled away.

"God help me." He straightened, closed his eyes and took a slow, deep breath.

In contrast, he heard Emma's breath catch in her throat. He looked down at her.

"What is it?" he asked, troubled by her stricken

expression. "What's wrong?"

"Forgive me." She exhaled. "I've never been kissed before. I fear I disappointed you."

Speechless, he stared at her for a moment, then took her hand in his and placed it over his heart. "Feel it, Emma. Feel my heart, how it beats for the want of you. Aye, and there's yet another part of me that speaks loudly of wanting you. " He touched his lips to hers again. "Disappointed? I think not. Bewitched, aye." His fingers brushed across her cheek and traced a path down her nose. "You're beautiful. Magical, even."

She dug her teeth into her bottom lip. "Yet I have much to learn, it seems, about the art of love."

An amused smile crossed Stephen's face. "And I'm very pleased to hear it."

Something akin to hope flickered in her eyes. "If you decide to stay, perhaps you could teach me."

The decision, he knew, was already made. "If Alexander has no objection, I would be happy to stay a while. As for teaching you about love, my little faerie, I suspect I might be the one taught."

A contented sigh escaped her followed by a grin. "I think Alex awaits us."

Stephen pressed her hand to his lips as she rose to her feet. She studied him with thoughtful eyes for a moment, and left him to dress.

A smile accompanied him into the kitchen, but it slid away as he met Alex's gaze, noting the rise of the older man's eyebrows and the tension in the air. Apprehension tightened Stephen's chest. Had he overstepped some unknown boundary?

The knife in Alex's hand sliced through the apple he held, his thumb anchoring the morsel on the blade as he raised it to his mouth. His teeth scooped it off the sharp edge and he chewed with deliberation, his eyes fixed on

Stephen. Emma sat in silence beside him, a nervous expression on her face.

"You look well in my *cùra's* clothes," she said, in an obvious attempt to lighten the weight of the atmosphere.

Stephen acknowledged her comment with a nod. "Thank you, my lady."

Alex ignored both comments. "Remember whose roof shelters you, Stephen de Montfort." His voice was quiet but stern. "Do not dishonour us."

Stephen didn't flinch. "I would never disrespect you, Alexander. Nor Emma. You have my word on it."

Alex nodded. "As I thought, but it's pleasing to hear it from your mouth. Sit."

Stephen settled into a chair, at the same time raising his hand to catch the apple Alex tossed his way.

"Now, young knight. Tell me how you're involved in this futile quest."

Stephen shrugged. "King Henry heard of Argante's long time obsession with the stone and sent me to learn more. Argante found out I worked for the crown and tried to kill me."

"I see," said Alex. "Go on. I'm curious to hear what you've learned about the stone so far."

A strange prickle lifted the hair on Stephen's neck. "I'm curious, in turn, about how you acquired your knowledge of it, and how you know so much about Argante's reputation."

Thunder rattled the skies somewhere off in the distance. Shadows started to swallow the late afternoon light, and the corners of the room grew darker.

"How I know Argante is a tale for another time." Alex bent down and tucked his knife into his boot. "As for the stone, the Latin name is Lapis Exilis. I learned of it through a...friend, many years ago. 'Tis not, apparently, a pebble for the faint of heart. In the wrong hands, I'm told it can be deadly." He cast a stern look at Stephen. "Please tell me Argante has not found it."

Stephen pulled in a deep breath and winced as pain lanced through his ribs. "Nay, not yet," he said. "At least, he hadn't when I left Lowland Chase yesterday morning."

"So what wild rumour, then, led him to these Cumbrian hills?"

Stephen felt Emma's eyes on him and glanced at her. She offered him the wisp of a smile and a slight nod of her head. A thought landed in his brain with the lightness of a butterfly, yet the clarity of it could not be mistaken.

Trust him.

He turned his eyes back to Alex. "Some time ago, rumours started circulating at court about an old priest who resides at Creake Abbey. During a feverish spell, he'd spoken of a mystical stone that fell from the sky many centuries ago, a stone blessed with great power."

Alex sat back. "What is this priest's name?"

"His name is Francis, I believe. Father Francis." Stephen frowned, wondering if he'd imagined the glint of sadness in Alex's eyes. "According to the Abbot, the priest suffered some terrible tragedy years ago that compelled him to take his vows. Over the years, his mind has become detached, his thoughts confused and unclear. Argante got some information from him, but it makes little sense."

"What information?" Alex shifted in his seat. "Tell me what the priest said."

"He said the stone rests at the side of an ancient king and is protected by a shield of silver. He mentioned a Cumbrian estuary and some ancient circle. Do his words mean anything to you?"

Alex rose to his feet and went to stand by the window, his eyes searching the stormy skies. "Aye, they do," he said.

"They mean a dangerous man has leased Lowland Chase and will likely not leave until he finds what he's looking for."

A grumble of thunder bounced around the skies like an ominous agreement. It sounded closer this time.

Stephen studied Alex for a moment. The atmosphere in the small space had thickened. Emma's eyes were also on the older man, a puzzled expression on her face. Tension hung in the air like an invisible mist.

"Just how are you involved in this, Alexander?" Stephen shifted in his chair. "For I know with certainty you are."

Alex turned to face them, his expression grim. "Let me just say Argante and I have shared history between us, none of it good. May God help us all if he finds that stone. 'Tis an object too powerful for most mortals, even if they be kings."

Stephen looked around the humble cottage, curiosity churning the questions in his mind. "But there has to be more to your story. Why do you live like this? 'Tis very obvious you're not of common stock."

"I live this way by choice." Alex's gaze drifted to Emma. "I have my reasons. That's all you need to know."

Stephen persisted. "Do you hide from someone?"

Alex took his sword and drew it from the scabbard. "Do not test me, young knight," he murmured. "It would not be wise." He twirled the hilt in his hand, casting an eye along the shining length of steel.

"I've been truthful with you, Alexander. I merely ask the same in return."

Without warning, Alex tossed the sword to Stephen who, in a reaction gleaned from years of military training, snatched the hilt from the air. Pain lanced through his chest at the sudden movement.

Emma clapped a hand over her mouth, stifling a cry.

"Christ!" Stephen, his heart racing, felt sweat beading on his brow. "Have you lost your mind?"

A wicked grin settled on Alex's face. "Nay. I merely wanted to test the speed of your responses. Not bad, but your injury is slowing you down."

"You could have just asked me if I still hurt." Stephen lifted the blade and examined it. "This is nice work. A weapon of great quality, obviously made for a wealthy knight." He handed it back. "So what now, *Sir* Alex?"

Alex smiled, slid the sword back into the scabbard, and placed it back against the wall. "We do nothing," he said, "until you're fully recovered."

"But I must send a message to Henry."

"Not yet. Argante is likely still searching for you. Let him think you're dead." Alex's gaze drifted to Emma again. "I don't want the bastard sniffing around here."

Stephen followed his gaze and understood.

"He would have to kill me," he offered, "before he got to her."

Lightning flashed a warning and thundered the storm's arrival.

"Aye, I know it, lad." Alex closed the shutters with a bang. "But I pray to God it will never come to that."

Chapter 6

She used a solitary fingernail to draw an erotic map on his skin, grazing a blood-red trail from his throat to his groin. Argante's greedy shaft responded to the sensation of painful ecstasy as the wench opened all ten of her claws and raked them over his chest. Licking her generous lips, she ogled his growing erection.

"Hmm," she purred, breathing hot air across the sensitive tip of his manhood. "You're indeed a stallion, my lord."

He watched in silence, enjoying her skills yet resenting her willingness. Argante preferred females who put up a fight - a genuine fight. The thought of an innocent maid struggling beneath him hardened him even more and his shaft twitched.

She smiled, observing him through cat-like, slanted brown eyes that gleamed in the candlelight. The image of a serpent slithered into his mind and he glanced at her mouth, half expecting to see the flick of a forked tongue between her lips.

"A stallion like you should be ridden." Tossing back a mane of wild red hair, she rose up, bending her spine like a bow before straddling his hips and impaling herself on his rigid member. She groaned. "And ridden hard."

With a grunt he sat up, pushed the girl off him and snatched a thick handful of her hair, twisting her onto her stomach with a violent wrench. He ignored her scream, grabbed her hips and lifted her buttocks, a guttural growl rattling his throat. "'Tis the stallion who mounts the mare, *salope*," he snarled, yanking on her hair again. "Let's see if you can take him."

With a brutal thrust he buried himself deep inside her, excited by her whimpers of pain, pounding harder and harder until his body stiffened with climax. Shuddering, he sank his nails into her flesh, drawing blood, relishing the sound of her scream.

"How was that, my little mare?" he hissed, shoving her away. "Now get out. And tell Markus I want a bath. I need to wash your stench off me."

The girl slid off the bed, picked up her clothes from the floor and started to dress.

"I said get out," Argante growled. "I'll not say it again."

The girl uttered a curse and ran from the room, slamming the door behind her. Argante heard a loud whistle from the corridor, followed by a scream. A moment later, Iain, Argante's man-at-arms, stuck his grinning face around the door.

"Can I have her now?"

Argante chuckled. "Help yourself. But tell Markus I want a bath."

"Will do." Iain's grin widened. "I'll only be a few minutes. The wench is already naked and I'm as hard as a rock."

Argante laughed and stretched out on the bed.

Later, while relaxing in the tub, he heard the clatter of hooves in the courtyard. His men had returned from another day of searching. Argante clenched his fists under the water, thinking of how Henry's spy had almost fooled him.

Almost.

Three days had passed since the young knight had made his escape. So far, they'd found no sign of him other than the two corpses he'd left bleeding on the road.

Thoughts of Stephen de Montfort's deception wrung a string of curses from Argante's mouth as he left the warmth of the tub. He rubbed himself down with vigour, taking time to admire his superb physique. Argante knew he was in better shape than many men half his age.

The hour was late, so Argante dressed for comfort, pulling on dark hose and a plain velvet tunic. He sank his feet into soft leather and fastened his sword belt around him, running his thumb along the jewelled hilt. Rarely did he go anywhere without the familiar weight of honed steel resting at his side.

"Well?" All eyes turned to him as he strode into the hall. "Anything?"

"Nothing, my lord. The rain has covered any tracks he might have made."

"But you searched to the north, as I suggested?"

"Aye, we did, and found nothing. Wherever he is, he can't have travelled far. I gave him and his horse a fair swipe with my blade. 'Tis certain they both bled to death and now lie rotting in the forest."

Argante cursed under his breath, grabbed the man by his tunic and hauled him to his feet. Spittle flew, along with his bitter words. "You'd better be right, Thomas. Christ's blood, the man bested three of you." He threw him aside and kicked at a chair. "To hell with de Montfort, then. We've wasted enough time. From now on, we focus on finding what we came here for."

"Where do you propose we start?" Thomas asked, eyeing his lord like a rat might eye a snake. "What ancient king is buried in this God forsaken corner of England?"

Argante grunted. "We start by looking for this circle the old priest mentioned. There's an ancient stone circle on the slopes of Black Combe. Maybe there's a burial mound nearby."

"There's sickness over that way," said one of the soldiers. "We passed by there two days ago looking for the spy. Remember? The Scottish peasant who lived in the forest? His son was sick. Sounded like the plague."

Argante spat on the floor. "We'll not be mingling with the locals. Be ready at dawn." He spun on his heel, but something the soldier said froze him mid-step. Skin prickling, he turned around.

"Wait. What did you say?"

"There's sickness over that way, my lord."

"Aye, I heard that. But a Scot?"

Thomas nodded. "Sounded like. He had a bit of a Gaelic lilt to his voice."

"What did he look like?"

"Tall, with dark curly hair. Your age, maybe a bit older."

"Did you see this son of his?"

"It was his son-in-law who was sick. And nay, we didn't see him. Saw his daughter, though. Pretty little wench."

Argante stepped back into the room. *A daughter? Then it couldn't be him. Unless...*

"What did she look like?"

Thomas shrugged. "Hard to say. She was hidden behind her shawl. But she had the greenest eyes I've ever seen. I'll never forget those. Like emeralds, they were. Think she was getting sick too. Coughing and sneezing."

"Jesus Christ." Argante grasped the back of a chair, a cold hand of certainty clutching his heart as he thought of the old priest. "It has to be him. After all these years."

"My lord?"

"Where is this place?" He leaned over and grabbed Thomas by the wrist. "Tell me everything."

~o~

Warm winds had stripped the sky of clouds during the night. The sun had yet to burn a trail over the horizon, but a glow on the eastern hills hinted at its imminent arrival. Five men set out as the stars faded into the dawn. They turned their horses inland, following the river.

As they left the spread of the coastal estuary behind them, the riverbanks narrowed, squeezing the water between into a frantic cascade that tumbled over boulders and crags. Darkness still lingered in the forest, but the remains of night were already being picked apart by birdsong.

Argante noticed none of it.

He rode in stiff silence at the head of the group, grappling with his emotions. Sleep had evaded him that night, his rabid mind besieged by thoughts of things past, which had unearthed a long-buried desire for revenge. Yet Argante fought to restrain his rage, for it did not bode well to approach Alexander Mathanach with anything less than a sharp mind and a sharp blade. The Scottish knight had cunning equal to a leash of foxes.

What of this girl? Green eyes like emeralds, Thomas said.

Like those of her mother. Yet the girl couldn't be Mathanach's daughter. Could she?

His fingers tightened on the reins.

Another thought persisted, this one a constant reminder of why he'd come to this remote part of England in the first place. If Alexander Mathanach was indeed the Scot who lived in the forest, the stone had to be nearby.

"The path is up ahead, my lord." Thomas's voice broke through Argante's reverie. "By those large red boulders sitting in the river."

Argante pulled his horse to a halt and his men followed suit.

"It goes straight in?"

"Aye." Thomas shifted in his saddle. "It leads directly to the cottage. A little less than a league, I'd say."

Argante dismounted and handed the reins to Thomas. "Wait here, all of you. Hide yourselves in the woods and keep quiet. I'll be back before dark."

Thomas cast a puzzled look at the reins in Argante's hand. "What are you doing, my lord? You can't go in there alone. And on foot?"

"Aye, I can."

"But – "

"Don't argue." He pushed the reins into Thomas's hand. "Get yourselves off the trail and stay low. Do not follow me or come anywhere near the cottage. Understood?"

Thomas paused. "Aye. But I hope you know what you're doing."

Argante glared at him. "I've killed men for lesser insults. Now move."

Chapter 7

"But *Cùra*, please let me go. 'Tis such a beautiful morning and I'm tired of staying here. It's been more than three days and we haven't seen a soul."

"That doesn't mean no one is out there." Alex leaned on the pitchfork and smiled at the expression on Emma's face. "You're pouting, child. I haven't seen you do that for several years."

"I haven't been this bored for several years." Emma folded her arms and glared at him.

"Then here." He tilted the fork handle toward her. "Bart's stall needs to be cleaned out. The old fellow needs some fresh water as well. After that, you can help me with the thatch on the roof. There's a leak over the door."

Emma ignored the proffered pitchfork. "But would you not like fish for dinner? I could be back in a few hours with some fresh flooks. You know how much you enjoy them. Besides, Stephen said he'll come with me. He's well enough to travel such a short distance."

Alex dug the prongs into the dirty straw, pulled up a forkful, and tossed it into a wooden barrow. "How about we have eggs instead? That way, you'll only have to walk to the hen-hut. And your knight is a wanted man, not yet strong enough to wield a sword."

"I can wield my own sword."

Alex sighed. "You'd be no match for this particular demon. Do you have any idea what Argante would do if he captured you? I can't take that risk. You're too precious to me."

He sensed the unspoken curses tripping through her mind and chuckled inwardly.

"That's not very lady-like, *a ghràidh*." His brows lifted. "I don't remember teaching you such words."

Emma's mouth twitched in an apparent attempt to suppress a smile. This time, Alex chuckled out loud.

Stephen appeared in the doorway, his sword resting in his left hand. He swung it in a wide arc, only a hint of discomfort on his face. "I'll go with her, Alex. My wound has healed quickly. Besides, I can fight left handed if need be."

"Aye. 'Tis that 'need be' part which bothers me," Alex replied, frowning.

"Please, *Cùra*. I'll take my sword and bow, and I promise we'll stay in the forest until we reach the sands." She blinked at him, clasping her hands together beneath her chin. "We'll fish below the southern cliffs, out of sight. Plea-ease."

"Christ forgive me." Whenever she brandished her eyes like that, he was lost. A twinge of pain lanced his heart, for Emma's mother had also bent his will with similar ease. "Go, then. But step quietly and watch your surroundings at all times. Young knight, do not let her out of your sight. If you see or hear anyone – anyone at all – hide yourselves."

Emma leapt on him, knocked the pitchfork clean out of his hands, and planted a kiss on his cheek.

"Thank you, thank you, I love you." She clapped her hands in obvious delight. "We'll be very careful. I'll be right back, Stephen."

With a whoop of joy, she ran into the house, her long braid whipping out behind her. Alex watched a smile cross Stephen's face.

"Emma is not like the noble women you're used to, lad," he said, "and I take full responsibility for that. I raised her to value her own worth in this world."

"She's remarkable."

"Aye, she is."

"Will you not tell me why you raised her? How she came to be here with you?"

The young knight's questions probed an old and

painful wound.

"Maybe one day I'll tell you why." Alex retrieved the pitchfork and dropped all levity from his voice. "But before you go to catch your fish, Stephen de Montfort, know this: if any harm comes to her, I shall kill you."

Stephen met his gaze squarely. "If any harm comes to her, my lord, it will be because I'm already dead."

They left a short time later, Emma dressed in a loose kirtle, a sword strapped to her side and a bow and quiver strung across her shoulder. She looked back at Alex and blew him a kiss before disappearing into the forest with Stephen. Alex smiled and raised his hand in reply.

A shadow flew over the sun and a crow settled on the cottage roof. It cocked a blue-black head at Alex, fixing him with an obsidian stare. He watched the bird for a few moments and then looked about, his eyes following the tree line surrounding the cottage.

Nothing stirred his suspicions and he turned a questioning gaze back to the bird.

"What?" he muttered. "What is it?"

The bird cocked its head to the other side, offered up a raspy caw, and took to the sky. A wisp of wind stroked a chilly finger across the back of Alex's neck.

~o~

Emma grabbed Stephen's hand as soon as they entered the forest, guiding him with sure, silent footfalls through the dense woods. The lass distracted him to the point of carelessness, and he reminded himself several times that danger might lurk in the benign shadows.

In subdued voices, they shared idle chatter and teased each other. When conversation ceased, she turned to him every so often and blessed him with a smile. If he snapped a twig underfoot, she reprimanded him with a frown and a shake of her head. Each time, he grimaced and shrugged an apology.

The lightness of her mood stirred his blood and set his heart racing. He loved the way she moved through the woods, graceful and sure-footed.

"You are indeed a faerie." The soft breeze further gentled his hushed tone. "Or a wood-nymph, for no mortal can travel in silence through the forest as you do. Do your feet even touch the ground?"

Emma grinned. "Never. My invisible wings carry me over it. Too bad you don't have them yourself. A herd of deer makes less noise than your two big feet."

He stifled a laugh. "How much farther?"

"Why?" Concern flitted across her face and erased her smile. "Does your wound hurt?"

"Nay, sweetheart, but your insult did. I've a sudden urge to heave you over my shoulder, wade into the sea with my two big feet, and drop you in it."

Emma giggled. "It would do you no good, sir. This faerie can swim like a mermaid."

"That doesn't surprise me." Stephen glanced around him. "How do you know where we are?"

"I know every part of these woods. We're almost there. Do you not smell the sea?"

She tugged on his hand and turned down a narrow path leading through a dense thicket of elderberry. Stephen felt the ground subside, looked down and saw sand. A gull's plaintive cry descended from above and the sound of distant waves meandered into the shady grove.

"This way." Emma ducked under a curtain of leaf-laden branches. "Mind your head."

They emerged from the forest beneath the cliffs, where the river met the Irish Sea. The estuary lay ahead; a wide expanse of sand banks surrounded by placid pools of salt water and swirling eddies of tidal wash.

Warm sunlight poured over them, a cool breeze played around them, and the sea whispered a welcome as it swept onto the beach.

Emma let go of Stephen's hand, threw her arms wide and spun in a circle. "Isn't it beautiful?"

"Aye." Stephen looked about him. "'Tis very –"

She'd kicked off her shoes, dropped her bow and quiver on the sand, and unfastened her sword belt. He watched, speechless, as she pulled her kirtle off and dropped that on the sand too. Her thin shift moulded itself to her body in the breeze, leaving little to the imagination.

Stephen exhaled a lungful of air. "God help me."

"What?" Emma glanced down at herself. "I cannot fish fully clothed. Do I offend you?"

He chuckled. "Not in the least, little one, but I fear my vow to Alex will be sorely tested today. Tell me, do you intend to catch these fish with your bare hands?"

"Ah!" She looped her arm through his. "I wondered when you'd ask. Come. I'll show you."

She led him to the edge of a tidal pool of shallow water, circling around a large sandbank.

"Flooks are flat fish," she explained. "They lie on the bottom, buried just under the sand. Watch me."

"With pleasure." Stephen stuck his thumbs into his sword belt. "Believe me, I'm enjoying the view."

Emma wrinkled her nose at him and waded out to knee depth, taking small deliberate steps. Her cotton shift floated out around her legs, but she paid it no attention. Sunlight glanced off the ripples she made, casting a halo of sparkles around her. Stephen held his breath, spellbound by the extraordinary scene before him. All at once she stopped, her eyes widening, and then reached down.

"Got one!" Emma pulled a fish from the water and raised it in the air, a bright smile on her face.

Stephen laughed. "You felt it with your feet?"

"Aye, it's easy. Want to try it?"

"I can't wait." He gave a wry grin, kicked off his shoes and stepped into the water.

"Your sword, sir knight." Emma pointed at the scabbard, which trailed through the waves.

"My sword stays with me, my lady." He paddled to her side, wrapped his arms around her waist and pulled her to him. She gasped and dropped the fish.

"Hmm, look what I caught."

She raised her chin. "Aye, and you didn't even have to use your feet."

"My two big feet?" His gaze shifted from the captivating green of her eyes to the softness of her lips, his body burning with desire. This unique woodland creature presented a temptation unlike any he had ever met.

The smile she offered him faltered. "Why do you look at me that way, my lord?"

Stephen sighed. "Because, my lady, I'm more accustomed to noble women draped in silk and lace, with jewels in their hair and gold on their fingers. So when I saw you just now, standing knee-deep in the Irish Sea wearing naught but your shift and waving a fish at me, I found it very strange."

Dismay shadowed her face and she stiffened in his arms.. "Oh. So I'm not...I mean, you don't – "

He pressed a finger to her lips. "Without a doubt, my little faerie, it was the most beautiful thing I've ever seen."

Unable to resist any longer, Stephen bent and kissed her, groaning when she opened for him, inviting his tongue to explore and taste. Everything he knew vanished behind a veil of desire as she settled against him, warm and soft in his arms.

Perhaps he had not found the stone, but he had found a rare treasure, nonetheless. He lifted his head, her sweetness still damp on his lips, his voice grating with passion.

"'Tis a strong magic you possess, sweetheart."

They stayed there, splashing in the waves, catching fish and sharing kisses, until the sun lengthened their shadows on the sand and changed the sparkles on the sea from silver to gold.

"It has been a perfect day." Emma leaned into Stephen's chest with a contented sigh. "But I think it's time to go. Alex will be worrying."

He tugged gently on her braid and offered up a soft gibe. "Do you remember the way back?"

Emma gave him a withering look. "Aye, I believe I do. Have no fear, sir big-feet. Your lady will see you home safe."

With a laugh he released her and lifted their catch from the sand; six fine flooks, speared onto a sturdy cutting of hazel.

"Then lead on, my lady."

Shadows wrapped around them as they ducked beneath the forest canopy. The murmur of waves faded into the distance, replaced by hushed whispers of wind in the leaves and sweet evening birdsong.

They had not travelled too far before Stephen stopped to pull Emma into his arms and kiss her, relishing the taste of salt on her lips.

"I cannot resist you," he whispered against her ear. "'The way you move is like a graceful spirit."

A twinkle brightened the green of her eyes and she grinned. "But the night will not wait and neither will these fish."

Stephen laughed. "Aye, you have a point. I suspect Alex is imagining his sword through my gut as we speak."

"Darius." Emma grabbed Stephen's hand and pulled him along the path. "This way."

"Darius?"

"Aye. Darius. 'Tis the name of my *cùra's* sword. When I was a child, he told me stories of magical kings and mighty warriors. Darius was a king of Persia, born many years before the birth of our Lord. He had a magic sword of great power and a bewitched carpet that flew on the wind. He also had –" Emma stopped and raised her hand.

Foreboding lifted the hair on Stephen's neck and he caressed his sword hilt. "What is it, Emma?"

She turned to him with a finger over her lips and gestured to the left. "There are horses over there. And men."

They stood in frozen silence, listening to the faint jingle of harness and a hum of voices drifting through the trees.

"They're some distance away, by the river." Emma turned down a narrow trail to the right. "Come. We'll circle around this way."

Stephen cursed under his breath. He knew, without a doubt, who the men were.

"I hope they haven't been to the house." Too late, he voiced his thoughts, cursing again as Emma's face paled.

"*Cùra*! Dear God."

Stephen grabbed her arm, stopping her mid-stride.

"Nay. We must be careful."

She struggled against him, breathless in her panic. "But he may be hurt!"

"I doubt it, sweetheart." Silently berating himself for his thoughtless outburst, he cupped his hand to Emma's cheek. "Don't worry. Alexander is no fool and well able to defend himself."

The sound of flapping wings drew their gaze upwards. A large crow settled onto an overhead branch and cocked a blue-black head at them. It cawed once before flying off down the path.

Stephen looked at Emma and raised an eyebrow. "Friend of yours?"

Emma frowned and gestured with her head. "This way."

Dusk had already cast a grey pallor across the clearing. The house showed no signs of life, but neither did it show signs of fighting or trouble. Upon leaving the shelter of the forest, Stephen moved Emma behind him and headed toward the door. He paused for a moment, listening, then took a cautious step forward.

A chicken ambled past, clucking quietly, and from his secret vantage in the woods, an owl hooted an early call. Stephen glanced back at Emma with a shrug and drew his sword.

The door swung open and Alex stood on the threshold, eyeing them with a puzzled expression.

"What in Heaven's name are you doing?" He glanced up at the darkening sky. "It's about time you two got back. I was wondering where you were."

Emma gave a squeal, ran to him and threw her arms around his neck.

He returned her hug. "What on earth is wrong, child?"

"We heard men and horses on the river trail," she mumbled, her face buried in his shirt. "I was scared they'd been here."

Alex grimaced. "They haven't, but I fear someone has. Ah! Flooks. Good. I'm starving. Put your sword away, young knight, and hand me those fish. You can let go of me, *a ghràidh*. I'm unharmed."

"Argante?" Stephen sheathed his sword and followed them into the house.

"Most likely." Alex laid the fish on the table and pulled a knife from his belt. "Do you know how to clean these?"

Stephen shook his head, wondering at Alex's nonchalance. "Nay. Are you not worried about Argante?"

"Then you shall learn how to clean them and aye, I'm worried about Argante." Alex glanced at Emma. "Very worried."

"What if he comes back tonight?" Stephen asked. "Should we set up a watch?"

"He'll not do that."

"How can you be so sure?"

Alex sighed. "Because Argante rarely acts on impulse, unless it's with some poor wench. Because you were gone today and I kept out of sight, so he cannot be certain whose house this is. And because he fears the dark, and more than that, he fears me."

"Argante fears you?"

"Aye. 'Tis why I fear for Emma. She's my one weakness. Argante would happily use her to get at me."

Stephen's eyes narrowed as thoughts galloped relentlessly through his mind. "To get at you? Or to get at what you know about the stone?"

Alex shrugged. "'Tis the same thing."

"This Argante does not frighten me." Emma sat on a chair hugging her knees to her chin. "I do not fear him, Cùra."

Some ancient Gaelic curse flew out of Alex's mouth as he stuck the knife blade into the table. Emma gasped and jumped up with a small cry.

Stephen frowned, for it felt for a moment as if the ground had shifted beneath his feet. "What the hell?"

"You do not fear him, Emma? Let me tell you some truths, then, about this devil's servant." Alex's eyes darkened, and he ground out his words through gritted teeth. "After that, perhaps you'll fear him as you should and also understand why you must leave here tomorrow."

Chapter 8

"Damn the Scottish pox-ridden son of a whore."

Argante paced the Great Hall like a caged tiger. Except for Iain, who hadn't been involved in the day's events, none of the men stayed after dinner, fearful of the fierce rage controlling their lord. Alexander Mathanach's name had lodged itself into Argante's thoughts like a poisoned splinter, which now festered with hate.

"But if you saw no one, m' lord, why didn't you try to search inside the house?" Iain sniffed loudly and spat into the empty hearth. "You can't know for sure it's Mathanach who lives there."

Argante cursed, drew his sword, and swiped at a goblet on the table. The cup flew across the room and slammed against the wall. Iain winced.

"Do not question my actions, Iain. Someone was there, and I know it was Mathanach. I could smell the bastard."

"Was he alone?"

"That I do not know. There's a fresh grave at the edge of the forest. Thomas said his son-in-law was sick. Maybe that part was true, and the man died. 'Tis the girl, this supposed daughter with green eyes, who interests me."

"If she is...was married, then she's no virgin, m' lord."

Argante stopped his pacing to glare at his man-at-arms. "You idiot. I care not about her virginity. I care about her importance to Mathanach." He dropped his gaze to the ground, his eyes blind to all but the thoughts tormenting his mind. "She can't be his daughter," he muttered. "Alicia died within days of his return to England. Who the hell is she?" He started pacing again. "Christ. I want that girl."

"The men are impatient, m' lord. Send them in to get the girl and the Scot. Let's finish this and find what we came here for."

Argante curled a corner of his lips. "You don't know who you're dealing with. They wouldn't get within an arrow's flight of the place."

Iain grunted and shifted in his chair. "What is he? A one-man army? Some kind of devil?"

"A Scottish demon, aye. I've seen things."

"Things?"

"Never mind. But I guarantee he knows exactly where the stone is. God's blood, he may even have it with him. I need this girl to force his cooperation." Argante stopped his pacing to fix Iain with a fierce stare. "You've failed me, Iain."

"My lord?"

"You were gone most of the day, yet you bring back not even a whore for me. Are there no damn wenches in this county? 'Tis not like you to return empty handed."

"Ah! Well, in truth, the pickings are few. I wouldn't let a flea-bitten dog fuck the women I saw today." He grinned. "Or maybe I would."

Argante's face relaxed into a reluctant smile. "That bad?"

Iain shrugged. "There was a pretty young thing at a farm a couple of leagues east of here. But she had a brother the size of yon mountain and I couldn't get her alone, so I brought back only the pheasants we had for supper."

"'Tis the hunting of women I keep you for, not food. Bring Bess to my chamber again, and tell Markus I'll need a hot bath. Be sure to wake me before dawn. In the meantime, try to figure out how to get this wench away from Mathanach."

"Aye, m'lord."

~o~

Emma said and ate little throughout the meal. Lost in misery, she fiddled with her food, avoiding eye contact with Alex. How could he insist she leave? This was her home. When at last she met his gaze she saw only sadness in his eyes. Alex cursed and pushed his unfinished plate away.

"I've known Argante since my youth," he began. "He fostered for a short time with my family. Even as a lad he was a bully, picking on those weaker than him. He and I fought often. Then one night he just disappeared, taking one of my father's best horses with him. Strangely, my own horse died the next day. A twisted gut, they said, but I always suspected Argante was responsible somehow. Poison, maybe." He smiled. "Yet a blessing emerged from that particular horror in the shape of old Bart. As for Argante, I heard talk of his evil once in a while, but didn't actually see him again until I was serving in the Holy Land."

Stephen gasped. "Argante went on a crusade?"

Alex shook his head. "Not exactly. He'd heard the stone had made its way there, so he was trying to track it down. We met and had words again. Later that night, I heard screams and went to investigate. I found him standing over the naked body of an Arab girl, little more than a child. She bled to death on the sand from his tearing of her."

"God save us. Why did you not kill him then?" Emma asked, shivering inwardly.

Alex sighed. "I beat him to within a hair's breadth of his life before some knights pulled me off him. It must be said that Argante was not the only one guilty of such crimes. Many women were abused by crusading knights. Indeed, most commanders turned a blind eye. Christ, some of them even participated. Thing is, the wee Arab girl was not Argante's first victim. I'd heard similar stories of his depravity while still in England."

He paused and looked down at the table. "Sadly, the rape of a peasant girl is not seen as so terrible a crime. The nobility in this country, to their shame, spend little time worrying about such matters. Argante knows this and chooses the defenceless as his victims. He takes perverse pleasure in tearing the wombs of innocent girls, and leaving his bruises and teethmarks on the skin of serving maids. Those who don't survive his assault - and I understand there have been a few - are disposed of quietly. We have other history between us, which I'll not discuss now. This is why you must leave here, Emma. He would use you to get back at me."

The thought of leaving sickened her stomach. "But where will we go?"

"You will go to Malvern Priory, and you'll stay there until I deem it safe for you to return. I've decided to remain here. I wish to see what Argante does, if anything."

"Why don't you simply kill him and be done with it?" Stephen sighed and shook his head. "'Tis what I should have done."

"I can't murder him in cold blood, lad. If he gives me cause to kill, then I won't hesitate, but I don't want Emma to be that cause. You're in no condition to go up against him either. Argante is a strong and skilled fighter. Besides, he likely thinks you're dead. That gives us an edge, should we need one."

"Tell me, Alexander," said Stephen, "do you know where the stone is?"

Alex leaned forward, a smile playing on his lips. "If I do, then all the more reason to get the lass away from here."

Emma scowled. "But I don't want to stay with a group of boring nuns. It will be like a prison."

Alex raised an eyebrow. "Have you heard nothing of what I said? You will do as I tell you, child. We leave at dawn."

"I'm not a child." Emma's cheeks flushed as she glared at Alex, who laughed.

"Is that so? Then stop behaving like one. Go and pack some clothes. I'll tidy in here."

"I shall not leave you, and you can't make me." Despite her verbal bravado, Emma's legs trembled when she rose to clear her dish away. Alex moved so quickly, she didn't have time to react. The dish flew from her hands as he grabbed her arms and she cried out in surprise when he gave her a shake.

"Aye, I can make you. Now go and pack some clothes." His voice simmered with suppressed anger. "You're leaving here in the morning, and if you resist I'll tie you to the damn horse. Do you understand?"

Emma tore free from his grip and backed away, her heart racing.

"Nay, I don't understand." A sob caught in her throat. "I don't understand at all. This is my home. I belong here with you, not hiding in some convent." She turned and fled into her room, Stephen's words following her through the door.

"God's teeth, Alexander. Was that truly necessary?"

"Aye, sadly it was. Let her go."

Emma slammed the door and sat on her bed, shivering. Alex had never shown such anger toward her, and his harsh words cut deep.

How, though, could she not fear Argante after what she'd learned? Of course she did, but she also feared for Alex and Stephen. What if something happened to them? Angry, muffled voices drifted in from the other room and her rebellious spirit weakened. She'd seen the pain in Alex's eyes and knew he merely wanted to protect her, as he always had. To resist would only serve to hurt him more.

Sighing, Emma lifted the lid of the wooden chest at the foot of her bed and pulled out some clothes.

Much later, she opened her eyes to darkness, a slight ache pulsing in her temples. She sat up, wondering at the hour. All was quiet apart from the sound of faint snoring from beyond her door.

Emma had no window in her room. Her ceiling was the floor of a storage area directly under the thatched roof, accessible by a ladder leading up to an open trapdoor. The storage area had a small window set in the wall beneath the rafters. Through the day, or on nights when the moon shone full and unhindered, light trickled down through the opening in her ceiling. On this moonless night though, Emma saw only shadows.

Eager for some air, she climbed the ladder, eased herself into the attic, and tip-toed over to the small opening, which was covered by a patch of greased linen. She pulled it aside and looked out.

The edge of the forest appeared as a dense barricade of twisted shapes. With the absence of a dominant moon, the stars dared to shine brighter, stretching across the night sky as if someone had cast a fistful of diamonds onto a length of indigo-blue silk. The silence of the woods remained unbroken, tempting Emma with its alluring mystery. Tears filled her eyes. How she loved this place. The thought of leaving it, not knowing when she might return, tore at her heart.

As a child, she'd often sneak out at night to wander through the forest. It was easy enough to squeeze through the small opening, drop onto the thatched lean-to at the back of the cottage and slide to the ground. Getting back always proved to be more difficult, but she'd always managed. To her knowledge, Alex had never been aware of her night-time exploits.

It had been a few years since, but...could she? Surely it would do no harm. Alex had said that Argante wouldn't come at night and she'd be back well before dawn.

Moments later she felt cool bare earth beneath her feet. She glanced up at the house, a twinge of guilt twisting in her belly, but not compelling enough to change her mind. The forest beckoned with dark fingers, and she obeyed the summons, taking fearless steps into the shadows.

She did not get far.

Without warning, one of the shadows emerged from the undergrowth like a black demon. It slammed a rough hand across her mouth and pressed a cold steel blade against her throat.

"Hush." The demon had a man's voice and vile breath. "Don't fight, lass. Save it. Save it for later."

In the terrified depths of her mind, Emma screamed for Alex and Stephen. Her voice grated the skin at the back of her throat, unable to escape the thick barricade of calloused fingers. The brutal grip forced her teeth into her lips and a metallic ribbon of blood curled around her tongue, gagging her. An arm looped through her elbows, forcing them back, locking them in a clamp of iron-hard muscle. The knife blade trailed across her back, and she flinched in pain.

"Keep still, wench." His growl was hot against her ear.

Emma ignored the command and kicked violently at the undergrowth, hoping to attract the attention of those who slumbered in the cottage. She knew, though, her efforts would likely be in vain. The serenade of the night-time forest often included the conflicts of wild animals; wolf against deer, fox against rabbit. Discord among the trees would not be considered unusual.

She was no match for her captor, who never tired or

loosened his hold. By the time he'd dragged her as far as the river, her fight had weakened to little more than a feeble struggle. He threw her, face down, across the back of a waiting horse and climbed into the saddle behind her. Freed from his gagging fingers, she pulled in a deep breath.

"You bastard." Her words rattled over raw vocal chords and she reached up to rake her nails across his face. He grabbed her wrist and pushed her arm up behind her, forcing a cry of pain from her lips.

"Shut your mouth," he snarled, spurring his horse into a canter. The sudden jolt had her sliding from the saddle until the man wrapped an arm around her, his hand coming to rest on her breast. He grunted and squeezed so hard it brought tears to her eyes. In response, Emma sank her teeth into his inner thigh.

"You little bitch!" He yanked on her hair and pulled his horse to a halt. With a curse, he lifted her to sit astride in front of him. "Stop your squirming or I swear I'll beat you unconscious. I'm sorely tempted already."

Emma shuddered against the hard wall of his chest. "Why are you doing this?"

The man laughed. "Because my lord wants you, and I'm paid to give him what he wants. I'll be well rewarded for this night's work."

"Your...lord?" Emma's terrified mind absorbed the man's words. *So... this is not Argante?*

"Aye. You'll meet him soon enough. Now, be still, or I'll make good on my threat."

Bile burned the back of her throat. "I'm so sorry, *Cùra*," she whispered into the night. "So sorry."

Her terror grew when her captor rode past the trail leading to Lowland Chase.

"Where are you taking me?" she asked, bewildered.

His response numbed her mind. "A place where

Mathanach won't find you."

The night showed no sign of ending as they rode out of the forest. Ahead of them, its dark silhouette plastered against the starlit sky, lay the ominous outline of Black Combe. Emma shuddered when she realized where they were going.

"The Bastard's Keep!" With trembling fingers, she pulled at the iron grip of her captor's arm. "Nay, please. Don't take me there. 'Tis the devil's lair."

The large grey tower loomed out of the darkness and the man chuckled. "Aye, it is. And you're his honoured guest."

"I beg of you, don't do this," she cried. "Demons lurk within that place. I shall die in there."

"That you might, if you don't behave." He reined in his horse, dragged Emma from the saddle and cut off her screams with his hand. "Christ, but you're a noisy wench. Be silent!"

Long abandoned, the desolate tower had stood for over a century. The locals avoided it, believing it to be haunted. Some of the outer walls had crumbled over time, but the interior was undamaged and the dungeons were sound. It was there he took her, pushing her into one of the underground cells, closing the solid oak door and banging the iron bolt into place.

Even her screams could find no release from that terrible place. Trapped within the thick walls, they echoed back at her like a horde of demented spirits. Total darkness wrapped around her, thick and suffocating, and her cries dwindled to desperate whimpers. She reached into the blackness and touched cold, damp stone. With a sob, she crumpled to the ground, curled into a trembling ball, and whispered a distraught prayer.

Emma's terrified mind had no concept of the passing hours. She didn't know how much time had passed before a noise filtered through her nightmare. She heard muffled words, the scrape of metal against metal, and the squeak of a hinge. Her closed lids sensed light, flicked open, and squinted into the blinding flame of a candle.

"Watch her, my lord. She's a fighter." The voice of her captor wandered into the cell from the doorway. Then a different voice hissed off the damp walls and Emma's heart clenched. How could one speak so softly yet sound so evil?

"I'd be disappointed if she were not. You've excelled yourself, Iain."

Argante.

"Stand up," he said, "for I would see your face."

Emma struggled to rise, her limbs protesting against stiffness and cold. A hand grabbed her arm and pulled her upright. She cried out in fear and pain.

Argante thrust a candle flame close to her face. "Iain, bring me more light."

Emma blinked at the flame, unable to see details beyond its glare. She rubbed her eyes and stumbled back against the wall as dizziness washed over her. Another candle seemed to float through the darkness, held in a shadowy hand. It settled on a ledge and stayed there. The shadow that had carried it dissolved back into the dark.

"God's balls, look at her. Surely there can be no doubt." Argante's breath rippled across the flame. "Tell me your name, child."

"Em...Emma," she muttered, her teeth chattering with cold.

"And your mother's name?"

"My m...mother?"

"Aye. Give me her name."

"Al...Alicia."

"Jesus." Argante's breath brushed across her face. "Then Alexander Mathanach is your father?"

"N...nay. He's my guardian. My father is dead."

"His name?"

Emma shook her head, her mind choked by fear and confusion. Argante dug his nails into her arm and she yelped.

"Tell me your father's name," he snarled through gritted teeth.

"Edward," she whimpered. "His name was Edward Fitzhugh."

"Fitzhugh? Christ almighty. Alicia had Fitzhugh's bastard?" Uttering a low growl, he released her arm. "Wait outside, Iain, but don't bolt the damn door. 'Tis blacker than the belly of hell down here."

He stroked his knuckles down her cheek.

"So, you're Fitzhugh's bastard. What a surprise. And what a little beauty you are, Emma. Just like your mother." He fingered her throat before cupping his hand around her breast. Emma whimpered and thrust his arm away. Fitzhugh's bastard? What did he mean? Why was he asking about her parents?

"Stop touching me," she cried. "'Tis you the bastard, not I."

"Is that so?" He turned to place the candle on the small ledge and stepped close to her, placing his feet on either side of hers. "So tell me, sweetheart, how did your mother die?"

At last she saw Argante's face by candlelight. It surprised her to see how fine featured he was, his firm jaw darkened by the premature growth of a beard. The flame reflected in his unblinking eyes and picked out the silver threads running through his long black hair. She gasped when he leaned into her, pinning her tightly against the wall.

"Answer me. Tell me how she died." Emma cringed at the smell of stale wine and garlic on his breath.

"She...she died from an infection a few days after birthing me. Please don't hurt me."

Argante's fingers slipped beneath the fabric of her shift and pushed it off her shoulders. "And your father? What took his mortal soul from this earth?"

His arousal pressed like an iron rod into her belly and the image of the young, lifeless Arab girl flashed into Emma's mind. In silence she cried out for Alex and for Stephen and prayed to God for mercy. Out loud, she pleaded with her captor.

"Please, my lord. I beg of you."

"Answer my question, child."

"My father died in combat before I was born."

Argante laughed. "Is that what Mathanach told you?" He eased his weight off her, reached down and untied his braies. "Did he tell you why he became your guardian?"

"Because my parents were...were his friends." Her teeth chattered with fear and cold. "Alex prom...promised my mother he would take care of me. Please don't do this to me."

"He promised her, did he? How noble of him, considering." He tugged her skirt up around her hips, and she flinched as her bare skin pressed against the cold, hard stone. "I've always wanted to bring that Scottish whoreson to his knees. He has something I want, and I have something he wants. You're a fine prize, Emma."

"Nay!" Emma dug her nails into Argante's shoulders as he forced her legs apart with his knee. His foul breath brushed across her face. With a steel grip, he captured her hands with one of his and pinned them over her head. The other snaked around her bottom and lifted her against him. His cruel thrust sent a shard of pain deep into her belly. Her scream echoed off the walls as something tore within her.

Argante froze, his entire body stiffening against hers.

"God's blood. You're yet untouched. A virgin." His hand closed around her throat. "Mathanach lied. You lied. There was no sick husband. Who, then, lies in the grave by the woods?"

Emma closed her eyes against a wave of nausea.

"Answer me, wench. Is it de Montfort?" His grip tightened on her windpipe. "Is it? Tell me. Tell me the bastard died."

"Aye." Emma's head throbbed with pain and she gasped for air. "'Tis the knight who rests there. He was past saving when we found him."

Argante's body relaxed and the snarl on his lips widened. "Then it is indeed my night for pleasure."

Something in Emma's mind closed as Argante tore her innocence away, yet she could not shut out the guttural sounds of his depravity echoing off the stark walls.

"Christ, Emma." He tensed and shuddered against her, his vile heat filling her belly. "You're beyond sweet."

"And you're a demon," she whispered. "Alex will kill you for this."

Argante breathed hard in her ear. "As he killed your parents?"

With a strangled cry, she pushed against him. "'Tis truly evil you are, that you could spit out such lies."

"Lies?" Argante lifted his head and gazed at her, dragging a fingernail along her jaw. "'Tis you who have been fed lies, sweetheart. Allow me to set you straight and tell you the truth of it. Your mother was married to Mathanach, not Fitzhugh, but while your precious guardian was away in the Holy Land, it seems Fitzhugh got busy rutting with her. Mathanach heard rumours of the affair and came home early, only to find them together in his chamber. That's when he flew into an unholy rage and ran them both through with his blade. The story was the flavour at court for quite some time."

He chuckled.

"But I never knew she'd dropped his bastard. What a delicious, dirty little secret you are. She obviously hid you somehow. Mathanach must have found out and adopted you to soothe his conscience. It certainly explains why he raised you in these god-forsaken hills. He was probably ashamed to admit the truth of who, or what, you really are. In any case, he's lied to you, Emma. You're Fitzhugh's bastard, your mother was a whore, and Mathanach killed them both."

He left her there, shivering with cold and shock, pain lancing her frozen limbs. The smell of him polluted her skin like rancid sweat, but the violation, as vile as it was, had gone way beyond the physical.

Argante had defiled more than her innocence. He had befouled everything she valued.

His allegations against Alexander could not be true. Dear God, they could not be true. Yet there had been something resolute in his voice. Truth, vicious and raw, had edged every word.

Stephen. He would not want her now, shamed as she was. Who would?

Despair, unlike any Emma could have imagined, flowed through every vein. She curled herself into a ball, wrapped her arms around her legs, and buried her face in her bloodied shift.

But there was no escaping the nightmare. Argante's words echoed in her tormented mind, over and over again, tearing her soul to shreds.

"...he's lied to you, Emma. You're Fitzhugh's bastard, your mother was a whore, and Mathanach killed them both."

~o~

The cockerel lifted his scarlet-combed head and announced the arrival of a new day. His bold, raucous call hurtled through the cool morning air and his harem of hens clucked an excited response. Moments later he repeated himself with equal vigour, as if to make certain everyone understood his message.

Alex stirred at the sound, a dream taunting him at the moment of waking. For less than a heartbeat his mind beheld a terrible vision and a voice whispered an inconceivable truth in his ear. The sights and sounds sank into his subconscious as soon as he opened his eyes.

Yet a shadow of the dream remained. It hung over him, ominous and dark, an unwelcome twinge of fear nudging his gut. The sensation confused him, for Alexander Mathanach feared only one thing, and he had no reason to fear it, did he? Emma slept soundly in her room, safe under his roof. Didn't she?

He pushed the covers aside, got to his feet, and wandered over to the doorway. Stephen, well enough recovered, had insisted Alex reclaim the bedchamber, so the young knight now occupied the pallet in the kitchen. Alex peered out and squinted into the gloom. Stephen still slept, Emma's bedroom door was closed, and the locking bar on the front door sat firmly in its cradle. Nothing seemed out of place, yet a prickle crept over his scalp.

He raked a hand through his hair, Emma's distress the previous night playing over in his mind. Perhaps her sorrow was the shadow hovering over him, he mused, for he had never before shown such anger toward her. Aye, perhaps that's all it was - a twinge of conscience on his part.

He pulled a simple cotton tunic over his head, grabbed the empty water-pail and crept over to the door.

"Alexander." Stephen sat up, rubbing the sleep from his eyes. "Do you need help?"

"Nay, I can manage." Unable to shake his unease, Alex glanced toward Emma's room. "Have you heard anything this morning?"

"Not a sound." Stephen frowned and followed his gaze. "You look worried. Is everything alright?"

A cold hand of dread pressed itself against Alex's spine. *Nay, everything is not alright.* He set the bucket down and stepped over to Emma's door.

"I'm not sure. There's something... " He lifted the latch and pushed the door open. The bed lay empty and unmade, Emma's imprint still visible upon the linen covered feathers.

"Dear God in Heaven." A cold hand clenched his heart. "Let this be a nightmare and awaken me from it now."

Stephen stumbled to Alex's side. "What the hell? Where is she?"

Alex stepped into the room, his limbs sluggish as if filled with icy water. Panic, hard and sickening, tightened his chest. His thoughts frantic, he glanced up at the opening in the ceiling. A truth taunted his brain and almost pushed him to his knees.

"Oh, nay, Emma." He pulled himself up the ladder. "You wouldn't be so foolish. Sweet Christ, please tell me you didn't do this."

A pungent smell of thatch hung in the air and a soft breeze toyed with the tiny linen curtain. The fabric fluttered against the small opening, tapping out a lonely tune on the wooden walls. Alex knelt, pulled the fabric aside, and gazed out at the silent forest. It occurred to him that the birds were not singing.

A flock of crows rose into the air from the treetops, splintering the silence as they called to each other. They circled over the roof of the cottage like a black cloud, before settling back into their rookery.

Heart pounding, he sat back on his heels. Emma had been taken. The certainty of it shook him to his core. He closed his eyes and clenched his fists.

"Forgive me, Alicia," he whispered. "I've failed her."

Stephen spoke with conviction. "She's likely out there hunting rabbits and has lost track of time. I'm going to look for her."

Alex turned to him, envying the hope that still lingered in the young man's eyes. "You'd be wasting your time. Argante already has her. Out of the way, lad. I must leave."

Stephen climbed down the ladder, his face draining of colour. "But how can you be so sure?"

Alex gestured to Emma's bow standing by the door. "She's not hunting rabbits."

"Then we must find her." Stephen's voice trembled. "Before it's too late."

"It's already too late." Alex pulled on his boots, swallowing against the nausea in his belly. "And you're staying here."

"I think not." Stephen wriggled into his tunic. "You can't ask me to do that. What do you mean, it's too late? It can't be too late."

Alex picked up his sword and buckled it around him.

"I've only one horse, Stephen."

"Then he must carry both of us."

Alex shook his head. "Bart has been with me a quarter century. His spirit is strong, but his heart is not as it was. He cannot manage us both. Besides, it will slow us down."

"Then I'll follow on foot." Stephen fastened his sword belt. "But I won't stay here. Emma is...Christ, Alex. She's very important to me."

Alex paused at the door, halted by the emotion in Stephen's voice. "Aye," he said, " I know she is. Then hear me well, young knight, for it's essential you obey me. Stay out of sight. If I have need of you, you'll know it. They surely think you dead, so Argante will be expecting only me. 'Tis the stone he wants."

"Do you know where it is?"

"I do."

Stephen's eyes narrowed. "I suspected as much. But there are five of them besides Argante. You can't hope to defeat them all."

Alex smiled. He opened the door and fingered the hilt of his sword. "They'll all be dead before sunset this day. And you must take heed of my orders, or you'll be dead too."

Bart pranced in excitement as if sensing the urgency in his master's preparations. Stephen held the stallion steady as Alex swung into the saddle.

"Remember what I told you, lad."

Stephen looked up at a crow circling overhead and nodded. "Alex?"

"Aye."

"Will you find her alive?"

The desperation in the young man's voice brought tears to Alex's eyes.

"Aye, I'll find her alive. She's his weapon against me, so he won't kill her."

He gathered the reins and kicked Bart to a canter.

But she'll never be as she was. I can only pray he hasn't killed her spirit.

Chapter 9

Argante never prayed. Whenever God's name did manage to cross his lips, it always suffered the verbal escort of some evil rant or blasphemous curse. Heaven and Hell existed only in a man's heart, and there was naught beyond the grave. At least, that's what Argante believed. He respected the finality of death, but didn't fear it. Then again, he had no intention of dying anytime soon.

Such thoughts played in his mind as he rode back to Lowland Chase, thoughts prompted by the knowledge he would soon be facing his old adversary. Once he had the stone in his grasp, he planned to kill Mathanach and keep the girl to use as he pleased. He wondered if her disappearance had yet been discovered. Argante smiled, imagining Mathanach's pain upon learning the girl's innocence had been torn from her.

Emma. God's blood, the wench had been so fresh, so tight. He hardened at the thought. Her scent was all over him. The salt on his lips came from her throat, her shoulders, and her breasts. He could smell her on his fingers and in the folds of his shirt. The tight ache in his groin became uncomfortable and he slowed his horse to a walk.

"Can I have her now?" Iain had asked as Argante left the dungeon.

"Nay. You'll not put your cock anywhere near this one. Guard her, but don't touch her."

Strange reaction, he mused. He always shared his women with Iain, like throwing a bone to a dog. *So why not this one?* The image of Emma's startling green eyes wandered into his brain - eyes faceted, it seemed, like emeralds.

Emeralds?

"Jesus Christ."

He gave his head a shake, adjusted his crotch and

urged his horse into a canter, but despite his self-reproach, thoughts of Emma remained.

By the time he arrived at Lowland Chase the sun had lightened the sky to a milky blue and pulled the chill from the air. The stagnant moat circling the manor wrapped a cloying stink around the old house. Argante wrinkled his nose in disgust as his horse's hooves rattled across the rotting boards of the small bridge. He glanced down at the bloated carcass of some nondescript creature, recumbent on the moat's fetid surface. Its lips, in death, had curled into a hideous grin. Argante pulled his eyes away from the vile sight and looked to the house. Startled, he cursed and reined in his horse.

The door of Lowland Chase stood wide open and unguarded.

Other than a crow watching him from its perch on the roof, there was no sign of life. Argante slid from the saddle and drew his sword, the back of his neck prickling with apprehension. None of the men yet knew of Emma's capture or location. When he'd left the previous night, he warned them only of a possible attack and instructed them to be on alert.

He paused in the doorway.

"Thomas!" Argante's harsh whisper disappeared into an unsettling silence and the prickle on his neck wandered over his scalp. He took a deep breath, steeled his jaw and stepped over the threshold.

He made a rapid sweep of the lower rooms, his hand sweating against the hilt of his sword. Everything appeared normal. He saw no sign of struggle and nothing seemed out of place. The staircase to the Great Hall lay ahead. He paused on the bottom step, squinting up into the dark recesses. With a quick glance behind, he started up the stairs. He hesitated on the threshold, peered into the hall, and let out a sigh of relief.

"The devil take you, Thomas." Argante sheathed his sword and strode across the floor to where Thomas sat at the table. "Where the hell is everyone? I told you to be on your guard, yet the damn door is wide open."

Thomas didn't reply. Was he asleep? Drunk? His anger rising, Argante shoved the man's shoulder.

"Answer me, you useless piece of shit."

Thomas's head wobbled a little, then lolled back to reveal a razor-thin cut across his throat. Bubbles oozed and popped from the opening, throwing a dark, bloody spray into the air.

"God's bollocks!" Argante stepped back, feet slipping in his haste. He looked down and found himself standing in a pool of thick, dark blood.

A quiet voice filled the room like a cold mist. "You'll have to clean it up yourself, Richard. I gave your servants the day off."

It had been many years, but Argante knew well who spoke. Uttering a curse, he spun round, drawing his sword again. Alex leaned nonchalantly against the doorjamb, his sword sheathed, his hand relaxed on the hilt. A smile played on his lips.

"Mathanach! You whoreson. Where the hell are my men?"

"They're visiting a friend of yours. Where's the girl?"

"What do you mean? What friend?"

"The devil, of course. Where is she, Richard?"

Argante shivered inwardly. "God's teeth. You killed them all?"

Alex shook his head. "Not yet. There are two still alive."

"Where are they?"

"Well, you're here, and I've yet to find the wee slug who usually clings to your arse. Iain, is it?"

Argante sneered. "Don't forget, you Scottish slime,

that I have your little girl. Or, should I say, Alicia's bastard. If anything happens to me, the wee slug you mentioned will slice her throat." He glanced at Thomas. "And I'll warrant you have no desire to clean up that mess."

Alex pushed himself upright, his eyes narrowing.

"Have you hurt her?"

Argante stepped out of the bloody puddle and stood by the window, a smile on his lips. "Aye, but the lass liked it. She begged me for more."

A sudden gust of wind grabbed one of the window shutters and smashed it against the wall. The impact wrenched it from the hinges and it fell to the floor with a crash, barely missing Argante's head.

"Jesus!" Argante stepped away and looked down at the shattered boards. "You're a servant of the devil yourself, Mathanach, with your hellish magic."

"'Twas but a gust of wind, you fool. Tell me what you want."

"You know what I want. And please spare me your pathetic denials. I know you have it."

"The stone is a holy thing, not meant for a devil's hands. It will only do you harm."

Argante grunted. "Bollocks. The girl for the stone - those are my terms. Iain has instructions to kill her if I don't return to him by sunset, and I doubt her death will be swift or painless."

Alex pondered for a moment. "Very well. Meet me at sunset and bring the girl. I'll show you where the stone is."

"Meet you where? No tricks, Mathanach."

"Nay, no tricks. The Bastard's Keep."

Argante felt the blood drain from his face. "Where did you say?"

"The Bastard's Keep. The old grey tower at the foot of

Black Combe. Do you know it?"

"Aye." Argante could not believe what he was hearing. "I know it."

"What's wrong, Richard? Do the local ghost stories frighten you?"

"Of course not. Are you saying the stone is hidden in the keep?"

"Aye, but even if you took the walls apart, you'd never find it. Not without me. Sunset, then? Gives you plenty of time to clean up this mess."

Argante blinked, his mind reeling. "Sunset. Aye."

~o~

Twelve hooves thudded along the shady forest trail, churning up the dark, sweet-smelling earth. Four belonged to Bart, the other eight to two handsome geldings taken from Argante's stable. Guilt clung to Alex like a shadow as he rode into the woods. He blamed himself for what had happened to Emma. He blamed the breeze for bringing tears to his eyes.

Five men had died that morning. Alex killed them in less time than it took a man to shave. He was aware of that simple detail because he'd seen Thomas shaving at the table in the Great Hall when he first entered the Chase. The man had been humming to himself and hadn't seen Alex steal past the doorway.

Three of the men died in their sleep, meeting their judgement swiftly and without pain. The other two knew nothing until the final few moments of their lives. Thomas had been the last to die. He was still shaving and humming, sliding the blade over his stubbly throat. With a little help, the blade slid much deeper. He died quickly.

Argante would not be as fortunate.

"*...the lass liked it. She begged me for more.*"

Anger sank venomous teeth into Alex. An image of Emma, innocent and happy, shattered like glass. In its place he saw Argante hovering over her, his depravity extinguishing her pure light. With a furious cry, he spurred Bart into a merciless gallop. The old horse blew and wheezed beneath him.

Then he heard it; a familiar voice skimming over the rush of blood in his ears. It echoed through his mind, speaking to him from the past.

"Above all, Alexander, beware the reflections of anger. You must pay them no heed. Always remember who you are. What you are."

"Christ, give me strength."

Bart answered to his master's tug on the reins, and slid to a halt with the geldings following suit. Alex slid from the saddle, drew his sword and fell to his knees, pushing the blade deep into the soft ground. The sword rocked from the impact, the blade slicing off shards of sunlight and casting them into the shadows.

Although he sought peace, Alex had no need of a church. The earth served as his altar, and his sword, which had killed so many that morning, served as a cross.

He wrapped both hands around the hilt and brought it to rest against his forehead, closing his eyes while he voiced the familiar words of his predecessors.

"Guard the peace and keep the faith. May God forgive my transgressions."

He slowed his breath, relaxed his muscles and focused on the sweet sounds of the forest. Soon, his heart slowed, his anger relinquished its harsh grip and the echoes in his head subsided.

A loud caw broke into his meditation. It came from a large crow sitting on a nearby branch, head cocked, eyes bright. With another shout, it ruffled ink-black feathers and flew off into the forest. Alex stood, his gaze following the direction of the bird until it disappeared into the shadows. He sheathed his sword and pulled the bridle from Bart's head.

"Forgive me, old friend." He rubbed the stallion's nose. "I asked too much of you. Go home."

Bart rolled his eyes and blew through his nose. Alex smiled and slapped him on the rump.

"Home, I said."

The stallion snorted in apparent annoyance, lifted his tail and cantered off through the trees.

Alex grabbed the reins of the other two horses and pulled himself up onto one of them. Neither animal wore a saddle - he'd not taken the time to tack them fully. Pressing his heels to the horse, they headed into the woods, following the path indicated by the bird.

He knew it would lead to the person he sought.

Chapter 10

Stephen eyed the two horses, relief easing the tightness in his chest. "I thought it was Argante's men. What happened? Is Argante dead? Did you find Emma?"

"Argante still lives." Alex held out the reins of the spare horse. "All but one of his men are dead, and I think I know where Emma is. Mount up, young knight. We must go."

Stephen pulled himself onto the horse. "Where is she?"

"A place called the Bastard's Keep."

"What makes you think she's there?"

Alex took a slow breath, his eyes darkening. "She fought damn hard, Stephen. I followed their trail through the woods this morning. Whoever took her had a horse tethered nearby. The tracks followed the trail to Lowland Chase, but instead of turning they went straight on, along the river. There are few places beyond there where they could hide anyone. The old keep was my first guess. I told Argante that's where the stone was hidden and said to bring Emma and meet me there at sunset. He did a poor job of hiding his shock."

"You should've killed him."

Alex shook his head. "I need to see Emma first. I have to be sure she's there."

"Is the stone there, Alex?"

"One thing at a time, lad."

Stephen fell silent and looked down. He had no wish to face the truth, but it washed over him like a sickening scent.

"Nay, young knight." Alex heaved a weary sigh. "We'll not find her as she was."

Stephen's gut clenched. "Then as God is my witness," he snarled. "I'm going to cut Argante to pieces."

They headed east, keeping away from the main path,

slowing their pace as they drew near to the Keep. The two men studied the dismal tower from the sheltered sanctity of the woods. It spilled a harsh, black shadow across the sunlit ground and Stephen shuddered.

"Christ. It's a prison."

"That's exactly what it used to be. The Normans built it when William sent his army up here to fight the rebels."

"There's no sign of life."

"Emma's here."

"Are you sure?"

"Aye, and so is the wee snake who guards her." Alex threw his leg over the horse's back and dropped to the ground. "But Argante is not. He's likely still cleaning up the mess I left. Leave the horses here and follow me. We have some housekeeping of our own to do."

"How can you be certain Argante's not here?"

Alex looked at him and raised an eyebrow. "Does the air smell like shite to you?"

Stephen yielded to a grin. "Nay."

"Right. Stay close, young knight."

They paused at the doorway. Alex placed a finger over his lips then gestured to the right. Darkness swallowed them as soon as they stepped inside. Stephen hesitated for a moment, squinting into the blackness. He blinked suddenly, not quite believing his eyes.

An apparition appeared before him, a glowing outline in the form of a man. Every hair on Stephen's body bristled in fear and he gasped.

It spoke to him in a voice he knew well. "Good. I was hoping you'd be able to see it."

"Alex? What the hell? How...?" Stephen stepped back and glanced over his shoulder to the sunlit doorway.

"Stay where you are," Alex commanded. "There's nothing to fear."

"But how can – ?"

A sudden rapture gripped him, a wild exhilaration unlike anything he had ever known or felt before. He drew in a deep, ragged breath and fear left him as if snatched away by an unseen hand. For one beat of his heart, Stephen's world knew no boundaries. Awareness burned through his mind like the stars he'd seen falling through the night sky. It carried with it the answers to every question ever asked, laying bare the ignorance of man. But before his consciousness had a chance to grasp it, it vanished.

Euphoria remained, an exquisite sensation of floating in mid-air. He had an urge to look over his shoulder, convinced wings sprouted from his back. A desire to laugh bubbled in his throat and tears filled his eyes.

"Sweet Mother of God."

"Try to relax, Stephen." Alex's face shone in the darkness. "Slow your breathing and calm yourself. You're in the presence of a very great power. Don't let it overwhelm you."

"What is it?"

Alex smiled. "'Tis what Argante wants but will never have. He would not see what you are seeing, nor ever feel what you are feeling. His soul is too dark, too evil. The fact you're able to see and feel it says much about you. 'Tis as I thought and as I'd hoped."

"The stone?"

"Aye, and you're feeling but a mere touch of its fingers. You haven't yet felt its full embrace."

"So it is here?"

"The light you see around me is my connection to it. Come."

"But...will Iain not see you like that?"

The light on Alex's face dimmed. "Not like this. But I'll still be the last thing he ever sees."

Daylight had never penetrated the narrow, twisting

stairway to the cells. Stephen had rarely seen such darkness and was thankful for Alex's strange radiance. Dampness coated the walls with a permanent sheen and gave birth to a foul-smelling slime. A fury rumbled up inside him as thoughts of Emma, lying torn and bruised in such a hellish place, played in his mind. His anger pushed the euphoria aside, replacing it with a different thrill, menacing and hungry.

Alex whispered a warning. "'Tis the stone's reflection driving your anger, Stephen. Try to control it."

He sucked in a long slow breath and held it for as long as he could. The fury receded, yet he felt it lurking within him like a trapped entity.

The stairwell ended at the earthen floor of a dismal cavern where each gulp of air tasted old and rancid. Three candles flickered in the farthest corner, their puny flames casting a yellow halo around Iain, who sat in front of a wooden door.

The two men crept forward until they reached the halo's edge. Alex gave a ghostly nod to Stephen and they pulled their swords. The metallic hiss echoed off the dank walls and Iain jumped to his feet. "Who goes there?" He drew his weapon, squinting into the darkness. "My lord, is that you?"

"Nay." Alex stepped into the candlelight. "Although you'll be seeing him in hell soon enough."

Cold steel rammed into Iain's chest and he dropped to his knees with a choking gasp. Shock tightened his face into a rigid mask and the sword tumbled from his hand. His hands fumbled blindly with the blade, which pinned him in place as death closed in. Two blood-choked words bubbled from his lips.

"You bastard."

Alex did not respond. He jammed his foot against Iain's shoulder and shoved him off the sword with a merciless kick. Iain flew backwards, hit the ground with a thud, and blew out his final breath.

Stephen threw back the bolt, and the heavy door swung open with a weary creak. A small cry of fear leapt across the dark space. It came from Emma, who sat huddled in the corner, arms wrapped around her knees, her face buried in the blood-stained folds of her shift.

The shift had been torn from her shoulders, leaving the bruised skin bare but for her long hair, which draped over her like a cloak. Her wrists bore cruel marks of captivity and her bare feet were black with dirt. Quiet sobs shook her body as she rocked back and forth.

"Jesus Christ have mercy." Stephen's heart lurched and the fury that had threatened him earlier writhed like a serpent in his chest. He felt Alex's hand on his arm.

"Easy, young knight. Let's just get her out of here." Alex sheathed his sword, crouched at her side and placed a gentle hand on her head. "*A ghràidh.*"

She flinched and curled herself even tighter.

"Don't call me that." The fabric muffled her harsh whisper. "And don't touch me."

Stephen saw the bewildered expression on Alex's face and answered to it.

"She's frightened, Alex." He crouched at her feet and pushed his fingers through her knotted hands. "Emma, it's us. Don't be afraid. You're safe now, sweetheart. Look at me."

He heard her breath catch and felt her fingers tighten around his.

"St...Stephen?" She lifted her head, drawing a sharp breath from him at the sight of her shadowed eyes and bruised throat.

"Aye, little one. We're here. You're safe now."

She gave a pitiful cry and held out her arms. Stephen gathered her close and lifted her from the ground. "My

God," he murmured into her hair. "You're so cold."

Emma buried her face in his tunic. "I'm so sorry," she sobbed. "Please don't leave me, Stephen. Please."

"Hush, my love. I'm not going anywhere. Hush, now."

Tears filled his eyes as she trembled against him. The smell of Argante's assault flared his nostrils and he gritted his teeth in distaste. He looked at Alex.

"May the bastard rot in hell."

Alex nodded, his expression grim. "Let's get her out of here before he returns."

They stepped into blinding sunlight and hurried to where the horses waited within the shelter of the forest. Stephen set Emma down, all the while whispering soft words of comfort and reassurance. She clung to him, trembling, her face buried in his chest, and flinched when Alex stroked her hair.

"Emma, my precious child," he murmured, his voice cracking with emotion. His hand drifted to grasp his sword hilt, knuckles whitening as his grip tightened. "I've failed you. Please forgive me."

But Emma didn't answer Alex, or even look at him. Stephen frowned at her lack of response, sensing her anger and resentment. He wondered what poison Argante had visited upon her mind, what damage had been done beyond what they could see. Such hidden wounds, he knew, often left the ugliest scars.

Visibly, things were already bad enough. Stephen bit down hard, fighting his rage at the physical evidence of Emma's ordeal.

Her clothing was torn, bloodied and dirty. Her legs and feet bore deep scratches, no doubt from her struggle with Iain in the woods. Thorns had already started to fester beneath her skin and a vivid rash of nettle-stings tracked a bold path around her ankles. Her neck was marred by teethmarks and bruises, as was her chest.

Most alarming, though, was the bleeding. Stephen had felt the wetness through Emma's shift as he carried her, and his arm now bore her bloodstains. She bled still, the dark stream winding a thin, chaotic path down her legs. This was no battlefield injury, or anything he could relate to. His words echoed the fear of his ignorance.

"Christ help me, Alexander. I don't know what to do."

"We're of little use to her in this." Alex sighed. "She needs a woman's help."

"Do you know of anyone?"

He nodded. "Take her and head east. Follow the trail around the base of Black Combe until you come to a small white cottage with an apple tree in front. 'Tis the home of Althena, the healer. She'll know what to do."

"You're not coming with us?"

"I have to wait here for Argante, remember?" Alex's expression hardened. "I've a nasty wee surprise planned for our friend."

Stephen gave a grim smile, wrapped his arm about Emma's waist and lifted her onto his horse. "Shall I return here?" He pulled himself up behind her.

"Nay, stay with her. I'll come to you. Go now." Alex looked at Emma. "And hurry, lad."

The horse, responding to the urgent demands of his rider, launched into a gallop. Stephen murmured words of comfort against Emma's ear, but if she heard them, she showed no sign. She trembled against him, hands gripping his sleeve like a frightened child. He held her close, aware of the anguished pace of her heart beneath her ribs.

Stephen followed the trail around Black Combe, his frustration growing as the path seemed to stretch ever onward. His tired eyes narrowed, desperate to see the small white cottage Alex had described. A sigh of relief escaped him when it came into sight, nestled in a bracken-choked vale.

"We're almost there, my love." He slowed the horse to a canter and dropped a kiss on Emma's head. This time she responded, but her whisper was not for him, and her words laced his blood with ice.

"Who am I, *Cùra*?"

She let go of his sleeve and collapsed against him. Stephen's heart froze mid-beat.

"Emma?" He lifted her in the crook of his arm, his eyes sweeping over her smudged, ashen face. "Oh nay, little one. Don't give up."

A sharp gust of wind swirled around them, fierce and unexpected. It brought with it a shadow, swift and dark, like that of a bird swooping down from the sky. So real was it that Stephen ducked, expecting to be struck. But moments later, when he lifted his head, he heard only the whisper of the summer breeze wandering across empty skies. Emma lay pale and still against him.

Breathing hard, he stopped the horse by the gnarled trunk of the ancient apple tree, its leafy branches casting cooling shade over the tired animal. No sooner had Stephen's feet touched the ground than the cottage door swung open and a woman stepped into the sunlight.

Perhaps it was the word 'healer' that had created the image of an older woman in his mind, someone with wizened skin, silver hair and failing eyes. How wrong he had been. This woman, of a similar age to Alex, was an exotic beauty, with fine features and wide dark eyes. The breeze played in her long black hair, which hung loose about her shoulders. Her gaze swept over him with the calculated intensity of a cat eyeing its prey. Stephen didn't fail to notice the dagger tucked into her belt.

"Mistress Althena?"

"Who's asking?" She didn't wait for an answer, but gasped. "By all the Saints, 'tis little Emma you hold in your arms. What the...?" She glanced past him. "Where's

Alexander?"

"He'll be here. He sent me to you. Emma is hurt, bleeding. She has been...she needs your help."

"Sweet Mary. Bring her in. Bring her in."

She ushered him into her cottage, and the interior also belied his expectations. This was not the dark, dismal hovel of a crone. A sweet smell of fresh-cut hay and lavender hung in the air, and a carpet of soft rushes cushioned his feet. The windows were uncovered, allowing sunlight to spill into the small space. Stephen had seen royal castles less welcoming than this modest home.

"In here." Althena lifted a pale linen curtain at the back of the cottage and gestured toward a small bedchamber beyond. "What happened?"

He took a deep breath, placed Emma on the bed and stepped back. "She was kidnapped by a madman."

"God have mercy," Althena muttered. "She's been violated?"

"Aye, and she's...she's bleeding from it. Will you help her?"

"And who are you?"

"My name is Stephen de Montfort and I'm..." *Who am I, indeed?* He was lost - lost to the beautiful girl lying so quiet and pale before him, already pledged to her in his heart. "I'm her betrothed."

"I see." She glanced at Emma. "So, Stephen de Montfort, tell me true. Was this man her first?"

Stephen clenched his fists and forced the answer from his mouth. "Aye, he was her first."

"I'm so sorry." Althena touched a hand to his cheek and nodded toward the door. "You'll find a small stream running behind the house. Light a fire in the hearth and put some water on to boil. If you hunger and thirst, there's ale and bread on the table. Help yourself."

He set about doing as she asked, finding some comfort in busying himself. Before long, a pot of water hung over a smouldering peat fire. He had no appetite but, consumed by an intense thirst, he downed a cup of ale with great relish.

Althena's voice crooned through the thin curtain. The words she spoke were unintelligible to him, but he recognized the kindness in her tone and wondered if Emma could hear her. He straddled a chair, dropped his forehead onto his folded arms, and heaved a great sigh.

"Stephen." A hand squeezed his shoulder and he lifted his head, blinking up at Althena's dark gaze.

He frowned. "Please tell me, mistress, that I didn't fall asleep."

She shrugged. "You were gone for a while, but don't feel bad." She glanced up at the roof, where bunches of herbs hung from the rafters. "'Tis the lavender which soothes a busy mind. It will have done you good."

"Emma?"

"She awoke and drank a tisane. She's now sleeping naturally and the bleeding has stopped."

He looked at her, seeking the words to ask a question. Understanding showed as a smile, and she answered him.

"The bleeding was not from her womb. The tear is lower down and will heal. The rest of her wounds are disturbing, but don't threaten her life and will heal." She sighed and tapped a fingertip to her temple. "Her mind will bear the ugliest scar. It always does, in these cases. Emma told me what happened, but I suspect there's yet more to her tale. Something beyond the physical attack."

Stephen ran a hand through his hair. "I agree with you and I believe it has to do with Alex. When we found her, she refused to speak to him but I don't know why." He twisted around and looked through the window at late afternoon sunlight. "He's supposed to meet Argante at sunset."

"Argante?" Althena's eyes widened. "He's meeting the man who took Emma?"

"Aye, to discuss the...ransom. He doesn't yet know we've rescued her."

"Ah. Then Argante does not have long for this world. No one can harm Alex's child and be permitted to live."

Stephen shifted in his chair. "Emma isn't really Alex's child."

"Perhaps he's not her true sire, but he loves her as a father might. Nay, more yet."

"What do you know of him?"

She tilted her head. "Alex? Likely as much as you do, Stephen de Montfort. And if I should know more, I'll not discuss it without his presence in the room." She turned away for a moment and took something from a basket by the fire. Stephen jumped as the headless body of a freshly killed chicken slammed onto the table in front of him.

Althena smiled. "Hungry?"

Chapter 11

"The past does not stay in the past. It circles around to greet us as we step into the future. One becomes the other. Thus has it always been."

Alex stood as a statue inside the cell, watching the candle's steady burn. Not a breath of air disturbed the small fiery wisp. Oppressive darkness formed a black wall beyond the feeble flame and the silence almost had a voice, such was the strength of it. Emma had lain here with no light at all, alone and terrified.

Anger consumed him. He closed his eyes, struggling against the reflective power of the stone. It linked to his impassioned mind, absorbing his strengths and weaknesses before returning them two-fold back to the source. Few men were strong enough to take it. Indeed, the stone would drive most mortals into madness.

Alexander Mathanach was not like most mortals.

Yet fierce emotion tore at the edges of his self-control. Argante had ripped away Emma's virtue and left her bleeding in the dark, but he had not stopped there. Alex had seen the revulsion in her eyes. He knew vile whispers had been uttered, destroying that most tenuous of bonds between parent and child.

Trust.

Secrets of the past, shaken from their quiet slumbers, clawed at his soul. For sixteen years they had lain hidden behind a cloak of anger and denial. And there they would remain unless Emma demanded he drag them out and lay them bare. Even then, he would have to make a decision. Which was less painful: falsehood or reality? Should he hurt the living, or protect the dead?

"I'm lost, *Cùra*".

Her whisper had been snatched by the wind and hurled at him with the force of a lance. He had reached out to her but felt nothing.

Damn Argante. Damn him to hell. Curse my failure to protect her.

Iain's body sat hidden in a dark corner, amusing the rats. Two candles burned outside the cell door, which stood slightly ajar, enough for the single candle burning within to be seen.

Although sunset was still a few hours away, Alex heard a footfall on the stair and saw a flicker of torchlight in the dark. His hand tightened on the hilt.

"Iain." Argante's harsh voice cut into the silence. "God's balls. I told you to leave the wench alone. If you touched her, you're dead."

The door burst open and Argante stormed into the cell, a flaming torch in one hand and his sword in the other.

"You're right." Alex stepped out of the shadows behind the door, sword ready. "Iain is very dead. What kept you?"

Argante gasped and spun round, dropping the torch, his blade arcing through the air. Alex reacted with the speed of a striking cobra and sparks flew as steel clashed with steel. Each man held his ground, weapons locked.

"I'm disappointed," Argante sneered. "I was looking forward to another rut with Fitzhugh's bastard. Sweet little thing, she is. You should try her yourself."

A surge of rage narrowed Alex's eyes as his blade came alive, twisting with a speed barely perceptible to human eyes. It wrenched Argante's weapon from his grasp and flung it into the air. Alex reached up and caught it neatly by the hilt.

"Death doesn't scare me, you Scottish bastard." Argante's voice held a semblance of truth, but the tight expression on his face belied his unease.

"Och, I'm just playing with you." Alex shrugged. " I'm not ready to kill you yet."

Argante snorted. "You'll have to. You'll never take me

out of here alive."

"Nay, don't misunderstand me. You are going to die. Just not right now." He gestured to where the torch lay, its flame crackling against the damp earth. "I wonder how long that will last? And the candle? Not too long, I think. Enjoy your last night on this earth, Argante. Enjoy a wee taste of what Emma suffered at your devilish hands. I'll be back with my blade in the morning. May your ghosts keep you awake."

Alex raised his sword in a cold salute, stepped back, and pulled the door closed. Argante's angry cry barely made it through the heavy door oak as the bolt slammed into place.

~o~

He turned Argante's horse loose with some regret. The stallion was a tempting bounty, but Alex knew Bart would not take well to being usurped. He took the gelding again, kicking him into a furious gallop.

The western horizon shouldered a line of fiery clouds, set alight by a dying sun. Alex lifted his chin to the breeze, savouring the warmth and fresh air after the stale dungeon. Althena's cottage came into view, with Stephen's horse grazing on sweet grass beneath the apple tree. The animal raised its head as they approached, and nickered a welcome.

Alex left the two horses together, rapped twice on the door and stepped inside. The smell of roasting chicken reminded him that he had not eaten that day. His stomach clenched in protest.

Stephen shot to his feet. "At last. What happened?"

Alex ignored the question, needing an answer to his own first. His eyes flicked around the room, coming to rest on the linen curtain.

"How does she fare?"

The curtain lifted and Althena stepped into the room. Alex studied her face, relieved to see the smile upon it.

"Physically, Emma will be fine," she said. "She's sleeping and no longer bleeds. The damage to her body will heal."

Alex sighed. "May God help her mind to heal as well." He pulled her into his arms and kissed her forehead. "Thank you.'Tis a sight for sore eyes you are, bonny lass. Can I see her?"

"'Tis good to see you too, you Scottish devil. Of course you can see her. But first, I must echo Stephen's question. What happened? Where is this Argante?"

Alex released her. "He's still at the keep."

Stephen frowned. "What do you mean?"

"Argante is locked in a cell at the keep. We'll hand him to the Devil in the morning."

"You're giving him a night to think about his demise?" A corner of Stephen's mouth lifted in a smile.

"Aye, there is that, although that's not exactly why I did it. I mentioned something to you the other day, lad, but perhaps you don't recall. Argante has only one true terror, a biting fear, learned from his father, who used to shut him in a trunk for punishment when he was a child."

He looked from one to the other, only to be greeted by blank stares.

"The dark," he said. "Argante is terrified of the dark."

Althena blew out a soft breath. "Alex, don't misunderstand me, but I know something of such intense fears. What you have done is enough to drive a man from his mind."

Stephen snorted. "The bastard is already out of his mind. I hope he suffers."

"Oh, he'll suffer." Althena wandered over to turn the chicken, skewered and roasting over a small fire in the hearth. "I doubt you'll find him to be the same person you left. I urge you both to be very careful."

Alex stood by Emma's bedside for a while, watching her sleep. He felt Althena's gentle hand on his shoulder.

"Come away," she whispered. "The child is safe. Come and eat. I fear your pallor is worse than hers."

So he ate, if only to appease his growling stomach, for the food held no flavour for him. Bitter bile coated his tongue, left there by the evil he had tasted that day. His child, aye, his child in every way that mattered, lay behind the flimsy curtain, her body torn, her mind corrupted.

She cried out several times during the evening. Each time, Althena went to her side, waving the men away with a resolute hand.

"'Tis the comfort of a woman's voice which is needed," she said. "Not that of a man. Not yet."

With a final declaration of fatigue, Althena tossed each man a meagre blanket before retreating to the small chamber to share the tiny bed with Emma.

Stephen dozed on the floor by the hearth, fidgeting in restless discomfort. Alex sat at the table, his busy mind quelling any desire to sleep. Frustrated and weary, he took his sword and went outside.

A pallid new moon had risen above Black Combe's ancient slopes, casting a feeble light across the land. Even the stars appeared bereft of strength, as if a translucent veil had been pulled across the cloudless sky. It was that deepest and loneliest part of night, when time itself seemed to stop for a while.

Alex settled himself beneath the apple tree and lifted his gaze to the skies in a silent prayer.

A star fell, burning a silver trail across the heavens. It prompted his fingers to play along the sword's hilt, tracing the familiar carvings with quiet deliberation. The ancient words engraved on the guard echoed in his mind, and his turbulent thoughts subsided a little.

Behind him, the cottage door squeaked open and footfalls trudged across the grass.

"Alex." Stephen settled himself at Alex's feet.

"Aye."

"I have questions."

Alex smiled. "And you believe I have answers?"

"Aye, but I'm not sure you're willing to share them with me."

Alex leaned forward, fixing Stephen with a steady gaze. "That depends."

Stephen frowned. "On what?"

"Your intentions." Alex nodded toward the cottage. "Most men would cast Emma aside now, used as she is. Do you still intend to pursue her?"

Stephen looked him straight in the eye. "With your permission, I intend to marry her."

Alex felt a weight lift from his shoulders. By all the saints, this young knight had a pure heart. "I give it willingly. And what of the stone?"

"What of it?"

"You act for Henry. What will you tell him?"

Stephen shrugged. "That the tale is a myth."

"You would lie to your king?"

"To protect you and him, aye."

"So, you do not intend to speak of it to anyone?"

"Nay, Alex, I swear with God as my witness." Stephen sighed and pushed the hair back from his eyes. "Besides, I can truthfully tell Henry there's no ancient king with a shield of silver."

Alex bit back a smile, amused by Stephen's obvious disappointment. "And what, pray, has led you to that conclusion?"

"You said it yourself. The stone lies hidden within the keep."

Alex chuckled. "That's not exactly what I said, but I can see how you might think so."

Stephen shook his head. "What do you mean? It must be there. I saw your... your light. I felt the power of it. It was..."

"Exciting?"

"Unlike anything I've ever felt."

Alex knew the connection had been made. He slid the sword from its scabbard and eyed the blade.

"Tell me, young knight, have you heard the name 'Darius' before?"

"Darius? Aye. Emma said it was the name of your sword. He was a king of Persia?"

"Aye, an ancient king of Persia." Alex presented the hilt to Stephen. "Take it."

Stephen looked at him sideways. "Why?"

"Take it. Examine the guard and the pommel." He glanced up at the moon. "If there's enough light, tell me what you see."

Stephen brought the hilt to his face, squinting in the gloom. He turned it, tracing the carving with his fingers.

"There are some words engraved on the guard. I can't..." He shook his head. "Nay, I can't read them. There's not enough light."

"Guard the peace and keep the faith." Alex leaned back against the tree. "The adage of the Guardians."

"A fine adage, indeed. Who are the Guardians?"

Alex ignored the question. "And the pommel? What do you see?"

Stephen's fingers traced the raised silver piping that wound itself around the egg-shaped pommel. "'Tis like a knot. But...there's no end, no beginning. An unusual design. Does it mean something?"

Alex smiled. "Aye, lad. It does. 'Tis the knot of Gordias. Have you heard of it?"

Stephen shook his head. "Nay."

"Legend tells of a knot, created by Midas, son of Gordias. It was proclaimed that whoever untied it would become the king of Asia. But, since it had no end and no beginning, it could never be undone. A king named Alexander, refusing to accept defeat, took his sword and sliced through it."

Stephen pondered for a moment. "You speak of Alexander, the great conqueror of Asia?"

"I do. I'm named for him. He was the first Guardian. There have been many since."

"Guardian of what?"

Alex sighed. "Young knight, take heed. You're holding a sword named for an ancient king and the hilt is made from pure silver. But it's more than a hilt and it's more than a sword. The pommel guards that which I must guard with my life, for I am one of the chosen. I am the present Guardian of Alexander's stone, Lapis Exilis." He glanced up at the stars. "The priest didn't lie. The stone rests with Darius, an ancient king, and is protected by a shield of silver. 'Tis what you hold in your hand."

He waited, watching the array of expressions flitting across Stephen's face. The young man had yet to blink or take in a lungful of air.

"Breathe, lad," Alex urged with a chuckle. "I swear I can hear your poor heart cursing in your chest."

"But, I can't believe...." Stephen stared at the sword's pommel, turning it over in his hand and running his fingers across it. He lifted wide eyes to Alex. "Nay, you jest. If the stone is truly resting in my hand, then how come I can't feel it? Like I did at the keep?"

"A jest, is it?" Alex leaned forward. "You felt the power at the keep because I allowed you to feel it. I wanted to see your reaction. Still, if it's further proof you need...."

A sudden gust of wind lifted the grass around them and shook the old branches of the apple tree. At the same time, the pommel of the sword began to perspire tiny, brilliant, pin-pricks of light. They swarmed over the hilt like a thousand luminescent ants, blending and merging together until they covered it completely. The sword glowed and pulsed with a strong, steady rhythm. Alex knew that each luminous beat coincided with the throb of Stephen's heart.

"Sweet Christ." Stephen's voice trembled with emotion.

Alex smiled and sat back. The light pulsed once more, then disappeared.

"Do you still have doubts, young knight? Or would you like to see it light up Black Combe as well?"

Stephen pulled in a deep breath. "So 'tis you who controls it?"

"Aye. At least, enough to keep it from doing harm." Alex held out his hand. "The sword, if you please."

"But how?" Stephen leaned forward and placed the hilt in Alex's hand. "And what harm can it do?"

"'Tis controlled with a quiet, clear mind. That's partly why I choose to live as I do, away from the loud pretensions of men. In the wrong hands, the stone becomes an evil, malignant force, eventually destroying even he who holds it."

"Does Emma know of it?"

Alex nodded. "Aye, although she doesn't know everything. I'll have your word, lad, that you'll say nothing of our conversation to her or anyone else."

Stephen frowned. "I already gave you my word."

Alex could almost hear the thoughts tumbling through Stephen's mind. The young knight had not been told everything either, nor would he be. Not yet. Not before the Circle had been consulted. The others had to be informed, investigations carried out. A decision would be made only after any trace of doubt had been removed.

Alex had no doubt. None at all. The certainty of who Stephen was - would be - burned in him like a sacred flame.

"I have more questions." Stephen's voice pulled Alex from his musings.

"Aye, I'm sure you do, but they'll have to wait." Alex got to his feet and glanced over at the thin silver filament gleaming on the eastern horizon. "'Twill be light soon, and we have a killing to do."

By the time they reined in their horses at the keep the night had retreated, leaving behind a frail new-born light. The entrance yawned at them from the grey walls, dark and forbidding, daring them to step into the blackness beyond.

They didn't hesitate. Alex once again appeared as an apparition, his soft glow thrusting the shadows aside. The stench assailed his nostrils as soon as he reached the staircase.

Stephen stole Alex's thought and spoke it out loud. "I smell burning."

Alex didn't reply. He drew his sword and headed down the stairs.

The smell grew stronger as he descended the damp, narrow steps. A grey wisp rose up to greet him, wrapping itself around him like a misty cloak. It was no mist, he realized, but smoke, curling around him as he stepped onto the floor of the cavern. He paused, his narrowed eyes stinging, his mind searching for an answer.

A terrible understanding crept into his thoughts and his heart missed a beat. He groaned inwardly, cursing his lack of foresight, his weakness, and his desire for revenge.

"Sweet Mother of God."

"What?" The scrape of Stephen's sword leaving the

scabbard accompanied his voice. "Alex, what is it?"

Alex strode over to the cell door, and Stephen followed. It was still closed and bolted, yet the ancient oak now bore the charred scars of fire, which ran up the wood in flaking black lines, like the gnarled fingers of some hellish beast. The bottom edge of the door had been burnt away in the centre, the hole forming a scorched, ragged arch. Alex felt sick, unwilling to accept the likely truth.

Nay, surely not. It's not big enough for Argante to crawl through. Besides, the smoke must have killed him, suffocated him. He could not have survived.

"Stand back, lad."

"But I don't understand. How did he – ?"

"Stand back, I said."

Alex reached over and slid the bolt. It clattered into the cradle, the sound splitting the depressed silence of the cavern. He glanced over at Stephen in an unspoken signal. Stephen acknowledged with a nod and Alex kicked the door open, sending it crashing into the wall.

Darkness greeted them, and something else - a vile smell, acrid and bitter. Alex could almost taste it. But nothing stirred in the blackness. Nothing leapt from the shadows or cowered in the corner. No one whimpered or cried out. Only the door creaked painfully on its hinges as it pulled away from the wall. Alex stepped into the cell, his physical glow intensifying until the light reached into every corner.

The room was empty and Alex's gut twisted as the truth took hold. Argante had escaped.

"Jesus Christ."

"Alex, how the hell...? Where did he get the flame?"

"I left him with a torch and a candle."

"You...?" Stephen gasped. "For God's sake, why?"

Alex sighed. "A moment of folly. I wanted him to

suffer, watching the light die, leaving him alone in the darkness. God knows, I didn't think he would do this."

Stephen paused for a moment, as if absorbing the truth. "Well, he's gone, and your regret won't change that. We can still catch him. But what's that stench? It's vile."

"It smells like burnt flesh."

Alex pulled the door toward him, looking to see the damage on the inside. A chill ran over his skin.

" Look at this!"

Deep scratches, line upon line of them, had been gouged into the wood, as if a rabid animal had clawed frantically at the door. Alex reached over and pulled something from the blackened oak - a bloodied fingernail - no doubt torn from Argante's hand in sheer madness as he attempted to escape.

Stephen crouched down at the threshold and poked at the ground. "'Tis this ash which stinks."

Alex bent and studied the floor. Small remnants of clothing could be seen mixed in with the fine dark ash. He gathered some on his fingertip, rubbed it between finger and thumb, and sniffed it.

"Nay," he whispered, the horror of it dawning on him.

"What is it?"

"Argante's madness. The remains of burnt hair and flesh."

Stephen rose to his feet. "We can do naught else here." He stepped out of the cell. "Let's go. He must have left tracks. He's likely crawled off into the woods somewhere and died."

Alex threw one last glance around the room. "I hope you're right, lad, but something tells me otherwise. Madness is a formidable beast with a relentless spirit. I fear the man we seek today is far more dangerous than the one I left here yesterday."

Stephen paused outside the cell door and glanced over

to the dark corner where Iain's body sat. The relaxed silhouette gave the impression of a man sleeping, but a faint bitter-sweet odour mixing with the smoky air told the grim truth of it.

"Another ghost for the locals to fear." His eyes swept around the dark cavern, Alex's eerie glow the only source of light. "I can understand why they stay away from this hellish place."

Alex followed his gaze. "Aye. Although 'tis not the dead who would do us harm, only the living. Come, lad. We must find Argante and finish him."

They stepped outside into cloying, sea-soaked air that hung in a curtain of salty drizzle, drenching them in moments.

"God's teeth. Where did this come from?" Stephen eyed the heavy clouds above, their tendrils almost brushing the top of the keep's thick grey walls. He looked over toward Black Combe, its rugged slopes now obscured beneath a dreary, wet veil. "It was clear when we arrived."

"'Tis the tide. It drags the rain in with it." Alex studied the ground and stepped around some prints in the soft earth. "Here, look." His narrowed eyes followed the direction of the tracks, anticipation lifting his mood. "He's headed south, toward the river. And he's injured."

At least he's headed away from Emma.

Stephen announced the same thought out loud. "Thank God he's not heading toward Emma." He crouched and studied the footprints, a puzzled expression on his face. "How can you tell he's injured?"

"The prints are unevenly spaced. See? He's favouring his left leg." Alex stooped to dip a fingertip into a rain-filled footprint and studied the pink-tinged fluid that stuck to his skin. "And he's bleeding. Let's go."

Before long, the lively rush of the river caught Alex's

ears. He reined in his horse at the bank and straightened in the saddle, his back aching from stooping over his horse's neck to follow the tracks.

"Did he cross here?" Stephen pulled up beside him, eyeing the exuberant white water gushing noisily over rocks and stones. At this point, the river was not wide, but flowed at a rate fast enough to unsettle even the most surefooted person. Even if the pull of the water did not upend a man, the slippery, jagged rocks beneath certainly would.

Alex shifted his seat and squinted across the rapids. He saw no sign of prints or disturbance on the other side. Yet the footprints ended there, at the bank. His mind struggled to find an explanation.

"Nay. So where the hell...?" Alex fingered the hilt of his sword and looked to the skies.

"He must have gone into the river." Stephen slid from his horse and examined the ground around them.

A crow dropped out of the clouds and circled overhead, silent, watchful. It settled on a nearby branch, shook the rain from its feathers, and threw a loud caw into the air. Alex studied the bird for a few moments then looked downstream.

"That's another thing I have questions about." Stephen's eyes flicked from Alex to the crow.

"Not now, lad."

"But what's the meaning of – "

"Not now, I said. Mount up." Alex turned his horse and started along the bank. "Argante is headed for the shore."

~o~

"I don't understand." Stephen reined in alongside Alex at the forest's edge, and looked out across the mist-shrouded estuary. "Why would Argante come here?"

Alex didn't answer, although the same question had been burning in his mind for the past mile. They had found Argante's footprints again, farther along the bank. He had obviously managed to navigate the river bed, hoping, no doubt, to obscure his tracks. Or perhaps, Alex mused, to soothe his burns in the cold water. Later, the tracks had stopped again, at a point where the river widened and calmed. Since then, there had been no sign.

The tide ran high and fast across the estuary's dangerous sands, churning with angry currents easily capable of dragging a man out to sea, along with his horse. Drizzle still tumbled from the thick, grey swathe above them, soaking both men to the skin. Alex contemplated the violent waters. If Argante had tried to cross the estuary, he would not have survived.

"If he tried to cross the estuary, he's a dead man," Stephen declared, watching the waves claw at the sand.

Alex swallowed a smile. Stephen's mind had started to reach beyond the boundaries of most men's abilities, and was linking to Alex's thoughts. Such behaviour was considered offensive among the Guardians, but Alex knew it to be an innocent intrusion, another sign of Stephen's connection to the stone. For now it would be tolerated.

"True, he would not have survived the crossing." Alex twisted in the saddle and looked back along the trail. "We'll return and cross the river at the last point we saw his footprints, then head east along the other bank. If we don't see any other sign of him, we'll head back to Althena's. I don't like leaving the women alone."

Stephen fixed Alex with a solid stare. "Where's the crow? Can't he tell you where Argante is?"

Alex smiled. "Young knight, 'tis surely the drizzle which addles your brain. Did no one ever tell you that crows cannot speak?"

Chapter 12

They searched all morning, battling rain and wind in what turned out to be a futile mission. No trace of Argante could be found, other than what they had discovered already.

As Black Combe loomed out of the damp haze, the dread already nudging Alex kicked him a little harder. He knew Emma carried more than physical wounds. A poison surely festered in her mind, put there by Argante's depravity and venomous tongue. The stone reflected his fears and toyed with his emotions, heightening his pain. He suffered in silence, trying to reconcile his guilt and sense of failure, while regret leached into his heart.

Stephen, no doubt fighting his own internal demons, had said little as they rode. Only when Althena's small white cottage appeared did he speak.

"Thank God," he muttered.

Despite his fears, Alex silently echoed the sentiment. He was tired, wet, and weary of the saddle.

The cottage smelled delicious, the aroma of soup mingling with the soothing scents of herbs. The weather had obscured the time-telling trek of the sun across the sky. Still, Alex knew it was well past noon, for his stomach clenched as soon as he stepped through the door.

Althena, stirring a pot over the fire, looked up as the men entered.

"God love us. Two drowned rats, and starving, no doubt." She met Alex's gaze and her eyes narrowed. "What happened? You've been gone a long time."

Alex threw his wet cloak across the chair and nodded toward the curtain. "How is she?"

Althena smiled. "Rested. She has eaten and her strength is returning." She glanced at Stephen. "She asked for you."

Stephen frowned and looked at Alex, who nodded.

"Go to her," he said. "You don't need my permission."

"So?" Althena asked, before Stephen had barely stepped behind the curtain. "I know you well enough, Alexander. What's wrong?"

"He escaped."

Althena closed her eyes for a moment. "Good Christ. How?"

"Set fire to the cell door. Made a hole barely big enough for a fox to get through, yet somehow, he got through it. We tracked him to the tip of the estuary, then lost him." Alex shook his head. "Twice now, Althena. Twice have I failed."

"Oh, nay."

She stepped into his arms, her warmth and sweet smell a balm for his tender nerves.

"Do not think such things," she murmured against his chest. "'Twas through no fault of yours."

Alex rested his cheek on her hair. "I'm afraid the blame lies squarely on my shoulders, bonny lass. I failed to protect Emma and now Argante may still live due to my stupidity."

A movement caught his eye. He lifted his head to see Emma leaning against the doorjamb, her hand hooked through Stephen's arm. She stared, unblinking, studying Alex with eyes that held no glimmer of warmth. Her long hair swung loose around her shoulders, her pale face and slender neck still bearing the marks of Argante's assault.

"Emma." He released Althena and took a step toward her.

"Is it true?"

The chilled tone of her voice stopped him dead.

"Is what true?"

"That you were married to my mother?"

Emma's words twisted in his heart like a knife. He heard Althena's surprised gasp behind him and saw confusion flash across Stephen's face.

"Answer me, Alexander. Were you married to my mother?"

Alexander? Never had he thought to be so wounded by the simple utterance of his name.

"Do not disrespect me, Emma." *Yet why should she not? Do I deserve aught else?*

"Will you answer me?"

"Aye, Alicia was my wife."

Anguished tears flashed at him. "Then what Argante said is true? I'm naught but a bastard?"

"Don't say that, lass."

Her voice faded to a whisper. "Tell me, please. Is it true?"

Alex bit down hard.

"Aye, you were born out of wedlock."

Emma hiccuped on a sob. "Then is it also true you killed my mother?"

There. There it was. The question he'd expected. Yet he wasn't prepared for the crushing impact it made. Memories from the past tore open wounds not fully healed by the touch of time and the images bled afresh into his mind.

His wife lying on the floor at his feet. The body of Edward, his most trusted friend, lying in a patch of sunlight by the window. And blood. So much blood.

Alicia had made her choice.

What now, wife? What of your child? What of her pain? The truth is the same, whichever way it is told. How shall I tell it, Alicia?

Alex pulled in a ragged breath and looked straight into Emma's beautiful eyes.

"I cannot lie. Your mother died at my hands."

Something between them crumbled and a precious bond snapped. A cry burst from Emma's lips, a hopeless sound that plunged straight into Alex's heart.

For a brief moment, part of him wished she'd never found Stephen in the forest, that none of this had happened. Yet, in that same moment, he understood unavoidable destinies had already been forged by actions in the past. The walls of fate could never be breached. The future would always play out as intended.

He took a cautious step toward her, reached out, and touched her hair.

"Forgive me," he whispered, pulling his hand away when she flinched.

"Never!" Eyes bright with tears, Emma spat her pain at him. "You say you cannot lie? My entire life has been a lie. I shall never forgive you for this."

She turned and fled into the bedroom, each heart-wrenching sob like a whip against Alex's skin.

Stephen's face was tight with shock. "For God's sake, why, Alex?" he whispered. "Why would you keep this from her?"

Alex frowned and looked at the ground, seeking answers that might make sense, but finding none. When he raised his eyes again, Stephen had already gone to Emma's side.

He turned to Althena, taking in her shocked expression and pale face, hands clasped prayer-like at her chin.

Desolation threatened to drown him. "Have I lost you too, lass?"

She shook her head. "Nay, you haven't. Nor will I judge you, for I'm not without secrets of my own. But what damage has this madman done?"

A sigh tore from his chest. "Immeasurable. I'm not sure it can ever be repaired."

He glanced back at the bedchamber. Stephen's soothing voice could be heard above Emma's quiet sobs.

"'Tis better, I think, if I leave. She needs time. They need time."

"You're going home?"

"Aye. They'll follow when they're ready." *I hope.* "I'm in your debt, Althena."

"You owe me naught, Alex. They can stay here as long as they wish."

~o~

Alex clambered into the saddle and spurred his horse into an easy trot. The oppressive mist had disappeared, dragged back out to sea by the retreating tide. It left a salty taste in the air, which also bore the heady scent of saturated turf and wet bracken. Sunlight managed to find gaps in the thinning clouds, descending to earth in wide, silver beams, fanning out in glorious splendour across the horizon.

He looked up at the wondrous sight and drew a wistful breath. In his mind he saw Emma, no more than eight years old, sitting before him on Bart's back and pointing at the sky.

"Look, Cùra! Heaven has opened a window."

Aye, and Hell had recently opened a door, releasing a demon that might yet live to do more harm.

He pulled his horse to a halt at the edge of the forest, listening, his eyes scouring the dark recesses of the woods. Nothing untoward caught his attention. The sights and sounds were merely that of a summer's day; flecks of sun through the trees, a rabbit peeking out from beneath a bramble patch, a woodpecker drumming on dead wood, water dancing over ancient stones.

"Where are you, Argante?" he muttered. "Does your cursed heart still beat?"

A shadow passed overhead; a solitary crow, silent in

flight. It told him nothing.

By the time he arrived home the sun's silver rays had changed to gold. Bart - still wearing his saddle from the previous day - whinnied through a mouthful of hay from the barn's open doorway and rolled his eyes at the gelding.

"Och," Alex slid from the saddle, trying to ignore a lonely ache in his soul. "Dinnae fash yourself, old friend. This one's not about to take your place. Come, let's get you both settled."

Until he entered the house that evening, Alex had never considered the torment of silence. Previously, it had always been something he'd associated with calm and meditation. Now he discovered its sharp edges, cutting him without mercy.

Emma's bed was as she'd left it, the imprint of her body still visible on the pallet. Her bow and quiver stood propped up by the door, her sword wedged onto a shelf above her bed. Alex took it down and examined it. He'd had it made for her and taught her how to use it. She'd learned quickly, proving herself a good student, ever eager to please him.

Maybe if you'd thought to take it with you, lass.

He set it back on the shelf, turned his back on the quiet room, and closed the door.

Alex spent the next few days in weary contemplation, finding little peace in prayer, nor in the brief snatches of dream-filled sleep. The house felt strangely claustrophobic in its emptiness, and fatigue weakened his ability to counter the effects of the stone, which only served to torment him further.

The daylight hours were spent on Bart's back, searching the surrounding forest for any indication of Argante's presence. But the man, it seemed, had vanished. Dead? Alex acknowledged the likelihood, indeed prayed for it. Yet even dead men left their bones behind and filled the air with a rotten stench. Perhaps the tide had taken him, or perhaps the bastard was hidden somewhere, licking his wounds.

Unease, with a stench of its own, clung to Alex like a shadow.

After yet another restless night, Alex headed for the barn, intent on seeing to the horses. Stars still peppered the sky, although most had already vanished behind dawn's grey pallor. A mild chill pinched the air, hinting that summer was at the point of surrender.

The cockerel greeted him with several loud crows and Bart whinnied a welcome. Alex rested Darius against the wall and set about his chores, changing the bedding straw and drawing water from the well. Weighed down with unease, he worked in morose silence. Bart nuzzled him, blowing into his hair as he set the water bucket down.

"Ach, don't worry, my friend." Alex ran his hand down the stallion's sleek neck. "My sadness is for the wee lass, not for myself."

Bart's ears pricked up, and he nickered softly, his head turned toward the doorway. Alex heard it too; the unmistakable sound of a horse approaching.

"And it seems," he murmured, knowing full well who it was, "the wee lass has come home."

Something stopped him from stepping outside. A passive thought. *Let them come to me*. He heard the cottage door open, followed moments later by the sound of footsteps crossing to the barn.

A shadow fell across the doorway.

"Alex." Stephen's voice was cautious, his face pale and tight. It appeared the young knight had not slept much either.

"Good to see you, lad. How does Emma fare?" Alex looked past him toward the house. "Did she returned home willingly?"

"She's improving, but still...conflicted," said Stephen, obviously choosing his words with care. "Did you find any sign of Argante?"

Alex shook his head. "Not a trace."

"Then surely he's dead."

"I hope so. Answer my question. Has she returned willingly?"

Stephen grimaced and gave a slight shake of his head, unspoken words clearly hanging in the air.

Alex sighed. "Say what you have to say, young knight."

"I'm leaving today, Alexander. I'm going to Thurston, my brother's demesne in Yorkshire. My work here is done, and my family are no doubt wondering where I am. Henry, too, is likely awaiting my report. Thing is..." he glanced over his shoulder toward the house, "...Emma wants to come with me, but I told her she can't unless you give your permission."

Emma leave? God above, Alex had not expected this. His response was immediate and not a little harsh. "Nay, I shall not give it."

Stephen nodded, disappointment evident in his expression. "I understand. Then she must stay with you, of course. With your leave, however, I should like to return here within the month. We wish to marry as soon as possible. I think she fears that I might abandon her since.... " He looked down and kicked at a pebble on the ground.

Alex cursed inwardly, his mind faltering over his initial gut reaction. That the lad loved Emma was beyond any doubt. Still, to let her go with him now, unmarried as they were, went against propriety. But could he keep her here against her will, bitter and resentful? Worse yet, fearful that Stephen might not return? Would that not serve only to push her farther away?

Stephen cleared his throat. "Alexander, you should know that Emma – "

"Has no desire to stay with me." How bitter the words tasted. "Faced with the truth, then, it seems I have little choice in the matter. Where is she?"

"Inside."

"Packing, no doubt." Alex took his sword and stepped out of the stall. "You'll need two horses. Take the other gelding."

"Oh, nay, Alex. One horse will carry us both. We'll take our time."

"It was not an offer, lad. Get him ready." He strode past Stephen and went into the house.

Emma's chamber door stood open. She wandered out, a cloth bag and her bow strung across her shoulder. Her head was bent, focused on buckling her belt.

"Did you tell him? How did he take it?" She looked up into Alex's eyes and gasped. "*Cùra*! I thought you were –"

"How did I take it? Ach, my wee lass. I think I took it well enough." Alex ran his fingers through his hair, his gut twisting as he observed the child he loved so well. Althena had obviously given Emma some clothes. They hung loosely on her small frame.

"You can't force me to stay."

The tremor in her voice belied her resolve. Alex saw past her defiant chin, the flush of anger on her cheeks, the way she held herself upright, stubborn and resolute. It was all a facade, an attempt to hide the pain and confusion that haunted her beautiful eyes.

"Aye, I can, but I won't. Indeed, you may go with my blessing, for what it's worth. Stephen is a good man, a fine knight, and I know he'll take care of you. But if you ever have need of me...." He swallowed over the lump in his throat. "Despite what you might think or believe, child, I've always loved you with a heart free from guilt or obligation. That will never change."

A tear fell and traced a silver trail across Emma's cheek. "I'm not as I was, *Cùra*. My world is not as it was. I doubt all I once held true." She looked toward the door. "Stephen is the only one I trust. If I lose him, I have nothing."

Alex closed his eyes. "I'm so sorry, Emma."

He felt the brush of air as she stepped past him, and heard the quiet click of the door. An exchange of voices disturbed the dreadful silence and the door opened again. He turned to see Stephen on the threshold, his expression drawn.

"Do not fear for her," he said. "I'll protect her with my life and honour her as promised. I'll send word as soon as we arrive."

Alex forced a sad smile and nodded. "I have complete faith in you, young knight."

"I'm sure..." Stephen fidgeted on his feet. "...I'm sure she'll forgive you. 'Tis only time she needs."

"May that be the truth of it."

"Thank you for everything." He glanced at Alex's sword. "For your confidence and faith in me. I swear I shall not speak of what I've learned to anyone. I...we must leave now. There's a three day ride ahead of us."

Alex raised an eyebrow. "You're dwelling on your words, lad. Farewell is quickly said, so say it."

Stephen sighed. "God be with you, Alexander."

"And with you both."

Once again, the door closed with a quiet click. Alex stood, unmoving, waiting until the sound of horses hooves faded into the distance.

Only then did he stir.

He set Darius against the wall, pulled out a chair and sat at the table. Emotions leaned heavily upon him, but he fought them off with the skill of a Guardian, a skill honed from years of practise. He would not weaken. He would not.

A mere heartbeat later, the soft laughter of a child echoed through his mind and his resolve crumbled.

Alexander Mathanach dropped his head into his hands and wept.

Chapter 13

At a time when the Roman Legions were leaving Britain's shores forever, a young oak tree in a northern forest unfurled its first leaves. It took root in the dark crevice of a granite boulder, managing to thrive where little else would grow. As the years passed, the trunk thickened, only to find itself surrounded on all sides by walls of solid, immovable stone. Undaunted, determined to endure, the tree fought doggedly against that which restrained it.

Several years later, on a bright spring morning beneath a naked blue sky, a crack like that of thunder burst through the forest. So loud was it, that a nearby flock of crows took to the air in fright, cawing madly. The birds remained aloft for some time, wary of returning to their roost and whatever had disturbed their peaceful glade.

They need not have feared. The noise was simply that of a granite boulder being split apart by the trunk of a young oak.

Over seven hundred years had passed since that morning, yet the mighty oak still stretched its limbs across the forest glade. Gnarled, they were, twisted by time and ravaged by three thousand seasons. At the foot of the tree lay four pieces of granite, mere pebbles, trapped between the toes of a giant.

Alex waited until nightfall, leaving the house only when the evening star had risen up from the horizon to hover over the trees. Moonlight draped the forest in a silver cloak, turning the palest shadows to darkest black. He saddled Bart and led him from the barn, pausing for a moment to gaze up at infinity, his hand drifting to the hilt of his sword.

"Where are you, Argante?" he murmured, shifting his gaze to the surrounding forest.

An owl hooted, the eerie call echoing through the

trees. Alex swung onto Bart's back, took one last glance around him, and rode into the shadows.

They were waiting for him at the sacred oak. When a Guardian issued a summons, the others were obliged to respond. Only one other time had he felt the need to call them together. That had been sixteen years ago when he'd taken charge of a tiny girl, vowing to protect and care for her.

Emma.

Alex left Bart at the edge of the clearing and approached the ancient tree on foot. He paused beneath the branches, glancing up at the majestic tangle. The stone pulsed beneath his touch.

They were there, as he knew they would be.

He drew the sword, first raising the hilt to his lips before pushing the point of the blade into the earth. As before, his actions served to create the semblance of a cross resting in the ground before him. This time, though, he did not kneel and pray, but spoke openly to the air.

"My lords. It has been many years since I approached the Circle."

Indefinable shadows moved through the trees ahead of him, and the air around him chilled, lifting the hair on his skin.

"We sensed your distress, Alexander. Your inner balance has been compromised."

Alex shrugged. "Temporarily. I'm not immune to discord. You're all aware of the disturbances in my past. Their ripples have caught up to me, and the innocence of the child has been corrupted through my failings."

The atmosphere bristled with a sense of impatience.

"While we regret such an occurrence, Guardian, it's none of our concern. Our interest lies solely in that which you guard. We trust, then, you have a valid reason for this summons."

"I have two reasons." He paused and took a breath. "One is a young knight, who has connected to the stone, although he does not yet know it. He exhibits the required traits and has the qualities you seek. I ask your leave to bring him to the Circle for your consideration."

"What of this knight's soul?"

"Without stain."

A soft breeze whispered through the leaves of the oak and something stirred in the branches above his head. Alex glanced up, but could see nothing.

"And the second reason?"

Alex shifted on his feet and took another deep breath, knowing what he sought would not be easily given.

"I seek permission to use the shield."

He thought he heard faint laughter ringing through the trees before the woods fell silent. Moments passed and Alex turned to look about him, puzzled at the delay.

"My lords?"

"We're still here, Alexander."

A warrior emerged from the shadows, tall and strong, clothing as black as night, one hand resting on the hilt of his sword. Long white hair shone like frost in the moonlight, and his skin glowed as if lit from within. His dark eyes held an unearthly gleam, as well as a mortal spark of amusement.

"There's stunned silence within the Circle, my friend, for we are truly amazed at the size of your Celtic balls. The shield, is it? Have you lost your mind?" The warrior gestured back toward the trees. "There's one or two back there who are ready to strip you of your status. I told them not to mess with a Scottish warlock."

Alex grinned. "'Tis good to see you, Finn."

"You too, my friend." The warrior raised a brow. "What do you need it for?"

"What does any Guardian need the shield for? To be

visible, yet hidden. I only need it for a short time, for my own peace of mind."

"To keep an eye on the little lass?"

"Aye."

"Where has she gone?"

"Yorkshire. The young knight's family has holdings there."

"Ah. A love match, is it? Then perhaps you should just let her go."

"I cannot. The child is deeply troubled."

"But the shield, Alex? I hardly need remind you of the risks. Using it weakens the Guardian's emotional resolve. Your emotions are already under duress. It would not be wise to place the stone among men under such circumstances."

Alex lifted his chin. "My resolve is yet strong, but I fear for Emma's well-being. Will you at least consider my request?"

Finn nodded. "Of course. Everything you've said will be considered. Go home and await our decision. But before you do...."

He reached out and grasped Darius's hilt, his lips curving into a smile.

Alex grinned. "Miss it, do you, Finn?"

"Aye. It reminds me of an Irish lass who came close to giving me similar sensations."

A harsh gust of wind cut through the clearing, creaking the old boughs of the oak.

Finn rolled his eyes, pulled the sword from the earth, and handed it to Alex. "There are those within the Circle who lack a sense of humour. Sadly for them, they don't appreciate a jocular being like myself. Go now. You'll hear from us before nightfall tomorrow."

Alex's weary heart took strength and beat with a lighter rhythm as he left the meeting place. If nothing else, it felt good to have connected with his peers, men who knew and understood what it meant to be a Guardian. The fact that they had not immediately rejected his request also buoyed his spirits. Bart must have sensed it too, for the stallion pricked up both ears and feet on the way home.

~o~

His mind clouded by fatigue, Alex sought out his bed and succumbed to some much needed sleep. When he next awoke, the sun was resting on the western horizon, stretching cool shadows across the forest.

He sat up, his thoughts clawing their way back to mental clarity and balance. The few hours of sleep, though laced with now-forgotten dreams, had done much to restore his resolve.

As his mind cleared, his lethargic muscles demanded release. Eager to move, he grabbed the sword and headed for the barn. He stepped into the sweet, hay-scented shade, closed the door, and peeled off his shirt.

Both hands gripped the hilt as he centred the weapon before him. He pulled in a deep breath, locking it under his ribs, sharpening his focus to match the deadly edge of his blade. Only when his lungs burned did he allow the breath to escape, guiding it slowly over his lips in a controlled release. It surrendered any remaining tension and allowed him to settle into a relaxed stance, combining perfect balance with finely tuned form.

Using slow, deliberate moves, Alex cut the blade through the air.

As his muscles warmed, he increased the pace and intensity, opening himself up, allowing the stone to reflect energy back to him. He arced the sword in wide, powerful swings, thrusting and parrying against imagined foes with formidable strength. Slivers of evening sun pierced gaps in the barn-boards, catching a swarm of dust motes and slanting off the sweat that glistened on his muscle-honed chest and arms.

Alex did not slow for a moment, devouring the power in his grasp with the fierce craving of an addict who had long been deprived. The surges flowing through him were highly charged, arousing, and absolutely lethal to any mortal who would dare challenge him while he was thus immersed.

Behind him, Bart gave a sudden loud snort, and another sword purred as it was pulled from its scabbard.

"Not bad for a puny Highlander. How about a real challenge, Mathanach?"

Alex's heart clenched. He spun round, his gaze flicking to the closed door before he smiled.

"Finn. I didn't hear you knock."

The silver-haired warrior stepped out of the shadows with sword drawn and a strange gleam in his eyes. He was not alone.

A second warrior emerged from the darkness, equally as tall, with long hair as black as the clothes he wore.

Alex's smile turned into a grin. "And Keir, you sly devil. 'Tis good to see you both." His grin disappeared as he looked from one warrior to the other. "I hope."

Keir gave a nod, the trace of a smile on his lips. "'Tis good to see you too, Alexander."

"We'll give you the bad news later." Finn waved his sword in the air. "But right now, my Gaelic friend, I feel like sparring."

"Against Darius?" Alex shook his head, trying to ignore Finn's remark about bad news. "Not even you are that good, my lord."

"Nay, not against Darius. Set it aside and use Keir's blade." Finn nodded at his fellow warrior. "It will even out the match."

"Hardly an even match, Finn." Keir drew his sword and handed it, hilt first, to Alex. "You're fighting a mere mortal."

"A mere mortal? I think not." Finn shrugged, his blade whistling as it cut a figure eight in the air. "But I'll go easy on him. Is Keir's sword a worthy enough weapon for you, Alexander? Not too heavy?"

Alex grinned, balancing the sword in his hand. "It feels fine."

The gleam in Finn's eyes seemed to flare for a moment before his blade arced. Alex blocked it and sparks flew.

Finn pushed Alex away and attacked again. "Tell me, my friend, do you miss the wee lass?"

Alex felt a stab of pain that had nothing to do with a blade. He dodged a thrust and countered with one of his own.

He ground his teeth as he swung the sword. "Of course I do."

Finn raised his eyebrows as he locked weapons with Alex. "But you must surely welcome the freedom your solitude brings. When are the women coming over?"

"What women?" Alex swung again and more sparks flew. "My Lord Keir, please ensure my barn does not catch fire while I silence this Irish demon."

"Bah! Let Emma go, ungrateful child that she is. Lose your saintly lifestyle and have some fun for a change." Finn's blade flashed as it cut through the air. Alex cursed and jumped back, but not before the point scoured a thin line across his chest.

Finn chuckled. "First blood to me. I'm telling you, scratch the itch between your legs and you'll soothe the ache in your heart. What about that healer wench that lives yonder? Did you bed her yet? Wouldn't mind parting her thighs myself. As I recall, she's in possession of a fine pair of – "

"Christ almighty, Finn." Alex pushed his anger aside as he parried a thrust. "I know what you're trying to do, and it won't work. My emotions are under control."

Finn stepped back and lowered his sword, his expression at once serious. "Not so, Alexander. You're compromised by your grief."

"Aye, as I was once before." Alex felt a surge of determination and glanced over at Darius, acknowledging the source. "But I prevailed then and shall do so again. The stone is not at risk and you both know it. 'Tis the sanity of my child that is at risk, thanks to the perversity of one man and the lies of another. I can't just let her go and absolve myself of all responsibility for her well-being."

Keir spoke. "But she's with this young knight. He must be of pure heart, since you've recommended him to the Circle."

"Aye, he is, and he'll protect her with his life, but my fear is for her mind. I would hear your thoughts and know of your decision."

Finn narrowed his eyes. "And you will honour that decision? Even if it's not what you wish to hear?"

Alex flinched inwardly, but spoke truthfully. "Aye, my lords. I shall honour and abide by any decision you've made."

Finn glanced at Keir, who nodded a silent response to unspoken words.

"Night approaches." Finn gestured to the door. "Come. There's much to discuss and a barn is not the place for such discourse." He lifted Alex's sword from where it rested against the wall. A sublime smile drifted across his face as the hilt settled into his palm. "I would have bested you easily, Alexander."

Alex studied the faces of the warriors seated at his table. Their expressions remained impassive, although the gleam lingered in Finn's eyes. Since they did not display auras in the mortal sense, Alex could only wonder at their mindset.

Each warrior had, in his time, been a Guardian of the stone. The essence of that honour emanated like veiled moonlight from their skin, casting a faint glow into the gathering gloom.

"Tell me, Alexander." Keir's eyes swept over the sparse surroundings. "Do you ever miss court life?"

"I did at first." Alex pulled on his shirt. "But my sacrifice was not as great as you might think. I gave up the noble lifestyle, but kept much of my wealth. If I need something, I have the means to obtain it. I want for – "

"Nothing?" Keir finished, pinning Alex with an intense gaze. "Then why are we here?"

"Don't twist my words, Keir. I've no interest in baubles, other than the one in my sword, and you well know I cannot buy what it has to offer." Alex leaned forward. "Only the Circle can grant me permission to use it. I'm eager to hear your decision."

Keir sighed and leaned back in his chair. "It's been many years since the Circle has been this - shall we say - stimulated? You stirred up a lot of passion with your bold request. Using the shield has always been considered an abuse of the stone's power. Also, it weakens the Guardian's composure, which leaves the stone vulnerable. It's deemed too great a risk."

"What are you saying?" Alex's heart quickened as he looked from one to the other.

The two warriors exchanged glances before Finn spoke. "We are saying, my friend, that the nays took the vote."

Disappointment kicked hard.

"I see." Alex managed a grim smile. "Very well. The problems I face are, of course, mine to deal with. I respect your decision."

He was suddenly aware of how dark the room had become and rose to light a candle.

"Sit down, Alexander," Keir commanded quietly. "Our business with you is not yet finished."

Alex sat, puzzled by Keir's remark. "What do you mean?"

A few moments of raw silence filled the room and a curious prickle wandered over Alex's scalp.

Finn looked down at the table, his face thoughtful. "'Tis natural that you fear for your child's well-being, my friend. We understand your concerns."

Alex nodded. "Emma is very important to me."

Finn gestured toward Darius, which stood against the wall. "But as Guardian of yon jewel, you have an even greater responsibility. The Circle expects much from you."

Alex stiffened. "Have I not met those expectations?"

Finn chuckled. "Aye, you have. Met and exceeded them, which became the basis of our argument last night. How can we refuse to help you when you have given and sacrificed so much?"

"Yet, you just said – "

"The Circle voted against you using the shield on your own, but we managed to strike a compromise that would seem to suit all concerned."

"A compromise?" Hope fluttered in Alex's chest. "What compromise?"

Finn looked over at Keir. "I think we've tormented him enough. Put the poor bastard out of his misery, will you?"

"Gladly." Keir smiled and his dark eyes took on a similar gleam to Finn's. "The Circle has agreed to let you invoke the shield, providing it's done under surveillance and with additional protection for the stone. That being so, Finn and I have volunteered our time. We will assume certain identities in this god-forsaken Yorkshire castle where Emma will be staying. I shall investigate the young knight to see if he's as worthy as you say, and Finn will support your role as Guardian for as long as you need him. He will, in effect, be your second."

A ribbon of warmth wrapped itself around Alex's heart. He closed his eyes for a moment.

"You have my complete gratitude, my lords. This means a great deal to me."

"Ach, don't get maudlin on us, my friend. It doesn't suit your ballsy persona." Finn rubbed his hands together, a wide grin on his face. "'Tis a perfect solution though, is it not? I must say, I'm looking forward to a relapse from my saintly existence. I hear there are some fine wenches in Yorkshire." He fidgeted in his chair. "Indeed, I believe I'm already aroused."

Keir rolled his eyes. "And so it begins. Christ help us."

"There's much to do before we leave." Finn frowned and reached over to lift a candle from the table. He passed his hand over the wick, which caught with an instant flame. "'Tis very dark in here."

Alex chuckled. "You must show me how you do that."

"We must show you how to create the shield." Keir stood and drew Darius from its scabbard. "It takes much practice to perfect the illusion. Only those chosen will see what you wish them to see. Everyone else will see your true image. The fewer people you manipulate, the easier it will be on you."

"There are only two who I wish to...that I will..."

"Deceive?" Keir gave a wry smile. "Say it as it is, Alex. The shield is a ruse. A lie. Which is another reason we hesitate to allow it."

"We'll need a week to prepare," Finn mused. "And you'll need another horse, so dig out some of your hidden wealth and buy yourself a new animal. Bart would never make the journey to Yorkshire."

Alex pondered for a moment. "I'll leave him with Althena."

"Althena!" Finn slapped his hand on the table. "That's the wench's name. I'll go with you when you visit."

Alex grinned. "Will I need to protect her?"

Finn grinned back. "Nay. The lass will be all over me like flies on —"

"Enough frivolity." Keir drew Alex's sword from the scabbard. "I was never one to waste time. Let us begin, Guardian."

Chapter 14

Three days after leaving Cumbria, Emma's feelings still lay in a tangled heap of disbelief and hurt. Innocence had become a mere word, a thing she had once possessed, never realizing its worth until it was stolen from her by a vile and corrupt soul. More painful yet, in a mind-numbing distortion, the person she'd always turned to for protection and assurance had betrayed her.

That Alex had lied about her parents was beyond her comprehension. Her waking hours were spent seeking an understanding, an explanation of why he had hidden the truth from her, but she could not make sense of it.

Nor could she forget the deep sadness in his eyes on the day she left. Anger prevented her from saying goodbye in a gentle fashion, and now guilt gnawed at her conscience. It seemed that a lifetime of love and caring had been carelessly cast aside. After all, Alex was still, in every way that mattered, her father. She missed him. Worse than that, she mourned him.

Sleep, when it came, brought little relief. Merciless, it opened a door in her mind, giving freedom to the terrors lurking within. She heard Argante's voice muttering guttural obscenities, felt his hands on her throat and a tearing pain deep in her belly. Something warm and wet gushed down her legs as the door slammed shut, leaving her to scream at the silent blackness.

Only then did she awaken, gasping for breath, sweat soaking her pillow. Instinctively, she would reach for Stephen, her beloved knight, who would hold her close and whisper words of love to soothe her fears.

He rode at her side now, never more than an arm's length away, always vigilant and protective. More than ever, Emma needed to feel his closeness, and in a strange twist, relished the protective response her nightmares always wrought from him.

Her faith in all she held true had gone, her confidence crushed beneath a burden of self-doubt. Each night, lying next to him, she wondered about Stephen's hesitation to touch her. Certainly he held her, and tenderly, but not with any great show of passion. Since leaving Cumbria he hadn't even kissed her, except for an occasional brush of his lips against hers.

She silently questioned this behaviour, fearful his feelings for her had been blemished by the loss of her innocence. Was it merely his honour, his vow to Alex that quieted his touch? Or did he, Heaven forbid, consider her stained, used, undesirable as a lover or a wife?

Her eyes filled with tears as she wrestled the questions in her mind.

"Tired, sweetheart?" Stephen studied her face. "Just a few more hours. We'll be at Thurston before sunset."

"I am a little tired." She offered him a tearful smile "Don't worry. I'm fine."

"Ah, I think not." Without slowing the pace of his horse, he reached over, wrapped a strong arm about her waist and pulled her into his lap. "There. Now you can sleep. But first, you'll tell me why you have tears in your eyes. Are you thinking about Alex?"

Emma sighed. "I think about him all the time."

"Only to be expected, my love. He's an important part of your life."

"He's lied to me all my life, Stephen."

"Perhaps, but I refuse to believe he killed your parents in cold blood. He's not capable of such an act. There must be another explanation."

"What explanation? He admitted to it. Argante said –"

"Argante!" Stephen turned his head and spat on the ground. "The man is the Devil's spawn and spews the Devil's words. I hope he's burning in his sire's hell."

Emma tensed at Stephen's outburst. He groaned and

tightened his arm around her.

"Forgive me, little one. My ire is for Argante, not you."

She fidgeted against him, seeking further solace for her troubled mind. "There's something else I must ask you, Stephen. Please be honest with your answer."

"Ask it. I shall not lie to you."

"I need to know if you still want...I mean...what Argante did to me. Has it changed – "

Stephen cursed and pulled the horses to a halt. His fingers slid under her chin and lifted her head so that her gaze met his.

"I know the question your tongue struggles with, Emma. Look at me as I answer you, for you must see the truth as well as hear it."

She searched his hazel eyes, remembering the first time she had done so barely two weeks earlier. Now, as then, she saw no sign of deception in their soft depths. He smiled and brushed her bottom lip with his thumb.

"Aye, I remember it too; the first time I saw you, stepping out from behind that tree, your arrow pointing here." He touched his chest. "I thought you were a creation of my feverish mind, such was the vision I beheld. Believe me, my brave little faerie, I wanted you then and I want you now."

"Yet you hesitate to touch me. I wonder if you no longer desire me because of what happened."

"No longer desire...?" He groaned and pulled her closer. There was no mistaking the hard arousal nudging against her thigh. "There, lass, is my want of you. Christ knows, I'm beyond tormented whenever you're close to me. 'Tis a wonder I manage to sit the damn horse. But I'll not act upon that desire. Not until we're wed." He cupped her face with his hand. "Besides, you're still healing. Argante hurt you, damn him to hell, and I need to be sure you harbour no more fear of what happens between a man and woman. 'Tis a beautiful thing when shared as it should be, when both are willing."

"When shared with someone you love, you mean." Regret dulled her voice. "I wanted it to be you, Stephen. Only you, and forever. But Argante took it from me. He stole that which I wanted you to have. 'Twas my fault for leaving that night. I'm so sorry. Please tell me you will not abandon me."

"Abandon you? Oh, Emma, heed your own words. Argante *took* what he wanted. You didn't give him anything. Don't you see? Your love is still yours to give. That you want to give it to me makes me the luckiest man under Heaven." He stroked her tears away with his fingers. "Set your fears aside, sweetheart, and stop tormenting yourself. I love you very much."

She shivered again, snuggling her head against his chest. "I love you too."

"Then I'm blessed." Stephen urged the horses onward. "Sleep a little, if you can. Tonight you'll have a hot bath and sleep in a proper bed. Thurston's a fine place. I'm eager for you to meet my family."

"Is Christophe much older than you?"

"Nay. Five years only, and there are four years between me and my little sister. You'll like Beatrice."

"I hope they like me."

"They'll love you."

Not if they knew of my shame. They would surely think me unworthy of their brother.

"Uh oh. There's that look again. I know it well." Stephen smiled down at her. "Tell me the cause."

"Please don't mention Argante," she murmured. "Don't tell them what he did to me."

"I swear I shall not speak of it, my love. You're an orphan of noble birth who has been raised by an adoptive father. 'Tis the truth, and all they need to know."

Somewhat placated, Emma allowed her gaze to wander across the vastness of the moors to the north. A carpet of purple heather stretched out as far as the eye could see, the tiny flowers rippling beneath the gentle touch of the breeze. The beauty of it managed to creep into her tortured mind, pushing away a little of the darkness.

Lulled by the sound of Stephen's heartbeat, the gentle sway of the horse and the sweet scent in the air, Emma fell asleep.

Stephen eased off the reins, content with the steady pace in this latter part of their journey. He bent his head and kissed Emma's cheek, glad that she slept, frowning at the bluish circles beneath her eyes. How she suffered, and how helpless he felt. What solace could he offer to one so bereft, so tortured?

In quiet reflection, his mind explored the fateful path they had followed over the past few weeks. Until that moment, he hadn't really considered just how much his life had changed by what he had seen and learned. Everything had happened so quickly, spurred on by bursts of urgency and emotion.

Unwilling to surrender to melancholy, he turned his mind away from the recent ugliness and focused on that which had enriched his life. The sleeping beauty in his arms, if she did but know it, had stolen his heart. Alexander's friendship and trust could only be described as a special gift, and the contact with the stone had been beyond description. His heart quickened at the thought of the strange unearthly object whose power touched the depths of his soul.

The mysterious jewel had, after all, been the reason for his mission to Cumbria. He reminded himself he'd been sent there by his king, who no doubt waited impatiently for news. Stephen knew he'd have to journey to London eventually, but not until Emma had settled into Thurston. If, indeed, she was able to settle into Thurston.

Emotion welled up inside him as he turned his focus back to the young woman in his arms.

Even as she slept, her fear and uncertainty spilled into his thoughts and magnified his need to protect her. He longed to know the truth, for he was certain Alex held onto other secrets. Who was Emma, really? What had happened to her parents? So many questions and so many miles until they reached Thurston. Plenty of time to ponder.

The light faded when they entered the thick forest surrounding Thurston. The sun was blazing just above the horizon, lancing spears of light through the trees. One of them flashed across Emma's face and she stirred, blinked, and smiled at Stephen. Then she shifted and stretched, wriggling in his lap. He groaned inwardly. Such sweet torture!

"You slept well, sweetheart?"

"I think so. Where are we?"

"We're almost home."

Emma tensed and Stephen silently cursed his tactless choice of words. How easily he read her mind. Thurston was his home, not hers. She had none, or so she thought.

She sat upright and gazed around her like a lost child.

"Forgive me," he said. "I didn't mean to upset you. I hope you'll come to think of Thurston as home."

"I know you didn't, and I'm sure I shall." She sighed and leaned against him. "But it'll be very different to what I'm used to."

"True." He nuzzled her hair. "But there's nothing to fear. I'll be at your side."

"Even so, your home is a castle, not a cottage in the

forest. How many people live there?"

"'Tis really not that large, as castles go. Including the knights, the men-at-arms and the servants, probably about forty."

She chewed on her lip. "And are they all as nice as you?"

Stephen laughed. "Nay. You're stuck with the best. They're all good, kindhearted people. You'll see."

A shout of recognition rang out from the battlements as they approached the castle gates. In response, the drawbridge dropped and the portcullis groaned and rattled a lazy ascent. Emma's fingers tightened around Stephen's as the horses rumbled over the bridge and entered the bailey.

The de Montfort banner sat atop its pole on the battlements, snapping under the playful hands of the breeze. Shadows from errant clouds flitted across the castle walls as the sounds and smells of the bailey drifted through the air. A horse whinnied and another responded as the smithy's hammer took its toll on an anvil. Maids chatted and laughed over soapy laundry tubs. Outside the armoury, sandstone rasped against metal as several young squires sharpened a number of swords.

Familiarity wrapped around Stephen with all the warmth of a mother's embrace. This was his home, his birthplace. His childhood at Thurston had been brief, because like most young noble sons, he had been fostered out at age seven. Even so, the walls surrounding him held nothing but good memories.

"Welcome to Thurston, little faerie. 'Tis a very peaceful place." Stephen reined in the horses and slid from the saddle just as a woman's shriek echoed around the castle walls. "Except for that," he finished, reaching for Emma.

Her eyes widened as she dropped into Stephen's arms.

"What in Heaven's name is that?"

He grinned, fully aware of the female-form hurtling toward them across the courtyard, her skirts lifted and hair flying.

"'Tis more of a who than a what. I'm afraid Beatrice is not known for her subtlety. I have to let you go for a moment, my love, or we will both be flattened. Trust me."

He turned just in time to catch the girl, who launched herself at him from a good two paces away.

"Stephen," she yelled, flinging her arms around his neck in a strangle-hold. "You've come home!"

"Your powers of observation almost match the power of your lungs, dear sister." Stephen returned her hug. "I'm sure all of Yorkshire now know we are safely arrived to Thurston."

"We?" Beatrice looked past him at Emma. "Brother mine, you have brought us a guest?"

"Aye, would that I live to introduce her." Stephen feigned choking as he unhooked himself from his sister's embrace. He placed a gentle arm around Emma's waist and drew her to his side. "Emma, this is my sister, Beatrice. Or Bee, as we call her. Bee, this is Emma, my betrothed."

Another shriek had the horses veering away in fright, and a young stable-lad scrambled to grab their reins.

"Betrothed?" Beatrice looked from Stephen to Emma in wide-eyed excitement, unkempt chestnut curls floating in complete disarray about her shoulders. "Betrothed? God's teeth. Since when? Christophe and Miriam will be so surprised."

Stephen chuckled, cleared his throat and gave Emma a squeeze. "I apologize, my love, for my sister's rudeness. She sadly needs reminding that you have a pair of ears and a tongue in your head. Care to show her how it should be done?"

"'Tis my pleasure to meet you, Bee." Emma smiled and grasped Beatrice's hand. "Stephen has told me so much about you."

"The pleasure is mine, and please forgive my manners." Bee wrinkled her nose at Stephen and squeezed Emma's hand. "But my favourite brother has been gone for months. I've missed him terribly, and now I find out he's to be married. I haven't been this excited since Anne fell in the moat. Where are your things? Are they to arrive later?"

Emma shook her head and gestured to the horses, which had at last been caught by the fraught young groom. "Nay, there's nothing to follow. Everything I own is on the back of that horse."

"Everything?" Bee threw a questioning glance at Stephen.

He slanted a cautionary glance back at her, a silent plea for tact.

"Emma grew up in the country with her male guardian. She's never had much use for silks and velvets."

Sibling blood shared a silent understanding and Bee performed with grace, offering a warm smile to Emma.

"I take it this means you don't like sewing?"

Emma laughed. "I hate it."

"Then I love you already, for I cannot abide it either." Bee grinned at Stephen and linked her arm with Emma's. "Will you hurry inside, brother dear? I'm fair itching to see Christophe's face upon hearing your news."

Stephen fought an urge to grab his sister and swing her around in grateful abandon. In a matter of moments, the blessed girl had lifted Emma's spirit, ignited a tiny spark in a pair of haunted green eyes, and made his sad little faerie laugh again.

I wish you could see her now, Alex.

In that instant, it seemed to Stephen that the sun blinked.

A shadow swooped across the bailey and a baleful caw pulled Stephen's gaze skyward. A crow landed atop the flag pole, fluttering its wings to steady itself against the breeze. He watched as a harsh gust of wind toppled it from its precarious perch. The bird dropped as if struck by a stone, smashed into the cobbles, and lay twisted and broken at his feet.

"What in God's name...?" He stepped back, his confused mind unable to grasp what he had just witnessed.

A voice spoke. It came from nowhere, from everywhere, from without and within. Stephen knew the voice well, for it belonged to a man he loved and respected.

A man who was many miles away.

"Take heed, young knight. She is but a feather in the wind."

His heart clenched and the hair on his neck lifted. "Alex? How the hell – ?"

He looked over at Emma and Bee, who were strolling toward the castle door. It appeared they had not noticed the bird nor even witnessed the strange event. Bee hung onto Emma's arm, chatting as if nothing had happened. Obviously, they hadn't heard Alex's voice.

An explosion of memories ignited in his mind, each one a cherished image. Emma, running silently through the forest, catching flat-fish with her bare feet, shooting deadly arrows, and healing the wounds of a dying knight.

A beautiful girl, confident, courageous, intelligent and happy.

The images faded. Stephen had a growing awareness of Alex's mental intrusion, but no longer questioned the inexplicable link. All at once, the impossible felt as natural as breathing.

"Look at her now, Stephen. See her as I do."

Stephen watched Emma through Alex's eyes and what he saw shocked him.

A gloomy aura, a grey outline, void of light or colour, surrounded her. Her head was bent as she listened to Bee's endless chatter. Her shoulders, previously square and proud, drooped as if bearing an unseen weight. The bounce had disappeared from her stride. There was no sense of purpose in her movements, but rather a weary deliberation driven by necessity and sheer effort.

The symbolism of the crow's death became clear, and the clarity of it sickened Stephen's stomach. Now he understood the meaning. Emma fought her demonic winds every day and, like the bird on the pole, struggled to keep from falling.

Anyone who had not known her previously would be no wiser, but Stephen now saw what he had not seen before.

Damn it to hell. Had he really been that blind? Things were far worse than he realized.

"Christ, Alex. I'm sorry." He closed his eyes. "She's lost her spirit, hasn't she?"

"Worse. She has lost her faith. Guard her well, lad."

"Stephen? Is something wrong?" Emma's sweet voice caressed him, drowning out the gut-wrenching whispers of truth. *Her sweet voice.* When, he wondered, had he last heard her sing? He glanced down at the cobbles. The bird had disappeared.

Ignoring Bee's puzzled expression, he strode over to Emma and pulled her into his arms, revelling in the feel of her, the scent of her. "Nothing's wrong. I was only thinking about how much I love you." He trailed his fingers along her jaw. "Come. I'm eager for my brother to meet the faerie I captured."

Emma grinned. "You have it backwards. 'Tis the faerie who captured the knight."

Stephen laughed. "Aye, that she did. And he has no desire to escape."

The evening sun poured through the windows of Thurston's Great Hall, highlighting an ever-present cloud of fine dust. Certainly, there were far bigger halls in castles all over England, but if Thurston lacked in grandeur, it overflowed with character.

Years of woodsmoke had stained the thick oak beams in the roof, turning them from soft gold to rich brown. The lofty canopy of darkened wood sat in stark contrast atop the rough white walls, which were decorated with an array of brilliant tapestries and battle-dented shields bearing the de Montfort coat of arms. The large fireplace at the far end of the hall had been built only two winters before at great expense. A tall man could easily stand inside and look up the new chimney. Of course, the hearth was bare of flame. The weather did not yet demand the warm crackle of burning logs.

Fresh rushes, already trampled flat beneath human feet, cast off a sweet scent, which mingled demurely with mellow aromas of roasted meats and stewed vegetables. A faint odour of unwashed bodies also tinged the air.

The evening repast had finished, but folks still lingered at the tables, relaxed by good food, well-brewed ale, and pleasant conversation. Memories flooded Stephen's mind as he stood on the threshold, and a smile spread over his face as he absorbed the atmosphere.

Christophe de Montfort, Stephen's older brother and lord of Thurston, sat at the head table with his pretty dark-haired wife, Miriam. Both were deep in conversation with another beautiful dark-haired lady sitting with them. Stephen's whimsical mood dissolved at the sight of her.

"By all the saints, Bee. You might have warned me she was here." He glared at his sister, who shrugged.

"Sorry, brother. I didn't want to spoil the joy of your return. She arrived three days ago."

Stephen groaned. "God give me strength."

"Who is she?" Emma asked.

"Anne," Stephen replied, his voice bitter. "Miriam's charming sister."

"The same Anne who fell in the moat?" Emma looked at Bee, who giggled.

"Aye, one and the same. Slipped on the bank and went straight in, so she did. I fell to my knees and whispered a fervent prayer, which God chose to ignore. 'Twas a very sad moment in my life when the wench surfaced again."

Emma laughed. "Why don't you like her?"

"You'll see." Stephen wrapped his arm about Emma's waist and led her into the hall. "Take little notice of anything she says. She has a serpent's forked tongue."

A momentary hush fell over the room when Stephen entered, followed immediately by a cascade of greetings from serfs and servants alike. Christophe looked up at the interruption, his puzzled frown turning into an expression of absolute delight as he rose to his feet

"God be praised!" Christophe held out his arms. "Welcome home, brother. We were in despair of ever seeing you again."

Stephen stepped into his brother's strong embrace.

"'Tis good to be back, Christophe. Miriam, you're as beautiful as ever. Anne, you haven't changed at all."

Bee had a sudden coughing fit.

"'Tis good to see you, Stephen." Miriam held out a delicate hand, which Stephen brushed with polite lips. "We've been quite worried. Anne was asking about you only yesterday, weren't you dearest?"

"Indeed I was," Anne purred. "Thurston is not the

same when its most handsome knight is absent."

Stephen smiled. "I haven't returned to Thurston alone this time."

"I see that." Christophe raised a brow. "I'm curious to learn who stands so quiet and serious at your side."

"As am I." Anne's dark eyes snaked over Emma's form. "Who might this be, Stephen?"

"This is Emma." Stephen wrapped an arm around her. "The most precious person in the world to me. She's to be my wife."

Christophe's jaw dropped open and Miriam gasped.

"Your..." Anne gave a short laugh. "Surely not."

"Aye, Emma and I are betrothed."

"Isn't she beautiful?" Bee shot a smug glance at Anne. "I love her already."

"Well, congratulations, little brother. 'Tis long overdue. In fact, I had recently considered choosing a wife for you." Christophe smiled at Emma. "But it appears you have already chosen, and chosen well. She's beautiful indeed. Lady Emma, this is my wife, the lady Miriam, and my sister-in-law, lady Anne. Welcome to Thurston, lass."

Chapter 15

Sleep held Emma captive, forcing her to face a darkness so thick it suggested substance. Someone moved within it, hiding, stalking, waiting. She flinched at the familiar stench of foul breath and stale sweat. A shadow separated itself from the darkness and pressed against her, muttering familiar words.

...beyond sweet, Emma...beyond sweet...

Terror chilled her to the bone as strong arms folded around her, solid, unyielding. She attempted to scream, but her petrified voice could only whimper.

"Emma, hush. You're safe. Wake up."

"Nooo...please. Please don't."

"It's alright. Sshh."

Stephen's voice reached into her mind and peeled the darkness away. Relief shuddered through her as the terror subsided.

"Stephen."

"I'm here, love."

"Argante – "

"'Twas a dream, little one." His hand stroked her back. "Only a dream."

Two heartbeats drummed in her ears; Stephen's strong and steady, her own galloping like the hooves of a runaway horse. She drew several long deep breaths, and her heart slowed.

A blackbird's sweet song drifted through the window, confirming the imminent arrival of a new day. Somewhere in the distance a rooster crowed, his raucous call a harsh contrast to the glorious voice of his smaller cousin. Emma turned her head and blinked in the darkness, her eyes picking up a hint of dawn's approaching light.

A gentle snore at her side told her Stephen had drifted back to sleep. Drowsiness enticed her to do the same, but she fought it, fearful of returning to the dark recesses of her subconscious.

Instead, she eased herself from Stephen's arms, slipped quietly out of bed and tiptoed to the window. She squeezed herself onto the cold sill, pulled her knees up under her chin and leaned back against the rough stone.

Absorbed in thought, she nibbled on the remains of a fingernail and stared out across the awakening countryside.

Over a week had passed since her arrival at Thurston. In that time, Emma had learned to love Bee, admire Christophe, and tolerate Miriam. Despite her best efforts, she could not find any liking for Anne, sensing both animosity and jealousy from the dark-eyed beauty, who made it quite clear she wanted Stephen for herself.

Emma no longer had any doubt about where Stephen's heart lay. He demonstrated his love for her often, both privately and openly, making it clear to all that she was his. Still, Anne persisted with her flirtatious remarks to Stephen and a condescending attitude toward Emma.

Bee avoided Anne whenever possible and made sure Emma did the same.

"Tell me," Bee had reasoned, "would you go into a room where a viper was on the loose?"

As daylight crept across a cloudy sky, the forests beyond the castle came alive with birdsong. The sights and sounds prompted memories of her humble woodland home. Over the past few days, Emma's anger toward Alex had faded. She discovered, however, that her anger had served as a shield against the painful emotions that lay beneath. Those emotions were now exposed like raw wounds, which bled grief and confusion.

Why had he lied to her? Alicia, her mother, had been his wife. His wife! Why would he hide that? And how could he kill his own wife? It just didn't fit the image of the gentle man she thought she knew, the man who had raised her and loved her. Everything had changed and little of it made sense. Despair twisted her heart. She leant her head against the cold stone and fought back tears. She missed Alex and her home so much.

"We can go back if you like, little one." Stephen's voice made her jump and she turned to look at him. He sat up in bed, arms resting on his knees, hair ruffled from sleep, his soft gaze on her. "I know how much you miss it. I miss it too."

"How do you do that?" A surge of love for her gentle knight quickened her heart. "How do you always know what I'm thinking?"

He smiled and shrugged. "You were looking out across the forest, the birds were singing. I knew you were pining."

"I do miss it. But I don't think I'm ready to face Alex yet. I'm too scared of what he might have to say."

"As you wish. But if you ever feel the need to return, you'll tell me. Promise?"

Emma nodded. "I promise."

She turned and looked out beyond the castle walls. The morning light revealed a soft white mist blanketing the forest. Only the tree tops were visible above it, their crowns decorated with the jewelled colours of early autumn.

"It's beautiful here too, Stephen." Overcome with a sudden need to escape, she reached out and touched the stone in front of her. Thurston's walls had been built to defend against those without. It occurred to Emma those same walls also served to confine those who lived within. "Do you think we could go for a ride today? Perhaps practice some archery in the forest?"

"I was just about to suggest it, my love. We haven't left the castle since we arrived." He slid off the bed and grabbed Emma's cloak from the back of a chair. "Put this on and come with me. There's something I want to show you."

"What?"

"It's a surprise. Come."

Mystified, Emma grabbed his hand and followed him from the chamber. He led her to the end of the hallway, where a small door sat flush in the wall.

It opened reluctantly, the bottom of it scraping against the wooden floor. Emma blinked into the gloom beyond and saw a small staircase winding up into blackness.

"Christophe and I used to sneak up here when we were children, even though our father forbade it." Stephen pulled her into the shadows. "I remember he caught us one time. We spent a week mucking out the stables as punishment."

"Where does it go?" Nerves fluttered in her stomach as darkness surrounded them.

He grinned. "You'll see. Don't let go of my hand."

"Is it safe?"

"Of course. I'd never put you in danger."

The steps finished at a trapdoor. Stephen pushed it open and it fell back with a crash.

He climbed out and turned to lift Emma through the gap.

"Close your eyes."

"Stephen!"

"Trust me. Close them."

She giggled and did as he asked. He turned her, pulled her back against his chest, and whispered in her ear.

"I lay the world at your feet, little faerie."

Emma opened her eyes and gasped. For a heartbeat, she felt as though she was hovering in mid-air. Miles of countryside stretched out around her, an endless patchwork of colour and texture.

"Oh, Stephen," she whispered. "It's beautiful."

They were on the roof of the keep, or at least, the ledge that surrounded it. Only a waist-high wall separated them from the drop to the cobbles below.

"On a clear day you can see the city of York." Stephen gestured into the mist. "If this cloud clears, we'll come back tonight and watch the stars."

"I would like that." Emma peered over the wall and shivered."'Tis a terrible drop."

"Aye, which is why our father didn't want us playing up here. Come, you're shivering. Let's go back.

Emma had refused the services of a lady's maid, much to Miriam's surprise and Anne's scornful huff. Although her bruises and cuts were gone, the thought of a stranger touching her body still discomforted her.

So, she washed and dressed herself, grabbed her bow and quiver and ran down the stairs. The thought of escaping the confines of Thurston put a smile on her face. With her mind already riding through the forests, she leapt off the bottom step, turned the corner and collided with Anne.

"For Heaven's sake." Anne scowled and smoothed her skirts. "Watch where you're going. 'Tis not ladylike to run."

Emma grimaced. "I'm sorry, my lady. I meant no harm." She tried to push past, but Anne grabbed her by the arm, eyeing the bow and quiver.

"You shoot?"

Emma wrenched her arm free, fighting a surge of annoyance. "Aye, I do."

Anne laughed. "I suppose you sword-fight as well."

"That too."

"By all the saints. Stephen has found himself quite the

little *gamine*. Archery and sword-fighting?" Anne stepped back and raked a vicious gaze over Emma. "Such vulgar behaviour for a lady. But I'm not surprised. You seem quite comfortable having a man in your bed ere your marriage as well. He'll be hard pressed to show proof of your virginity after your wedding night."

Emma gasped and her stomach twisted. A flush of heat swept over her skin as her mind swam with a stupefying mix of shock and shame.

"Enough!"

Stephen's shout carried over the strange hum that had settled in Emma's ears. She turned to look at him, noticing the flush on his skin. Why was he so angry? Her mind, still numb, could not fathom at first what drove his temper. She blinked, and her frozen thoughts began to thaw.

Anne spun round. "My lord, I did not see you there."

His eyes narrowed as he stepped toward her, his hand resting on the hilt of his sword. "'Tis a vicious bitch you are, Anne." He spat at her feet. "If you were a man, you'd be feeling the sting of my blade. You speak of things you know naught about."

Anne stiffened. "Stephen, open your eyes. Can you not see what she is? Or rather, what she is not? I doubt the girl is even of noble blood, and your brother has also voiced his doubts – "

She yelped when he pinned her against the wall, his words hissing at her through gritted teeth. "Still your tongue, woman." His hand held her in place, pressed on her chest at the base of her throat. "And apologize to my lady."

"I'm...I didn't... I..." Anne wrapped her hands around his wrist in an effort to push him away but he held her fast. Her eyes searched his face in an apparent plea for mercy. "Please don't hurt me, my lord."

"Then apologize," Stephen snarled. "We're waiting."

Emma's heart lurched with pity at Anne's expression of fear, which was obviously real. She stepped forward and placed a hand on Stephen's arm. "Stop," she said. "Leave her be."

He shook his head. "Not until the witch apologizes to you."

"'Tis of no consequence, truly." Emma tugged at his sleeve. "Please, Stephen."

He grunted and stepped back, his eyes still fixed on Anne's face. "Very well. But if I ever see you near my lady again, I swear – "

"What the hell is going on?" Christophe strode toward them, shoulders stiff, brows knitted in a frown. "I've just had a servant tell me my brother was strangling my sister-in-law."

"The woman needs strangling." Stephen scowled and wrapped a protective arm around Emma, who saw Anne flinch at Stephen's words.

"And why is that?" Christophe looked from Anne to Stephen. "What did she do to merit your hands around her throat?"

"She insulted Emma." Stephen's lips curled in disgust. "The woman possesses a venomous tongue, brother, and well you know it. And my hands were not around her throat, even though the thought was in my head."

Christophe frowned at Emma. "What was said that so insulted you, my lady?"

Caught between pity and a sense of shame, Emma swallowed a sob. "'Twas – "

"'Twas all a misunderstanding, my lord," Anne interrupted. "Emma bumped into me and I confess I lost my temper. I said some things I do now regret."

"God's teeth, woman." Stephen ran his hand through

his hair. "That's your idea of an apology? Or could it be you don't want my brother to hear the filth you spewed?"

"Enough!" Christophe cursed and blew an exasperated breath. "Christ, give me strength. Last night, a servant's babe was stillborn. This morning, I find I've lost the fealty of two fine knights to a Baron in Northumberland. As lord of Thurston, these are things I might expect to hear. I do not expect to hear that my family are behaving as spoiled children and fighting in the hallways."

"Yet your sweet sister-in-law also implicated you in her little tongue lashing." Stephen eyed his brother angrily. "If you have concerns about my choice of bride, my lord, perhaps you should discuss them with me rather than the women." He glared at Anne. "Especially this one."

"Stephen, please." Emma clutched at his shirt, desperate for the arguing to stop. "No more, I beg you."

Christophe's jaw tensed. "Watch your tongue, little brother." His eyes flicked briefly to Emma. "I have no concerns about the choices you've made, but there are indeed things to discuss before you wed. Until God sees fit to grant me a son, you're still heir to Thurston. With that comes certain...expectations."

"Then you and I will discuss those in private." Stephen shot another scowl at Anne. "I find the air in here unpleasant. Excuse us, my lord. Emma and I are going for a ride."

Emma wrinkled her nose as they stepped outside, her nostrils flaring at the odours of stagnant water and human waste.

"Actually, the air out here is no less unpleasant. It really does stink." She cast a sideways glance at Stephen, whose taut expression told her his thoughts were elsewhere. She hung onto his arm, trotting at his side as he strode toward the stables. "There's something I'd like you to do for me, Stephen."

His jaw relaxed a little, although he still did not look at her. "Aye, sweetheart, and what is that?"

"Slow down. Unless this is a race, in which case I do willingly forfeit."

She smiled, noticing the twitch at the corner of his mouth. He stopped and swung her into his arms, laughing at her squeal of delight.

He relaxed his shoulders. "I swear that woman makes me so angry."

"I noticed." She wrapped her arms around his neck and kissed his cheek. "I love you so much."

"I love you too, little one." His chest rose and fell against her. "With all my heart."

The pleasure and beauty of a late summer morning awaited them outside the castle gates. Pale sunlight seeped through thinning clouds, reflecting off a mist that blurred the finer details of field and forest. The horses' hooves kicked odours of wet leaves and dew-kissed earth into the air. Stephen insisted they kept the animals to a walk, since the mist obscured much of the road ahead.

Emma didn't care whether they walked, trotted or galloped. Her entire being soaked up the release from Thurston without reserve, every pore in her body savouring the space, the scent of the forest, and the sounds that reminded her of home. Her lungs welcomed the deep breaths of fresh air, which she savoured until her head swam with dizziness.

Content and relaxed, she reflected on the morning's events with little discomfort, and a question came out midway through her thoughts. "Why is she not married?"

Stephen looked at her. "Who? Beatrice?"

"Nay, Anne. Well, aye, Beatrice too, I suppose. But I was wondering about Anne."

"She was married. Anne's a widow."

Emma pondered for a moment. "But she's so young. How sad. Was he ill?"

"He was old. 'Twas an arranged marriage. He died only months after they wed. Death was likely preferable to the poor bastard."

"Stephen! Did you know him?"

"I met him once, when they came to Christophe and Miriam's wedding."

"And?"

Stephen gave her a bemused glance. "What is this, Emma? Are you wondering if Anne suffers from a broken heart? I can save you some time. Anne suffers from a poisonous tongue. Nothing more."

Emma shrugged. "I suspect he beat her."

"I don't blame him."

"Stephen, that's not funny."

"Maybe not. But she pushes me to my limit."

"And what of Bee?"

"Aye, when she was five. I came home for a visit once, and she took my wooden sword and broke it, so I dropped her in the horse trough. I got a thrashing from my father for that."

"Pfft! Nay, that's not what I meant. I meant, why has she never married?"

Stephen chuckled. "Christophe is scouring England for a suitable husband as we speak, much to my sister's disgust. It'll take a special kind of man to handle Bee. She's not exactly pious, hardly delicate, and she could teach an innkeeper a curse word or two."

Emma grinned at him. "Half a dozen, from what I've heard."

Stephen laughed. "Aye, no doubt."

Emma's eyes caught movement in the air and looked up at a crow circling over their heads. The bird screeched his harsh lament as he floated aloft, his black outline softened by the haze. As she watched, a strange sense of excitement fluttered beneath her ribs, a feeling of anticipation. She frowned, wondering at it. Stephen's voice startled her.

"Do they mean anything to you?"

"What?" She looked at him, puzzled.

He gestured to the bird.

"Crows. They appear to follow Alex around."

"Aye, that they do." Her heart quickened at the thought of it. "He has some kind of connection to them. To all creatures, it seems. I'm not sure what it is."

"You never speak of his abilities." Stephen's tone softened. "Nor the stone, yet you know he has it."

She looked at him, wondering, deciding. His eyes met hers, unwavering, glowing like dark honey. Her decision made, she pulled her horse to a halt.

"There are some things I've always known, Stephen. I've known about Darius and the stone and Alex's abilities for as long as I can remember." She took a long slow breath. "But there are other things I remember, too. Things I've never spoken of, not even to Alex, because they are so...strange. Memories, images in my head that I can't explain because I'm not sure how they came to be."

"Tell me."

"You must swear not to tell anyone else, nor think me insane."

"I would never do that." He reached over and touched her cheek. "You have my word, little one."

"Very well. I have a memory of a woman weeping. I'm in her arms, looking up at her. She has green eyes, like mine."

"Your mother?"

"Aye, my mother." Emma took another deep breath. " And she is, or was, frightened. Even now, when I think of it, I can feel her fear."

"Frightened of what?"

"I don't know. Alex, perhaps? Maybe he was about to kill her."

"I refuse to believe that."

"I don't want to believe it. But the strange thing is, my next image is of Alex. I'm lying in a crib, crying, surrounded by strangers. Then I see Alex's face looking down at me. I stop crying and reach for him, for I know for certain I'm meant to be with him and I believe he has come for me." Emma closed her eyes as the reality of the image cut deep into her heart. "But he turns from me and walks away. He leaves me, Stephen. I can hear his footsteps fading away and I cry and scream, but he doesn't come back."

Stephen reached over and took her hand in his.

"Well, obviously he came back."

"Aye, although I've no memory of that. But you don't understand."

"What?"

"When Alex leaned over the crib and looked at me..." Emma took a deep breath, fighting her emotion, "...I reached for him because I recognized him. I knew, beyond any doubt, that he was my father."

Stephen sighed and lifted her hand to his lips. "Ah, my love. The mind's a strange thing. It gives us those things we want but can never have."

She looked up at the crow, still circling overhead. "Aye, I know. But the images are so real."

"When you're ready, you must ask Alex what happened. You have to find out the truth."

"How will I know if it's the truth he speaks?"

"You will...ah...someone's coming." Stephen's hand drifted to his sword. "Stay behind me, sweetheart."

The mist muffled the sound of hooves, but Emma

could tell at least three horsemen were heading toward them. She peered into the haze, aware of Stephen's tension, although she sensed no threat.

At that moment, the sun found a gap in the clouds and leapt through it, dropping into the surrounding mist as a shaft of blinding light. Emma blinked, squinting into the brilliance and Stephen rose up in his stirrups, his sword half-drawn.

Three men rode out of the light, their silhouettes darkened by the sun at their backs.

One, tall and handsome, had long silver hair that fell well past his shoulders. He stared at Emma with eyes as black as night. For an instant, she though she saw a light in them, like the quick flare of a candle-flame. The man at his left had straight black hair of similar length, a noble, serious face and eyes equally as black. He glanced at Emma for a mere moment before turning his gaze to Stephen.

The third man, strong featured, yet gentle of expression, had long dark hair that curled as it settled upon his shoulders. He nodded at Emma, studying her with eyes of an indefinable colour. A tingle ran across her skin, lifting the hair on her arms and neck. Her strange feeling of anticipation grew.

They have much presence, these men. Knights. They can surely be nothing else.

Stephen settled back in the saddle, pushed his sword into its scabbard and repeated her conclusion.

"Knights," he murmured. "And they can only be going to Thurston. Stay behind me, Emma. Let us see who they are and what they want."

As quickly as it had appeared the shaft of sunlight vanished, smothered by the persistent blanket of cloud. Stephen turned his horse diagonally across the path, keeping Emma behind him, forcing the three riders to halt.

The air stilled except for the gentle rattle of bridles and the soft breath of horses. Emma's heart thudded so hard she wondered if everyone could hear it. She willed herself to slow her breathing, noticing a hint of mirth on the face of the silver-haired knight as he addressed Stephen with a gentle Irish lilt.

"You're either very brave or very foolish to challenge us." He gestured to his companions. "Do I need to point out we are three blades to your one?"

Stephen shrugged. "Aye, I noticed. 'Tis indeed an unfair match. You should have brought a fourth."

The man struggled to suppress a smile. "I'm surprised your horse can carry the weight of your balls, young knight." He nodded to Emma. "Begging your pardon, my lady."

The serious, black-haired knight leaned forward. "What gives you the right to delay our passage? We have presented no threat."

Stephen lifted his chin. "I am Sir Stephen de Montfort, brother of Lord Christophe de Montfort of Thurston. Since this road leads only to Thurston's gates, I'm curious as to your business there."

"Your vigilance is to be commended, but your methods are questionable." The knight relaxed back into his saddle. "I am Keir, this is Finn and that is Caleb. We seek to establish ourselves with a demesne of good renown. We offer fealty and services in exchange for a fresh pallet and nourishment."

Stephen studied the three for a moment, his eyes coming to rest on the one who had yet to speak. "Sir, you do not have a tongue?"

The knight met Stephen's gaze. "What would you have me say, my lord?"

Emma's heart leapt at the sound of his voice and eased

her horse forward. "You're a Scot."

He nodded. "Aye, my lady. Does that pose a problem?"

Warmth spread across her skin, as if someone had wrapped her in soft fur.

"Nay, not at all." She tugged on Stephen's sleeve. "Stephen - I mean, my lord -did your brother not say, just this morning, that two of his knights had left for another holding in Northumberland?"

"Aye, he did."

The one called Finn leaned back in the saddle. "Indeed? What a coincidence. 'Tis fortunate, then, we happened along. We can replace those two and throw in another for good measure."

Stephen paused a moment before pulling his horse to the side. "Very well, you may pass and approach Thurston, but permission to serve must be granted by my brother. When you get to the gate, ask for Marcus. Tell him you have spoken with me. He'll let Lord Christophe know of your arrival."

"Thank you, my lord." Finn nodded at Emma. "My lady."

He touched his spurs to his horse and trotted off into the mist, with Keir close behind.

Caleb lingered, gesturing to Emma's bow. "You're going hunting, my lady?"

She shivered inwardly. His voice reminded her so much of Alex.

"Nay, Sir Caleb. Just practising."

He studied her for a moment then looked at Stephen. "Keir is right. Your vigilance is to be commended."

"Thank you." Stephen's eyes narrowed. "Perhaps it's merely because you remind me of someone, but have we met before?"

Caleb shrugged and gathered up the reins. "If so, 'twas

not here. This is my first visit to Thurston. I trust I shall see you both later. Enjoy your practice, my lady."

As man and horse vanished into the mist Emma realized she had tears in her eyes.

"He reminded me very much of Alex," said Stephen, reaching over to tuck an errant strand of hair behind Emma's ear. "They give the impression of being decent men. I hope Christophe accepts them."

Emma sniffed. "You're doing it again."

"What?"

"Reading my mind."

Chapter 16

Where once he had feared darkness, Argante now relished its soft cloak. Night didn't hurt him, unlike the ferocious light of day, which flayed his burned skin without mercy. He lifted his deformed face to the stars, sniffed the rancid air, and eyed the stark grey tower. The stench of death wafted from the doorway and he curled his lips in distaste.

Although the keep appeared as a shadowy blur to his burned eyes, his demented mind toyed with a sense of familiarity. He'd been here before, searching for something, someone. There had been others here too. His twisted mind shuffled his thoughts like a deck of cards.

Before Emma. After Emma.

Emma.

He didn't know how much time had passed. A day. A week. A month. It didn't matter. She'd been there in the dungeon with him. An angel with emerald eyes, crying, fearful of the dark. Her cries had aroused him, so he'd coupled with her. He'd been her first. He hardened just thinking of it.

Yet as she struggled against him, something had leapt into his soul, into his mind. It was an unfamiliar emotion, one that weakened him. Even now he fought against it, resenting its presence.

I shall not yield.

Afterwards, she'd left him alone in the dark with nothing but a dying flame.

Nay, not her.

It was it the other one. The one he hated. The one who held the secret of the stone.

The stone.

Bah! He didn't want the stone. He wanted her. She was his ecstasy now. In the depths of his fear, he had smelled her essence, her blood, the aroma of their joining. She had driven him to escape.

Even as the fire blistered the flesh on his face and hands he thought of her, calling her name between his screams of agony. Consumed by his want of her and his fear of the dark, he had pushed his charred skin through the hole in the door, smelled his burning hair, felt the warm flow of blood from his torn fingers.

He had to find her.

She belongs to me.

After his escape, he'd stumbled blindly through a forest already shrouded by night, guided by the sound of running water somewhere off in the distance. The river gave him some relief as long as he remained submerged in its cool waters, so he followed it until it rolled into the sea. There, the vicious tide grabbed him, its salty waves peeling away burnt remnants of flesh from his face and hands as he struggled to fight against the swirling currents.

Crippled with agony, he'd managed to crawl ashore, finding shelter in sea-carved niches at the base of the sandstone cliffs. His will to survive was sustained by a glorious madness and a growing obsession with a green-eyed girl.

Now he was back where it all began. His wounds, though still painful, were healing. But where Emma had burned his soul, the fire still raged.

Ah, sweet Emma. Sweet, sweet Emma.

Bitch.

Can I have her now?

Nay. You'll not put your cock near this one. You're dead, you little runt.

Aye, Iain is very dead. What kept you?

Some of the images puzzled him and he tried to frown, but the healing flesh pulled too tightly across his face. Any attempt at facial expression pained him.

Where was she? Where was the stone?

Christ. Forget the damn stone.

Another memory surfaced from the slimy folds of his brain and his heart missed a beat.

The cottage. Of course. That's where she would be waiting for him. If only he could remember the way.

Where was it?

Such was his power. All he had to do, it seemed, was wish for something and it appeared. For had he not just wished to find Emma's house? And now here it sat in the clearing below him, silent and dark, nestled deep in the forest. He glanced back along the trail, unaware of ever having walked it.

"Quiet, Richard." He raised a blackened finger to his crusted lips. "Or Mathanach will hear you."

Mathanach? Scottish bastard, pox-ridden son of a whore. Married to a whore.

"I said be quiet, Richard." His laugh emerged as a saliva-choked gurgle and he limped toward the house.

Mathanach isn't here. He'd never let you get this close.

I've seen things. He knows where it is. He knows where she is.

Tell me de Montfort rots in the grave. Tell me the bastard died.

Nothing stirred.

Argante pulled a scab from his cheek, and flicked it into the air. "Let me know as soon as you return, Emma." He snorted as he ambled back into the forest.

"I'll be waiting."

Chapter 17

"I like Yorkshire." Finn leaned back against the wall and stuck his feet up on the bench, his eyes glued to the shapely backside of the serving maid as she sauntered away. "Very friendly people. Lord Christophe accepted us quite readily."

Keir's goblet of ale paused midway to his mouth as he threw Finn a pained look. "'Tis your persuasive tongue. The poor man didn't stand a chance."

Finn pointed his chin toward the maid. "Wouldn't mind persuading her with my tongue."

Keir choked on his drink. "God's teeth, you don't waste any time, do you? The bench beneath your arse is barely warm. Please try to remember why we're here."

"I haven't forgotten, nor will I." Finn took a gulp of ale. "But that doesn't mean I can't enjoy the local scenery. Right, Alexander?"

"And watch what you're saying." Keir glanced around. "His name is Caleb, remember?"

Alex smiled at Keir. "He's doing it on purpose, my lord. I believe he enjoys goading you."

Keir returned the smile with a scowl. "'Twould seem you also need reminding, Caleb. I told you, while we're here we're equal, so drop the formal address."

"Keir, give the man a little rein. His mind is occupied." Finn looked at Alex, his expression all at once serious. "Emma is a beautiful young woman, my friend. How did she seem to you?"

Alex swirled the ale in his goblet as he considered the question. "Her aura is still dark, but it brightened a little when she heard my voice." He wrestled with a twinge of guilt. "She's still very...conflicted. Her outer image belies the torment inside."

Keir grunted. "I sense you're also conflicted where she's concerned. Stop blaming yourself, or the shield will weaken."

"I'm about to say something I've never said before." Finn leaned over and patted Alex's shoulder. "Keir is right."

Alex laughed and fingered the sword's hilt, which had been wound with a strip of leather to disguise it. "'Tis a strange sensation, like looking through a mist, yet I see everything clearly."

Keir nodded. "You're controlling it well. Let us know if you need to rest. Don't try to do more than you're able."

"So far it's not been difficult," said Alex. "I'm curious. What did you think of Stephen?"

"First impression?" Keir shrugged. "Impetuous. Courageous to the point of foolish. A little too sure of himself."

"Young, you mean?"

Keir chuckled. "Indeed. I don't doubt your judgement, but I need to spend time with him to form an opinion. I want to see what he's made of."

"Ah, I smell food." Finn sat up and rubbed his stomach. "'Tis indeed a treat to have both feet back in the mortal world. Be warned, Guardians, for I intend to make a pig of myself."

Most people had finished eating by the time Stephen and Emma entered the hall. A touch of sadness squeezed Alex's heart when he saw Emma searching the crowd. He knew instinctively she was looking for him, even if he was - as far as she knew - a complete stranger. She caught his gaze and nodded at him, her face lit by a smile.

"I wonder how she'd react if you revealed your true identity," Finn mused, his greasy fingers wrapped around the remains of a chicken leg.

"I don't know." Alex watched as Emma turned to speak to Stephen. "Before today, I would have said she'd be angry, but after the way she reacted to me this morning, I'm no longer sure."

"This morning she reacted to a stranger who only reminds her of you," Keir observed. "'Tis not the same thing as reacting to you directly."

"Aye, true enough. As I am now, I present no threat. Caleb does not stand accused of killing her parents."

"Then use that to help her," Keir suggested. "The shield will be serving its purpose."

"I'm tempted to say I knew her mother."

"Why?" Keir looked puzzled. "I see no reason for that."

"It may prompt her to speak of her past. Perhaps I can ease her mind a little."

"She's the image of her mother." Finn dropped the bone on the table and licked his fingers. "It's remarkable."

"What's remarkable is the amount of food you just consumed." Keir eyed the pile of chicken bones stacked up in front of Finn. "Are you even able to stand?"

Finn rolled his eyes. "Pah! Too much food has never stopped me from standing. Too much ale, aye. Oh, and there was that wild night in Kildare when I woke up naked in a stable with – "

"God help us, will you never cease?" Tears of mirth in Keir's eyes belied his tone of disapproval. "I must check the scrolls when we return. Your acceptance to the Circle was obviously an error."

"I think not. But I must confess, I miss all this." Finn's eyes swept around the room. "Which is why I intend to enjoy it while I can. Caleb, methinks we have a visitor."

Alex turned to see Emma approaching, alone. He thought she looked better than she had that morning. Her cheeks had a soft blush of pink and her eyes shone. But he didn't fail to notice dark shadows under her eyes and the uncertainty in her step. He watched her as a father might watch his child, painfully aware of her courage as her body and mind still coped with a shattered soul and a broken heart.

It tore at him, knowing that the carefree girl he had raised had gone, and likely forever.

"Easy, Guardian." Finn's whisper drifted into his thoughts. "Take it slow."

"Aye." Alex sighed, the pain under his ribs forcing the air from his lungs. "I will."

As she drew near, all three men stood.

"My lady." Alex smiled at her. "'Tis a pleasure to see you again. Did you enjoy your archery practice?"

"I did, thank you." Her eyes flicked briefly to Keir and Finn before her gaze returned to Alex. "I'm pleased Lord de Montfort saw fit to accept your services."

"As are we," Keir replied. "You're Lady Emma, are you not? We were not formally introduced this morning."

Emma nodded. "Aye, my name is Emma. Stephen, I mean, Sir Stephen is speaking with his brother, so I thought I might come over and welcome you all to Thurston."

Keir nodded. "'Tis very kind of you, my lady."

She chewed on her bottom lip and looked at Alex. This gesture he recognized, and it gladdened his heart. Emma was awaiting his permission.

He gave it.

"Would you care to join us?" He gestured to the seat at his side.

"I won't be in the way?" She sat down before he could answer and he bit back a chuckle. He glanced at Finn and Keir, seeing hints of smiles on their faces too.

"Nay, my lady." He sat down next to her. " You won't be in the way at all."

Christophe's voice faded into the background as Stephen watched Emma from across the room. She sat chatting with Caleb, her hands moving as she spoke, her face lit with a shy smile. It had been a while since Stephen had seen her so animated. The pleasure he got from her reaction to the Scottish knight cushioned a mild stab of jealousy. If anything, Caleb's uncanny resemblance to Alex gave Stephen some comfort as well. As if aware of being scrutinized, Caleb turned and met his gaze. A familiar tingle of excitement lifted the hair on Stephen's arms and his eyes drifted to the sword sitting at Caleb's side.

"Nay," Stephen murmured to himself. "It can't be."

"What can't be?" Christophe's voice finally broke through. "Stephen, are you even listening to me?"

"What? Oh, aye. I mean, nay. Sorry. My mind was elsewhere." Stephen kept his eyes fixed on Caleb's sword.

Christophe followed his gaze. "Is something wrong? Does Emma know those men?"

"Nay, there's nothing wrong. The Scot reminds her of her guardian. 'Tis likely why she's drawn to him."

"They seem honourable enough, and their arrival was timely. Speaking of Emma and her guardian, I need to ask you about them."

Stephen faced his brother and glanced at Miriam. "Not here."

"Nay, not here. Father's writing room."

"Now?"

"Aye, now. This morning's little fracas caused quite a stir. I'm tired of the evasive answers about your future wife. There are things I must know."

His father's writing-room had always been Stephen's favourite as a child. Memories flooded back when he stepped through the door. The smell of musty leather, parchment, and beeswax all combined to transport him back to his childhood. Even his father's chess set sat where it always had, beneath the tall lancet window. Long before Stephen learned the game, he would play with the wooden figures, creating mock battles between the two colours.

Christophe settled himself at the desk and gestured to a chair. "Sit, please."

Stephen straddled the seat. "Before you begin, let me say that Anne was entirely to blame for the morning's events. I overheard what she said to Emma, and there was no excuse for it."

Christophe cleared his throat. "But perhaps there is reason, even if Anne's handling of it was misplaced. I cannot say I approve of the...behaviour I've seen since Emma's arrival. The girl does not act as most noble women would. Her interests are, shall we say, less than ladylike. I have concerns."

Christophe's remarks prompted an immediate and defensive response. "So, you've changed your mind about my choice of a bride?"

"Don't put words in my mouth, Stephen." Christophe's jaw tensed. "I didn't say Emma wasn't suitable. I'm merely curious about her ancestry."

Stephen fidgeted in the chair. He'd seen this conversation looming on the horizon and dreaded its arrival.

"I've told you. Emma's ancestry is as pure as ours."

"So you keep saying, but I should like to know more about it. I've never heard of this guardian, this Alexander Mathanach. And why the guardian? Who were her true parents?" Christophe leaned forward, elbows resting on the desk, hands folded in front of him, eyes fixed on Stephen's face. "Stephen, I need to know who it is you are bringing into our family. 'Tis not an unreasonable demand. So far, you've managed to avoid answering any of my questions."

Stephen's gaze drifted to the signet ring on his brother's right hand. It had been his father's ring. Even from where he sat, he could make out the shape of the Rampant Lion, carved into the dark gold face.

A memory surfaced of himself as a little boy, clambering into his father's lap. He remembered his father's hands, strong yet gentle, folding themselves around Stephen's small body. He remembered the patience in his father's voice as he explained to his youngest son, for the umpteenth time, what the engraving on the ring meant.

The de Montfort crest.

Even as a child, Stephen nursed a strong sense of pride in his family's name. That pride surfaced again as the childhood memory played out.

Christophe and Miriam had been wed almost two years. Stephen knew how desperately his brother wanted a son and heir for Thurston, yet so far there had been no sign. For as long as his brother's marriage proved barren of a male child, Stephen remained next in line. He decided to speak the truth as he knew it.

"What I have to tell you must not go beyond this room. I insist on your vow of discretion, my brother, before I answer."

Christophe sat back, his eyes narrowing. "You have it."

"Thank you." Stephen sighed. "Emma's parents are dead. Her father was a knight by the name of Edward Fitzhugh. Her mother's name was Alicia. Lady Alicia Mathanach."

He watched the changing expression on his brother's face, not quite sure what to expect. Understanding of Emma's situation showed itself through a brief shake of the head and a soft exhale of breath.

"You're telling me the girl is illegitimate." Christophe's gaze dropped briefly to the warm amber surface of the oak desk. "So, Lady Alicia was Alexander Mathanach's sister?"

"Nay." Stephen swallowed. "Alicia Mathanach was Alexander's wife."

"My God. The woman had an affair? Where was her husband?"

"In the Holy Land."

Christophe leaned forward again, frowning. "I don't understand. Why would a man raise his wife's bastard? What happened to Alicia and this lover of hers? This Fitzhugh?"

Irritation hardened Stephen's voice. "Do not call Emma a bastard."

"Forgive me. 'Twas a slip of the tongue. Will you answer the question?"

"I will, and then we're done with this conversation." Stephen ran his fingers through his hair. "From what I understand, Alexander came back and found his wife with Fitzhugh. There was a fight, an altercation. Both Alicia and Fitzhugh were killed."

"The man killed his own wife?"

"It would seem so. Maybe he adopted Emma to appease his conscience and chose to live quietly thereafter. But he never told her the truth. She only recently discovered what supposedly happened, which is why she left Alex and came back to Thurston with me. She's very hurt by what she's learned." He would not - could not - tell Christophe about Argante.

"What *supposedly* happened, you say? Do you believe otherwise?"

Stephen shrugged. "I don't believe Alex told her the entire story. I don't believe the man capable of killing in cold blood."

Christophe closed his eyes for a moment and rubbed his temples. "So, you arrive home with an illegitimate girl, raised by a guardian who killed his wife and her lover and appears to be hiding some secret. Then you proceed to openly share a bed with the lass under my roof. And you expect me to approve of this?"

"I don't...that is...we don't...oh, Christ. What does it matter?" Stephen had no desire to explain the situation. "I don't expect anything from you. I'm going to marry Emma whether you approve or not. Is there anything else, my lord? I haven't eaten today, and my stomach is grumbling almost as loudly as yourself."

"Oh, I've no doubt you'll ignore any reservations I might have." Christophe's lips lifted in the semblance of a smile. "If I'm to be honest with you in return, I suppose I can confess to some envy. Miriam and I are not unhappy, but our marriage lacks the affection I see so clearly between you and Emma. And I do like the girl, Stephen. She's missing a certain...noble polish, but she possesses a unique charm."

"I consider myself fortunate to have found her."

"Oh, and there's something else." Christophe reached behind him and picked up a letter from a small table. "This came for you earlier."

Stephen's heart clenched, for he recognized the seal at once - an armoured knight, sword aloft, sitting astride a horse

The seal of King Henry.

Stephen snapped the wax seal and unfolded the parchment, already knowing what the letter demanded. He read Henry's words as guilt soured his stomach. Not that he couldn't provide what his liege asked of him - Henry would have his report on the mysterious stone. Stephen would go to London, look his king straight in the eye, tell him what he had learned.

Perjure himself. Commit treason.

May God forgive me.

"If you were not already sitting, I would tell you to do so." Christophe's quiet voice interrupted Stephen's guilty contemplation. "What has Henry said to cast such a pallor upon your skin?"

Stephen lifted troubled eyes to his brother's face.

"I have to go to London. He's asking for a report."

"On this mysterious investigation you were asked to complete?"

"Aye."

"Do you have a report to give?"

"Aye, I do."

Christophe raised a brow. "Then might I suggest you remove your mask of guilt beforehand, or His Grace may be inclined to question the sincerity of your words."

A smile tugged at Stephen's mouth. "I forget how well you know me."

"You're my brother." He heaved a sigh. "Are you in some kind of trouble, Stephen?"

"Nay. 'Tis simply that I find my loyalties conflicted."

"Indeed? Would this conflict have anything to do with your future wife?"

A flare of anger lifted Stephen to his feet. "Absolutely not. God's blood, but how you misjudge her. You ask if I'm troubled? Aye, perhaps I'm troubled by my family's recent hostility toward my betrothed."

Christophe shook his head. "Calm yourself, little brother. 'Tis you who misjudges me. I harbour no hostility toward the girl. Emma will be well cared for and protected in your absence. I swear it."

"Good, for there are things..." Stephen grimaced as dark thoughts tripped through his mind. "There are things of which I cannot speak, except to say that Emma is fragile, vulnerable. I need to know she'll be safe here, Christophe, for her life is...is...like a feather in the wind." A chill ran across his skin as the image of a crow's mangled and twisted body drifted unbidden into his thoughts. "I'll delay my journey for a week, maybe a little longer. But I shall tell Emma of the summons today. Give her time to accept it."

"She'll be safe here, I promise. I just don't understand why you won't tell me what troubles her."

Stephen shook his head. "I gave my word. But if you still doubt the girl at all...." He lifted his shirt, exposing the recent wound, which trailed a ragged red furrow across his ribs.

"Sweet Mother of God." Christophe jumped to his feet and strode around the desk to touch the scar with his fingertips. "Who the hell did this?"

"I cannot say. But if not for Emma..." Stephen smiled at the memory, "...if not for a little forest faerie who found me bleeding to death, I wouldn't be standing here now."

Christophe's eyes widened. "I see. Then it would seem I'm in her debt for saving my brother's life." He sighed and patted Stephen's shoulder. "'Tis quite remarkable that you can say so much, yet say nothing at all. Perhaps you should take up politics."

Stephen grinned. "Will you speak to Anne before I leave for London? Order her to leave Emma alone? Or would you rather I did it, using my special political talent?"

Christophe chuckled. "Leave Anne to me. The poor woman almost expired of fright this morning."

Stephen felt a pinch of regret. "Aye, I was perhaps a little harsh. I'll try to make amends, for your sake."

"It would be much appreciated. Now, go and eat."

Chapter 18

Alex sat beside Emma, feigning polite interest in her chatter, fighting his emotions as he studied her in depth. Faint shadows clouded the delicate skin beneath her eyes, and her slender hands, conducting her story in the air, trembled as she spoke.

She had lost weight too. Most disturbing, though, was the colourless grey aura surrounding her, almost void of spirit. Yet it flickered weakly as she spoke to him and brightened a little whenever he responded. He searched her eyes for a glimmer of hope, but saw only pain and confusion.

Oh, Emma.

He made a decision, and interrupted her mid-sentence as she continued to relate the events of her ride that morning.

"May I say that you're the image of your mother, my lady."

His words brought a loud gasp of shock from Emma and twitches of discomfort from Keir and Finn.

"My mother? But...how...how could you know that?"

"I knew who you were as soon as I saw you." Alex smiled. "If naught else, your eyes would tell me who delivered you. Identical to hers, they are."

"And my...her...husband. Alexander?" she stammered. "Do you know him too?"

"Aye, I do." The stone vibrated at his side, responding to the strength of Emma's emotion. "Forgive me, my lady. I didn't mean to distress you."

"Nay, 'tis not you. I'm shocked, is all. " She glanced around wildly. Alex knew whom she sought.

"Sir Stephen left with his brother a few moments ago. Would you like me to fetch him for you?"

"Nay." Emma turned tearful eyes on him. "But I'd rather not talk here. Please Caleb, will you walk with me?

The bailey, perhaps? I have questions."

Alex threw a glance at Keir and Finn. Emma saw it and apparently misunderstood its meaning, drawing a sharp breath as she pushed herself to her feet, her voice shaking as she spoke. "I do beg your pardon. Pay me no heed, my lords. Sir Caleb, I...I did not mean to impose upon you. Perhaps another time?"

"You are not imposing on me at all, my lady." Alex rose and offered his arm. "I would be honoured to walk with you, although I'm not sure I can answer the questions you have. My friends can manage well enough without me."

"Caleb speaks true." Keir smiled. "Go with him and bear us no thought, my lady."

"Aye." Finn gave Alex a telling look. "He knows where we'll be."

Emma almost dragged Alex outside, her eagerness evident in the pull on his arm and the quickness of her stride. They stepped into a bailey topped by dull grey skies. The fog had vanished, leaving behind cool, damp air. Emma didn't slow her steps until they approached the gardens, which lay at the south side of the castle. She glanced around, apparently satisfied at seeing no one, before turning her eyes to his. A shiver ran through her, so violent that it travelled through her hand and up Alex's arm. The sword at his side trembled.

Stimulated by Emma's intense emotion and profiting from Alex's compromised resolve, the stone sent an unexpected burst of immaculate energy through every cell in his body. His sight blurred as he struggled to maintain command over the unearthly forces swamping him. All at once, a second rush of energy warmed his skin and calmed his mind.

Breathe easy, Guardian. We have you.

Finn.

Alex managed to focus his eyes on Emma's face.

"My lady?"

"Please sir, I beg you, tell me how you know of my mother and my guar...my father."

He flinched inwardly at Emma's denial of her illegitimacy, at the same time noticing her shivering had not stopped.

"You're cold, child," he murmured, pulling off his cloak and settling it around her shoulders.

She appeared not to even notice the gesture. Alex realized her desperate mind saw only what she believed to be a link back to her home, back to her past.

Back to him.

God help me. How can any of this ever be put right?

"You say I remind you of my mother." Emma's teeth chattered as she spoke. "Well, you remind me of him. Of Alex...my father. It's incredible, uncanny. Your voice, your eyes. The way you look at me." A sob rose in her throat. "I left him. I left...angry. He...I found out... God forgive me, I didn't even say goodbye."

"Please try to calm yourself, my lady. Ask me your questions. I'll tell you what I can."

Emma nodded, her eyes bright. "How do you know them? My parents?"

Alex's mind slid back over many years, yet it might have only been a few days. Bending the truth a little, he spoke.

"I met Alicia many years ago, in London. She looked exactly as you do now." He lifted a hand, intent on brushing an errant strand of hair from her eyes. At the last moment, he stopped himself. "She was promised to Alexander, and they were married just before he left to serve in the Holy Land. As I recall, they had very little time together after the wedding."

"So you knew Alex...I mean, my father...before that?"

He smiled, gave in to the urge, and lifted the curl from her brow. "I've known Alexander for as long as I can remember."

Emma frowned and looked at the ground, the loose curl once again tumbling over her face. "'Tis strange he never mentioned you."

"Och, perhaps not that strange. Alexander Mathanach knew many people."

She looked at him, calmer now. "Do you happen to know if he loved her?"

Alex bit the inside of his cheek until it bled. The pain felt mild compared to the savage wound that had just opened in his heart.

"Oh, aye, lass." His voice dropped almost to a whisper. "You can take my word for it. Alexander Mathanach loved your mother more than anything in the world."

Emma tightened her grip on Alex's arm and closed her eyes. He waited, knowing exactly what she was about to say, knowing he couldn't fully enlighten her with the answers she sought. At least, not yet. Not as Caleb. Still, perhaps he could lift some of the weight from her young shoulders.

Her eyes opened and she spoke the words he expected to hear.

"Are you aware he murdered her?"

Despite his anticipation of it, Emma's question hit him hard. He breathed deeply, thankful for Finn and Keir's emotional scaffold.

"I heard about Alicia's death and I know Alexander was involved." He reached up and stroked her cheek. "But murder? Knowing Alexander as I do, I doubt him to be guilty of murder."

"He told me he did it." She swallowed, tears in her eyes and anguish in her voice. "And he also killed her...her..."

"Lover?" Alex finished, the word bitter on his tongue even after so many years. "I'm familiar with the story."

"Aye, her lover. He murdered both of them."

"He actually admitted to murder?"

Emma chewed on her lip and looked away. That small familiar action almost crushed Alex's resolve. All at once she was his child again, puzzling over something he'd asked, seeking the right answer before she spoke. His jaw tensed as he blinked away tears of his own.

"He said...he said they died at his hands." She turned back to him, a different light playing in her eyes this time. Hope? "Aye, 'tis what he said. I'm sure of it. What else could it mean?"

"Only Alexander can tell you that. But he never actually said he murdered them?"

"Well, not exactly." A tear rolled down her cheek. "But he didn't deny it, either. And there's something else I must tell you."

He wiped away the tear with his thumb. "You don't have to tell me anything else, child."

"Aye, I do." She blinked at him, a soft tinge of colour brushing her cheeks. "I lied to you, Caleb."

He frowned. "About what?"

"My father. Alexander isn't really my father. He's my guardian."

"I already know that, my lady. You see, I knew Alex when – "

"Emma!"

They turned to see Stephen striding toward them, an anxious expression on his face. He reached Emma's side and pulled her into his arms, dropping a kiss on her forehead.

"Thank God. I was worried." He fingered the cloak wrapped around Emma's shoulders and looked at Alex.

"May I know why you brought the lady out here?"

Alex inclined his head. "We were merely conversing, my lord. I can assure you she's quite safe, other than being chilled by the damp air."

"I asked Sir Caleb to walk with me, Stephen." Emma smiled up at him. "He knew my mother, and he's known Alex for years. Isn't that strange?"

Stephen's eyes flicked briefly to Alex's sword. "Aye, 'tis a remarkable coincidence. Almost beyond belief. Do you know Alexander well, Sir Caleb?"

"Quite well, aye."

"When did you last see him?"

Alex shrugged. "I don't recall exactly. Is it important, my lord?"

"Nay, it's not important." Stephen looked up at the sky. "But was it recently?"

"Stephen." Emma tugged at his sleeve. "Is anything wrong? Surely you don't doubt Caleb's word?"

Stephen turned to Emma and smiled. "Nay, my love. Nothing is wrong. I'm only concerned for your safety." He looked at Alex. "Forgive me, Caleb. Recent events have made me very protective of my lady."

"I understand," Alex replied. "And I swear, as a knight of the realm, she has my full protection also."

"Aye." Stephen's gaze dropped to Alex's sword again. "I'm certain she does." He turned back to Emma and ran his thumb along her jaw. "Sweetheart, Bee was looking for you. She said to meet her in the mews."

Emma's eyes widened. "I'd forgotten. She's going to let me hold Arthur."

Alex raised a brow. "Arthur?"

"Her falcon." Emma removed the cloak and handed it to Alex. "Will you excuse me? Thank you, Caleb, for everything. You have given me much to think on. May we speak again later?"

"Whenever you wish, my lady."

She turned to Stephen, rising up on her toes, her meaning obvious. He bent his head and kissed her.

"Be careful, little one," he murmured, pushing back the same errant curl from her eyes. "Arthur has a sharp beak."

She nodded, smiled, and hurried away.

Alex watched, gratified to see a brighter edge to her aura, and lightness in her step he had not noticed earlier.

"My thanks for raising Emma's spirits, Caleb." Stephen's voice held a hint of amusement. "Though something tells me 'Caleb' is not your real name."

A sudden gust of wind snatched at a handful of leaves, tossing them in the air. Stephen looked up again, searching the skies. Alex tensed as a door opened in his mind but, fascinated by what was happening, didn't attempt to resist the foreign intrusion.

He felt a burst of heat through the hilt of his sword and saw Stephen flinch. At that moment Alex knew, without a grain of doubt, he was looking at a future Guardian. The young knight's connection to the stone was indisputable. His mind had managed to bypass two other Guardians, breach the shield and connect with Alex, albeit innocently.

Keir's investigation of Stephen's suitability would be nothing more than a formal exercise. How could they deny him after this?

For now though, Alex decided to play the game, prolong the moment. He pushed Stephen's mind away and fixed the young man with a steady gaze. "You doubt my identity, my lord?"

Stephen shrugged and held out his hand. "Perhaps my instincts are wrong. May I see your sword? I'm curious about the leather on the hilt, why you have it wrapped in such a manner."

Alex fingered the hilt. "Aye, you may see it if you wish. But I'm also curious to know, young knight, what you were searching for just now."

"Young knight?" Stephen chuckled. "What happened to 'my lord'? I was looking for crows."

"Crows?"

"Aye, crows." He glanced around. "I don't see any, which is strange, for if you are who I think you are, they tend to follow you about."

Alex smiled. Game over. "Ah. Well in that case, lad, I'd hate to disappoint you."

A shadow dropped from the sky, black, swift as an arrow. The draught from its wings kissed Stephen's hair as the crow flew past, cawing as it circled back up to the clouds.

Stephen ducked. "Alexander. God help me, I knew it. As He is my witness, I sensed it. But how the hell...?"

Alex patted Stephen's shoulder. "I'm more than impressed by your instincts, Stephen. I suppose I should explain."

He paused as a misty curtain of rain descended, its soft whisper muffling the sounds of Thurston's bailey. He pulled his cloak around his shoulders and grimaced at the sky, wondering how to begin, where to begin and how much to say. Stephen's intense wide-eyed stare amused him.

"Get used to it, lad, and stop gawking."

"Forgive me." Stephen scratched his head. "I'd like to say it's good to see you, but it wouldn't be quite accurate, since it's not you I see. If I didn't already know of your strange talents and that wretched jewel, I'd swear it was the devil's work."

Alex caressed the hilt of his sword. "'Tis the wretched jewel which betrayed me. Or at least, your consciousness of it. Let's get out of this rain."

Stephen continued to examine Alex's face as they walked. "How is it done? Some kind of wizardry?"

"Nay. Just a manipulation of the stone's power. Nothing to fear."

"Will you tell Emma the truth of it?"

"I will not and neither will you."

"But you're deceiving her."

"Aye, I am, and not without some guilt. But tell me, do you think I should reveal my identity? Given what she's learned about her parents, would she speak to me as she speaks to Caleb?" He sighed. "Stephen, I might not be her sire, but she's still my child. After everything she's been through, I feared for her mind. I had to do something."

Stephen echoed Alex's sigh and looked up at the castle walls. "'Tis certain she has not found it easy at Thurston. I know she's missed you, missed her home. There have been times when I feared for her sanity." He wiped the rain from his face. "Truthfully, Alex, I'm glad you're here."

"But?" Alex paused on the steps. "I sense unspoken questions."

"I'm curious why you lied about her father." Stephen pushed the door open. " And did you really kill her parents?"

Alex shook his head. "Those questions are for Emma to ask. I can't...ah." He halted mid-stride as pain wrapped around his heart.

Stephen frowned. "What is it? Are you ill?"

Alex gasped for breath. "In God's name, Keir, stop. 'Tis not what you think."

The pain vanished as Keir stepped out from behind the door, his expression hard with anger. Stephen's hand drifted to his sword.

"Nay, lad." Alex placed his hand atop Stephen's. "Believe me, it would not be a wise move."

Keir's eyes narrowed as he regarded Alex. "I heard what he called you just now. I hope I'm mistaken in my assumption. A betrayal of the shield will not be forgiven."

"You heard him correctly." Alex met Keir's icy gaze. " But your assumption is wrong. There has been no betrayal."

~o~

Despite the sombre light of a dreary autumn afternoon, the candles stayed unlit in Stephen's chamber. Their fragile flames were not needed, for an unearthly glow illuminated the room, pushing shadows deep into the corners. It emanated from the two Guardians who circled Stephen, studying him as wolves might study a newcomer to their pack.

But this newcomer had already stepped into their realm undetected, without invitation, and that left them with questions. Stephen's ability to invade Alex's mind was notable enough, but to do so while under the protection of two other Guardians and the shield shocked them, disturbed them.

No mortal had ever done such a thing before.

Finn's humour had vanished, replaced by a silent, serious scrutiny. And despite Alex's assurance that Stephen could be trusted, Keir's suspicions continued to leach into the atmosphere. The stone absorbed, magnified, and reflected all the circling emotions, tightening the air with ribbons of invisible tension.

Alex knew Stephen sensed the danger facing them, for the young man stood silent and wary, yet to Alex's gratification, apparently fearless.

"You're certain you gave him no indication of who you were?" The gleam in Keir's eyes intensified as he spoke, his gaze still fixed on Stephen's face.

"None." Alex looped his thumbs into his sword belt, realizing with some shame he was enjoying the bemused reaction of his powerful companions. "He entered my mind unbidden."

"But I sensed nothing. Finn sensed nothing." Keir stopped pacing and looked at Alex. "Can you explain that?"

Alex shrugged. "Nay, other than to suggest his abilities are stronger than I thought."

Finn also examined Stephen, inspecting him, studying him. "Tell us what you felt, young man. What you sensed. How did you know it was Alexander who stood before you?"

"Truthfully, I didn't know. At least, not at first. Of course, the Scottish accent reminded me of Alex." Stephen gestured to Alex's sword. "But I sensed the stone as I stood with Christophe in the Great Hall. 'Twas unmistakable to me, for it's a sensation unlike any other. Then I noticed the binding on the hilt, and wondered at it. When I saw Caleb outside with Emma I just knew he was Alex, even though I found it hard to believe."

"Were you aware of my thoughts?" Alex asked. "Did you realize where your mind was?"

Stephen pondered for a moment, then shook his head. "I cannot say I was fully aware of them. Although I've noticed whenever you're nearby my awareness of everything heightens, sharpens. Thoughts arrive unbidden and take me by surprise."

Alex chuckled. "Aye. They often take me by surprise too."

Keir scowled. "This is very serious, Guardian. Do you

know what this breach implies?"

"It implies my instincts were correct, my lord." Alex suppressed a flutter of irritation at Keir's tone. "Stephen merits the Circle's consideration, as I suggested."

"Perhaps," Keir acknowledged. "Yet I still question the ease with which he saw through the shield."

"And slipped past our defenses," Finn added.

Stephen tensed. "'Twas not Alex's failure. He never betrayed you or the presence of the stone. Nor can I actually see through this...this shield he hides behind. Even now, 'tis Caleb's face upon his shoulders. I just knew —"

"You don't have to defend me, lad," Alex interrupted, his irritation growing. "They have no cause to question my integrity. They're deciding whether or not to trust you."

"Or kill you." Keir's voice sliced through the charged air like the arc of an executioner's blade.

Alex's hand gripped the hilt of his sword, his breath catching at the ominous words. Stephen's brow creased as he stared at Keir, but he said nothing.

"God's blood, Keir." Finn muttered under his breath. "You have such a charming way with words."

"There will be no killing." Alex moved toward Stephen. "I swear the lad is no threat."

Stephen continued to stare at Keir, who gasped. "What...what the hell...?" He lifted a hand to his temple.

Stephen smiled. "I applaud your effort to intimidate me, my lord, but it won't work. I know what you want from me, and I'm quite willing to allow your observations. However, I would appreciate a little more respect while you decide upon my worth as a future Guardian."

Keir uttered a curse and stepped back. Alex looked at the floor, fighting an urge to laugh. Finn failed in his effort. His shout of laughter filled the room, shattering the tension.

"Well, Keir, there's your answer," He stepped forward and gripped Keir's shoulder. "May I suggest the first thing you teach our young knight is how to control his remarkable abilities. Reading minds without permission is very impolite. 'Tis also dangerous. Heaven help him if he stumbles into my thoughts."

Stephen visibly relaxed as a grin spread over his face. "Why do I get the feeling I should be warning the women of Thurston about you?"

Finn's eyes twinkled as he shrugged. "Go ahead. They won't listen. They're all smitten as soon as they lay eyes on me."

Keir cleared his throat, his face now expressing reluctant admiration. "When you've both finished, there are things to discuss. Stephen, it would appear your talents do merit our sincere investigation. I'll need to spend time with you. Despite what has happened here today, you still have to face the Circle. There's much to learn."

Stephen nodded. "Aye. Well, we have a week. Maybe ten days. Is that long enough for this Circle of yours?"

Finn and Keir exchanged amused glances.

Alex gave a wry smile. "It takes years, lad. I'm still learning what this jewel can do. Today is an example of that."

"What's happening in a week?" Keir asked.

"I must leave for London." Stephen reached into his shirt and pulled out the letter. "Henry is looking for me. He wants a report on my findings."

"On the stone, you mean," said Finn. "Alex told us of your...mission."

"Aye, I'm not happy about lying to my king. But I understand why I must."

"I shall travel with you," announced Keir. "'Tis the

perfect opportunity to learn more of your potential as a Guardian."

"And to make sure I don't betray you to His Grace," Stephen added. "I don't need to read your mind to understand that."

Keir smiled. "You're learning already."

"Does Emma know you're leaving?" Alex asked. "You're not taking her with you, surely."

"Nay and nay." Stephen sighed. "Leaving her will be difficult for her and me. 'Tis another reason I'm glad you're here."

"Speaking of Emma," Alex tapped a finger on his temple. "Remember, once we leave this room, I am Caleb again. She must know nothing of this discussion."

Chapter 19

Stephen stifled a yawn, squinting at the early morning light that poked through gaps in the shutters. He had slept little, his turbulent mind giving him no rest. His meeting with the Guardians had excited and overwhelmed him, yet left him with more questions than answers. The combination of euphoria and fear had eased, but his thoughts still raced and his skin tingled with anticipation.

In contrast, Emma's night had been peaceful, apparently free from the dark dreams that usually disturbed her. Even now, her breaths were soft and serene as she lay at his side. He turned to look at her.

His incessant thoughts slowed, subdued by his contemplation of the sleeping girl. It could not be denied. Alex's - or Caleb's - presence at Thurston had already made a visible difference to Emma's spirits. He had succeeded where Stephen had failed, calming Emma's distress and bringing a light back into her eyes. It was uncanny, especially since she didn't even know that Caleb was actually Alex. She'd reached out to an apparent stranger, who only reminded her of Alex, and taken comfort from him.

Stephen searched for some jealousy on his part, but couldn't find any. Emma had a connection to Alex that defied any external resentment, a bond as natural as the sun to the earth.

Strange for a man to have such an affinity with a child not of his loins. Moreover, the child of his wife's lover. Unusual. Puzzling, even.

As he pondered, a migrant thought slipped into his mind, a revelation, the meaning of it so inconceivable it stopped the breath in his lungs. But it vanished before his brain could grasp it, leaving no imprint. He tensed, dredging through his thoughts, searching for the elusive information, but it had already gone. Was it something about Emma? Aye. Maybe. And something about her mother. Some kind of impossible truth. But gleaned from where? The thought had not been his, surely?

He rubbed his eyes, frustrated, deciding to blame fatigue for the strange experience.

Overcome by a sudden need to hold her, he gathered Emma in his arms and pressed a kiss to her head. Her mouth curved into a sleepy smile.

"Stephen."

"Good morning, little one." His lips brushed against her ear, his body hardening as she snuggled up to him. God help him. He resolved to marry the girl as soon as he returned from London. "You slept well, I think?"

"Uh-huh." She opened her eyes. "Did you?"

He trailed a fingertip across her brow. "Liquid emeralds."

"What?"

"Your eyes. They really are remarkable." He kissed the tip of her nose. "And your nose is absolutely perfect."

She placed a hand on his cheek. "What is it, Stephen?"

"Your nose? It's what you use to smell with."

She blinked at him and grinned.

"Stop teasing me. I know something's troubling you. I sensed it last night. Tell me what it is."

"Hmm. You know me too well." He traced a finger down her cheek. "I had a missive from Henry yesterday."

Emma frowned. "Henry who?"

Stephen chuckled. "You know. Henry. The man who rules England?"

"Oh, him." She chewed on her bottom lip. "He wants to see you?"

"Aye."

"So, we're leaving Thurston?"

Stephen's gut clenched. He sat up, punched the pillow behind him and settled back, pulling Emma against his chest. He knew he was about to hurt her feelings.

"I have to leave Thurston, Emma, but I want you to stay here."

Her body stiffened against his. "Why? Nay, please. I can't stay here on my own." She tried to pull away, but he held her firmly.

"Sweetheart, listen to me. The journey will be exhausting, for I intend to ride hard and fast. And, since we're not wed, you'd have to share a chamber with several other courtiers once we arrive at Westminster. Have you ever been to court? Do you have any idea what it's like?" He stroked her hair. "Besides, you'll not be on your own here."

He waited, feeling the fall and rise of her chest against his, aware of the rapid tumble of thoughts in her head. Finally, she spoke, her tone one of sad resignation.

"When are you leaving?"

"The sooner I leave the sooner I can return. But I can delay my departure a few more days yet."

"How long will you be gone?"

"Three or four weeks. Maybe a little more."

A sigh shuddered through her. Stephen placed a gentle finger under her chin, lifting her face to look at her.

"I've no wish to leave you, little faerie, believe me. I'll deliver my report to Henry and return to Thurston immediately after. And when I do return..." he bent and kissed her mouth," ...we'll plan our wedding. I want you, Emma. I want to make you mine. 'Tis torturous for me to lie with you like this and not make love to you."

Emma half rolled onto him, her expression serious. "Then make love to me, Stephen. I long for it too. If we're to be married, what does it matter?" She grimaced. "It's not like I'm a —"

"Nay." Stephen placed his fingers across her lips. " We'll not use Argante's depravity as any kind of excuse.

You're as innocent as you ever were, and will remain so until my ring is on your finger. Besides, I'll not break the vow I made to Alex."

He sat up, lifted her from him and slipped out of bed. "I have something for you. I meant to give it to you last night, but you fell asleep so quickly."

Emma sat and pulled her knees up under her chin. "Really? What is it?"

Stephen dug a small leather pouch from his discarded shirt, smiling at the childlike excitement in her voice and soft flush on her cheeks. He bounced onto the bed and pulled her back into his arms.

"This." He grabbed her hand, opened the pouch and tipped the contents into her palm. "It belonged to my mother. In fact, it was one of her favourite pieces. I want you to have it."

The tiny brooch was a delicate circle of finely carved gold leaves, set with small brilliant red rubies and startling blue sapphires.

Emma gasped. "Oh, Stephen. It's beautiful. But should it not go to Bee?"

Stephen shook his head. "Nay. My mother gave it to me. Of course, it would be more fitting if it had emeralds in it. To match your eyes, I mean."

"Oh, no. I love it as it is. I shall treasure it and wear it always." She looked at him, her eyes shining. "Thank you."

"You're welcome." He kissed her again, soft at first then with more passion as she leaned into him. God help him, but it would not be easy to leave her.

~o~

Morning sunlight reflected off honed steel, dazzling the several pairs of eyes that watched as Alex and Emma battled against each other in the practise yard.

"She fights well," Keir observed. "Although I find it unnatural to see a woman with a sword."

"I find it quite stimulating." Finn nudged Stephen. "Do you not find it a little warm out here, young knight?"

Stephen gave him a withering glance. "Be careful, sir. 'Tis my betrothed you speak of."

Keir grunted, his gaze still on Alex and Emma. "Ignore him, Stephen. Finn was born in the forest during rutting season. He truly cannot help himself."

Finn chuckled and leaned back against the wall.

"Tell me, gentlemen." Keir's eyes narrowed as he watched Alex correcting one of Emma's moves. "What do you see when you look at them?"

Stephen frowned. "What should I see? I don't understand the question."

Finn straightened. "I do. I noticed it last night in the Great Hall and wondered at it."

"So did I." Keir looked at Stephen. "Don't even think about searching my mind. Just watch them and tell me what you see, independent of my thoughts."

Stephen watched for a few moments and shook his head. "I see nothing untoward. Besides, she thinks he's Caleb. You can't expect her to react exactly as she would to Alex."

"That's not what I mean. Perhaps you're too close to them emotionally." Keir tilted his head as he watched them. "They share something, yet it appears neither one is aware of it. A link of some sort. A connection that transcends even the shield. 'Tis almost as if..." He turned dark eyes to Stephen. "How much do you know of Emma's mother?"

A prickle ran across Stephen's scalp as a vague memory teased his mind. "I know little of her. Only that she died with her lover, although Alex will not say how exactly."

"Aye, we know that much. The child had been placed in some abbey in Norfolk." Keir frowned. "Where was it, Finn?"

"Creake Abbey."

"Aye, that's right. Creake Abbey."

The hair on Stephen's neck lifted. "God's teeth. Are you sure?"

Keir nodded. "Certain. Why? Is that significant?"

"It might be. That's where Argante went looking for clues about the stone. There's an old priest there who supposedly had knowledge of its location."

Keir's eyes widened. "Father Francis?"

"Aye. You know him?"

"We know him very well." Keir glanced at Finn then turned back to Stephen. "I fear our trip to London may take longer than planned. I'd like to make a detour. I have questions for Father Francis."

"If he still lives." Stephen grimaced. "He was at death's door the last time we were there.

Keir smiled. "Oh, I can assure you, young knight, Francis still lives."

"But what's this about?" Stephen gestured toward Emma. "Is something wrong?"

"I hesitate to use the word 'wrong'. 'Tis more a sense that something is not quite right." Keir raised his eyes to the sky as if seeking an answer from above. "But I'm not sure what it is."

"What's so special about this old priest?" Stephen asked. "How can he know so much?"

Keir didn't answer, but pondered for a moment. "What did he tell Argante about the stone? He must have said something to lead you to Cumbria."

"I can't be sure of all that was said between them. Argante told us the stone lay buried south of the great estuary, next to an ancient king, protected by a shield of silver." The mere mention of Argante's name left a bitter taste on Stephen's tongue. "The riddle meant little to me at the time."

Finn raised an eyebrow. "'Tis precise, yet still vague enough. 'Twas only circumstance, then, which led Argante to Alex."

"Perhaps," said Keir. "But I'm still surprised Francis said anything at all."

"So who is this priest?" Stephen fought with his rising impatience. "And what is his connection to the stone?"

Finn nodded at Keir's questioning glance. "Aye. Tell him."

Keir's eyes lit with a strange gleam. "Father Francis used to be one of us."

Stephen hesitated as his mind fumbled with Keir's information. "A Guardian?"

Keir nodded. "He chose to leave the Circle and take the holy vows instead." He looked over toward the practice yard, his eyes thoughtful. "His mind must be deteriorating. I can't believe he would intentionally betray his only son."

Stephen followed Keir's gaze. Alex feigned a move and Emma's sword clattered to the ground. Her shriek of laughter echoed around the courtyard, followed by Alex's exaggerated shout of victory.

As the meaning of Keir's words sank into Stephen's brain, his breath slowed. "Christ above. You're telling me the old priest is Alex's father?"

"Aye." Keir smiled grimly. "But they haven't spoken for many years."

Finn shifted on his feet. "They haven't spoken since Alex adopted Emma."

"But why?" Stephen thought of his own father and the closeness they'd shared. What could possibly drive a father and son apart? Besides, these were extraordinary men leading extraordinary lives. Surely they would be above the petty tribulations reserved for mortal existence.

Keir shrugged. "Neither of them would ever speak of it. But something is plainly amiss here, and I intend to find out what."

Stephen felt a sudden need to protect Alex. "Perhaps they both prefer to leave the past where it is."

"Perhaps you're right." Keir sighed. "But I suspect Alex simply refuses to see the truth."

"What truth?" Stephen demanded. "What is it he refuses to see?"

"That's what I'm hoping Francis will tell us."

Another shout of laughter echoed across the courtyard, drawing their attention. Still wondering at Keir's words, Stephen watched Emma, her sword in hand, hair wild, and skirts whirling. He couldn't help but smile. By all the saints, he loved her so much.

Keir's voice cut into his thoughts. "The change in her since Alexander arrived is remarkable."

Finn cast a grim look at Keir. " We're being very careless of late, my friend. As you take such pleasure in reminding us, his name, for now, is Caleb."

"True," Keir acknowledged. "But you're usually more careless than I, and need reminding. 'Tis merely this brush with mortality that has clouded my otherwise perfect mind."

Finn snorted. "Curse your balls, Guardian. It obviously hasn't affected your lack of modesty."

"Nor your lack of discretion," Keir shot back. "Which reminds me, where did you disappear to last night?"

"Christ, what are you? My damn nursemaid?" Finn's eyes twinkled as he looked at Stephen. "If you must know, I was battling with Bee."

"You and my sister? Who won?"

"Me, of course." Finn grinned. "Mated her easily. Three times."

Keir looked at the sky. "Dear God, please tell me he's talking about chess."

Finn chuckled and shoved his thumbs into his sword belt. "Ach, but she's a lovely wee girl. Parts of me just sit up and take notice whenever she's near."

"Aye, well, just remember who she is," said Stephen. "You'd better keep your wayward parts in check."

Finn frowned. "I would never disrespect the lass, young knight. In fact, I've grown quite fond of the little filly."

"Good." Keir nodded toward the castle. "Because the little filly is galloping this way."

All eyes turned to watch Bee approach, the quickness of her step not quite a gallop, but certainly not sedate, unlike Anne and Miriam who followed at some length behind.

"God's teeth," Stephen mumbled. "I hope they aren't going to start any trouble."

An expression of amusement settled on Keir's face. "I doubt it. Emma has a sword."

"Brother!" Bee arrived, panting, her breath clouding in the cool autumn air. She lifted her face for a kiss.

Stephen obliged, dropping one on each cheek, his eyes on Anne and Miriam. "Did you have to bring them with you?"

"I had no choice. Word of your dragon-slaying bride has spread through the castle. They wanted to come and watch. Thought I'd better come too, in case you need support."

Finn gave Stephan a nudge. "By all that's holy, you're a lucky man, my lord. All these women willing to fight for you. What's your secret?"

Bee flashed a sweet smile at Finn. "For one thing, my brother's more gentle with me on the chessboard than some I could mention."

"Ah." Finn grinned at her. "Well, if that's what it takes to gain your favour, *mo chroí*, I promise to go easy on you tonight."

Stephen found himself juggling both pleasure and concern at the happiness on Bee's face as she chatted with Finn. Her attraction to the Irish knight was both obvious and surprising. Normally, she spurned men's advances, declaring them all to be forced and insincere, but it appeared she'd fallen for this one, and Stephen's gut clenched. Hell, she knew nothing about him.

He was a Guardian, a member of an ancient assembly, a powerful being, free from the bonds of mortality and belonging to a realm beyond human comprehension.

Finn could never be hers.

Keir leaned over and murmured in his ear. "He'll not hurt her, Stephen. In fact, I guarantee she'll only benefit from his good grace."

Stephen grunted. "I don't fear for her safety. I fear for her heart."

Keir smiled. "Don't. You'll see. He'll ensure her future happiness before he leaves. 'Tis another part of what we do and who we are. When Guardians visit in friendship, they rarely leave a place, or the people within it, untouched or unaffected in some positive way."

Stephen opened his mouth to respond, but another voice cut in.

"Good day, my lords."

Stephen forced his mouth into what he hoped was a believable smile.

"Lady Miriam, Lady Anne."

"We heard about Emma's prowess with the sword. I

wanted to see it for myself." Miriam looked over to where Alex and Emma stood talking, swords resting quietly in their hands. Alex nodded toward them and said something to Emma, who shook her head.

Stephen shrugged. "Well, unless I'm mistaken, dear ladies, it appears you're too late."

"Oh, that's too bad. I expect our presence intimidated her." Anne's voice purred with false regret. "Personally, I fail to see the attraction of such unladylike activities."

Bee rolled her eyes at Stephen who opened his mouth to respond just as a shadow skimmed over their heads, blue-black wings flashing in the sunlight. The crow settled on the outer wall and peered down at them in silence. Stephen chuckled. A new spectator? Perhaps Alex and Emma were not done after all.

The answer came in a clash of steel as blade met blade. No one spoke, only watched as Emma's slight form moved with a grace and speed learned from childhood at the hands of a master swordsman.

Of course, Stephen was fully aware of Alex's gentle sword-play, recognizing the intentional errors and false moves, which appeared to give Emma an upper hand. But the ladies watched in silence, apparently unaware of the pretence.

After a while, when both mutually conceded and sheathed their swords, Emma strode from the practice field at Alex's side, her chin held high. Without hesitation, she stepped into Stephen's embrace. He didn't balk at the sweat on her brow or the tangle of her hair, but swung her around in his arms and joined his laughter with hers.

Stephen's heart raced. Emma's face glowed with confidence. Her eyes were bright, her demeanour relaxed and happy. Alex met Stephen's gaze and a silent acknowledgement passed between them.

Finally, he thought, he could leave her without fear for

her safety or her well-being. All was well. He had nothing to worry about.

Later - much later - he thought back to that day.

And how terribly wrong he had been.

Chapter 20

Darkness retreated from the Cumbrian hills, leaving behind the damp chill of a bleak autumn morning. Clouds scurried across the sky, chased by a western wind, which chose to remain aloft, unhindered by hill or vale. Only a gentle breeze explored the earth below, skimming over the summit and slopes of Black Combe. It fussed around Althena, playing with her skirts and her long, dark hair.

She pulled her shawl across her shoulders, searching the skies for hints of what the weather might yet bring. The fragrance of autumn carried on the breeze, captured from nearby forests and lakes. Stronger yet was the scent of horseflesh, for Bart stood at Althena's side, his warm breath brushing her shoulder. She scratched his cheek.

"I think the tide is on its way out, old friend. May God grant we stay dry as we travel."

The stallion snorted and nodded his head in apparent agreement. Althena patted his neck and, with a final glance at her little cottage, led him down the track toward the river.

An entire moon's cycle had passed since Alex had left Bart in her care. Through the day, the horse grazed the land around her home, and took shelter in her small lean-to at night, enjoying a further feast of hay and oats. But the advancing chill of autumn pained the stallion's old bones. Althena could tell by the increased stiffness of his gait and his occasional limp.

She realized he needed the warmth and shelter of a barn. His barn. So, she decided to take the old fellow home, intending to stay with him until Alex returned.

"Whenever that might be," she muttered, voicing her thoughts, for Alex had been gone longer than she'd expected.

I wonder how he fares? And Emma too, bless her heart. May God have granted them some peace.

She thought about Finn and Keir, a grin spreading across her face as she recalled the Irish knight's unabashed flirtations with her. The man was utterly incorrigible!

But Finn wasn't the one she wanted. He wasn't the one she loved.

Althena's shoulders slumped and she parted with a heart-felt sigh, followed by a muttered curse.

"Oh, for God's sake. What am I? Some love-sick maiden?" She pulled her shoulders back, stuck out her tongue and blew in self-disgust. Bart jerked his head at the sound, his ears twitching.

"Sorry, old man. Ignore me. I'm just being foolish." She reached up and rubbed Bart's nose.

Althena chose to lead the animal rather than ride him. Despite his gentle nature and advanced years, Bart was still a full-blooded war-horse, accustomed to obeying the commands of only one master. She wasn't sure how he might respond to someone else sitting on his back. Besides, she didn't mind the walk. Much of the trail ran alongside the river. Althena enjoyed watching the water, recently invigorated by several days of rain, tumble and bounce its way over the rocks.

Around midday they reached the forest trail leading to Alex's home. Althena eyed the dark path with some reluctance, chiding herself for her nervousness as she led Bart deeper into the woods.

Still draped in autumn colours, the trees allowed little light to descend to the forest floor and the lack of sun only strengthened the woodland gloom. The breeze pushed its way through the branches and dying leaves fell silently all around them.

Althena chatted to Bart, her trivial discourse intended, for the most part, to dispel the loneliness of the forest. Bart's mighty hooves fell sure and steady alongside

Althena's quiet steps, his ears twitching at the sound of her voice. Once in a while, he would snort or shake his head. Such actions were often timely, as if he agreed with her words or understood her questions, and Athena's amused laughter often echoed through the trees.

They were almost home when the feeling crept up on her, a sense someone was watching from the shadows. The hair on her arms and neck lifted. Was it her imagination, or had the woods become unusually quiet? The breeze had died. The leaves no longer fell. Even the birds were silent. Then, somewhere off in the trees, a twig snapped.

Althena stopped, her breath trapped in her lungs, her fingers gripping Bart's lead-rein so tightly her knuckles whitened. Cursing under her breath, she peered into the gloom, half-expecting to see someone step out from behind a tree. But no one did.

She glanced at Bart. Had he heard something, noticed anyone? Apparently not. He showed no indication anything was amiss. In fact, his head hung in lazy contentment while his tail swished away the few remaining flies of the season.

Althena swallowed her fear, uttered a quick prayer, and walked on.

By the time they reached the house, her anxiety had subsided. Even so, she let out a sigh of relief at the familiar sight of Alex's home. She could no longer ignore the ache in her feet and the slight throb in her temples. After all, they'd been travelling for more than half the day.

"I'll settle you in, my friend, and then I'm going to make myself a tisane and rest my poor feet."

Bart needed no encouragement. He dragged Althena into the musty barn, his nostrils quivering with apparent excitement at being home again. He looked about him, lifted his head and neighed loudly. She understood his question.

"Nay, lad. Alex isn't here." She pulled the saddle bags from Bart's back, unhooked his lead rein, and slapped his rear as he stepped into his stall. He turned to face her, resting his chin on the gate as she latched it. To her surprise, he bared his teeth, pulled his ears back and kicked the door. "Oi, watch your manners." Althena frowned and picked up an empty bucket. "I'll be back in a moment."

She stepped outside, looked over to the house and froze.

Something was propped up by the front door. Nay, not propped up, standing. Standing by the door. *A man?* Nay. The shape was similar, but... *Some kind of animal, maybe?* It blended into the background, almost as if it was had torn itself away from the earth, the trees, the walls of the house.

Her eyes narrowed, squinting as she tried to make it out. She took a step forward. The thing didn't move. She took another step.

The creature turned its head and looked at her.

Althena gasped, her guts twisting in fear. "Sweet Mary. Oh, dear Mother of God."

It defied belief. Such a creature shouldn't be alive - nay - couldn't be alive. Not even the devil could have spawned such a being. At one time, it might have been a man. Now, half its skull was bare of hair, the raw skin stretched, like rough leather, down one side of a face that bore little resemblance to a human. One eye was sealed shut by strings of scar tissue. The other eye watched her, void of lashes and a brow. When it blinked, Althena screamed and dropped the pail.

She turned to run, tripping over the pail in her terror. Her skirts tangled around her ankles and she stumbled to her knees. Bart squealed in anger, and the barn shook with the impact of his hooves hitting the door.

A hand grabbed her hair and hauled her upright. She screamed again and tried to pull the vice-like fingers free from her scalp. An arm wrapped itself around her throat, cutting off her cries.

"Where is she?"

Althena cringed at the stench of rotten flesh, sweat and human waste. She whimpered, her voice choked by her captor. The fist in her hair twisted her head, pulling her face around to meet his. She closed her eyes, unwilling to look at him. His vile breath violated her nostrils. Her stomach clenched and she heaved.

"Where. Is. She?" Each word spat saliva in her face.

"Wh...Who?" she croaked, fighting for breath.

A name gurgled from his throat. "Emma."

The realisation of who held her turned her blood to ice. *Argante.*

Althena opened her eyes, her head throbbing from lack of air and the pain of his grip.

"P...please," she rasped. "You're killing me."

He let her go and she dropped to the ground, trembling and gasping.

"Who are you?" His hand drifted to his crotch and spittle pooled at the corners of his lips.

"I...I am Al...Althena." She rested on her knees and summoned the courage to study him, searching for any sign of humanity on his scar-ridden face. She found none.

"Althena." A globule of saliva escaped his deformed mouth and hit the ground in front of her. He licked his lips. "I want Emma."

Tears rolled down her face. "Emma has gone. She isn't coming back."

His one eye blinked several times. "You lie. She is coming back. Emma belongs to me." He pulled his erect penis from the torn remnants of his britches and stroked it.

"See? I only have to speak her name. Hard as a rock."

Althena sobbed, her desperate mind trying to calm itself, seeking a way to survive. She sensed the depth of his insanity and it terrified her. Should she try reasoning with him? Make a run for it?

Bart continued to squeal and kick at his door. If only he could free himself. She knew the horse would attack Argante.

Still fondling himself, he bent over her. She cringed and turned away.

"Emma is coming back." He spat on the ground. "You lying whore. Maybe I'll give you to Iain. He'll fuck anything." He picked something up and closed his fingers around it. "That horse is giving me a headache."

He raised his fist, a twisted smile stretching across his scarred lips. "Liar."

His eye blinked once more and his fist came down hard, striking her on the side of her head. It sounded like an egg breaking close to her ear. For one glorious insane moment, she thought he'd merely picked up a hen's egg from the ground and hit her with it. Then she felt a warm rush of blood coursing down her neck. A moment later, blinding pain flashed behind her eyes, stabbing deep into her brain.

She vomited and fell backwards, gagging on the contents of her stomach.

Dear God. What has he done? Alex, I need you. Please, help me. Please.

Coughing, she turned her head, spitting out vomit. The flow of blood changed course and ran across her eyes. She wiped it away in time to see Argante disappearing through the barn door.

Only moments later Bart stopped squealing, but the sickening silence that followed lasted but a moment.

Faint at first, the sound grew louder, filling the space

around and above Althena with the steady beat of wings and a distinct chorus. Behind the pain and shock, her injured brain recognized the familiar cries. With a groan, she turned blood-filled eyes to the heavens.

Geese, hundreds of them, were flying overhead in majestic formations, leaving behind the cold grip of a northern winter, heading south.

Seeking survival.

Just before darkness consumed her, Althena stretched a trembling hand to the sky.

"Alex."

~o~

The west wind continued its journey toward the German Sea, herding huge swaths of clouds across the wild expanses of Yorkshire. It grazed the top of Thurston's battlements and blew into the bailey, snatching at Alex's hair and lifting the cloak from his shoulders. He paid it little attention. His focus was elsewhere.

Beneath his right hand, which rested on the sword's hilt, the stone gave off a soft vibration. At the same time, a sense of foreboding nibbled at him, unsettling his stomach.

An elusive dream had wrenched him from sleep just before dawn, the images in his head vanishing the moment he opened his eyes. Yet remnants of the dream taunted him still, unreachable and indiscernible.

The lingering sensation reminded him of the morning he'd awoken to find Emma gone, yet he knew she was not the cause of his unease this time. So what, or who, was? The answer eluded him.

His gaze shifted from the sky and wandered over the forest, seeking the source of...*what?* He turned toward the vast moorland of Yorkshire. Beyond that, to the northwest, lay the distant fells of Cumbria.

The breath caught in his chest and a prickle of apprehension stroked the back of his neck. *There. An anomaly. An imbalance.*

Argante? Nay, surely not. Argante's evil influence couldn't stretch this far.

Could it?

A crow settled on the wall next to him, flapping its wings against the pull of the wind. Alex looked at the bird, who puffed out its blue-black feathers and cawed loudly.

The unease in his stomach settled a little. "Aye, I'd be grateful."

The crow spread its wings and soared skyward.

"Remarkable." Finn's voice cut through the rush of the wind. Alex turned to see him watching the flight of the crow as it disappeared into the clouds. "You're troubled today, Alexander. Anything I should know about?"

Alex gave a grim smile. "I'd tell you if I knew what it was."

"Well, beware." Finn glanced at Alex's sword. "Your emotions are a little...scattered. Go easy on yourself. Our control of the shield is weaker since Keir left."

Alex took a slow breath and relaxed his shoulders. "'Tis a feeling of unease, but I can find no reason for it."

"Probably something you ate." Finn grinned and gestured toward the bailey. "I saddled your horse. Our ladies await."

~o~

The moor stretched to the horizon, a ragged patchwork of windswept grasses, bedraggled heather and rusty bracken. Here and there, patches of cotton grass waved their white flags in the breeze, betraying the location of boggy ground. An endless multitude of clouds, caught in the wind's grasp, rushed across the sky.

Alex and Finn reined in their horses at the top of a gentle rise and turned to watch Bee and Emma, who, moments later, pulled their own horses to a halt alongside. Bee, panting, uttered a string of curses and glared at Finn. Alex, struggling with an urge to laugh, sat back in his saddle and waited.

"*A chailín mo chroí.*" Finn met Bee's glare, his lips twitching with suppressed laughter. "Such language for a lady. What, pray, have I done now?"

"You cheated." Bee's eyes narrowed. "Again."

Finn placed a hand on his chest, his eyes twinkling. "Me? How this wench, whom I adore, does cut me with her sharp words. I'm beyond bereft."

Emma burst out laughing. "She does have a point, Finn. You yelled 'race you to the top' only after you'd kicked your poor horse into a gallop. We didn't stand a chance."

Alex stifled a chuckle and looked at the ground.

"And you're no better, Caleb." Bee scowled at him. "I saw the silent exchange between you both. You're in league with this Irish devil. Move aside." She urged her horse forward, brushing past them, her nose in the air.

Finn shrugged, gave Emma and Alex a sheepish grin, and turned his horse to follow Bee's. "Please excuse me," he said. "It seems this Irish devil must endeavour to embrace the backside of a wee English angel."

Emma gasped and looked at Alex with wide eyes. "He's incorrigible!"

Alex laughed. "Aye. But quite harmless. She couldn't be in safer hands."

"I know. It's nice to see her so happy." Emma sighed and looked out across the moor. He watched her fingering a small gold brooch through the opening in her cloak. He didn't recognize the jewel.

A gift from Stephen?

Alex sensed her thoughts as he urged his horse onward, following Bee and Finn's path. Emma's horse fell into step beside his.

"Stephen will return soon, my lady. It's been what...a fortnight already?"

"It's been fifteen nights since he left." She turned and gave him a wistful smile. The fresh air had brushed roses on her cheeks, but shadows lingered beneath her eyes. Her aura was still bright, though. *A good sign.* "And one half day," she finished.

His eyes flicked to the skies, his sense of foreboding all at once stronger. "'Tis not easy being apart from someone you love," he murmured, a chill peppering his skin.

"Is something wrong, Caleb?" The hint of fear in her voice caught his attention.

"Nay, lass." He tore his gaze away from the clouds and smiled at her. "I was merely wondering if it might rain. Being caught on the moors in a rainstorm would not be pleasant."

"Ah. You appeared...worried for a moment." She glanced at Bee and Finn up ahead. "I have something to tell you. Something in confidence."

"Of course, my lady."

"I came to a decision last night. Nay. Truth is, I came to it many days ago, but only admitted it to myself last night." Her eyes softened. "I've decided I want to go home. I want to get married in Cumbria. I have to talk to my...to Alex and ask him what happened to my mother."

Alex cursed inwardly, leaned over, and pulled Emma's horse to a halt. He studied her, wondering if she could hear the thud of his heart. "Are you sure, Emma?"

Emma frowned. "About what? Going home? Or

getting married?"

"About asking Alex for the truth. It might not be what you want to hear."

"All I've been told is that he killed my parents. Murdered them. How much worse can it be?" She chewed on her bottom lip. "I've given it much thought. Indeed, I've thought of little else. I agree with Stephen, and I agree with you. My *cùra* would never do such a thing. There must be more to this tale."

My cùra.

Those two words sank into the depths of Alex's soul and soothed the pain within.

"'Tis a good decision," he said. "He'll be pleased to see you. Both of you. Of that, I have no doubt."

Emma wriggled in the saddle. "I can't wait to tell Stephen. I know he wants to go back as well. He and Alex became good friends."

"Aye, he told me."

"Do you intend to stay at Thurston?"

A twinge of guilt plucked at his conscience. He was, after all, deceiving her.

"I'm not sure what my future holds, lass."

"Why don't you travel with us when we go? Come and visit Alex. I'm sure he'd be surprised to see you."

Alex chuckled. "Aye, that he would."

A sound carried on the wind, faint, but distinctive. Emma, still smiling, raised her eyes to the sky and pointed.

"Caleb, look. Oh, how splendid! There must be hundreds of them."

Alex followed her gaze. Thin dark lines were strung across the sky from horizon to horizon. Geese, he realized, on their way to warmer climes before winter arrived.

The air purred with the beat of a thousand wings, and

the wind snatched up the crescendo of melancholy cries. It was an exodus unlike any Alex had ever seen. His spirit lifted at the impressive sight, and he smiled with the sheer pleasure of witnessing the event.

Then, above the cacophony of noise, he heard someone call his name.

Who...?

It sounded like a cry for help. A woman, and, dear God, he knew her voice. But it didn't belong in Yorkshire. It belonged...

Everything around him blurred as a sharp pain exploded in head. The dream he'd tried so hard to recall came back to him in a heartbeat, every terrible detail of it. Only now he knew for certain it was no dream, but a vision.

Althena. Argante. Oh, nay. What has he done?

"Jesus Christ."

Alex doubled over in the saddle, vaguely aware of Emma's panicked cry.

"Caleb?"

She sounded so far away. The earth seemed to reach up and grab him. What was happening? Why could he not see?

Shouts echoed through his mind. Emma again, panic in her voice. He reached out a hand, trying to reassure her. The air still vibrated with the sound of wings, but now the earth around him shook with the thud of hooves. He tried to move, sit up, open his eyes. His limbs would not respond, but his eyes opened to a nauseating blur of black and grey.

"God help me."

"Easy, my friend." Finn's voice cut into Alex's nightmare. A gentle hand rested on his head and subdued his terrible thoughts. "I have you. Try to focus."

"The birds... they saw. I have to go back. Althena..."

Say naught else. I know it hit you hard. I felt the shock of it myself.

Finn's voice was barely a whisper. Nay, it wasn't his voice anymore, but his thoughts.

Focus on my strength and use it. You must focus, Alexander. The shield is failing.

With his eyes squeezed shut, Alex focused on Finn's touch, absorbing his energy and strength. A warm tingle ran across his skin and his heartbeat slowed, the sound of it pulsing in his ears. He flinched when a sudden and intense light flared behind his eyelids.

Open your eyes, Guardian. The energy must have a release.

He opened his eyes and blinked, his sight clearing as Finn's thoughts continued to speak to him.

Better, but your heart is still pounding like a whore's bed. Slow your breathing. You're scaring the ladies.

"Nice turn of phrase, Finn," he murmured, rubbing his eyes. "The shield?"

"Is intact. Can you stand?" Finn wrapped his arm around Alex's shoulders, lifting him.

"I think so." He pushed the heel of his thumb against a pain in his temple. " I need my horse. I must leave right away. Did you see what I saw?"

"I did, but gather your strength. You need a few moments yet." Finn gestured over his shoulder. "Besides, we have the ladies to think about. We can't leave until they've been escorted back to Thurston."

Alex shook his head. " Nay, I'm going from here. I want you to stay at Thurston until Stephen gets back." He looked over at the girls, who stood silent and grim by the horses. His eyes met Emma's and saw fear reflected in them. "Please, Finn. The shield will no longer be needed once I leave, and I'll rest easier knowing you're still here."

Finn blew an exasperated breath. "Christ, but you're an obstinate bastard. Aye, I'll stay. But you'll take my horse too, as a spare. I've no doubt you'll be flying across both counties like the winds of Aran." He followed Alex's gaze and nodded at the girls. "What will you tell them?"

Alex sighed. "Some sorry version of the truth."

Finn looked to the northwest. "The wee lass lives yet. But she's very weak."

"I know. Which is why I must leave right away."

"Alexander, if Althena should die —"

"She'll not die." Determination stiffened his jaw as he strode toward the girls. "I'll not let her die."

Emma's eyes didn't leave Alex's face as he approached, but it was Bee who spoke. "Thank God you're unhurt, Caleb. You scared us."

"Please forgive me, ladies. I had an...attack. It came upon me unawares."

"Is it an affliction you have?" Bee asked, her eyes wide.

"Of sorts, aye." Alex glanced at Emma, wondering why she had not spoken. "'Tis something I've learned to endure."

"God's truth, you have my sympathy." Bee gave him a warm smile.

Alex inclined his head. "'Thank you. I'm sorry if it disturbed you." He looked at Emma again. "May I speak with you privately, my lady?"

Emma nodded, her eyes softening with tears as they stepped away. The breeze played around them, whistling a quiet tune as it wandered over the land. Alex glanced at the sky, empty now apart from a lonely crow circling above.

Emma followed his gaze and then turned sad eyes back to him. "You're leaving, aren't you? It has something to do with what happened just now. You're leaving Thurston."

Alex took her hand and raised it to his lips, surprised at her perception. "Aye, lass. I must leave right away. 'Tis a decision forced upon me." He placed a hand on her cheek. "Stephen will be back soon. In the meantime, if you're in need of help for any reason, go to Finn. Swear to me that you will."

She nodded, biting her bottom lip as she always did when nervous or pondering.

"I swear. But will I see you again?"

The anguish in her voice landed like a weight on his chest. He forced a smile, forming his answer with care. "I'm certain I'll see you again, Emma." He reached over and pulled her cloak around her. "You're shivering, child. Come. Let Finn take you home."

"Home? Nay. Thurston is not my home." She hiccupped a sob and gestured toward the horizon behind him. "My true home is that way. I thank you for all you've done for me, Caleb. May God bless and keep you safe." She turned, but not before Alex saw tears escape from her eyes.

He watched as she hurried back to her horse and climbed into the saddle. Her pain reached out and touched him, winding its way around his heart, intensifying the ache already there. He gripped his sword, fighting his emotions, still unsettled from the horrific revelation about Althena. Finn approached with the horses, his dark eyes gleaming with subdued light.

"Have no fear, my friend. I'll watch over the wee lass." He handed the reins to Alex. "Release the shield as soon as we're out of sight, but prepare yourself. 'Tis like throwing a sack full of lead from your shoulders." He grinned. "You'll think you've sprouted wings."

"What will you tell Christophe?"

"That you're needed urgently elsewhere." The light in Finn's eyes brightened. "'Don't trouble your mind with such trivial thoughts. His lordship and all at Thurston will believe whatever this Irish devil tells them. Go and take care of Althena. You know what to do if you need help."

Alex swung into the saddle and looked up at the sky. The crow still circled, silent, waiting. "Thank you, my friend."

Finn chuckled. "Are you talking to me, or the bird? God keep you, Alexander."

"And you." Alex looked over to Emma and Bee, raising his hand in a solemn salute. Turning his horse, he touched his spurs to its belly and set off at a good canter across the moor. Moments later, he heard a frantic shout behind him.

"Wait!"

He heaved on the reins and twisted in the saddle to see Emma riding toward him in a flat-out gallop. She pulled her horse to a sliding halt next to his, her chest heaving, her face wet with tears.

"Tell me true, Caleb," she sobbed. "Did he send you? Did Alex send you to me?"

In the time it took his heart to beat once, he thrust temptation aside. He knew what his answer must be.

"Nay, my lady. Alex didn't send me." At his words, an expression of bleak disappointment settled on Emma's face. Her need of him - the real him - tore at his conscience. He leaned over to wipe the tears from her cheeks, but she uttered a small cry and turned her head away.

"Emma, please don't cry." His fingers slid under her chin and forced her to face him. He looked into her eyes, into her mother's eyes. "Listen to me, lass, for I tell you this from my heart. Alex loves you very much. Never doubt it. Not for a moment."

"But how can you know that for certain?" she whispered.

He smiled. "He raised you as his own. How could he not love you? Now, promise me you'll stay strong. Promise. I need your word if I'm to go in peace."

"Aye, I promise." She sniffed and tilted her head, studying his face intently. "And if you should see Alex before I do, tell him I love him too, and I'll see him again soon."

As Emma rode back to Finn and Bee, a shocking thought wandered through Alex's brain, looking for a place to settle. Nay, not a thought. A realisation - a startling truth.

He'd seen it reflected in her tears, heard it in her declaration of love, and sensed it in her thoughts. Perhaps it was her need of him, her desire to see what she wanted to see. Whatever the reason, he knew, beyond any doubt, that Emma had seen through the shield.

He rode hard and fast, ignoring the twists and turns of the well-trodden roads, following his black-winged guide along a rugged but more direct path. Freed from the weight of the shield and Finn's suppression of the stone's power, a familiar euphoria swept over him. Alex embraced it with fervour, unaware, until that moment, of how much he'd missed it.

It erased his fatigue, infusing his spirit with light and energy. He relaxed his own rules and allowed the stone's power to drive the horses. Under its influence, the animals did not tire or falter. Only when daylight faded did Alex slow the pace, fearful of the horses stumbling in the dark. Even so, he rested little, but pushed on through the night, crossing into Cumbria as darkness departed.

Dawn unveiled a cold grey sky over the Cumbrian

hills. Alex's airborne escort had long since vanished, no doubt to seek shelter and rest his weary wings.

The wind had died. Thick mist draped over Black Combe, hiding the soft lines of the summit. Without the wind to move them, the clouds settled into place and dropped a steady saturating drizzle to the earth. Alex eyed the sky with dismay, worrying about Althena's survival as he urged the horses onward. Cold and damp were deadly to an unprotected body, especially one already weakened by injury.

At last, he turned the horses onto the forest path leading to his home. His fingers played on the hilt of his sword, yet he sensed nothing untoward, no danger. The forest surrounded him with silence. Even the horses' hooves fell noiselessly on the thick carpet of leaves. Despite the stone's influence, both animals were now close to collapse, their heads drooping with fatigue.

The sight of Althena, lying so still on the muddy ground, was like a kick in Alex's stomach.

"Mother of God."

The words tore from his throat as he dismounted and knelt at her side. He lifted her gently, tears burning his eyes. Blood, mud and vomit soiled her face and matted her hair. Beneath the grime, Althena's skin was deathly pale, her lips and eyelids edged with a chilling blue tinge. Raindrops, stained red with her blood, trickled through Alex's fingers as he held her.

"Ah, Christ. My poor wee lass. What has he done to you?"

He took the corner of his cloak and wiped the filth from her mouth and eyes. Then his fingers explored beneath her jaw, searching for a sign of life, hoping, praying.

"Give me your heart, *leannan*. Please."

There. A pulse. It fluttered weakly, but hope clutched

at his heart. "Praise be."

He scooped her into his arms, meaning to take her into the house, but as he passed the barn door, a chill ran across his skin.

Bart.

He stepped into the barn. The two weary horses had already found their way in there, and were busy munching on some loose hay.

Little remained of Bart's stall. Splintered boards were strewn across the floor and the door was smashed, as were the partition walls. Alex groaned at the sight of a large bloodstain on the ground. But there was no sign of the stallion.

"What happened to you, old friend?" He glanced around. "Where have you gone?"

With a glance at the woman lying deathlike in his arms, Alex swallowed his emotion and fatigue, turned on his heel and headed into the house.

As soon as he opened the door he grimaced at the stale, damp air. Althena needed warmth if she was to survive.

He set her down on his bed, unbuckled his sword and placed it next to her. Its power stimulated the body's natural ability to heal itself. That's why Stephen had recovered so quickly from his wound, Alex mused, his weary mind wandering for a moment.

Using the stone to aid healing was discouraged by the Circle. They believed life to be cyclical, and death was a natural and integral part of that cycle. But, Alex reasoned, Althena had not succumbed to a natural sickness, nor an injury of war. She was another innocent victim of Argante's evil.

Alex blamed himself for all of it. He'd failed to protect Emma and had allowed Argante to live. God forgive him, he'd even provided the bastard with a means to escape.

The repercussions of that one stupid decision had been devastating to the people he loved.

Many years before, someone else he loved had died because of his actions.

Not this time.

He'd known for some time that Althena loved him but, consumed by memories of the past, he'd always hesitated to return her love. She had never pursued him, made uncomfortable demands, or attempted to lure him with typical female wiles. The lass had always maintained her pride, even though he'd often seen the longing in her eyes.

Remorse overcame him. He lifted a strand of hair from her face and lowered his mouth to hers, embracing her frigid lips.

"You shall not die, my sweet lass. Not here, not now. I swear it."

He wiped the blood from her wound and the mud from her face. Then he removed her wet clothing, and rubbed her body down with a soft cloth, massaging her limbs and torso, stimulating her sluggish circulation.

The damp air persisted. Alex tucked a blanket around Althena and went into the kitchen. Before long, a hearty fire burned in the kitchen hearth. With the atmosphere warming at last, he returned to his bedchamber.

Finally, he placed the sword under the pillows, with the hilt directly beneath Althena's head. Then he removed his own clothes and slid into bed beside her. The clammy chill of her flesh shocked him. Beneath the blanket, he gathered her body against his, covering it with his warmth, skin against skin.

"I'm here, *leannan*," he whispered, holding her close. "You're safe now. Argante will not harm you again."

Overcome with fatigue and comforted by Althena's steady breath against his chest, he succumbed to the depths of sleep.

His mind staggered awake some hours later, leaving behind vague shadows of troubled dreams. Althena lay on her side, facing him, her breathing steady, her body warm and soft against his. Alex pushed himself onto an elbow and studied her. Although pale, her skin was fresher, the blueness gone from her eyelids and lips. His fingers stroked her hair and hovered over the gash on her head. It appeared dry, no sign of infection, but he couldn't tell how deep the wound was.

What if her brain has been injured?

He ran a thumb across her cheekbone. "Althena, can you hear me? Can you open your eyes?"

Her eyes rolled beneath the papery skin of her lids and a small frown creased her brow. He held his breath for a moment. Had she heard him?

"Althena."

She groaned, her frown deepening. Her eyelids fluttered but didn't open.

Alex's thumb continued its caress, following the hollow of her cheek and the outline of her bottom lip. "Do you know who I am?"

A tear slid from one corner of her eye and fell onto the pillow. Her lips parted and soundlessly mouthed one word.

"Alex."

Relief choked his immediate response. He took a deep breath. "Thank God."

With her eyes still closed, Althena's hand explored his chest, his throat, his lips. He smiled against her fingertips and kissed them.

"Alex?" This time she murmured his name. Her eyes fluttered open, blinking against the light. "Do I dream?"

He saw the confusion in her expression and pressed his lips to her forehead. "Nay, lass. 'Tis no dream."

She tried to move and groaned, her fingers reaching for the gash on her head.

Alex caught her hand. "Hush. Lie still."

"But...I don't understand. Why are we...?" Her eyes squinted at his bare chest, her pale cheeks flushing pink as her hand went to her throat. "You're...I'm..."

Naked. God's teeth. What must she think?

"I found you outside, unconscious and chilled to the bone," he explained. "I had to warm you somehow."

"But I don't...how..." She squeezed her eyes shut. "Sweet Mary, help me."

"Do you remember anything?"

Her eyes opened again, clouded with misery and confusion.

"Nay. My head, Alex...it hurts so much."

"I know. Take it slow, lass. Are you thirsty?"

"Aye." She cleared her throat. "I am a little."

"Don't try to move. I'll be right back."

Alex pulled on his britches and headed to the kitchen, taking a few moments to stoke up the fire before settling again at Althena's side with two goblets of spiced ale.

It pleased him to see her drink with obvious relish, but all at once her body tensed. She choked and turned shocked eyes to his, coughing as she fought for air.

"Sweet Mother of God," she sputtered, her fingers finding the wound on her head. "I do remember now. 'Twas Argante. He attacked me, struck me with something. And...oh, poor Bart. Alex, I'm so sorry."

"Nay, hush." He took the goblet from her and set it down, alarmed by the sudden grey pallor of her skin. "'Tis not your fault."

"But it is." Her eyes shimmered with tears. "'Tis entirely my fault. I brought Bart here to get him out of the cold and Argante killed him. How can you ever forgive me for that? If I'd stayed at my cottage, he never would –"

"Enough." Alex could not bear to hear the regret in her voice. "Listen to me, lass. None of this is your fault. None of it. 'Tis I who should ask your forgiveness. That bastard is still crawling around the forest because of my foolishness. And the truth is, I don't know what happened to Bart. He's disappeared, but that doesn't mean he's dead." He groaned. "'Tis I who am sorry. Sorry beyond words. I almost lost you. Christ knows, such a thought is unbearable to me."

As he spoke, he noticed a flicker of fear in her eyes and felt her body stiffen against his.

"Where's Emma?" she asked. "Did she return with you?"

Alex hesitated for a moment, his stomach twisting at the fear in her voice. "Nay. She's still in Yorkshire."

"How is she?"

"Frail yet, but much improved."

"Is she coming home?"

"Aye, in a week or two. When Stephen returns from London."

Althena whimpered and her fingers clutched at his arm.

"What is it, *leannan*?"

"Argante. Dear God. He's a monster."

He sighed. "Aye, he is. But he'll not hurt you again. I swear it."

"Nay, you don't understand. I mean he's monstrous to look upon. He's horribly burned, scarred beyond belief. His face, his appearance, is grotesque. And the man is insane, Alex. His mind is sick, twisted." Her voice faltered. "He...he wants Emma. He said she belongs to him. He's watching and waiting for her return."

A sense of dread rose up, like a forgotten nightmare, from the depths of Alex's mind. He recognized the sensation. It had plagued him on and off since Argante's escape from the Keep.

"Then I must find the bastard and kill him," he murmured, "before Emma returns."

Although they came from his heart, his words sounded meaningless to his ears. They dissolved in the air like warm breath on a winter's day. Sweet Jesus, he wanted nothing more than to see the bastard's blood on his blade. But something about Argante had changed. What, though? What had changed?

"I haven't told you everything." Althena's voice broke into his musings. "There was something else about him. Something so strange, I'm not quite sure how to explain it."

God's blood. The answer he sought lay with the woman resting in his arms.

"Tell me."

Her head dropped against his chest. "Perhaps it was my imagination."

"Let me be the judge of that. Tell me what you saw, lass."

She sighed. "'Twas like he was part of the scenery, at one with his surroundings. Only when he moved did I truly see him. At first, I couldn't tell what it...he was. I only saw a shape, something standing by the door, but it - he - blended with the colours around him, the house, the earth, everything. Then he turned to look at me, and his face..." She shuddered. "Never have I seen such a horror."

Althena's words swirled in his head. How could it be? Alex knew of creatures blessed with the ability to hide in plain sight. But a human? Nay, Argante was not human. He was a demon and, dear God, a demon obsessed with Emma. Argante was far more dangerous than Alex had supposed.

"Maybe the blow to my head confuses my thoughts." Althena yawned and snuggled against him. "Yet my memory of it does seem quite clear."

"There's naught wrong with your memory." Alex settled back against the pillow. "I believe you saw him as you say."

Several moments of silence passed while Alex's mind searched for ways to track and kill Argante. Dogs, perhaps? Even an invisible man must have a scent. Between him and Stephen, Emma would not be left alone for a moment when she returned, whether she liked it or not. Not until Argante lay rotting on the ground.

"How did you know?" Althena's sleepy voice carried into his thoughts. She yawned again and rubbed her eyes like a child. He smiled.

"How did I know what, *leannan*?"

"That I had been injured. Or was your return home merely a coincidence?"

Alex decided to tell her the truth. There would be no more deceit. "Nay, not a coincidence. I rode all night to get to you. I knew you'd been hurt."

"How?"

"The birds told me."

"Ah. Well, that explains it." She reached for his hand and wound her fingers through his. "I love you, Alexander."

Time stopped, unsheathed a hidden blade, and thrust it into Alex's heart. Sixteen years peeled away like dead skin, layer by layer, taking him back. Back to that terrible day.

Back to Alicia.

"I love you, Alexander."

A damn lie. The final words of a guilty wife. Nay, not her final words. But spoken as she lay dying in his arms, her blood spreading across the floor, mixing with that of her lover.

A lie, followed by a confession. One that almost drove

him to join his blood with theirs.

Alicia's final thoughts were not for Alex. Apart from a false declaration of love, she gave nothing to him. No expression of regret, no outpouring of grief at her wrongdoing. Nay, he was not in her mind as she went to God. Her final thoughts were for someone else.

"We have a child," she said, the light fading in her splendid eyes. "At Creake Abbey. Take care of her, Alexander. Please. Give me your word. Her name is Emma."

A numbing confession. The existence of a child. Her lover's child. Fitzhugh's bastard.

Alex hated Alicia at that moment and almost cast her aside to lay by her lover's corpse on the cold stone floor. Perhaps she deserved to die looking into Edward Fitzhugh's unseeing eyes.

But Alex could not push her away, for even in the midst of hate he loved her more than life. His soul was devastated, his heart ripped to shreds, but he held his wife until her heart stopped beating. And, as she drew her last few breaths, he gave her what she'd asked for.

He gave her his word.

The past does not stay in the past. It circles around to greet us as we step into the future. One becomes the other. Thus has it always been.

His father's words drifted back to him. They had not spoken to each other since Alex had taken Emma from the abbey. At that time, harsh things had been said, unjust accusations made, impossible truths sworn upon the Holy Book.

He'd been confronted by a tapestry of lies, woven by people he had loved and trusted. But, God forgive him, was he not guilty of the same sins? Had he not lied to Emma? Destroyed her trust, broken her heart?

Time moved forward, shrugged off the memories and

carried him back to the present. He took in a deep breath and gazed at Althena. She slept, her chest rising and falling in a soft rhythm, her dark lashes resting against pale cheeks. It surprised him that she'd accepted his explanation of the birds without question.

Ah, to trust a woman again, to discard that other shield wrapped so tightly around his heart. Could he?

He only had to give himself permission, he realized, whispering a belated, but very honest, response.

"I love you too, Althena."

Chapter 21

Stephen fought with his conscience unarmed, struggling to reconcile right and wrong. It was impossible, he realized, since both decisions were right and wrong. He lied to Henry, straight faced, aware of Keir's eyes upon him. The story of the stone was merely a legend, he explained, with no basis in fact. The priest in the abbey had spoken only in riddles. There was no indication that such a stone existed.

Argante was a rogue, a mercenary leading a group of undisciplined men on a futile quest. They would find nothing, for there was nothing to be found.

Henry listened, thankfully showing little interest. His mind was otherwise occupied, strangely enough, by one of Stephen's distant cousins who was busy rallying the English barons to a rebellious cause. The 6th Earl of Leicester, Simon de Montfort, was giving the English king plenty to think about.

So, after telling Henry of his findings, Stephen was paid for his services and quickly dismissed.

~o~

Creake Abbey, Norfolk, England.

"Francis, do you know me?"

Francis frowned. An unfinished prayer died on his lips and his fingers paused on the polished wooden beads of his paternoster. He squinted through eyes misted with age, trying to make sense of the dark shape before him. The voice was familiar, and that of a man.

"Were you here yesterday?" Francis asked, searching his failing mind. "I think I do remember you from yesterday."

Another voice spoke, also that of a man. "Is he addled

as well as blind?"

Francis tensed with annoyance. *Who is this stranger with the insolent tongue?* "I may not see well," he said. "But I'm not deaf."

Soft laughter emerged from the shadows. "Please forgive my young companion, old friend. He tends to speak before he thinks. He means no offence. 'Tis I, Lord Keir. Do you remember me?"

"Lord Keir?" Francis's heart clenched. Of course he remembered. "Why are you here? Is it Alexander? Has he been hurt?"

"Nay. Rest easy. Alexander is in good health."

"Good." Francis nodded, wondering why tears burned behind his eyes. "Aye, very good. 'Tis many weeks since I've spoken to him, but I expect he's occupied. Does the babe yet thrive? They said she wouldn't live the summer."

He waited, frustrated by the silence. Had he imagined the voices? Sometimes he heard whispers in the night, ghosts from the past who refused to let him be. But these visitors weren't ghosts. So why did they not answer him?

A soft sigh echoed off the cell walls. "I fear we're wasting our time. I could enter his mind. I could see –"

"Nay, Stephen, you'll do no such thing."

"Does the wee lass live?" Francis interrupted, annoyed by their lack of response. "Does she?"

"Aye, she does." Cool breath brushed against Francis's face. "Tell me, Francis. Do you trust me?"

Francis blinked, puzzled at Keir's question. "Of course, my lord. I've always trusted you." He grinned and scratched his chin. "'Tis that Irish whelp who merits caution. Is he here too?"

"Nay." Keir chuckled. "Listen to me, old friend. In a moment, you'll feel my hand resting on your head. The sensation will be strange, painful even, and for that I'm truly sorry. But you must not resist me. Do you understand?"

"Aye. The other one hurt me too." Francis scowled at the blurred memory. "I forget his name. He wanted to know who held the stone, but I only told him a riddle. He was here yesterday, I think. Or maybe it was last week. "

"Argante," the unknown voice whispered.

"Aye." Francis nodded, his neck prickling. "That's him. The Devil's spawn. He stole my best horse. Do you know him?" His eyes closed at Keir's gentle touch. "What are you doing, my lord?"

"You've been too long away from our influence, Francis. I'm going to remedy that. Don't be afraid."

Francis thought the sun had burst through the walls. Instead of the grey mist, he found himself blinded by intense light. At the same time, fingers of ice lanced through his skull, freezing his skin, numbing his mind. He gasped, his fist tightening on his prayer beads.

"God help me. Keir, please..."

"Don't fight it, old friend."

Stimulated by Keir's touch, the disparity of time began to right itself in Francis's jumbled mind. The light picked up his scattered memories and gathered them together, shuffling them like a pack of cards. Days, weeks, months and years all took their proper place, each one clear and fresh, unfettered by age, grief or denial.

God's blood. So much anger and pain. So many regrets.

Behind closed lids, Francis watched his life unfurl like a long lost scroll, line by line, describing places and events that had remained hidden for years. Secrets, revelations, and miracles.

Aye, miracles.

He opened his eyes. The mist lingered, his physical world still clouded, but he was no longer without direction. Everything had circled around, just as he'd predicted. The truth could no longer be ignored or denied. After so many lost and wasted years, it was time for Francis Mathanach to step forward into the past.

"Sweet Christ. 'Tis not I who am blind." His voice shook with emotion. "'Tis my son."

He dropped his head into his hands and wept.

"'Tell us, Guardian." Keir's whisper brushed against his ear. "Tell us everything."

~o~

Seventeen years had passed since a cold winter's night in the depths of February, when Creake Abbey's great oak doors rattled beneath the frantic pounding of Francis's fist. A man's face appeared in the peephole, his eyes suspicious and not without fear. Francis asked him for help.

The doors were pulled open by two black-robed monks, torches clenched in their hands, the flames spitting and hissing at the frosty air. With solemn eyes, they scrutinized Francis and the silent young woman shivering at his side.

Her name was Lady Alicia Mathanach. She was Francis's daughter-in-law.

Alexander's wife.

Francis didn't know where else to take her. He didn't know what else to do.

Alicia's face, deathly pale against the night, had the look of a trapped animal. Hair the colour of dark honey swung freely about her shoulders and tumbled to her hips in a magnificent cloak. Her emerald eyes shimmered with tears that reflected the torchlight.

The obvious swell of her belly declared her delicate condition.

As planned, Francis told the monks a concocted tale

that Alicia was his daughter, her unborn child conceived by a knight who had since left to serve in the Holy Land. Her transgression, if discovered, he explained, would only bring shame to bear on the family. He needed to place her in the abbey, out of sight, until the child was delivered and adopted out, or kept by the church. After the birth, the girl would be allowed to return home.

"Wait here," one of the monks commanded. He turned and entered a nearby building, no doubt to fetch the abbot. Francis had heard the man was of good heart, benevolent and merciful. He hoped so, for his own mercy and benevolence was stretched to the limit.

In truth, Francis didn't know for sure whose child kicked beneath Alicia's robe. Her telling of its conception defied belief. As far as Francis knew, only God could perform such a miracle as she had described.

Alicia had sent him a message a few days earlier. Urgent, it said. Please come at once. Alarmed by the tone of her missive he wasted no time, and met her that afternoon in her chambers. The sight of her shocked Francis, for beneath the soft folds of her gown, he saw the telling outline of her condition. She was not alone. Alex's childhood friend, Edward Fitzhugh, stood white-faced and silent at her side as Alicia admitted she was with child.

Stunned with anger, Francis pulled his sword, assuming Edward to be the father. Alicia placed herself between them, swearing before God that Edward was not responsible. She told him six full months had passed since her last flow, but she never suspected she carried a child. Why would she? She had never betrayed Alexander. In fact, she claimed the child was his.

By all the saints, Francis thought her possessed by some evil madness. How in God's good name had she conceived a child with her husband when he was three thousand miles away, and had been for nigh on a year?

"When he came to me I thought it to be but a dream," she sobbed. "But a babe kicks beneath my ribs. A dream cannot do that."

Her story stunned him. It was beyond belief. Utterly preposterous. He accused her of lying, of betraying Alexander. He hurled insults at her, calling her a heretic and a whore as she sobbed into her hands. But Alicia's tale was so incredible, her fear so real, that Francis found himself pitying her, even entertaining the remote possibility she spoke the truth, absurd as it was. He knew Alicia, knew how much she loved his son. He didn't want to believe her capable of such wicked deceit.

His growing hesitation to discount Alicia's story also came from the fact she'd sought him out as soon as she realized the impossible truth of her condition. She was terrified and in a state of shock.

Why, Francis asked himself, would a deceitful adulteress be so quick to seek out her father-in-law, to admit she carried a child, especially with her lover at her side?

While he stood, still numb with doubt, she pleaded with him to help her, and something in her eyes and her voice touched the very depths of his soul.

Finally, with not a little trepidation, he relented and told her he would take care of things. Indeed, they would leave that very night.

He knew no one else would believe the tale. Alicia's claims would be deemed outrageous, the sorry babblings of a loose woman whose guilt had driven her mad. She would stand accused of breaking the seventh commandment while her poor husband fought to protect pilgrims travelling to and from the Holy Land. Francis forbade her to speak of her story to anyone else, for her own safety and that of her child.

Edward Fitzhugh was ordered to disappear, never to

show his face in Alexander's home again. At the time, Francis had no idea that his instructions would be disobeyed with such tragic consequences.

For the remainder of her term, Alicia stayed at the abbey hospital, sequestered in a private cell. Francis knew she hated it. He also knew she feared Alex's return. Would her beloved husband believe her story? Francis wondered the same thing and secretly shared her fear.

The worry took its toll on Alicia. Although her belly swelled with child, her limbs grew thin, her face gaunt. Her beautiful eyes lost their lustre, shadowed by uncertainty for her child's future and her own. Francis feared for her health and visited her daily, soothing her, insisting Alex would understand and believe her. In convincing her, he almost managed to convince himself.

A few months after entering the abbey, on a bright spring morning when the world outside was renewing itself, Alicia gave birth to a daughter. As she held the newborn child in her arms, she swore again before God that the babe belonged to her and Alexander.

She named her Emma.

Francis could hardly bear the sound of Alicia's heartbroken sobs as they took Emma from her. He reassured her, insisting it was all pretence, a temporary separation. He made a generous donation to the abbey, and told them to care for the child until he could find her a suitable home. Until, he told himself, Alex returned and Alicia revealed the truth about the child.

But she never got the chance.

Alex refused to speak of what happened the morning he arrived home unexpectedly. Francis only knew that two people had died, and his son's life was all but destroyed.

Still, he tried to redeem Alicia's name. He told Alex what she'd said, explained how the child was conceived.

But the telling of it sounded outlandish, even to Francis's ears. Alex sneered, called Francis a fool, and cursed him for hiding Alicia and allowing Edward to live, thus condoning their actions. Alicia's ridiculous claims were merely the sorry lies of betrayal. She'd been delusional, wracked with guilt. The child was Edward's bastard and Alex wanted nothing to do with her.

Francis visited Emma every day, his heart increasingly heavy with sorrow. She was a sickly, mewling child, and not thriving. He was told she would be with God before summer's end.

Hope flared in his heart a few days later when Alex showed up at the abbey. But his son regarded him coldly, saying he was there out of curiosity, nothing more. Emma had cried most of that morning, but to Francis's amazement, her crying stopped the moment Alex leaned over her crib. She smiled at him, reaching out with her scrawny little arms. Alex ignored Emma's obvious plea to be held, hardened his expression, turned and walked away, followed by the child's frantic screams.

Francis hated his son at that moment. He hated himself even more.

But only two days later, Alex returned. Without speaking to anyone, he went to the crib and lifted Emma from it. The child gave a squeal of joy and touched a tiny hand to Alex's face.

Something passed between his son and that frail little girl; a connection of spirit so strong it sparkled like sunlight on a lake. Perhaps it was divine, certainly it was magic, but most of all, it was truth. Francis felt the warm spill of tears down his cheeks. Any lingering suspicion he might have had about Emma's parentage evaporated.

Christ be praised, Alicia had not lied.

"Surely you can feel it, lad?" he'd demanded of his son. "Surely you can see it? 'Tis obvious whose child she is."

But Alex, the stubborn fool, refused to see, refused to accept what lay before his eyes. He would never believe such an impossible truth, such heresy. Aye, it was obvious whose child she was. Emma was Edward's bastard, but she could not be held responsible for the sins of her mother. He told Francis of the promise made to Alicia before she died. Foolish, perhaps, but as a man of his word, he'd decided to honour that vow and raise Emma as his own.

"One day, you'll be forced to see the truth, my son," said Francis. "The past does not stay in the past. It circles around to greet us as we step into the future. One becomes the other. Thus has it always been."

Alex looked at him with cold eyes and spoke the words that ripped through Francis's soul. "There is only one truth. The two people I loved most in the world betrayed me. My wife died in my arms. You both died in my heart. May God forgive you, Father."

He took Emma from the abbey that day, rode north, and disappeared into the forests of Cumbria. A few weeks later, unable to reconcile the parting words of his son, Francis renounced his vows to the Circle and entered the abbey.

He had not heard from Alexander in sixteen years.

~o~

Keir and Stephen left Creake Abbey at dawn, heading north, back to Thurston. Other than the soft clip of horses' hooves on the packed dirt road, nothing disturbed the tranquillity of the morning. Frost had descended during the night, covering the earth with ragged silver threads that glistened beneath the first rays of a feeble autumn sun. Even the birds had lapsed into silence, seeking shelter in the protection of the forest. The only sign of warmth came from the cloudy breath of horse and man.

Keir appeared calm, apparently accepting the incredible revelations of Alex's father with little difficulty. Stephen, on the other hand, could barely sit the saddle for the churning in his stomach. He glanced sideways, attempting to read his companion's face. He didn't dare try to read Keir's mind.

"A wise decision, young knight." Keir looked at him with knowing eyes "Your self-discipline is improving."

"I'm struggling, my lord."

Keir shrugged. "As a Guardian, you often will. It's tempting to use —"

"That's not what I meant." Stephen let out a deep breath. "I'm struggling with the ramblings of an old man whose mind has been twisted by time and grief."

"Ah. You speak of Francis." Keir raised an eyebrow. "You don't believe his story?"

"I'm finding it difficult to accept." Stephen shook his head. "His claims - Alicia's claims - are beyond impossible. Do you believe them?"

"I believe Francis told the truth as he sees it."

"Which means what? That he refuses to see the lies told by an unfaithful wife? That Emma is the result of some magical union? That Alicia died for naught?"

"Francis's tale warrants, and will receive, further investigation." Keir's eyes narrowed. "Yours is a powerful mind, Stephen. Do not close it to realms of the impossible. We have guarded the stone for sixteen centuries, yet still do not know all it can do."

"But transporting a man halfway across the earth in one night to lie with his wife?" Stephen rubbed the back of his neck, trying to visualize the images that Francis had described. "'Tis incredible. Besides, I do think Alex would remember such an experience."

"Whatever the case, truth has a way of emerging from even the darkest depths," said Keir. "Also, Alexander does possess some God-given abilities of his own, outside of what he has learned from us."

"Aye, that he does." Stephen gave a wry smile. "He has a special affinity for crows in particular."

"He connects with many living things, including humans, on a level beyond our comprehension. His mother was descended from a line of Highland women who were...gifted in certain ways."

"You mean witches?"

Keir scowled. "That is narrow-minded superstition. I mean gifted in certain ways. They shared a great knowledge of medicinal plants and herbs, some had the ability to glimpse into the future, and others could apparently connect with departed souls."

"Aye, like I said. Witches." Stephen waved away Keir's disapproving glance. "I jest with you, my lord. What happened to her?"

"She died of a wasting disease when Alex was but twelve. Francis brought him back to England and settled in Norfolk."

"Francis was a Guardian at that time?"

"Aye. But we all knew Alex would be the next one. Even at that young age, he showed great promise. He trained all through his adolescence, into manhood, and took the vows just before he left for the Holy Land."

Stephen pondered Keir's words. A thought surfaced in his mind, prompted by something Francis had said.

"How long did Alex intend to serve there?"

Keir frowned. "The Holy Land? I believe he said he'd be gone for two years. Why?"

"I'm wondering why he came home early. Do you know?"

"I have no idea. Perhaps he missed his wife."

"Or perhaps something motivated him to return earlier than planned."

"What are you getting at, Stephen?"

"I'm not sure yet." Stephen chewed on his lip, trying to reach another relevant thought that lay just out of his reach. "'Tis like a great puzzle."

"Has Emma shown any abilities? Any special talents?" Keir asked.

Stephen smiled, his heart quickening at the thought of her. "Several. She can walk through the forest as silent as a ghost. She can sing like an angel. I'm living proof of her talent for bringing wounded knights back from the brink of death. And she can catch fish with her bare feet."

Keir laughed. "All commendable. But is there anything she has done or said which might help solve this mystery?"

Emma's words flashed through Stephen's mind. His breath caught in his throat.

I knew he was my father.

"Dear God."

"I take it you've remembered something?"

"Aye. Something that happened to Emma as a child, something she never told Alex. She told me of it the day you arrived at Thurston, which is likely why I forgot about it until now." Stephen added an edge of sarcasm to his voice. "If you recall, my lord, that was also the day you threatened to kill me."

Keir grinned. "You must have misunderstood my meaning. You're still alive and I never make idle threats. What did Emma tell you?"

Stephen shook his head. "I promised her I'd say naught of it to anyone, but it does relate to Francis's story. All at once I find myself doubting my doubt."

"Hah! See what happens when you open your mind? Perhaps you can ask her about it upon our return. Do you think she might be willing to share the information with Alex? Or Caleb, I should say."

"She might." Stephen sighed, his thoughts clouding with doubt once again. "'Tis still difficult for me to believe a man can be transported halfway across the world and back in the space of one night."

"Perhaps he was not physically transported," Keir suggested. "Perhaps it was his essence, his soul. All that a man truly is beyond the body."

"'Tis more plausible. But I still don't understand why it would happen. Why would his...his essence do that? Was it prompted? And if so, would he not remember it? And how could he get his wife with child if he left his physical body behind?"

"All good questions, lad. Keep on asking them." Keir smiled. "Leave that door between your ears open, and see what happens. You might just find the answers you seek."

"Well, we've a week in the saddle to think about it." Stephen grimaced. "Too bad the stone couldn't pick us up and transport us back to Thurston in the blink of an eye."

Chapter 22

Emma rolled onto her back and blinked into soft candlelight. The bed linens were cold, the bed large and lonely. She ached for Stephen's touch, longed to hear his voice, to share her thoughts with him. As if missing Stephen wasn't bad enough, now Caleb had gone too.

She covered her face with her hands, pushing her fingertips into her eyes to stop the tears. Over a week had passed since the incident on the moors, since Caleb left, yet she still had difficulty dealing with what had happened.

Night after night, unanswered questions, unexplained memories, and unfounded suspicions ran ragged through her mind. And sleep, when it did come, was a restless affair, disturbed by a hoard of strange dreams and nightmares.

With a frustrated cry, Emma flung back the blankets, slipped out of bed and grabbed her cloak. She stumbled, her head spinning with familiar fatigue, nausea rolling through her belly. Her stomach clenched and she swallowed the bile that burned in her throat.

"Promise me you'll stay strong."
Damn all the lies. Damn them.

The dizziness gone, she wrapped her cloak around her and stepped into the hallway. A solitary candle burned on a small table at the top of the staircase, casting a feeble light across the walls. The flame flickered, as if disturbed by a sudden draught. Emma froze, her skin prickling, certain she'd seen a dark shape duck back into the shadows on the stairs. She held her breath and peered into the gloom, the sound of her heart thudding in her ears.

All else was quiet. The candle burned steadily, undisturbed. Emma took a deep breath, turned, and crept along to the oak door at the end of the hallway. With a quick glance of assurance behind her, she pulled the door open and started up the steep steps.

The rooftop had become her nighttime refuge. She relished the openness of it, the exhilaration of being so high up. It was a place to think, away from the confines of thick stone walls that kept people in as much as they kept people out. At first, she'd stayed away from the roof's edge. The low wall offered little defence against a stumble or, God forbid, one of her increasingly frequent dizzy spells.

But strangely, that same week, Christophe had arranged to have the wall heightened and crenellations added. The work was still ongoing, but parts of the wall already stood at chest height to Emma, which meant the heart-stopping drop to the bailey had been obscured.

She stepped out beneath a clear cold sky, drawing her cloak tightly around her. Not a whisper of wind stirred as she gazed across the countryside. A bright quarter moon hung in the eastern sky, surrounded by a halo of silver light. Below it, the meadows and forests of Yorkshire lay in peaceful shadow. Here and there, off in the distance, wisps of smoke from peat fires traced soft grey lines up to the heavens, their comforting smell wandering through the night.

She studied the stars, savouring the familiar sensation of wonder and amazement that gripped her. The universe was exciting, intriguing - a profound mystery beyond the understanding of men. Her life was also shrouded in mystery - a mystery she needed to solve.

Emma sighed. She still wasn't sure what happened that day on the moors, why Caleb - or Alex - had collapsed and tumbled to the ground. The event had terrified her, seeing him so helpless, not knowing what was wrong. Yet Finn knew, for he reacted with urgency rather than surprise. When Emma asked him why Caleb had left so suddenly, he mumbled a tale about a childhood affliction that coincided with some forgotten business in the north that required immediate attention.

He had told everyone else the same story. It amazed Emma that they accepted the Irishman's explanation so easily. She knew there was more to it than Finn's vague allegory.

Much more.

It had something to do with the geese, she decided. Alex had heard something in their cries, a message of some kind. But what? It must have been something terrible to put such an expression of fear in his eyes. Not fear for himself, mind. That, she had never seen. The fear was for someone else. But who?

The revelation about Caleb's true identity shocked her at first. What shocked her more was the sudden awareness that she'd known it all along. She realized she'd recognized Alex the moment she spoke with him in the forest on that misty morning over a month before. But she hadn't voiced it to anyone or even admitted it to herself. Why? Because logic told her such a thing was impossible, unacceptable. It was easier to deny it than accept it.

Denial. Was it not a convenient yet sometimes dangerous shield for those who chose to hide behind it?

Each time she visited the childhood memory of recognizing Alex at the abbey, denial stepped in, pushing her instincts aside. Recently though, that denial had been put to the test. Everything she thought she knew, whether dictated by logic or instinct, had changed since Alex had left Thurston.

"God help me," she whispered to the sky, for her tortured mind could find no peace.

As if in response, a different childhood memory emerged from her torment, the intensity of its arrival forcing a small cry from her lips. The stars blurred behind a haze of warm tears.

She saw herself as a small girl, clad in a thin cotton shift, padding barefoot into Alex's bedchamber in the middle of the night. She'd clambered up beside him and placed her lips to his ear.

"I cannot sleep, *Cùra*".

Alex merely grunted in response, so Emma lifted one of his eyelids with her finger. The eyeball beneath rolled around to look at her and she giggled with mischievous delight.

"*Cùra*, are you awake?"

In the gloom, she saw the hint of a smile on Alex's lips.

"Nay, *a ghràidh*. I'm sound asleep. And so should you be."

"But I cannot sleep."

"Why not?"

"My head is filled with too many thoughts."

"What thoughts? Tell me."

"'Twould be easier to count the stars in the sky."

"That many?"

"Aye, I swear it."

He sat up and studied her for a moment, then slid out of bed, opened a shutter and peered outside.

"Go and get your blanket, Emma."

"My blanket?"

"Aye. And don't dawdle."

Alex bridled Bart, but didn't saddle him. With Emma wrapped in her blanket, safe in his arms, they rode bareback, by starlight, to the shore. He stopped Bart at the water's edge, the estuary spread out before them like a large dark hand. Beyond that lay the wide expanse of the Irish Sea. Emma had never seen the sea at night before. How empty and black it was. She shivered, and Alex wrapped the blanket more tightly around her.

"Look up, *a ghràidh*, and tell me how many stars you

see."

Emma raised her eyes and scanned the expanse above. Without the hindrance of trees and mountains, the sky lay open from horizon to horizon.

"There are so many, *Cùra*. They go from one side of the sky to the other. I cannot count them all."

"Then guess."

"Maybe three hundred?"

She felt the warm breath of his laughter against her hair.

"A good guess, but there are many more than that. There are more stars up there than you could count in your lifetime."

The wonder of his words quieted her for a moment. Her eyes continued to search among the glittering milky splash that meandered across the sky.

"'Tis so big. Where is Heaven?"

"Only God knows the answer to that."

"Mama and Papa too, because that's where they are. Do you think they can see me from up there?"

Emma remembered the ripple of tension that ran through Alex's body. He didn't respond to her question, but tugged harshly on Bart's reins and set off toward home. She wondered what she had done, what she had said.

"I'm sorry, *Cùra*."

"For what?"

"For making you angry. Please forgive me."

She felt the harsh rise and fall of his chest against her as his arms pulled her close. He rested his cheek on the top of her head, his voice gentle as he spoke.

"Ach. There's naught to forgive, child. I'm not angry with you."

But words were left unsaid. And she didn't dare ask him what they were.

She would dare to ask him now, though. She knew his reaction that night had to do with the truth about her mother. And her father. As soon as she returned to Cumbria with Stephen, she would face all her fears, ask Alex all the unasked questions, and insist on truthful answers.

And, in turn, she would tell him what she knew. What she remembered.

"Emma?"

The voice made her jump.

"Finn! What are you doing here?"

He approached her, a rueful smile on his face. "Sorry, lass. I didn't mean to frighten you."

She studied the Irish knight for a moment. His gentle expression belied the fearlessness she knew he possessed. He was most striking in appearance, a tall strong silhouette against the backdrop of stars. Darkness suited him, she thought. Moonlight glinted off his long silver hair, and reflected in the depths of his eyes.

She wondered, as she had many times in the past week, about his true identity. So far, she hadn't found the courage to ask him about his connection to Alex. Something held her back, as if admitting she knew the truth about Caleb's identity would be unwise.

But perhaps the time for truth had arrived.

His eyes narrowed slightly as he looked at her. Had he just read her thoughts?

He glanced around the roof. "You'll catch cold up here, little one. 'Tis very late, too. Will you come downstairs?"

Emma frowned. Finn's vigilance for her since Caleb - Alex - left was notable, commendable even. Following instructions, no doubt.

"How did you know I was here?" she asked.

He hesitated for a moment. "You looked very pale at

supper, so I thought I'd check on you. When you weren't in your chamber, I became worried and began searching."

Emma, remembering the shadow on the stairs, didn't believe a word of it. "Ah. Well, I thank you. But as you can see, I'm quite well."

"I think not, lass. You're as white as death." He proffered his arm. "Please come inside. You need to rest."

His gentle concern brought tears to her eyes again. "Very well." She took his arm. "Thank you, Finn. 'Tis true I've not been sleeping lately."

"It pleases me that Christophe took my advice about heightening the walls." He gestured toward them. "'Tis much safer for anyone taken to wandering around up here at night."

Emma's eyes widened. Finn had obviously been watching her more closely than she realized. "The walls were your idea?"

He shrugged. "My suggestion. As I said, much safer. Do you not agree?"

"I do." She smiled at him. "Tell me, Finn. How do you do it?"

"How do I do what?"

"Manipulate people. Bend them to your will. Make them agree to your suggestions and believe your words without argument."

"Manipulate? Bend?" He feigned an expression of dismay. "My dear lady, how you wound my poor sensitive heart."

Emma took a deep breath. "Alex asked you to watch over me, didn't he?"

He tilted his head. "Who's Alex?"

"Finn, please."

A smile tugged at his lips. "Aye, he did. But even if he hadn't, I'd be watching over you anyway. At least until Stephen returns. Come away, now. Let me take you to bed." He winked, leaned in and whispered in her ear. "And don't ever tell that young knight of yours I said that. Fear not, *a chailín álainn*. He'll be home soon."

Emma took one last glance at the heavens, aware of Finn's scrutiny of her, sensing he saw more than his eyes beheld. For a brief moment, she was tempted to share her thoughts and fears with the gentle Irish knight.

'Twould be easier to count the stars in the sky.

And perhaps it would, for there were so many thoughts and unanswered questions in her mind. She decided to wait until Stephen and Keir returned to Thurston.

Keir. Aye, and there stood another mystery, another question. Who were these knights, really?

But of all the questions newly formed in her mind, one in particular insisted on pushing its way to the front.

How was Stephen involved in all of this?

~o~

Emma slept until mid-morning. By the time she wandered, bleary eyed, into the Great Hall, most people had finished the break of their nighttime fast. She glanced around, seeking a familiar face, squinting into the shadowed corners of the room. Only a few hints of daylight managed to filter through gaps in the shutters, which remained closed against the cold.

To atone for the resulting gloom, dozens of candles burned in several chandeliers, and a cheerful log fire roared in the hearth. Four men, including Christophe, occupied the chairs around it. Emma did not recognize his companions.

A thin veil of smoke hung in the air, softening the edges of whitewashed stone walls and ripened oak beams. Odours of roasting meat, crackling on spits in preparation for lunch, drifted in from the kitchen to mix with the cloying smell of melted tallow and woodsmoke. Emma cringed at the thick atmosphere. It filled her nostrils, stung her eyes, and tasted bitter on her tongue. She swallowed against a sudden wave of nausea and reached out to grasp the end of a table. A hand settled about her waist as a familiar voice murmured in her ear.

"Sit, *a chailín*. 'Tis the pale face of a ghost you have. Did you sleep at all after I left?"

"Aye, some. Thank you, Finn." She smiled gratefully at him and sank onto the nearest bench, her hand clutching her belly. "I don't know why, but lately the smell of food turns my stomach. Perhaps it was something I ate."

He sat beside her, a frown on his face. "Or perhaps you need to eat," he said, his hand summoning a serving girl who brought bread to their table.

Emma shook her head. "Nay. I couldn't right now. Truly."

He broke off a piece of bread and offered it to her.

"Try."

She sighed, took it from him, and nibbled on it.

"Where's Bee?" she asked after a few moments, glancing around the hall. "Have you seen her this morning?"

"Earlier, aye," Finn replied. "She's probably hiding in the mews."

Emma's gaze switched back to him, curious at his words. "Hiding? From whom?"

He ignored her question, instead gesturing to the bread. "Do you feel better?"

She looked at the remaining morsel in her hand, realizing her nausea had all but disappeared. "Actually, I do. But what do you mean by 'hiding'? Why would Bee need to hide? Is something wrong?"

He studied her with an unreadable expression. "Not exactly. Emma, you must listen to me. I think you need to prepare –"

"What do you mean, not exactly?" Emma heard something in his voice and a twinge of apprehension twisted inside her.

His eyes softened. "*Pie Jesú.* Fate is a cruel master." He took her hand and placed it between his palms, his chest heaving with a deep sigh. "Bee is...unsettled." He nodded toward the hearth, where Christophe sat chatting with the group of men. "See the fellow with reddish hair? The one wearing the green surcoat? He, and several of his knights, arrived this morning. His name is Lord Nathan de Maucier of Northumberland, and he's here to offer for Bee. Christophe has already agreed to the union."

Emma gasped and turned wide eyes back to Finn. "You mean marriage? But I thought...my God, Finn, I'm so sorry for you both."

Finn shook his head and squeezed Emma's hand. "On the contrary, 'tis a good match for the lass. I know Lord de Maucier will treat her well and I'm sure she'll learn to love him in time."

Emma pulled her hand from his grasp, irritated by his calm tone. "I don't understand. How can you be so accepting of it? Bee loves you; surely you know that. I thought you felt the same. She must be heartbroken."

"Easy now." Finn's voice softened. "I know Bee has strong feelings for me, as I do for her. But she also knew I could never be her husband. I've always made that very clear."

"But why? Why can't you marry her?"

He shrugged. "I'm something of a rogue knight, with no lands or wealth to offer. But 'tis not only that."

"Then what?"

"Well, for one thing, I'm too old for the wee *chailín.*

She deserves better."

"You're not that old," Emma protested, a small inner voice telling her more unspoken factors prompted Finn's excuses. "Older men often take young women to wife."

"I'm older than I look." He smiled and touched his fingers to Emma's cheek. "Bee knows how I feel. I opened my heart to her this morning. 'Tis many years since a woman compelled me to do that. Don't worry. She'll be fine. Indeed, I warrant she'll be very happy. Trust me."

"I don't know how you can be so certain." Emma glanced toward the door. "I think I should go to her."

A muscle twitched in Finn's jaw and his gaze dropped to her belly. "How long have you had this sickness, little one?"

"Only for the past few days, on and off. Mostly in the mornings. It's gone now, though. I feel much better." Emma popped the last small morsel of bread in her mouth and stood. "Thank you, my lord, for your concern, but you really don't have to worry. I'm perfectly well, and Stephen will be back any day. If you'll excuse me, I'm going to find Bee." She bent down and kissed his cheek, her heart touched by the sudden sadness in his eyes. "I believe Lord de Maucier has some very large shoes to fill."

Emma scurried across the bailey, her eyes drifting briefly to the skies, which had clouded over. The mews lay at the rear of the stables. It was a small wooden building with six stalls, each fitted with a perch for the valued birds of prey so revered by nobility. The door stood open, and Bee's gentle crooning drifted out of the darkness. Emma paused on the threshold, allowing her eyes to adjust to the dim light.

"Bee?"

"Emma." Bee's anguished sigh filled the air. She

turned and looked at Emma with eyes red and swollen from crying. Arthur, her Merlin falcon, sat on his perch, ruffling his speckled breast feathers. He lifted his head and gave a series of short sharp cries. Bee made a sound somewhere between a sob and a laugh. "I suppose you've heard. Even Arthur knows I'm upset."

"Dear God, I'm so sorry." Emma went to her and hugged her. "Finn told me."

"Did he indeed?" Bee's voice trembled. "And what, exactly, did the heartless Irish devil say?"

Emma frowned at the harsh words. "He told me Lord Nathan had offered for you, and Christophe had approved the union. But heartless? I think not. Finn is very upset. He said fate was a cruel master. I believe I've rarely seen such sadness in a man's eyes."

"Aye? Well, 'twas surely not for me. Did he happen to tell you how Lord Nathan came to be at Thurston?"

"Nay, he didn't."

"Then let me enlighten you, my dear Emma. Lord Nathan is here following Finn's recommendation to Christophe. Can you believe it?" Bee's shaky laugh was edged with emotion. "He took it upon himself to find me a husband. Finn! The man I love. The man I thought loved me too." She covered her face with her hands. "I'm such a damn fool."

"Nay, I can't believe it." Emma's mind spun with Bee's revelation. "He never said anything about that."

"Oh, I assure you, 'tis true enough. Christophe told me first and Finn admitted it later." She smiled through her tears. "But only when I tackled him about it."

Emma shook her head. "Why would he do such a thing?"

"Why indeed? Mind you, he always said he had nothing to offer me. No lands or wealth. I told him I didn't care and begged him to ask Christophe for my hand. After all, Stephen managed to sway him where you were concerned, so I thought...oh, Emma. Forgive me. I didn't mean that the way it sounded."

Bee's words cut with a sharp edge of truth and summoned up the ghost of Emma's self-doubt. She knew Stephen could have made a far nobler match for himself. Still, she managed to smile at Bee through the hurt. "I know you didn't. You're upset, and rightly so. Perhaps it won't be so bad. And I must say, from what I saw, Lord Nathan is very handsome." Knowing Bee's penchant for forthrightness, she added, "You weren't rude to him, were you?"

"Nay." Bee sighed. "I curtseyed to the man and babbled something halfway pleasant. I surprised myself, actually. I think it was because I didn't want to admit how hurt I was. And 'tis true he's not displeasing to look upon."

Emma nodded. "I'm glad you weren't...uncivil. After all, the poor man isn't to blame for your distress. Maybe you should give him a chance."

Bee grimaced. "I have no choice. You should've seen the warning look on Christophe's face when we were introduced. If I make a bollocks of this, I'll be put in chains and shipped off to some God-forsaken convent."

Emma bit back a smile at the paradox of Bee's statement. "I don't think he'd go quite that far."

"Aye, he would. He's threatened it before. Do you know what else the bastard said?"

Emma flinched at the epithet. "Christophe?"

"Nay, not Christophe. Finn." Tears spilled down Bee's cheeks again. "He said he'd never been so tempted to forfeit his existence and embrace the pleasures of a mortal life. He also told me I'll be forever in his heart and he'll always watch over me. What the hell does all that mean? Is the man's brain addled, for Christ's sake?"

Emma shivered inwardly. Finn's words roused a

familiar awareness within her, as a certain aroma might bring a long-forgotten memory to mind. But, as quickly as it surfaced, it disappeared again.

"I'm not sure what it all means," she said, glancing around the dark space. "But you can't hide out here all day. Christophe will come looking for you."

"I know." Bee sniffed and patted her hair. "And I'm sure I look a sight. I'm supposed to have lunch with my future husband." She stuck out her tongue like a rebellious child. "Will you come to my chamber and help me prepare? I suppose I should try to make an impression."

"Of course. I'd be happy to." Emma hooked her arm through Bee's and headed back across the bailey.

~o~

"I can't do this, Emma." Bee paused outside the Great Hall, fussing with her skirts. "I feel like a prize mare at an auction."

Emma smiled. "Don't be silly. You look beautiful. Lord Nathan is a lucky man."

"But what if I hate him? What if he smells? Or drinks too much? Or farts all the time?" Bee turned wide eyes to Emma. "Oh, shite. What if he has a sister who's like Anne?"

"And what if he's kind, gentle and loving?" Emma leant in and kissed her on the cheek. "Truly, no one else could have a sister like Anne. And don't use language like that in front of him. Please. Christophe would not be happy, and I've no desire to see you chained up in a convent." She gave Bee one last critical glance. "You're magnificent."

Indeed, Bee did look breathtaking in a forest-green velvet gown. Her chestnut curls, tamed and brushed until they shone, cascaded to her slender waist. She'd refused to cover her head, choosing to wear only a simple gold coronet that reflected the candlelight, giving the appearance of a halo.

"Well, here goes." Bee lifted her chin. "Wish me luck."

"You won't need it. Lord Nathan will be grovelling at your feet by the end of the first course."

Emma lingered in the doorway, blinking back tears as Bee stepped across the threshold. A hush fell across the room, followed by a low hum of approval rippling through the crowd.

Christophe's smile could not have been wider at the sight of his sister so exquisitely presented. Lord Nathan's expression was more subdued, but spoke plainly of his approval. And his desire, Emma thought. He rose to his feet as Bee approached, took her hand in his, and kissed it. Bee bowed her head and sat beside him, tension obvious in the stiffness of her spine and shoulders.

Emma studied Lord Nathan and liked what she saw. He was tall, with handsome features framed by rich chestnut hair that fell carelessly to his shoulders. Although he exuded authority and brandished a commanding presence, Emma sensed an air of gentleness about the man. She glanced around the room looking for Finn, silently thanking him for his discreet absence. His appearance would only have upset Bee.

Throughout the entire meal, Lord Nathan's intense blue eyes shone with unabashed pleasure. He chatted to Bee constantly, his hands moving in descriptive motions to accompany his words. Every nuance suggested he liked what he saw in the young woman sitting at his side. Bee's posture gradually relaxed as she responded to her betrothed's devoted attention.

Perhaps things might work out after all. Perhaps Lord Nathan would ease the pain in Bee's bruised heart. Emma glanced at the door. Perhaps Stephen would be back today.

Or tomorrow, please God.

Troubled by a twinge of sadness, she let her gaze wander around the hall, her lips curving into a smile when she saw Finn leaning against the back wall, arms folded, watching her. He returned her smile, nodded toward Bee and mouthed 'I told you so'. Emma looked down at her untouched food, shaking her head at his self-assurance. *Unbelievable.* How did he know the two would be so compatible?

A foolish question. She'd been raised by a man who demonstrated similar mystical traits, and she'd never questioned those. They were simply part of her life. And Finn, like Alex, possessed abilities beyond mortal understanding. She knew it had something to do with the stone.

Maybe the time had come to ask about Finn's true identity, how he was connected to Alex. She looked up to find his eyes still on her. He beckoned, his expression all at once serious.

She slowed on her way across the hall, her attention snared by the silhouette of a woman sitting alone by the fire. It was Anne, her eyes fixed on Bee and Nathan, her face drawn into an expression of misery. Emma stopped mid-stride and glanced at Finn, who frowned and followed her gaze to where Anne sat. He shook his head and the message, although unspoken, came through quite clearly.

Leave her be.

But something about Anne's expression tore at her. Emma glanced back at the dais. Bee and Nathan were smiling and chatting, each focused on the other. Christophe sat with his arm around Miriam in a rare display of affection. He bent his head to whisper something in her ear and she responded with a smile.

Emma turned back to Anne in time to see a tear roll down her cheek, the proof of her sadness quickly removed by a stroke of her hand. Despite everything, Emma felt a twinge of sympathy for the woman.

She conveyed her intentions to Finn with a subtle gesture of her head. He grimaced with disapproval, but Emma ignored him and stepped over to the hearth.

"It's damp in here today." She knelt down and held her hands out to the flames, surprised to realize she feared a rebuff. "But the fire is pleasing."

Anne wrinkled her nose and sniffed. "I suppose."

"Lord Nathan is a fine match for Bee, don't you agree?" Emma smiled as she searched Anne's face, trying to read what lay in those dark sad eyes. To her dismay, she saw them harden beneath a shadow of resentment.

"Nay. I pity him. He'll have his hands full with the little hellion." Anne flicked a crumb off her skirt. " I wonder if he knows she's been draping herself all over that strange Irish knight for the past few weeks. I guess he'll find out the truth of it on their wedding night. Trouble is, if she's already with child, we'll never be sure whose babe it is."

Emma gasped at Anne's words. For God's sake, could the woman never find anything nice to say? She deserved no sympathy after all. Emma clenched her fists in anger, Finn's advice still echoing in her head.

Leave her be.

Nay, she would not leave her be. She would not allow such slander to go unchallenged.

"What wicked lies are you spreading, Anne?" She glanced around to make sure no one could hear them. "I can assure you, Bee is not with child. Finn hasn't...I mean, I'm sure they haven't..."

"I hope you're right, for poor Lord Nathan's sake."

Anne smirked. "Mind you, 'twould be quite something, all these babes coming at once."

Emma frowned. "What do you mean?"

Anne gestured toward the head table. "Miriam. She hasn't announced it officially yet, but she carries Christophe's child."

Emma looked over at Christophe and Miriam again, her anger subsiding. "But that's wonderful news. They must be so pleased."

"They are. She's eager to announce it but wanted to wait until she felt the child quicken. Apparently, she felt it last night, so I've no doubt it'll be old news by tomorrow. Christophe, of course, is insisting she gives him a son and heir." Anne shook her head. "Men. They're all so damn selfish." She glanced at Emma's belly. "And what of you? What of your child? I don't suppose Stephen knows yet. It's to be hoped he arrives home safely, or you'll be left raising his bastard."

Emma sat back on her heels, stunned by Anne's words.

"His...bastard?" She stumbled over her response. "Nay, you're sorely mistaken. I'm not...I can assure you, I'm not carrying Stephen's child. He has never touched me...like that. We're waiting until we're properly wed."

Anne leaned forward, her narrowed eyes sweeping Emma's form. "Don't tell me he's spent every night in your bed and never coupled with you. I've been watching you, Emma. I notice things. You've missed meals, you sleep late and you're paler than usual."

Emma's stomach clenched. " 'Tis true I've been unwell, but not because I'm with child. 'Tis only something I ate which disagrees with me."

"Mother of God, surely you're not that naive?" Anne laughed. "You do know how a babe is conceived, do you not? Aye, you must, being raised as you were with the beasts of the forest."

"But I can't be with child." Emma turned her head and stared into the flames, her head reeling with confusion. "'Tis not possible."

"Indeed? Tell me, then, when you had your last flow. I made enquiries of the servants this morning after I witnessed your little spell of sickness and saw you nibbling on a morsel of bread. I discovered you've not once asked for cloths since you've been here. Nor have you disposed of any, which tells me you've not bled. I suspect, then, you must have already been carrying Stephen's child when you arrived at Thurston."

Emma blinked and looked at Anne, refusing to acknowledge a terrifying whisper of understanding. "When I arrived?"

"Aye." Anne sat back, a triumphant smile on her face. "Waiting until you wed? Pah! Do you think we're all fools here? You're no virgin bride. I don't know why you won't admit it. The truth will out when you give birth to a fully formed babe after only a few months of marriage."

Emma looked down at her belly and placed her hand upon it, trying to remember the last time she'd had her monthly flow.

Oh, sweet Jesus Christ.

Why had she not seen it? Why had she not realized?

She staggered to her feet, her heart frozen by a truth so abhorrent she could hardly breathe.

Dear God. No. Please, no. It can't be. There must be another explanation. There has to be.

In her peripheral vision, she noticed a tall silver-haired figure striding toward her. She recognized Finn, saw the concern on his face, the strange light in his eyes. His essence folded around her shivering body as her fragile world collapsed. His mind cradled hers, catching the shattered fragments of hopes and dreams as they exploded in her head.

But even Finn could not alter the reality of what had taken root in her womb.

Argante's seed.

The devil's spawn.

Reality spun a dark web in her mind, snaring her in a hopeless trap with no visible escape. Everything blurred into a nauseating haze and dissolved into a dull incomprehensible roar. Above it all she heard a cry of pain. 'Twas the lament of a mortally wounded creature, she thought, the final howl of a dying spirit, empty of all hope for the future. Better to finish off the poor thing than let it suffer such torment. Why were they waiting? Emma put her hands over her ears, unable to bear the noise any longer.

"Kill it," she whispered. "Please. Kill it."

As the room spun faster and the light faded to black, she felt strong arms holding her and heard a gentle voice in her ear.

"Hush, *a chailín*. Hush."

A soft murmur of voices floated in the light above her, pulling Emma from the quiet depths of oblivion. She closed her eyes and gritted her teeth against a sudden wave of nausea.

"Emma?" She recognized Bee's voice and felt a cool hand on her forehead. "Can you hear me?"

"Aye." The word grated against her parched throat. She opened her eyes, blinking in the candlelight, surprised to see the walls of her chamber. "How did I get here?"

"Finn carried you." Bee leaned over her. "Do you remember what happened?"

Emma's hand went to her belly. Had it been a dream? Nay, not a dream. A nightmare.

"Anne said something to me, I think. Did I fall?"

"You fainted. Anne tends to have that effect on

people." Bee slid her arm under Emma's shoulders. "Can you sit up? Drink a little, perhaps?"

Miriam's voice drifted in. "Or eat something? It seems you and I each share a blessing that needs to be fed."

A blessing? Emma struggled against her fear. 'Twas no blessing. 'Twas nothing but a curse. But they would never know whose child she really carried.

Never.

She took a deep breath, sat up, and even managed a smile. "I heard your news and I'm very happy for you, Lady Miriam. I'll take a sip of something, maybe. But I don't think I can eat anything."

Miriam sat on the edge of the bed, and took hold of Emma's hand. "Anne said you had no idea you were with child. Is that so?"

She nodded, swallowing against a lump of emotion. "I...I never paid any attention to...that. To myself. It never even occurred to me. There was so much happening, everything new and strange. Then Stephen left and I...."

Stephen.

God help her, how could she face him? There would be no marriage, of course. Not now. He would never accept Argante's child. The thought of him turning from her, rejecting her, pressed heavily on her heart. Dear God, she loved him so much.

Despair wrapped around her like a cold, dark cloud and tears tumbled down her face.

"Nay." Miriam squeezed her hand. "There's no need for sorrow, my dear. This child has come as a shock, no doubt, but I'm sure Stephen will be delighted. We'll bring the marriage date forward. Truly, 'tis of no consequence at all."

"I think the news is splendid. Here you are, silly girl." Bee handed Emma a goblet of ale. "I can't wait to see Stephen's face when he finds out." She clapped her hands.

"To think, God willing, I'm going to be an aunt twice over. 'Tis so exciting. I have to say, though, it scared me when you cried out like that. The way you wailed, I thought you'd burnt yourself in the fire or something. Trust Anne to bugger things up in style. I swear she pisses vinegar from both ends."

"Beatrice, please." Miriam sighed. "My sister has not had an easy life."

"'Tis no excuse to create a living hell for everyone else."

Bee and Miriam's trivial argument continued. Their words skimmed over Emma's mental turmoil, fading into the background as she tried desperately to see a way forward.

Cùra, tell me, please. What shall I do? Dear God, I'm so lost. So lost.

"Well, aside from all this excitement, I should tell you that I like Lord Nathan. We got along very well." Bee's voice intruded into Emma's thoughts.

"Good." Somehow she forced another smile, wishing they would leave her alone with her grief. "I'm very happy for you, Bee."

"Thank you. Ah, but you look so tired. We should leave you, let you get some rest."

"I would appreciate it. I must also ask a favour of you both."

Miriam and Bee exchanged glances. "What?" they asked, in unison.

"If Stephen should arrive home today, please don't tell him about the...our child. I would prefer he heard it from me first."

"Of course." Miriam patted Emma's hand. "'Tis something to be shared between the two of you in private. I'll send a maid with a platter right away. You really must try to eat something. It helps with the sickness and the babe needs nourishment too."

After they left, Emma slid from the bed and went to the window, eager for some air. She opened the shutters and peered out, startled to see an orange glow behind the clouds in the western sky. Until that moment, she hadn't realized the lateness of the hour.

The sight of day's end gave her a measure of relief. She knew Stephen likely wouldn't travel after dark unless he was really close to home. That meant she had, for at least another night, a respite from facing him, confessing to him.

Her hand wandered to the brooch he'd given her. She considered it a symbol of his love and wore it always, pinned to the shoulder of her dress. She caressed it with her fingertips, familiar with the shape of each tiny stone and each small bump on the delicately carved gold.

Tears spilled from her eyes again as she looked down at her belly. It showed no indication of what lay within, and a wild irrational stab of hope made her shiver. Perhaps they were all wrong. Perhaps she was actually ill, and not with child after all. *God, please let it be so.*

Yet she knew, from the weight of dread sitting on her shoulders, her hope was ill founded.

She heard a light tap on the door, and a man's voice. "Emma?"

Her breath caught in her throat. Stephen? God, no. Not yet. Please.

But the next moment, Finn stuck his head into the room. "Are you dressed and decent, *a chailín*? Aye, you are." He entered, a smile on his face, a platter of bread, cheese and fruit in his hand. "I stole this from the maid, who gave me strict instructions to feed you by force if necessary."

He set the platter on the table, strode over to the window and closed the shutters with a bang "And they say the Irish are daft. Here you are, looking like death, standing in a bone-chilling draught. Sit down lass, and eat something."

Emma didn't move. "You knew," she said, studying his face. "On the roof last night, and this morning in the hall. You knew about the babe, didn't you?"

He wiped one of her tears away with his thumb. "Let's just say I suspected."

Emma saw sympathy flare in his eyes. It answered another question she'd been afraid to ask, but she needed to hear him say it.

"What else do you suspect, Finn?"

"Sit down and eat something, will you?"

"Not until you tell me why you look at me with such pity. Are you not happy for Stephen and I?"

His expression softened as he glanced at her belly. "I know the truth of it, little one. The father of this babe is a sad circumstance, but what's done is done. 'Tis your well-being which concerns me."

"The father of this babe is a tragic circumstance to me," she whispered, her heart reaching out to his. "As it will be to those I love. I'm so very frightened, Finn. I don't know what to do, nor how I can even begin to survive this."

"Nay, don't be frightened." He took her in his arms, rocking her gently, stroking her hair. "I don't know why you've been given such a burden to carry, but I do know this. 'Tis not a burden you must carry alone. You have people who care for you, who love you deeply. You'll survive, I promise."

"But I'm so afraid I'll lose Stephen." She buried her face in his chest. "How can he possibly marry me now? He might be home any moment. I'm dreading it."

"Stephen won't be back until tomorrow evening."

She looked up at him. "How do you know that?"

He stroked the end of her nose with a fingertip. "I have my sources. Now, I believe I've answered your question, my lady. Will you at least try to eat a few bites?"

Under Finn's watchful eye, Emma managed to eat a decent helping, although it sat in her stomach like a weight.

"Rest now." He brought her hand to his lips. "I'll check on you later. If you need me before then, just say my name and I'll come to you. Fear not, little one."

Emma absorbed his words with wonder. "I need only say your name?"

"Aye." His eyes shone in the candlelight. *Ask me*, they said.

She took a deep breath. "Who are you really, Finn?"

He smiled at her. "You already know who I am, *a chailín*. Or rather, what I am. Stop doubting your instincts. I'm a Guardian. Just like Alex."

~o~

It stood at the other side of the clearing, watching her, lips twisted across a grotesque face. She couldn't make it out in detail. What was it? A creature of some kind, perhaps? Not human, yet there was something familiar about it. Strange, she thought, how it blends into the trees at its back. Almost as if it's made from the fabric of the forest. She had never seen such a thing.

The babe kicked hard. Emma looked down, placing her hand on the taut, stretched skin of her belly, feeling movement beneath. A moment later she felt breath on her face. Hot, foul, breath.

She lifted her head.

Emma awoke, a silent scream rasping from her open

mouth, her heart thudding hard against her ribs.

"God help me."

She gulped air and sat up, wiping cold sweat from her forehead, thankful the bedside candle had not burnt out. Still caught in the grasp of the fading nightmare, she searched the shadows, fearful something lurked within, watching her. Bile rose in her throat, bitter and hot. She slid from the bed, fell on all fours and heaved over the chamber pot.

"God help me," she said again, trembling, clutching at the bed covers to pull herself up. A gust of wind rattled the shutters and Emma jumped, her frayed nerves triggering tears of utter despair. The grotesque face she'd seen in her dream stayed in her head, drooling from a deformed mouth, one eye sealed shut with ribbons of skin, the other a window into a depraved mind.

She knew who he was, this monster, this wretched soul, this father of her child.

...the man is the devil's spawn...

Stephen's words echoed across the crumbling remains of her life. He would never accept a woman who carried the seed of Argante's evil. He would find and marry another, grow to love her instead, share her dreams, and give her children.

Her thoughts turned inward. What of herself and this bastard child? What path would they tread? Where would it lead? Back to Alex? What then?

Emma did not sense the departure of hope. It didn't subside like a burst of anger, or fade away like a happy moment. It stole away quietly, taking her future with it, to be replaced by the deadliest of all human miseries.

Hopelessness.

Promise me you'll stay strong.

"I can't," she whispered. "Forgive me, *Cùra*, but I can't do this any longer."

She stumbled across the room and pulled the door open. A cold breeze whirled past her and blew out the candle at her bedside, plunging the chamber into darkness. Barefoot and sobbing, she ran down the hall, clambered up the small staircase and staggered onto the roof.

The wind howled a welcome, snatching at her hair and skirts. She lifted her face to the heavens, where fragmented clouds hurtled across a star-splintered sky. Such beauty, such magnificence. Yet beneath it, evil had managed to survive and spread its seed. She went to the battlement wall and looked down at the dizzying drop.

Suicide was the ultimate blasphemy, a defiance of the Holy Spirit, an unpardonable sin. No one who took his or her own life would be allowed entry to Heaven. Nor would the body rest in consecrated ground, but be committed to some unmarked grave, abandoned and forgotten.

Yet hopelessness was without compunction, without guilt. It removed all reason, eradicated the need to justify an action. Nothing mattered to Emma anymore.

She grabbed the top of the wall and pulled herself upwards.

"Stop, Emma."

She hesitated, flinching at the sound of the beloved voice she'd known all her life. Her cruel imagination, she thought, for Alex was many miles away in Cumbria. He had no idea of her plight. He'd understand, though, once he knew the truth. And he would forgive her. They all would.

"*A ghràidh*, please. Turn around. Look at me."

A sob rose in her throat. "Nay," she cried. "I'll not turn around, for you can't be real. 'Tis my wicked mind playing tricks. If I look, you will not be there. And *Cùra*, I cannot bear such false hope. I cannot."

A soft sigh carried over the wailing of the wind.

"Come away from the darkness, child." Strong arms wrapped around her, solid, warm, and so sweetly familiar. "'Tis no trick of your mind. I'm here. I'm real."

The wind's lament ceased abruptly, as if a door had closed somewhere in the sky. Alex lifted Emma away from the wall and set her down. She clung to his sleeve, still disbelieving he was actually there.

She turned to look at him, tears blurring her vision. "God above," she said, stunned by what she saw. The moon lay hidden behind the clouds, yet Alex's skin had a faint glow to it, as if lit by moonlight. "You look like an angel, *Cùra*." She reached up with a hesitant hand and touched his face. "Is it really you?"

"It is." He lifted some strands of hair away from her eyes. "You need not doubt what you see."

With a small cry, she wrapped her arms around him, snuggling into his chest. She at once became a child again, seeking comfort from an adored parent, needing him to wipe away her tears and soothe her wounds. But this was no grazed knee or bumped head.

"Thank God for you," she murmured, her voice muffled by his cloak. "Thank God and all His saints. I'm so glad you're here. I've missed you so much. I need your help, please. I don't know what to do."

Alex slid a finger under her chin and lifted her head. "About what? Tell me, Emma, I need to know why..." his eyes filled with tears as he glanced at the wall behind her, "...I need to know why you would think, even for the briefest moment, that ending your life is the only solution to whatever your problem may be."

"But surely you're aware?" Emma shook her head in confusion. "Have you not spoken to Finn?"

Alex frowned. "I've spoken to no one."

"I don't understand. Then what brought you back–?"

She wondered if she should admit to knowing the truth about Caleb's identity and decided against it. "What brought you to Thurston? Why are you here?"

"I'm here because you have great need of me, *a ghràidh*. I'm here because you stood at death's door, ready to open it of your own accord. But I've yet to learn the reason for your despair."

His answer didn't make sense. How could he know of her suffering, yet not know the reason for it? It was as if he had been conjured out of thin air and dropped at her side, oblivious to all that had happened in the past two days.

"I...I despair because I'm with child," she said, her voice trembling. "Argante's child."

Alex's jaw tensed. "Argante's child," he repeated. "So this is why you wish to die? Because of a babe?"

"I have no wish to die, *Cùra*." She glanced at the battlement wall and shivered. "But the seed of a devil grows within me. 'Tis pure evil."

A bemused expression crossed his face. "Pure evil? Must we assume then, that the goodness in your soul was cast aside at the moment of conception?"

"Aye, we must," Emma cried, frustrated at his calm demeanour. "Don't you understand? 'Tis an aberration I carry. One that Stephen will never accept."

"He won't? Are you certain of that?"

"Of course I'm certain," she sobbed. "What man would raise another man's bastard as his own?"

Alex grimaced. "Do you forget so easily? 'Tis another man's child who means more to me than anything else in this world."

Emma's heart clenched as she grasped the meaning of his words. "Oh, dear God. I'm so sorry. Please forgive me. I didn't think, *Cùra*. It seems I'm unable to think clearly of late, as if my entire mind has descended into shadow."

"Shadow cannot exist without light." Alex raised his eyes to the heavens. "Look up, Emma. Tell me how many stars you see."

The familiar words struck deep into Emma's heart. She had played them in her mind only the night before, reliving that special night in her childhood. Did Alex know somehow? Was he in her head? Or was he in her blood? She lifted her face to the sky, longing to give him the answer she gave him once before.

Maybe three hundred?

But she couldn't, for on this night the conditions were very different.

"I barely see any stars at all. They are hidden by the clouds."

"But do they still shine?"

"Aye, of course they do."

"Of course they do," he repeated. "And if you wait long enough, the clouds will disappear and allow you to see the stars again. All three hundred of them." He laughed, his grey eyes twinkling with stars of their own. "I haven't forgotten our little trip to the seashore. Such memories I treasure beyond any price. I love you, Emma. I always have and I always will. You do not travel your path alone. Remember who I am, what I am, and know I'm always with you."

Something akin to a flame flickered inside her desolate soul. She looked at Alex and saw awareness on his face. What was this connection they shared? It went beyond what she had been led to believe about their relationship.

Stop doubting your instincts.

Perhaps it was time to speak of her memories, what she knew of her mother.

His wife.

"*Cùra*, there is something I–"

"'Tis hope you're feeling, child. Nurture it. Keep it alive always. If you ever doubt again, look to the heavens and remember what I said."

His words prevented her from voicing her thoughts. Although she didn't doubt Alex's presence at her side, there was something surreal about him. It occurred to her he'd only said what she needed to hear and nothing more. Just enough to save her life, just enough to give her some hope. The time was not right, she realized, to share her memories or ask him for truths.

That time had yet to come.

Filled with sudden longing, Emma turned from him and gazed across the darkened countryside toward Cumbria. A wisp of wind danced across the roof, teasing her with the aromas of frost-covered hillsides, crystal streams and damp salty air.

She closed her eyes, licked the salt from her lips and inhaled the smells of her childhood.

"I've been so blind, *Cùra*. My pride and my anger prevented me from seeing the truth. I don't belong here. I never will." She sighed. "I want to go home."

Alex leaned over and kissed Emma's cheek.

"Then why wait?" His voice sounded distant as if he'd stepped back. "Perhaps the time is nigh. There are memories to be shared and truths to be told."

She whirled around, her cry of surprise flung aside by a cold gust of air.

"*Cùra?*"

Heart racing, she spun around again, searching every shadowed corner, not believing her eyes.

The roof was empty.

The wind, freed from whatever force had held it captive, tore through the clouds to reveal the stars beyond.

A sob caught in her throat. Had any of it, then, been

real? Or had her weary mind created an illusion of Alex from some deep and desperate need? Nay, surely not. She had touched him, felt his warmth. She hugged herself, the scent of him still on her skin and in her hair. Was it some kind of magic perhaps? She'd noticed Darius resting at his side. Who knew what the stone, lying within the silver hilt, could do?

Emma pondered a moment. Dream or magic? It didn't matter, she decided, for although her future was uncertain, it was no longer without direction. But could she make the journey to Cumbria alone? She looked out across the foreboding forest, remembering the terror of her abduction. The prospect of setting out at night frightened her.

"Finn, I need you," she whispered. He would take her home, and keep her safe.

But what of Stephen? A twist of pain nudged beneath her ribs at the thought of never seeing him again.

Despite what Alex said about raising another man's child, Emma knew her circumstances were different. Stephen was not her husband. This child was not the result of a clandestine affair. She did not want to see pity in his eyes or watch his love for her wither and die in the ruins of an impossible future.

She simply didn't have the courage to face him.

If, by some miracle, he still wanted her after discovering the truth, he would know where to find her.

She could always hope. After all, she'd just acquired a fresh supply.

A shiver ran across her skin and she looked down at her bare feet, realizing how cold she was. With a last glance at the stars and a wish in her heart, she headed toward the stairwell.

~o~

Finn sat by the fire in the Great Hall, staring into the dying embers. The direction of his gaze belied his focus. His sight was turned inward, trying to figure out who had brushed against his mind a few minutes earlier. The presence had been familiar - certainly that of a Guardian - but indeterminate, not quite complete.

At first, he'd thought it was Keir. He'd even looked toward the doorway, half expecting to see his friend standing on the threshold, somehow spirited back to Thurston a day earlier than foreseen. Moments later, a gust of wind rattled the shutters and the presence vanished. All that remained was a vague impression.

"Finn, I need you."

Emma's whisper drifted into his mind and snapped it away from the enigmatic encounter. Without hesitation, he rose and went upstairs, pausing at Emma's open door, wondering whether to be amused or concerned.

She stood in the middle of the room, her head bent as she fastened her sword about her hips. Her bow and quiver lay on the bed and the handle of a dagger protruded from her belt. A sackcloth bag lay at her feet, obviously stuffed with clothing.

He leant against the doorjamb and folded his arms, deciding to be amused. "Are we under attack, little one?"

"Nay," she replied, lifting her head and smiling at him. "But I do need your help."

He stepped into the room and closed the door. "Well, it seems you're on a mission. Am I to know what it is? Does it involve drinking and fighting?"

Her smiled changed to a grin. "I hope not. I want you to take me home, Finn. To Cumbria."

Finn raised his eyebrows. "Home, is it? And when do you propose we leave?"

"Tonight. Now, actually, if you don't mind." She lifted

her chin, her eyes burning with a determined light he hadn't seen in days.

"Now?" He bit back a smile, wondering what on earth had brought this on. "You want to leave Thurston now? In the middle of the night?"

To his dismay, the light in her eyes faded behind a blur of tears. "Please, Finn. I can't face Bee or Miriam again. They're happy for me only because they think the babe is Stephen's. And I'm terrified of facing him tomorrow, telling him the truth, seeing his reaction when he finds out. Can you imagine what Anne will say when she hears this news? I just want to go home. Nay, I *need* to go home. And there's no one else I can turn to but you. I'm begging you, please."

"*Jesú.*" His heart aching, he strode over and took her in his arms. "Of course I'll take you home, *a chailín,* if it's what you really want."

She sniffed. "Do you think it wrong of me to sneak away?"

He chuckled. "Sneaking away got me out of many a sorry situation. But are you sure about this? You'll leave behind many questions, much worry and, I daresay, some heartbreak."

"Only until Stephen returns tomorrow night. Once they all learn the truth about whose child I carry, they'll be glad I've gone."

"You believe Stephen will betray you? Abandon you?"

"Don't say it like that."

Finn frowned at the pain in her eyes. "To tell you true, little one, I think you underestimate the strength of his love."

"I pray to God that I do. If so, he'll follow me home. If not, he can forget about me and get on with his life."

Finn nodded, thinking about the strange presence he'd

sensed earlier. "Did something happen tonight to bring this about?"

Colour flooded Emma's cheeks and she looked at the floor. "Well, in a way. I had...I had a dream. About going home."

"I see." Finn knew she was hiding something. "And was Alexander in this dream of yours, by any chance?"

"Aye, he was." She chewed on her lip and lifted her eyes back to his. "It was a very troubled dream. A nightmare, in fact. He...he helped me through it. And that's when I realized I wanted to go home."

There was more to her tale, he knew, but it could wait.

He glanced around her chamber. "Right, lass. Home it is, then. Stay here and count slowly to three hundred, then leave by the main stairs. I'll meet you at the portcullis."

Emma frowned. "But you can't open the portcullis without alerting the guard."

He feigned annoyance. "*A chailín álainn*, how you do wound my Irish heart. Trust me, the guards won't hear a thing." He rubbed his thumb across her chin and kissed her forehead. "There are a couple of things I must do before we leave. I'll see you in three hundred."

Finn's admiration for women went far beyond an enticing glimpse of cleavage or a sparkling pair of eyes. Women fascinated him. He loved being with them and genuinely enjoyed their company. But, since taking his vows with the Circle, none had ever tempted him to leave his chosen path.

Until he met Bee.

She stole Finn's heart without apology, and his battle to retrieve it had been one of the hardest he'd ever fought. He loved how she laughed so easily, was amused by how she angered just as quickly. When upset or sad, her tears remained unshed, hidden behind the proud lift of a noble chin. To cry would imply weakness, heaven forbid. Yet Finn knew Bee's heart to be a fragile thing well guarded, akin to a butterfly wing encased in armour.

She hated to lose at chess, looked beautiful in rich velvet or plain wool, and smelled of fresh summer flowers. She challenged God and church daily, yet her confessions were contrite and her prayers genuine.

And she could curse the ears off an executioner's dog.

He stood at her bedside watching her sleep, his immortal glow casting a soft light across the chamber. Her chest rose and fell in a peaceful rhythm. Her body, outlined beneath the covers, was perfect in form. The mortal within him stirred with desire. His eyes adored what he saw, his heart loved who she was, and his mind mourned that which he could never have.

Nathan would soon be burying his face in those silky strands of chestnut hair, kissing those sweet lips, feeling the flutter of soft eyelashes against his cheek. He would take her to his bed as his wife and taste her passion.

Finn envied him the feast.

He'd taken great care in choosing a husband for Bee and was unabashed in using his power of suggestion with Christophe. He knew Nathan de Maucier's family. More specifically, he'd known William, Nathan's great-grandfather. William had taken a pretty Irish princess to wife, and they'd shared a long and happy marriage. It pleased Finn to know that Bee's children would have some of the Irish in them. Royal blood, at that.

"You have blessed my life. I shall never forget you." He bent and kissed her cheek, his eyes softening at the hint of a smile that played on her lips. "And you must never forget what I told you. God be with you, *a stór mo chroí.*"

He would have stayed at her side longer, but he knew Emma awaited him. Besides, there was still one more person he had to see before leaving Thurston.

Even in sleep, Anne's face was drawn with tension. She'd been crying again, proof of recent tears evident on her cheeks. Finn studied her with pity and compassion.

When he first arrived at Thurston, Anne's self-destructive nature puzzled him. He wondered why the blood in her veins ran cold, why her heart beat with such a harsh cadence.

The Circle discouraged probing the minds of mortals. They viewed such action as an abuse of power and privilege. But Finn noticed the persistent sadness in Anne's dark eyes and was intrigued. Driven by curiosity, he slipped into her mind one night as she slept.

What he discovered shocked him.

He found a twelve-year- old girl on the cusp of womanhood, eager to learn and explore her unfolding world. He saw her skip across the bailey of her uncle's castle on a fresh spring evening and disappear into the stables to play with the kittens. Her harmless intent had been short lived, for Anne stumbled into the middle of a drunken dice game.

At first, the three men welcomed the pretty dark-haired child, teased her with some silly jokes, even let her throw the dice. Innocence blinded her to their true intentions and she'd sat with them willingly.

Her struggle was futile, her pitiful cries silenced by a filthy hand covering her mouth. She was found the next morning, lying in an unused stall mumbling incoherent prayers, bruised, bleeding and broken. The men were caught and sent to the scaffold, but their deaths did little to heal Anne's spirit.

Two years later, her father, embarrassed by what he perceived as his daughter's disgrace, gave her to a much older man, one who cared little about the stigma his pretty young wife carried. It proved to be a short, lonely marriage that did nothing to change Anne's perception of love between a husband and wife. She wept only tears of relief at his funeral two months later. Then she met Stephen and felt the first stirrings of attraction, a reason to hope.

Emma's arrival at Thurston changed all that.

Only Miriam and Christophe knew the truth of Anne's past. Finn did what he could for her, although her scars ran deep. He returned to her chamber every night while she slept, stepped into her dreams and pushed the demons aside. He only wished he could defeat them, banish them entirely, and allow a sad desecrated soul to renew itself.

Tonight would be the last time he'd place a gentle hand on her head, but she would remain in his thoughts, and he would continue to pray for her.

"Sleep well, my lady," he whispered. "May God grant you peace."

She sighed and snuggled deeper in the covers. Finn felt her slip past the nightmares in her mind to seek rest in a quieter place.

Ironic, he thought as he left her chamber. The one person Anne resented the most was probably the only one who would fully understand her torment.

A partial moon peeked through the scattering of clouds, casting subdued silver-blue light across the bailey. The soft hoot of an owl drifted through the air, followed by a dark shape swooping low across the cobbles.

Finn stood in the shadows holding the reins of Emma's horse, his eyes trained on the doorway to the keep. Emma should have been there by now.

"Where are you, *mo chailín?*" he murmured.

As if on cue, she stepped into the moonlight, her hair swinging loose, her bag and bow slung carelessly across her shoulders. She paused for a moment, looked right and left, and ran to him.

"Did you forget to stop counting at three hundred, lass?" He took her things and looped them over the saddle. "Your horse and I were getting worried."

"Forgive me," she said, her expression tight with anxiety. "I've been looking for something. I can't find it anywhere."

"What have you lost?"

"A brooch." She looked at him with moonlit eyes. "A little gold brooch that Stephen gave me. It means such a lot to me."

"Do you remember when you last saw it?"

"Tonight, in my chamber. It was pinned to my dress. I've looked everywhere, even on the roof."

"The roof?" He gazed up at the battlements. "You were on the roof tonight?"

She fidgeted on her feet. "Aye. After...after my nightmare, I...I couldn't sleep, so I went up there for a while. I feel terrible for losing it. It belonged to Stephen's mother."

He studied her for a moment, sensing her regret at mentioning her rooftop visit. What was she hiding? "I'm sorry, lass. We can go and look again if you like."

She hesitated and glanced back at the keep. "Nay, I think not. I'm sure someone will find it and return it to Stephen. I just want to leave here, Finn. I can't wait to get home." She gestured to her horse. "I forgot you gave your horse to Caleb. 'Twill be slow going with only one set of hooves."

He smiled at the blatant change of subject, lifted Emma onto the saddle, and swung up behind her. "I'll pick up another horse in York. And you can call Caleb by his real name, *a chailín*. I'm aware you recognized him."

I'm just not sure how.

They passed through the gates unnoticed and

unhindered. Emma twisted in the saddle to watch Thurston's walls disappear into the night.

"Thank you for helping me, Finn," she whispered.

He shrugged. "'Tis why I'm here."

She looked up at him. "Aye, I know. I have questions about that."

"I'm sure you do, little one. Ask away. We've plenty of time. 'Tis a three hour trek to York."

"You'll answer me honestly? No more secrets?"

"None. But only if you agree to the same. There are things I would also know."

She looked down, twisting her fingers through a strand of the horse's mane. "Very well," she mumbled. "I agree."

"Good." He gave her a gentle squeeze. "Off you go then. Ladies first."

She shifted her seat. "I want to know about that day on the moors. What happened to Alex? I didn't believe your tale of childhood affliction and unfinished business for a moment. Why did he fall, and why did he leave so suddenly?"

Finn looked dismayed. "You both surprise and hurt me, little one. I thought you'd ask me about Alexander's disguise. And I'm utterly devastated my lies didn't fool you."

Emma giggled. "Well, I know his disguise had something to do with the stone. But I've no idea why he left so suddenly, why he collapsed like that. Did it have something to do with those birds? It frightened me, Finn."

"No need to fear. The affliction was temporary, the result of a vision the birds shared with him about Althena. The shock of it interfered with his ability to maintain his disguise. That's why he collapsed and that's why he had to leave."

She tensed against him. "About Althena? What happened?"

"She was badly injured. Close to death."

"But...but she didn't die. Finn, please tell me she didn't die."

"Nay, she didn't die. Alex would have let me know."

Emma drew a sharp breath. "How was she injured?"

"She was attacked, Emma. Attacked and left for dead."

He waited, his heart heavy with sorrow for the anguish he knew she was about to feel.

"Attacked? Who...?" He felt her flinch as if she'd been struck. "Dear God. It was him, wasn't it? Argante?"

Dawn cast a pale glow across the eastern sky as they approached the great walls of York. Finn's mind played with several undeniable truths, many of which he'd already suspected. He'd answered Emma's questions, told her how Alex asked the Circle for help, how the shield worked, why they had gone to Thurston. She wept for a while, castigating her behaviour toward Alex, blaming herself for Argante's assault on Althena.

"You're being too hard on yourself," said Finn. "Think of what you've been through, what you're still going through. No one blames you for any of this, little one."

He never mentioned Stephen's growing connection to the stone or his awareness of the Circle. Emma never asked about it either, although Finn had the impression the question hovered on her lips more than once. *Poor wee thing.* He guessed it was just too painful for her to talk about, even though he felt certain Stephen would not abandon her.

Nor could she explain how she saw through Caleb's disguise. But she told him about the strange memories of her mother and Alex. She described the vile image of Argante in her nightmare and told him of the utter despair that had driven her to Thurston's roof.

Her words chilled his blood, but he said little. He simply leaned over, kissed her cheek, and silently thanked God for Alexander Mathanach.

Emma's strange tale of seeing Alex on the roof that night puzzled Finn above all the rest. Although she admitted to speaking with him and touching him, Emma had come to believe Alex's image was merely a dream. She needed a guardian angel and one had appeared, she explained, taking the form of a man who had guided her through life.

Even though he knew it hadn't been a dream, Finn didn't argue, nor did he admit to sensing a Guardian's presence. But it raised more questions. How had Alex managed such a feat? And why had he never mentioned this ability to the Circle? To hide such important information bespoke of deceit. Any attempt by a Guardian to deceive the Circle was a punishable offence.

A death sentence.

Unless, of course, Alex somehow wasn't aware? Nay. He discarded the foolish notion. How could a man not be aware of travelling halfway across England and back in the space of a night?

A stifled yawn caught Finn's attention.

"You need some sleep, *a chailín*. We'll stop in York for a few hours."

"Nay." Emma rubbed her eyes. "We don't need to do that."

"Aye, we do." His concern for her included his awareness of her delicate condition, although he knew better than to mention it. "I'll hear no argument. I have to find us a second horse anyway, and this one needs a rest. There's a decent inn close to the Minster. Hopefully, they'll have a room you can use."

She yawned again.

"Finn?"

"Aye."

"Do you think losing my brooch was a sign?"

"A sign of what?"

"That I'm to lose Stephen's love as well?"

"I think fatigue is twisting your thoughts." He pulled the curtain of thick hair back from her face. "Losing the brooch is a sign the catch was loose. Nothing more. Don't use superstitious reasoning to explain accidental events, lass. 'Tis an unhealthy pastime."

He saw her hand drop to her belly. She shivered and looked toward the west where the land still lay in darkness. Her sense of foreboding touched him like a cold hand.

"Argante's out there somewhere," she murmured. "I can feel him."

"Fear not, little one." He lifted her fingers to his lips. "Argante's days are numbered. He'll not hurt you again."

Chapter 23

The stars elongated, twisting into brilliant threads of heavenly silk, weaving a silver tapestry across the sky. Beyond that lay the black timeless realm of infinity, a kingdom without horizons.

Alex watched, entranced by the beauty, wondering why it all looked and felt so familiar. He reached out, searching for the one who brought him on this journey.

I'm always with you, Alicia. Always.

He waited, listening to silence as an understanding took shape in his mind. Alicia had not asked for him. Not this time. The cry for help had come from his child, more terrified of life than death, wandering aimlessly, lost and without hope.

Bless her soul, she'd called out to him, begging forgiveness as she approached the jagged edge of her life. He pulled her back just in time, showed her the light, and saw hope flare anew in her eyes. Alicia's eyes. Her child. Their child.

Dear God in Heaven, forgive me my doubt.

"Alex."

The voice startled him. His quiet heart leapt into a sudden gallop, the intensity of it squeezing the breath from his lungs.

"Alex, beloved. Please wake up. The horses are going crazy. I think there's someone in the barn."

Althena. She was calling him home, but he didn't want to return. Not yet. It would mean facing the truth.

"Alex, please. What's wrong? Alex."

The fear in her voice stirred a deep-rooted instinct within him, a need to protect and defend those in need, especially those he loved. He knew Emma was safe. He knew he had to go back.

With that simple thought, the stars stopped their wondrous frolic, folded in on themselves and disappeared.

Alex had the impression they'd been pulled into a deep dark hole. He heard a sickening snap, like the crack of a rib, and felt a burning stab of pain behind his eyes.

Something feather-light and cool caressed his brow.

"Please. Please wake up, my love."

He did so, and in a heartbeat all that he had seen in sleep was lost to him, washed away like a footprint in the tide.

"Althena?" The fear in her eyes jolted him awake. "What's wrong, lass?" He tried to sit up, wincing at the pain that lanced through every limb.

Christ, what the hell is going on?

"Oh, thank God. I couldn't wake you. I thought for a moment ..." She rested a cool hand against his cheek. "Do you feel ill? You look so tired. Mind you, I'm not surprised."

He took in a deep breath. Even that hurt. "Nay, I'm not ill. Just weary." He managed a wry smile. "I feel like I lost a fight. What do you mean, you're not surprised?"

A horse whinnied outside.

"Alex, the barn. I'm sure there's something or someone out there."

"Easy, my love. 'Tis probably nothing."

Since the attack, Althena lived in fear of what might be lurking in the forest. Alex cursed Argante daily, and persistently renewed his vow to hunt him down and kill him. But so far, Althena had flatly refused to be left alone at the cottage.

With a stifled groan, he struggled to his feet.

"But what if it's him?" Althena glanced at the shuttered window, where the first hint of daylight poked through the gaps.

"If it's him..." Alex pulled her close and kissed her forehead, "...he does not have long to live." He frowned at the sleeves covering his arms. When had he dressed? "Did

I get up in the night, lass?"

Althena blinked. "Aye. You were restless all night. Don't you remember? You rose soon after we went to bed, and you only came back a short while ago." She clutched a handful of his shirt as more whinnies sounded outside. "Do you hear that?"

"Aye, I do." He ignored the questions in his head and smiled at her. "I'll go and see what's upsetting them."

With another kiss, this one on her lips, he set her gently aside, lifted the scabbard from the table and drew his sword. "Bar the door after me, sweetheart."

She nodded, wide-eyed. "Be careful."

A fresh winter's morning awaited him outside, but little else, just as he expected. He sensed nothing, at least nothing threatening. Even the weather held a promise of kindness, albeit a chilly one. The sky above the eastern forest glowed with a soft, pale light, outlining the stark branches of ancient trees. A few clouds drifted overhead, but none were inflated with the weight of snow or rain.

Alex's warm breath took shape as it met the cold air. He twirled his blade upwards in a nonchalant gesture, resting it against his shoulder, his eyes turning to the west where a few stars still twinkled among the remnants of night. A prickle ran across his scalp at the sight of them.

Something had occurred last night, he knew for certain. But what? And why did he hurt so damn much? More importantly, why did he feel as though he'd experienced this before - the fatigue, the pain, the loss of time?

Somewhere off to the right a blackbird struck up a cheerful song, an echo of spring strangely out of place. Alex stood in silence, listening, focused on every layer of his surroundings. He scanned the edge of the forest, seeing only the twisted shadows of trees and hints of ghostly woodland mist. But nothing moved, nothing dangerous lurked in the dark.

The barn door was closed as he'd left it, but some marks on the ground caught his attention. He strode over and crouched down, running his fingertips across the indentations in the earth. *Hooves - large hooves - and only three of them shod.* The back left shoe had been cast. Someone had been here, after all, and Alex knew who it was.

A slow smile spread across his face.

A knight's relationship with his horse was iron-clad, forged from trust and a deep understanding of what one expected from the other. It was a partnership between warrior and beast made to stand the test of many challenges, time included.

Sadly, many did not survive the brutality of human conflict. Horses fell in battle just as men did. Under the protection of the stone Alex had been fortunate, as had the feisty, courageous animal who had been his companion for nigh on twenty-six years.

He knew those hoof prints as well as he knew the backs of his own hands.

"Bart, you sneaky old rogue." With a grimace of pain, he rose to his feet and glanced around. "Where are you, lad?"

Althena was on all fours in the bedroom when Alex returned. He stood in the doorway and cleared his throat. She jumped, uttered a quiet curse, and reached under the table for something.

Alex smiled at her reaction. "There's nothing to be scared of, *leannan*. Everything is secure."

"How do you do that?" she asked, without turning around.

"Do what?"

"Enter through a door that is barred on the inside."

Alex chuckled. "'Tis one of my many talents. And

right now, seeing you like that, I've an urge to show you another. Come out to the barn with me, Althena."

She sat back on her heels and twisted to look at him, a grin brightening her face. "The barn? Alexander Mathanach. What has gotten into you?"

"Me? You're the one crawling around on the floor with your sweet backside in the air. What on earth are you doing?"

"Picking up the contents of this box." It sat on the floor next to her. "I leaned over the table to watch you through the gap in the shutters and knocked it onto the floor. Nothing's broken though."

"Good. Then come out to the barn. There's something I need to show you."

She laughed. "Alright. I think I've got everything. Oh! Almost missed this." She bent over, reached under the bed and held out a small gold object. "A wedding band?"

He took the ring from her and placed it in his palm. So delicate, he thought, so precious. A tiny circle of Welsh gold.

"Alicia's wedding band," he murmured.

"You didn't...that is, she wasn't buried with it?" Althena's face showed surprise, then regret. "Forgive me. I didn't mean—"

"Nothing to forgive, lass. 'Tis a fair question. The answer is I didn't know where the ring was when she died. Turned out it was tucked into Emma's swaddling clothes against her chest."

More proof of your denied infidelity, Alicia? Guilt has a sharp edge, does it not? I can understand why you removed my token of love while you gave yourself to Edward. But why the hell would you place it next to his child's heart?

"Alex." Althena's fingers scooped up the ring and dropped it in the box. "You want to show me something?"

Love shone in her eyes, pure and uncomplicated. He tied his fraying trust back into a tight knot.

"Aye, I do. Follow me."

Althena wept as he knew she would. Hell's teeth, his own eyes were hot with unshed tears. Bart peered at them over his stall door, his noble features marked with the consequences of Argante's attack. A ragged line of dried blood ran down the side of his face, from his left ear to the edge of his mouth. His nose was one massive scab, parts of it oozing pus.

"I'm glad it's cold," said Alex, "or the flies would be troublesome for him."

"I can't believe it," Althena sobbed. "Thank God he's alive. I wonder where he's been all this time? I'll make a poultice for those wounds, the poor old man."

Alex reached out to stroke the stallion's neck. The horse rolled his eyes and jerked his head upwards, his message clear: Don't touch.

Alex sighed. "I'm not sure he'll let you near him. He wouldn't even let me lead him into the barn. I just opened the door and in he went. Even in battle, I've never seen him this nervous. I fear his scars go beyond what we see."

Emma, Althena and now Bart. All poisoned by that evil bastard.

"I'm so glad he came home." Althena slipped her fingers through Alex's. "Now we just have to wait for Emma and Stephen."

A twinge of apprehension twisted in Alex's gut and his mind once again toyed with an obscure memory. Yet nothing bad could have happened, or Finn would have contacted him. Then why the sense of foreboding? Did he fear telling Emma the truth? Nay, It was time she knew about her mother. Was it guilt, perhaps?

Aye, Alicia. Guilt does have a sharp edge. I know, for I feel it all the time, ripping into my own conscience.

None of this would have happened but for me. None of it.

As he had done so many times before, Alex silently cursed the night he'd let Argante live.

~o~

Like a displaced gargoyle, Argante stood on the summit of Black Combe, savouring the chill in the air, curling a distorted lip in disapproval of the sunrise. He abhorred the sun. It hurt him, lashing his tender skin with unbearable heat. He'd found comfort in the onset of winter and the cool Cumbrian rain was always a blessing. But nowadays he still preferred the night.

His chaotic mind had a vague awareness of the world spread out at his feet; a patchwork of subdued winter colours ending at the misty grey expanse of the Irish Sea. Behind him lay the fells of Cumbria, the ancient range of slate crags as dangerous as they were magnificent.

But his impaired vision was focused on a thin column of smoke rising up through the distant trees. It marked the location of the house. Alex's house.

"You Scottish fuck." He tried to shout, but his voice stumbled over heat-damaged vocal chords and finished in a fit of coughing. "You...you and your black-haired whore. I didn't hit her hard enough. You need to teach her some fucking manners, my lord. She was very rude, screaming like that for no reason."

He ran his fingers across his face, wiping ribbons of saliva from his chin. His beard would not grow on his burned skin. As a consequence, small patches of facial hair thrust out here and there along his jawline. He pulled on one and twirled it. "I must surmise I don't look as handsome as I used to. 'Tis your fault, Emma. All yours. Have no fear, I'm all yours. You set me on fire. My cock. My heart. My face."

Argante choked on his laughter, twisting his lips into a slobbering snarl. He took an unconscious step backwards, cringing at the smell of peat smoke drifting on the slight breeze. "You'll burn in hell with me, you son of a Scottish slut."

He gathered a wad of spittle behind his front teeth, aimed his mouth at the sky and launched a thick black-flecked mass into the air. "Fuck you, Mathanach." His face twisted into a deformed grin. "Although I'd rather fuck your wife's bastard."

His one good eye blinked several times, and the grin fell away, pulled downward by a harsh sullen droop.

"Oh, Christ. My sweet little Emma. Where are you? I've waited so long."

Everything else blurred as his mind took Emma's image and made it real. She lay on the ground in front of him, her head tilted back, thighs parted. "Ah, there you are, my love." With a gurgling moan, he stroked his bulging erection. "I knew you'd come back to me. You want me, don't you little girl? She lied to me, Iain. She's really a virgin. Why don't you watch me fuck her? You might learn something."

He fell to his knees and sank into her depths, groaning and thrusting until he shuddered in a frenzied climax.

"God's balls, you're cold. Nay, don't fret. I like cold." He raised his head and studied the girl's nipples, licking the spittle from his lips. A drop escaped, stretched into a glassy thread and pooled onto a curl of soft brown hair. Brown hair? Puzzled, Argante lifted it from a blood-smeared breast and let it slip between his fingers. He grunted and looked into a pair of dark, unseeing eyes. A stranger's eyes.

"Who the fuck are you?" He sniffed. "Have we met before? Were we properly introduced, my lady?"

A sliver of sun sliced across the horizon. It lit the girl's face with a golden glow, obscuring the grey pallor of her skin and the blueness of her lips. Argante trailed a smooth nail-free fingertip across the bite marks on her breast. He hummed a lullaby from childhood and fastened his hands around her neck, his fingers matching the existing bruises exactly.

"Christ, you're good. You had me going there for a minute. Or should I say coming?" He coughed through his laughter, spraying dark sputum across the girl's chest. "I thought you were Emma. You deceived me. I should kill you for deceiving me." The sun disappeared into the clouds, and the girl's skin faded back to its deathly hue. "But it looks like someone already did. Probably Iain."

Argante pushed himself to his knees and looked down at the old stone keep sitting at the foot of the mountain, the place he returned to every morning. A memory stirred and a strange twinge of regret wriggled its way into his gut.

"Iain. Iain. He always took care of me."

Chapter 24

Thurston's grey walls appeared as a black silhouette against the crisp evening twilight. The de Montfort banner hung limp in the chilled air while several torches flickered and danced in iron sconces beneath the gatehouse arch.

Stephen heaved a sigh of relief at the welcome sight. "Thank God. 'Tis good to be home. I'm of a mind to dismount and kiss the earth."

Keir nodded. "Aye. I confess I shall not be sorry to abandon the saddle."

More than a week had passed since leaving Creake Abbey. The journey had been uneventful and, Stephen thought, exceedingly long. The fascination he'd felt upon hearing Francis's tale had waned as the days and miles dragged behind them. It stirred anew within him now, as did his excitement at the thought of seeing Emma again.

"No offence, my lord Keir." He grinned at his companion. "But I'm eager to look upon a different face. A beautiful female face, with emerald eyes."

Keir frowned. "I'm sure you are, lad."

Stephen's grin faded at the sombre tone. Keir had been preoccupied all day, as if burdened with worrisome thoughts. Stephen had made several attempts to lift the mood, using light conversation, trying to pry the lid off his friend's closed mind. But he'd met with only guarded, quiet responses.

It no longer mattered. They were home at last.

A command from the battlements cut through the shadows and the portcullis began its slow ascent. At first, everything appeared normal. Stephen felt nothing but relief and anticipation as he entered Thurston's bailey. But he wondered why none of the guards shouted their usual salute, and why the groom mumbled an awkward greeting and avoided eye contact. A cloak of apprehension settled on him like a gentle rain.

"What's going on?" he murmured, glancing at Keir as they strode across the cobbled yard. "Is it just me? Or does everyone seem ill at ease?"

Keir had no time to respond. The main door to the keep opened and Christophe stepped onto the threshold, his hand resting on the hilt of his sword, two men-at-arms at his back. Stephen hesitated, confused by the serious expression on his brother's face.

"I'm arrived home safely, my lord." He approached, lifted his brother's right hand and kissed the gold ring on the third finger, the metal cold against his lips. "But I sense trouble. Is something wrong?"

"Come with me, Stephen." Christophe's voice held no hint of welcome. "We're gathered in my chambers."

"We?" Stephen's heart clenched. "What's happened?"

"You, sir,..." Christophe turned to Keir, "...will accompany the guard and wait in the hall until I send for you. I shall not offend by asking for your sword, but do not attempt to leave Thurston. My men have orders to stop you, using whatever force necessary."

Stephen gasped. "For God's sake, Christophe, what the hell is going on? Why would–?"

Keir placed his hand on Stephen's arm. "No doubt Lord de Montfort has a good reason for his actions, my friend. There'll be no resistance from me."

Stephen cast him a curious glance, for he heard the connotation in Keir's words. He knew something. Why had he not shared it?

The fire in Christophe's chamber burned bright in the hearth. At any other time, it would have been a most agreeable sight, begging warm seats, cups of good wine, and shared laughter.

But tonight it did little to take the ominous chill from the air. Miriam sat staring into the flames, Bee kneeling at her feet. Both women turned as Stephen entered. Bee gave a small cry, jumped up, and burst into tears.

Christophe closed the door. "Sit down, Stephen."

"Nay, I believe I'll stand." His gut twisted at the sight of Bee's tears and he resisted the urge to enter Christophe's mind. "God's teeth, will someone tell me what's going on? Where's Emma?"

Christophe stepped over to a small table, poured a goblet of wine and handed it to Stephen.

"Take it."

"Nay," he said, pushing it away. "Answer my question. Where is Emma?"

"That's what we'd like to know. Emma has left Thurston. She disappeared overnight."

"Disappeared?" Ignoring the rapid thud of his heart, he shook his head, trying to understand. "What do you mean, disappeared? How could she disappear?"

"It seems she left with the Irish knight, for he has vanished as well." Christophe glanced at Bee. "I'm also of the opinion she went willingly. All her things are gone - at least, everything she brought with her to Thurston. Her horse is gone too. We don't know how they left without being seen."

Bee wiped the tears from her cheek with a trembling hand. "I can hardly believe it, Stephen. I trusted her, yet it looks like she was betraying us the entire time. And as for him, the lying son of a–"

"Wait, please. Just wait a moment. You're telling me she left with Finn?" Stephen's heart steadied a little. Whatever Emma's reasons for leaving, Finn would not let any harm come to her. "But where's Al...where's Caleb?"

"Caleb left over a week ago," Christophe replied. "I was told he had urgent business up north, but I now find myself doubting the truth of that, which is why I wish to question your travelling companion. Something tells me these knights are not who they say they are."

"But why would Emma leave before my return?" Perplexed, he ran his hand through his hair, fighting the agony of disappointment. What would prompt Emma to leave Thurston with Finn? And why had Alex left? "I don't understand. There has to be a reason–"

"You haven't heard it all yet, brother." Christophe paused and took a deep breath. "Emma is...that is, we just found out she's with child."

Stephen heard the rush of blood in his ears and felt his legs weaken. He reached out and grasped Christophe's arm.

"With...child? Sweet Jesus Christ. Are you sure?"

"Certain." Miriam's voice carried over Bee's quiet sobs. "She didn't realize it herself until yesterday morning, but she has all the signs. I must say she didn't seem too happy at the news."

"Dear God above, have You no mercy?" Stephen collapsed into a chair and pushed his fingers against the sudden throb in his temples. All at once he understood Emma's need to flee. He also knew exactly where to find her.

Ah, my poor little faerie. You should have trusted me, sweetheart. You should have waited for me. I would have taken you home.

"Is it your child, Stephen?" Bee hiccuped through her tears. "It can't be Finn's. He's only been at Thurston for a month. Unless they knew each other before. Did they? Have they betrayed both of us?"

Stephen raised his head, ready to attack Bee's comment. But he caught the desolation in her voice, saw the raw pain on Christophe's face and the sorrow in Miriam's eyes. They were his family and they loved him. He understood their shock and disbelief.

No more lies.

He stood and took a deep breath. "Nay, the child isn't mine, nor is it Finn's."

Christophe uttered a curse, Miriam's hand flew to her mouth and Bee gave a small cry. "Then whose?" she wept. "Whose child is it?"

"Do you even know the answer to that, Stephen?" Christophe growled.

Stephen's eyes narrowed. "Aye, I do know the answer, and you'll cease with your judgemental slurs. All of you." He gritted his teeth against the pain of his words. "Two weeks before we came to Thurston, Emma was abducted by a man who is nothing more than a servant to the Devil. We - that is, her guardian and I - found her in time to save her life. But she was not unharmed. She had been defiled, her innocence taken in a brutal attack. This child she carries is the sad result. She has betrayed no one, and neither has Finn. I've no doubt she took him into her confidence and he's escorting her safely home. May God bless him for that. Emma left Thurston because she was frightened - frightened of your judgements and my reaction. She's the victim, not us. Indeed, she's the one betrayed by misplaced prejudice."

Stephen heard a sound behind him, a soft whimper followed by a rustle of cloth. He spun round to see Anne stepping out of the shadows, her face ghost-like and drawn.

At the sight of her, he let out a short bitter laugh. "Christ above, and here we have the most judgemental one of all. I'm certain we can expect no sympathy from you, my lady. I've no wish to hear your skewed opinions." He turned back to his family. "Make of it what you will, but know this. My plan to marry Emma has not changed. I'll be leaving for Cumbria in the morning, for I'm sure that's where she's gone. I don't expect any of you to support my decision, but I'll not be swayed from it."

Bee's face reddened and she uttered a string of curses. Miriam crossed herself and looked past Stephen to Anne, her eyes still soft with tears. Christophe rubbed a hand across his forehead. "God's blood." A muscle twitched in his jaw. "You're making a grave mistake, Stephen."

The words cut deep. Despite the bravado, Stephen had hoped for some compassion from his brother.

"Think what you will, my lord," he replied, the bitter taste of disappointment on his tongue. "As I said, I don't expect your support, but your disapproval changes nothing."

Christophe sighed. "Nay, lad. You misunderstand me. You're making a mistake in not expecting my support. You have it, and wholeheartedly. I'm impressed by your intent to stand by the little lass. Your biggest mistake was not telling me of this before now."

Stephen's heart thudded against his ribs and tears burned behind his eyes. He hadn't realized, until that moment, the true importance of his brother's approval.

"I couldn't tell you, Christophe. Emma begged me not to speak of it to anyone. She feared your judgement. She wanted so badly for you all to like her."

"Oh, Stephen." Bee went to him, stood on tiptoes and pressed a kiss to his cheek. "Please, please forgive me. I feel terrible for doubting her. I'm so sorry. Poor Emma. I had no idea. Did you catch whoever did this?"

"Nay. The bastard escaped and as far as I know is still at large." He lifted his chin and took a deep breath. "And there is something else you should all know. As far as I'm concerned, Emma is untouched. The reason I stayed in her chamber every night was because–"

"She had nightmares." Anne's voice drifted over Stephen's shoulder. He turned to look at her, surprised to see tears on her cheeks.

"Aye. She had nightmares."

Anne nodded, her face still pale and tight. Stephen frowned at the tremble in her hands, and the quiver on her lip.

"So, you found your conscience at last?" He shook his head. "'Tis a little late for that, my lady."

"Stephen, please." Miriam stepped forward, reaching for her sister. At the same time, Anne let out a sob and fled the room, but not before Stephen saw what lay within her broken mind.

He turned shocked, questioning eyes to Miriam.

~o~

Rank curiosity permeated the atmosphere of the Great Hall. It anchored people in their seats and edged their hushed voices. They all knew about the midnight flight of Lord Stephen's betrothed with the mysterious Irish knight. Strange that it coincided with Lady Beatrice's betrothal to Lord de Maucier, and rumour had it that Lady Miriam was not the only one with child.

So now everyone waited, eager for more tasty tattle since learning of the young lord's return, speculating at what his reaction might be. Keir's presence, in the company of two sullen-faced guards, also prompted suspicious scrutiny and whispers.

Keir ignored the tireless buzz of scandal and bent to pet the wolfhound lying at his feet. The dog grunted, thumped his long grey tail against the floor and lifted his muzzle in pleasure. The men-at-arms tensed at the sudden movement, hands hovering over hilts. Keir smiled to himself, amused by their eagerness to draw swords.

There had been a time in Keir's life when he intentionally provoked confrontation, a time when his blade spoke more sharply than his tongue. The desire to fight had little to do with the personal defeat of an unfortunate opponent. It came from a need to tempt and triumph over that most invincible of foes - death itself.

Disguised as sickness, death had taken his parents and his brother without mercy. Why not him? Why had he been left alive? Guilt had ravaged his soul. Flirting with death became an obsession and he threw the gauntlet down at every opportunity. He lived by his sword, each challenge pushing him closer to a time when he would surely die by it.

One day, he challenged a man who carried an unusual, silver-handled sword at his side. Keir hankered after the remarkable weapon, meaning to keep it for himself once he'd dispatched the owner. At first the man had refused to fight, brushing Keir's insults away like troublesome flies. But Keir had persisted, taunting and mocking until the man finally pulled the mighty blade. Moments later, defeated and humiliated, Keir had lain at the man's feet, awaiting the final, fatal thrust of honed steel. Instead, the man extended a hand, pulled Keir to his feet and changed his life.

Some time later, he took possession of that incredible, magical sword and in a bizarre twist, triumphed over his oldest foe. Death became something to respect, but nothing to fear.

His reflections faded as a hush descended on the hall. All eyes turned to see Stephen standing on the threshold, scanning the shadowed faces in the candlelit room. At the sight of Keir, he strode over and dismissed the two men-at-arms.

"I would speak with you, my lord," he murmured, his expression troubled. "But not here. We will use my father's...I mean, my brother's office."

Keir nodded and followed Stephen. The small room was cozy, even though the fire had all but burnt out in the hearth. Only a few glowing embers remained, sharing their feeble light with that of a solitary candle flame.

"You knew about this, didn't you?" Accusation shone bright in Stephen's eyes. He folded his arms and perched on the edge of the desk. "That's why you were quiet all day. Why did you not tell me, for Christ's sake?"

Keir offered a grim smile. "I'm curious, Stephen. What would you have done had I told you?"

Stephen gasped. "What do you think? I would have ridden hard and—"

"Killed your horse? Feigned surprise upon hearing the announcement from your brother? It served no purpose to tell you, lad. None at all. Finn and Emma had already left. Your reaction to the news had to be genuine, without any hint of precognition. The Circle has risked exposure like never before over the past few weeks. Indeed, Christophe's suspicions about us are already heightened to dangerous levels. We don't regret our involvement in this, but we must always remember where our true allegiance lies." Keir sighed. "Rest assured, Emma is safe with Finn. And for what it's worth, I'm am proud of your decision to stand by her."

Stephen looked at him, aghast. "Did you truly believe I'd abandon her?"

Keir smiled. He knew few men with a heart as honourable as the one beating in Stephen's chest, or with a mind as open to accept that which most would find unacceptable. The young knight's only real fault lay in his tendency to act first and think later - a trait familiar to Keir - and one that could easily be curbed.

"Nay, lad," he said, patting Stephen on the shoulder. "I never doubted you. Not for a moment."

Stephen nodded. "Good. That said, I shall be leaving for Cumbria at dawn."

Keir chuckled. "I didn't doubt that either. I shall be at

your side, of course."

Stephen closed his eyes for a moment. "It won't be easy for her, carrying this child. I cannot begin to understand how she must feel. "

"Emma is fortunate."

"Fortunate? Surely you jest."

Keir shrugged. "She's surrounded by people who love her, who are willing to stand by her. There are those who would not be treated thus, who instead would be blamed, cast aside and shunned. Such women must suffer terribly."

Stephen looked thoughtful for a moment. "I'm sure they must."

"But I understand not all the news is bleak." Keir tilted his head. "I overheard some talk in the hall. It seems you're to be an uncle, and you're to acquire a new brother-in-law."

Stephen gave a bitter laugh. "Aye. God does work in mysterious ways."

"Nay, there's no mystery." Keir drew his sword, placed one finger beneath the blade just below the hilt, and raised it to eye level. The weapon did not waver upon its narrow perch. "'Tis a simple question of balance, young knight. Balance in all things."

The horses were saddled and ready to go just before dawn. A soft, cold drizzle fell from the sky, typical rain of the North Country, gentle in its assault yet miserable in its effect.

Christophe and Bee had risen early and splashed across the bailey to see the two men off. Bee pulled her cloak around her and shivered. "'Twill be slow travelling in this. Perhaps you should wait a while to see if it clears."

Stephen shook his head and swung himself into the saddle. "Nay, I think not. I'm eager to leave. We'll be fine."

"You'll rust before you get to York." Christophe grinned, but the rain could not disguise the softness in his eyes. "Take care, little brother. Tell Emma...tell her she'll always be welcome at Thurston. Let us know how she fares." He turned to Keir, who already sat astride his horse. "I'm no fool, Sir Knight. I know there's some mystery surrounding you and your friends. Stephen tells me you're somehow involved in this secret mission for the king, but will say no more. I'm not sure why, but it gives me great comfort to know you ride at my brother's side."

Keir smiled, touched by Christophe's candid approach. "I never took you for a fool, my lord, and I value your faith in me. 'Tis well placed. You need not fear for your brother's safety."

Stephen shifted in the saddle, his impatience obvious. "We must go," he said. "I'll try to return for the wedding, but it will depend on—"

"Don't worry, Stephen." Bee smiled up at him, her tears mixing with rain. "Just take care of Emma. Please give her my love and tell Finn...tell him I'll never forget what he told me."

Stephen nodded and urged his horse forward. "I'll send word to let you know what's happening. May God be with you both."

The cry echoed across the courtyard just as they got to the gate.

"Wait!"

They turned to see Anne running toward them, skirts lifted, hair hanging loose, silk slippers splashing through the mud. She stopped at the side of Stephen's horse, panting, her breath clouding in the air, rain dripping from her chin.

"Please," she said, holding out a small packet wrapped in oilskin. "Please give this to Emma."

Stephen's eyes narrowed. "What is it?"

"'Tis just a letter explaining how...how sorry I am for my unkindness. Stephen, can you forgive me? I cannot forgive myself unless you forgive me first."

Stephen frowned and took the scroll from her. "'Tis Emma's forgiveness you should seek, my lady. Not mine."

Anne nodded. "Indeed, but I don't doubt Emma's forgiveness, my lord. She...she's such a kind, sweet soul, without reproach. 'Tis your absolution that, I fear, might be more difficult to obtain."

Keir smiled, wondering if Stephen recognized the gentle insult embedded in Anne's words.

"Very well." Stephen tucked the letter into his tunic. "You have my forgiveness, for what it's worth. And I'll make sure Emma gets your letter. I know it will mean a lot to her."

Anne's eyes blurred with tears. "Thank you, my lord. Thank you with all my heart. May God keep you safe."

With Anne's blessing still hanging in the air, the two knights spurred their horses through the gates and rode into the dreary gloom of a November morning.

Chapter 25

"He's healing well." Althena stepped back and wiped her hands on her apron. "'Tis good to see."

"Aye, you've worked wonders, my love." Alex reached up and ruffled Bart's forelock. The horse twitched his ears and snorted through his wounded nose. "He's not as fearful as he was."

"He was in pain, the poor old soul. Besides, his improvement is due to more than my remedies. You have a special way with God's creatures, Alexander." She bent down and picked up the wooden bowl and cloth at her feet. "I'll go and clean this up. Are you staying here?"

Alex cocked his head, a spark of mischief flaring in his mind. "Now, why would I stay out here when I can sit by a warm fire and watch you cook my dinner?"

He resisted chuckling at Althena's indignant expression. "Alexander Mathanach. I've a good mind to...to...make you cook your own dinner. And here's me thinking you were a chivalrous knight."

"I am, my lady. What are we having?"

She laughed. "Trout."

"And for dessert?" He grinned and gave her rump a playful pat. "Do you have something sweet for your chivalrous knight?"

"I swear, my lord, you're quite beyond hope. I'm sure I don't know why I love you as much as I do." She tossed back her long dark hair and headed for the door, grimacing at the sky. "It's raining again. If it carries on like this much longer, we'll be...." She froze mid-step. At the same time, Bart whinnied and shook his head.

Alex's smile faded. "Althena?" With his sword half-drawn, he rushed to her side and followed her gaze across the clearing. "What...?" His voice failed him, caught up in a sudden wave of surprise and emotion. The sword slid back into the scabbard as he stepped out into the cold

Cumbrian rain. Not that he cared about the chill at that moment, for the sight before him warmed his heart.

"She has returned at last," he murmured. "'Tis a day I've prayed for."

Althena stepped to his side and voiced his unspoken thoughts. "But why is she with Finn? Where's Stephen?"

Alex frowned. "I'm wondering the same thing."

A moment later, Finn's response brushed across his mind.

She knows who and what I am, my friend. As to the rest....

Emma reined in her horse some distance from the barn and slid from the saddle. She took a hesitant step, her face pale and drawn, her aura grey and bleak as the sky. Her obvious uncertainty confused Alex. Did she doubt his joy at seeing her?

Unable to speak, he simply held out his arms in the timeless, loving gesture of a parent summoning his child. She let out a cry and ran to him, wet hair flying, feet splashing in the mud. With a sob in her throat she threw herself into his embrace.

"Please, *Cùra*, forgive me. I didn't mean the things I said when I left. I've missed you so much."

Sweet Jesus, but she was thin. His chest tightened with grief at the feel of her tiny frame in his arms, every bone discernible to his touch, her heart rattling against his body at an alarming rate. Not quite two weeks had passed since he'd left Thurston, but in that time Emma had obviously languished. Something was wrong. Very wrong.

He lifted her chin and studied her, dismayed to see dark circles under her eyes as he stroked the wet hair back from her face. She looked tired and sad, her tears mixing with the icy rain. The stone vibrated gently at his side as he fought to contain his emotions.

"Hush, *a ghràidh*. Calm yourself. There's nothing to

forgive. 'Tis beyond a blessing that you've returned. But where's Stephen?"

Before she could answer, Finn rode up, threw his leg over the saddle and jumped to the ground.

"Greetings, Alex." He nodded at Althena. "It pleases me to see you in good health, mistress."

"My lord Finn." Alex managed a smile and shook his friend's hand. "Welcome, and thank you for bringing my child home safe. But where is Stephen and Lord Keir?"

Emma turned to Finn. "See? He doesn't know." She shivered. "I told you 'twas but a dream."

"Doesn't know what?" Confused, Alex glanced at the sky, the stone amplifying his anxiety as he scowled at the rainclouds. He pulled Emma into the shelter of the barn. "Curse this weather. What is it I don't know?"

"Alexander," Finn interrupted, "we've travelled far. The little lass is cold, wet and tired. Perhaps we should get her settled before we discuss anything further?"

Something in Finn's dark eyes struck deep into Alex's soul.

"Aye, of course. Forgive me." He took a slow breath, cupped Emma's face in his hands and kissed her forehead. "Get yourself inside where it's warm, little one. I'll be with you as soon as we've seen to the horses."

"Come with me, Emma." Althena held out her hand, her smile failing to disguise the concern in her eyes. "We'll get you dried off and warm some broth for you."

Alex watched them disappear into the house and then spun round, no longer caring to restrain his anger. The stone pulsed in time with his heartbeat. "God's blood, Finn. What happened after I left Thurston? The lass weighs less than a barn cat. What is this thing I know nothing about? This...this dream she spoke of? And where's Stephen, for Christ's sake?"

"Calm yourself, Guardian." Finn gestured to the

sword. "You're treading dangerous ground. There's indeed much to tell, but Emma must relate most of it herself. 'Tis not my place to do so. I suggest we see to these poor beasts then follow the women to the fireside. You'll learn everything then." Finn pulled the saddle off his horse and took a deep breath. "I'll say this, there's more to the wee *chailín* than meets the eye. Her instincts are remarkable. She's either unaware of her abilities or, for some reason, denying them. I suspect the latter. You know, don't you, that she recognized you at Thurston? Saw through the shield, just as Stephen did?"

"Aye." Alex swallowed against his declining anger as he looked toward the cottage door. "That I know."

Finn raised an eyebrow. "Can you explain how she was able to do that?"

"Nay, my lord." A different sensation stirred deep within him, one he could not quite define. "I cannot."

The cottage smelled of woodsmoke, vegetable broth and freshly fried trout. Rain thrummed against the thatch in a steady rhythm, enhancing the cozy feel of the kitchen. Candlelight poked into the dismal corners, and the fire cast dancing shadows across the ceiling. Emma sat staring into the flames, a blanket around her shoulders, a bowl of steaming broth in her hands. She looked up and gave a weak smile when Alex and Finn entered.

"Feeling better, *a ghràidh?*" Alex unbuckled his sword, propped it against the wall, and went to her. He crouched at her side and looked into her troubled eyes, wondering what demon ate so ravenously at her soul. "Warmer now?"

"A little." She let out a shaky breath and handed the bowl to Alex. "Take this, please, *Cùra*. I can't eat anymore."

"But you've hardly touched it." He stood and set the bowl on the table. "Please tell me what ails you."

Emma glanced at Finn, who lifted Alex's sword from the wall and nodded to her. "Go ahead, little one."

She rose and faced them, her expression tight with anguish. "I'm...I'm with child. Argante's child."

A cold hand of reality reached into Alex's chest and squeezed his heart. His world stilled for a moment, the only noticeable sound being a soft cry of dismay from Althena. Everything else faded into a blurred silence as Emma's sad confession engraved itself on his mind. Certainly, the possibility of her conceiving Argante's child had occurred to him, but he'd denied the likelihood. He voiced his reasoning in a ragged breath.

"God cannot be that cruel."

"My same thought." Finn ran his thumb over the sword's hilt. "But for whatever reason, He has seen fit to visit a harsh burden on your little lass."

"Oh, Emma. I'm so sorry, love." Althena went to her and pressed a kiss against her damp hair. "Whether it be God's will or fate's wicked hand, you don't deserve this."

Emma pushed her fingers against her temples. "'Tis a nightmare unlike any I could ever have imagined. But I do deserve it. I should have listened to you, *Cùra*. I should have stayed in the house that night. But I disobeyed, and now I'm being punished. 'Tis my fault, all of it."

"Christ." Alex pulled her into his arms. "You're wrong, sweetheart. None of this is your fault. 'Tis the fault of that bastard who might yet live because of me. Don't blame yourself. But where's Stephen? I can't believe he would abandon you at a time like this."

Emma shook her head. "I left Thurston before he returned. I couldn't bear to face him, see the rejection in his eyes. He'll not want me, now I carry the seed of a monster. 'Tis a devil's child, an evil thing."

"Evil, is it?" Alex said, his heart breaking at the despair in her voice. "Must we assume then, that the goodness in your soul was cast aside at the moment of conception?"

Emma gasped. "That's what you said when....that's what you said in my dream."

"Your dream?" Alex sensed Finn's dark stare and glanced at him. "What dream?"

"You came to me the other night in a...a vision. I was in such despair, but you comforted me, told me to look to the stars for hope. And you told me to come home."

Finn cleared his throat and sat down at the table. Alex had the distinct impression of a question left unspoken.

"May I speak with you in private, lass?" Althena linked Emma's arm and gestured toward the bedroom. "There are things I would say that are not for the ears of men."

Emma rubbed her eyes and nodded. "Aye, of course."

"Althena has a strong spirit," Finn observed, after the women left.

"Yet not immune to your manipulation it seems." Alex straddled a chair. "Now you've got rid of them, what did you want to ask me? I know you have a question."

"Aye, I do." Finn cleared his throat. "How do you feel?"

Alex gave a bitter laugh and gestured to the sword. "You're holding the answer to that in your hand. I know you're shielding me and I thank you, but for Christ's sake how do you think I feel? I suffer with my child. I feel her pain, her fear and her sadness. I only pray she's wrong about Stephen."

"No need to pray for that, my friend. Stephen and Keir will be here tomorrow." Finn chuckled. "Apparently, Keir's having difficulty keeping up with him."

"Thank God." Alex heaved a sigh. "I didn't think he would forsake her. She needs to be told."

"Nay, she does not, Alex. You know full well we do

not speak of foreseen events. Nothing in the future is known for sure. If it is to be, she'll see him soon enough. And that's not my question, by the way."

"What do you mean?"

"'How do you feel' is not my question."

Alex frowned. "Then what is?"

Finn stood and placed the sword back against the wall. "I want you to think back three nights ago. Did anything untoward happen? Anything strange?"

A vague sense of apprehension surfaced in Alex's mind. "Might I ask why?"

"Nay. I want to hear what you have to say first."

Alex straightened and took a slow breath. "I believe something did happen that night, aye. But I'm not sure what."

Finn's eyes narrowed. "Explain."

Alex gave half a shrug. " I remember undressing and going to bed the night before, yet when Althena woke me the next morning, I was fully clothed. She said I'd got up in the night, but I have no memory of it. That was the morning Bart returned."

Finn nodded. "Anything else?"

"I was in pain."

"Pain?"

"Felt liked I'd been trampled by a horse."

Finn nodded again. "Has this ever happened before?"

Aye it had, and in that moment Alex remembered when, but he had no desire to admit it. He shook his head and looked at the floor.

Finn leaned forward. "This is important, Alex. When? How many times?"

"Once before." Alex met Finn's gaze. "Many years ago, when I was serving in the Holy Land. We always slept fully clothed in readiness for battle, so being dressed was normal, but I remember waking up one morning with the same pain. Except, that time it was more severe. So bad, in fact, I couldn't leave my bed until close to noon. One of the men said I'd left the tent in the night and not returned for several hours, but I had no recollection of doing that."

"That's the only other time this loss of memory has occurred?"

"Aye." Alex couldn't resist a wry smile. "As far as I can remember."

Finn ignored the quip and looked thoughtful. "Hmm. Well, here's why I ask. Three nights ago, Emma awoke from a nightmare. She was frightened, distraught and unable to sleep. Apparently, she went up to the roof, seeking some kind of...release." He frowned. "She told me you appeared out of nowhere. You spoke to her, held her, and showed her hope where none existed. Then you simply vanished. That experience is what prompted her to return home. She thinks she had a dream, a vision of sorts. But I'm curious, Alexander. Am I stirring a memory? Can you offer any kind of explanation?"

It couldn't be. Not again.

Alex shifted in his seat, his heart racing mercilessly as his mind fought to suppress memories long since buried. "I can only surmise Emma needed a guardian angel. In her desperation, perhaps her mind created one, and it took the form of the man who has guided her through life. 'Tis not so strange when you consider it."

Finn narrowed his eyes. "I find it strange you should use her exact words, and here's my problem with that theory. Although I didn't actually see anyone, I sensed an arrival at Thurston that night. A presence. Granted, the identity was vague, indefinable in fact, but definitely a Guardian. Of that I have no doubt. At first I thought it was Keir, but of course, it wasn't." He paused, as if to place more emphasis on his words. "I happen to believe something remarkable happened three nights ago. Something beyond any sort of dream or vision. I believe that you, or a tangible likeness of you, appeared at Thurston and physically interacted with Emma."

"Nay," Alex murmured, his mind numb with denial. "'Tis not possible."

"Not possible?" Finn smiled and glanced at the sword. "They aren't words I expect to hear from a Guardian. Why are you so quick to dismiss the likelihood of such an event? Will you not even consider it?"

One day, you'll be forced to see the truth, my son.

"Nay," he repeated, his gaze drifting to Emma's door. "It can't be possible."

Sleep eluded Alex that night. Restlessness consumed him to the point of exasperation. Taking care not to wake Althena, he left the warmth of their bed, pulled on his clothes, and padded out to the kitchen. Finn had kept the fire stoked, and the flames cast a soft glow across the darkness.

"You needn't worry about Emma, Alex." Finn did not lift his gaze from the hearth. "She hasn't stirred all night. The poor wee lass was beyond fatigue yesterday."

Alex poured himself a cup of spiced wine and settled himself at the table, aware of a slight throb in his temples. "I worry about her anyway. She's facing such a trial."

"She's not facing it alone."

"But for me, she would not be facing it at all."

Finn sighed. " Lose the guilt, my friend. What could you have done differently? Boarded up the window? Chained the lass to her bed? She doesn't blame you, so stop blaming yourself."

"She's my child and this is my house. I'm responsible for her safety."

Finn turned to face him, his eyes reflecting the firelight. "But Emma's not really yours, is she? Indeed, I find your commitment remarkable. Few men would even consider caring for another man's child with such devotion. Especially one resulting from an affair between your wife and your friend while you sweated in the Palestinian desert."

Alex tensed with suppressed anger. "You well know I made a vow to her mother. Besides, 'tis not that unusual. According to you, Stephen is about to make a similar commitment."

Finn shrugged. "Hardly the same situation. Emma's child was forced upon her, whereas Alicia gave herself to Edward willingly, did she not?"

"Christ, Finn." Alex clenched his fists on the table. Behind him, the sword trembled against the wall. "If you're trying to anger me, you're succeeding. But I can't think what you hope to gain from it."

"An admission."

"An admission of what?"

"That your connection to–" Finn looked past Alex and flinched. "Emma. Ach, I'm sorry. Did we wake you?"

Alex turned to see Emma yawning in the doorway to her room. "Nay. 'Twas a dream that woke me." She wandered over to stand behind Alex, put her hands on his shoulders and kissed the top of his head. "It took me a moment to realize where I was, but I'm so glad to be home. *Cùra*, why are you not sleeping?"

Alex heard a hint of tears buried in her voice. "I'm restless tonight," he answered. "Was it a bad dream, little one?"

"Nay, not exactly bad. Sad, though." She flopped into the chair next to him. "I dreamed of Stephen."

"Don't despair. I think you're underestimating him." Alex ignored Finn's subtle shake of the head. "You'll see. He'll likely show up here any day." He reached over and stroked her hair, shocked anew at her thin form. "How are you feeling? Could you eat something?"

"I feel a little better, but I'm not hungry." Emma parted with another sigh, looked down, and drew an imaginary line on the table top with a fingertip. "Has it stopped raining, *Cùra*?"

Overcome with sudden emotion, Alex closed his eyes for a moment. He knew exactly why she'd asked the question. "Aye, little one, I believe it has."

"Then maybe the stars are out." She raised her head and blinked at him, chewing on her bottom lip. "In that case, I wonder if we could...I really need to talk to you. Please. I wonder if you would consider...."

Her pleading eyes followed him as he stood, took his sword and buckled it around his hips. "Dress warmly, *a ghràidh*." He gestured toward her door. "And bring a blanket."

Emma gave a squeal of delight, leapt to her feet, and ran into her bedroom.

"Alex, if you need privacy to talk, I can leave," said Finn. "You don't need to go."

"My thanks, but this wee excursion is meaningful to the lass." *And me.* "I would appreciate you staying here in case Althena wakes up. Ever since Argante's visit, she's fearful of being left alone."

"Aye, and there's him to consider. What if he's still lurking out there?"

"If there's any justice, his corpse is feeding the crows. But if he still lives, he'll not be out and about at night. He hates the dark." Alex patted the sword. "He'd never get anywhere near her, Finn."

"Emma's going to ask about her mother. You know that, don't you?"

Alex pulled his cloak around his shoulders and fastened it. "I do."

"Are you ready for that? Ready to tell her the truth?"

Emma emerged from her room, wrapped in her cloak, a blanket tucked under her arm. Her eyes shone in the firelight and a faint brush of colour played on her cheeks. She was breathless, obviously excited.

"I'm ready, *Cùra*," she said. "Can we go now?"

"Aye." Alex cast a telling glance at Finn. "I'm ready too."

Chapter 26

Cumbria rested in peace beneath moonlit skies. Off in the distance, Alex heard the frantic rush of tumbling water as the river made its way to the shore. The only other sound was that of the horse's hooves making a soft rhythmic thud against the damp forest floor.

Alex knew, with sad certainty, this was the last time he would take such a trip with his child. He gave himself a mental shake, admonishing the parental sentiment, for Emma was no longer a child, but a young woman carrying a child herself. Tomorrow - nay, today - Stephen would return and claim her, make her his again.

As it should be.

Yet of all the things Alex had shared with her, all the experiences and lessons she had learned from him, this was by far the most important and the hardest. He had to right a wrong, but in doing so he would hurt her. He prayed the wounds would heal, that she could forgive him.

"Emma."

She shook her head. "Not here, *Cùra*. Not yet. When we reach the shore, please. I want to look up and see Heaven when you tell me about Mama."

He suppressed a sigh. *Alicia, help me. Dear God, help me.*

They followed the river in silence until at last the sea stretched out before them, paved with a silver path of moonlight. The tide had retreated, baring the estuary sands to the night sky. Alex pull the horse to a halt and Emma tensed against him. He leaned down and whispered in her ear.

"What I'm about to tell you is still very painful for me, and it will hurt you too. For that, I'm eternally sorry."

He felt her chest rise and fall.

"It's alright." Emma wrapped her left hand around the

hilt of the sword, covering the stone in a protective gesture that stunned Alex, for he felt the immediate calming influence of her touch. "Please don't be afraid, *Cùra*. I believe in you and I love you. I didn't realize how much until I went to Thurston. Nothing will ever change that." She snuggled closer to him and lifted her eyes to the stars. "I'm ready now."

~o~

The Holy Land, Anno Domini 1247.

Alex listened to the story in growing disbelief, watching a sneer of satisfaction creep across Argante's face as he finished his sordid tale. It was all nonsense, servants gossip, vicious rumour without foundation. Alicia would never betray him. Never. She was his, and only his.

Indeed, Alex's desire for his wife would not be quelled until he held her again, tasted her sweet lips, made love to her. He missed her beyond reason. Many nights he awoke beneath the rippling canvas of his tent, grasping at fading remnants of dreams, reaching into the shadows for a woman who slept almost three thousand miles away.

In battle Alex was quietly invincible, aided by the protection of the stone, supported by the will of the Circle. A Saracen's sword held no threat for him. His true fight always began after dark, when solitude and yearning clashed head on. Then the stone switched sides and became his adversary, enhancing his emotions, heightening his need, stretching his frustrations as taut as a bowstring.

So it was perhaps fortunate for Argante that the afternoon sun hovered above the sweeping fronds of date palms and cast sparkles on the water as he spewed his malicious words. Alex's anger rippled like the hot desert sand, but it had yet to erupt. Even so, the accusations against Alicia tore at him, and his sword hummed as he pulled it from its scabbard.

"Wash the filth from your mouth, you lying bastard." Sunlight glanced off honed steel, matching the flashes of anger that heated his blood and set the stone pulsing. He pressed the point of his blade into the hollow at the base of Argante's throat. "Or continue with this false tirade and allow me to finish your miserable life. I doubt anyone will mourn your passing."

Argante's lips curled into a scornful grin. He wrapped his fingers around Alex's blade, squeezing until blood leached through them and dripped to the ground.

"Wash the sand from your ears, Mathanach. I speak no falsehoods. While you toil to defend these pathetic pilgrims, Fitzhugh is strutting around your English estate with his cock erect and ready for your wife. Believe me, you stupid fool. Alicia isn't lamenting your absence. She's too busy rutting with Edward Fitzhugh, and in your own chambers, no less."

"Lies." The tip of the sword dug deeper and Alex watched as a line of blood snaked down Argante's chest. "All lies."

"Why would your steward lie? The man was drowning his sorrows that night in the inn and his tongue was well loosened with wine. He wanted Fitzhugh's head on a pike and spat each time he mentioned Alicia's name." Argante leaned forward, challenging the blade at his throat, his eyes narrowing as he flinched in pain. "Such hatred does not stem from trivial hearsay. Nor did he tell me everything, I fear. I sensed there was yet more to this miserable deception."

Alex tilted his head and studied Argante. "Why are you here really? Surely you did not travel this far merely to spout your fountain of filth. What brings you, a Godless man, to the Holy Land?"

"Godless? Nay, not I. Now I've taken up the cause, all my sins will be forgiven." Argante smirked. "I'm on the trail of the stone, old friend, and have been led to believe it now resides in this barren wilderness. 'Tis strange, I must say, how the clues I discover always seem to lead back to you."

Alex smiled. "Ah. So not only are you spreading myths, you're still seeking them."

"The stone's existence is no myth." Argante stepped back from the blade and eyed his bloodied hand. "And neither is your wife's infidelity. Believe what you will. 'Tis of no consequence to me. I gain nothing from her philandering, nor the telling of it. Are you going to put that blade through my heart or not? I tire of this hellish heat and would seek a cool spot to rest awhile."

Despite his desire to thread his blade through Argante's ribs, Alex let him live, cursing the man's scornful laughter as he walked away. It was a decision he came to regret later that night when he heard screams. He left his tent to find Argante nearby, panting and adjusting his clothing, standing over the body of a young Arab girl, while the sand between her legs darkened as the blood flowed from her.

"You're too late," Argante said, fastening his sword about his hips. "If you'd been here five minutes ago, I'd have let you have a turn. Nice and tight, she was."

A sharp throb of pain lanced through Alex's head. Sickened to his core, he surrendered to the stone's demands and freed his rage, but put the sword aside. A blade was too swift, too merciful. Instead, he set about Argante with his fists, intent on breaking every bone and beating every spark of life from the man's body. Hatred consumed him. For the first time since taking guardianship of the stone, Alex lost control. And he didn't care.

It was a short-lived lapse. Several of his comrades dragged him off Argante's bruised body. Argante, barely conscious, pushed himself onto an elbow and twisted his bloody mouth into a grin.

"Alicia's a whore, Mathanach," he mumbled through swollen lips. "Go home and beat the life out of her. That's what I'd do in your place."

Argante disappeared that night and Alex never learned where he'd gone. But he left behind a seed of doubt that took root. To Alex's dismay it thrived, fed by a growing sense of suspicion and dread. After weeks of torture, haunted by unbearable imaginings, he reneged on his pledge to God and left the Holy Land a full year sooner than planned.

Three months later, he stood at the bow of a ship tasting the salty spray of the English Channel. Although he travelled light in the way of worldly goods, anguish weighed heavy on his heart. With the white cliffs of England resplendent on the horizon, he was but a two-day ride from home and the truth.

It was the height of summer. The days were long, the sun rising after only a few hours of darkness. It had barely begun its journey across the empty skies when Alex rode through the gates of his manor. By the time he'd dismounted, led Bart into the stable and headed for the main door, he knew the shock of his unexpected return had started to ripple through his household.

Mary, his housekeeper, met him in the doorway, her wimple askew, a rosy flush on her face and her aura dark with anxiety.

"My lord. This is a...a surprise. We did not expect you."

Alex glanced up the stairs toward his chambers.

"Don't fret, woman. 'Tis understandable, since I'm come home a full year early. My wife is still abed?"

"Aye." Mary twisted her fingers in her apron. "But please allow me to wake her, my lord. Let me tell her you've come home. The shock of seeing you unannounced might send her into a faint."

Alex chuckled, yet his guts twisted, for the servant's suggestion was an obvious ruse. Why did Alicia need to be warned of his arrival?

"My lady is not prone to fainting," he said. "I shall wake her myself. I'm right eager to see her after so long apart."

"But, my lord—"

He cast her a look then, stern and dark. Her mouth closed, her face paled, and she turned away, crossing herself. Alex saw the gesture and his heart leapt. Christ. Had Argante spoken the truth? He grasped the hilt of his sword, feeling the tingle of heavenly power through his fingers.

It did not allay his fears.

The chamber door stood before him, thick golden oak studded with black metal. He frowned and glanced behind, realizing he couldn't remember climbing the stairs. His hand reached for the latch, lifted it, and pushed. He fully expected the door to be locked. It wasn't.

It swung open with a slow grace, noiseless, revealing. The chamber faced southeast, so on this bright and beautiful morning, golden sunlight poured through the window, slanting across the floor and across the blue-canopied bed. The bed stood unmade and empty.

For a moment, Alex grasped a shred of relief, of hope. Perhaps Alicia was alone after all. Then he saw them standing by the window, drenched in sunlight, as yet unaware of his presence. Alicia's head rested against Edward's shoulder, her eyes closed. Her kirtle was rumpled and her long hair hung loose, draped about her shoulders like a cloak. Edward was fully clothed, sword strapped to his side, his arms around Alicia. He murmured something to her, stroked his hand across her cheek, and pressed his lips to her forehead.

And Alex's world shattered.

A spark of hatred lit within him as he watched them embrace. Within moments it grew, burning through his veins like venom, destroying his trust, leaching into his love for her.

Guard your heart and mind, Alexander. Beware your weaknesses, for the stone will seek them out and use them against you.

How could she?

"How could you?" His whisper was ice cold, filled with pain.

Alicia's eyes opened and her head lifted.

"Alexander?" She gasped, and pushed herself away from Edward like a culprit caught in the act.

"Aye, my lady." He drew his sword and stepped into the room, closing the door behind him with a gentle push. "Alexander, your husband."

The stone pulsed against Alex's palm, shooting ribbons of energy down his arm, into his chest, around his racing heart, intensifying his emotions. His gaze swept over his wife's body, disturbed to see her bright aura dimming beneath his scrutiny. She had lost weight, and her eyes were circled by shadows in contrast to her pale skin, but her beauty had not waned. God's blood, how he loved her, wanted her.

Ah, lass. If you'd thrust a blade into my heart it would have done me less harm, been more merciful than this vile deceit.

"'Tis really you?" Alicia took a hesitant step toward him, her hands clenched together as if in prayer. She glanced at the sword in his hand and then at Edward, shock and fear evident in her expression. "What...what are you doing here?"

"What am I doing here?" He moved closer, struggling with his growing rage. "Sweet Christ. I live here, do I not? This is my home, you are my wife, and this–" he took a deep breath and turned furious eyes to Edward, "–is my chamber. Damn you to hell, Fitzhugh, you treacherous bastard. Take up your sword."

Edward held up a hand. "Wait, Alexander. Things are not as they might appear."

"Indeed? Did my eyes, then, deceive me just now?" Alex took a step closer, his lips curled in a snarl. "Nay, I think not. Draw your weapon."

"Alex, please," Alicia pleaded. "Edward has done nothing wrong. I...I was in need of comfort after you left. I've been...unwell."

A sliver of concern pricked at Alex's anger.

"Do you still ail?"

"Nay, I was...I mean...'tis just that I...I missed you."

"You missed me?" His anger swelled again. "Ah, I see. You missed me so much that you thought to seek comfort in Edward's arms. How very touching. But I'm returned now, so let me hold you, whisper soothing words in your ear, press my lips to your skin." He spat on the floor at her feet. "In truth, I would rather kiss a viper. Take up your sword, Fitzhugh. I'll end this debauchery today. All in my household know I'm betrayed. I saw the sympathy in their eyes, sympathy for me, their liege-lord. Such shame I have never known. Christ, news of your rutting has spread even to the Holy Land. 'Tis where I learned of it. 'Tis what brought me back to these shores a full year early. 'Tis what brought me back to the whore who is my wife."

The words tasted good as they were spoken, but they

left a bitter aftertaste on his tongue. He saw Alicia drop her face to her hands, heard her harsh, painful sobs. God knows he wept with her, invisible tears from deep inside, out of sight, untouched even by the power of the stone.

Edward's quiet voice cut into Alex's tragic reverie. "Do not speak to her that way." His hand drifted to his sword hilt. "'Tis apparent you know not the full truth of it. Alicia has something to tell –"

"Nay!" Alicia cried. "Please, Edward, say no more."

Alex's veins turned to ice as the stone reflected back his sorrow and hate. The violent sensations all but pushed him to his knees.

"His silence will serve no purpose, Alicia. He's already a dead man. Draw your sword, Fitzhugh. You can either die fighting or in cold blood. I care not, nor will anyone else. No man will condemn me for taking the life of my wife's lover." He stepped forward and pressed his blade to Fitzhugh's throat. "Any last words for my wife? How about you, my lady? Any sweet words for your paramour before I dispatch him?"

"Nay!" Alicia stepped between them, grabbing at Alex's arm, trying to pull the blade away. "Please, Alexander, stop this. You're sorely mistaken in your beliefs. I haven't betrayed you. I love you. I've always loved you. Edward has done no wrong, I swear it."

He looked into her eyes, wanting only to see her love for him. They looked back at him, glorious in their beauty, their depths obscured by a mist of tears.

By all that was holy, he ached to take her in his arms, feel her body pressed against his, smell the sweetness of her hair. He wanted to believe her. More than anything, he wanted to believe her.

Christ, Alicia. What have you done?

"Then explain to me, wife, why the tale of your love affair has crossed continents. Explain why my housekeeper cowered in fear when I arrived home just now." He gritted his teeth against a surge of fury. "Most of all, explain why Edward is in our chamber at the break of dawn, holding you and kissing you. Explain it, Alicia."

"I...'tis difficult, Alexander." Her voice trembled. "I fear you would not believe me."

She blinked as her eyes left his face and looked to Edward. Alex saw their desperate exchange of glances and the intimate transfer of unspoken understanding before she returned her gaze back to him.

God's blood. It was lies. All of it. Nay, he would not be swayed.

Beware your weaknesses...

Was it weak to succumb to a justified rage, or weak to show mercy to those who betrayed him? Alex's spirit was human, his heart broken, his emotions raw. All his defences crumbled beneath the crush of grief and anger as the power of the stone overwhelmed him. He blinked back tears of fury.

"Your lies mean nothing to me, wife. Take yourself from here, for I would see you gone from my home today. You're already gone from my heart." With little care, he thrust her aside. She stumbled and fell, crying out as she collided with a small table before hitting the floor. Alex was at once sickened by his action, for he had never before raised a hand to any woman, least of all his wife.

Struck by a spark of remorse, he started to turn, meaning to help her. But he heard the scrape of metal on leather, saw Edward's sword leaving its scabbard and, in an instinctive reaction honed by years of practice, defended himself. He heard Alicia's scream, and within the flutter of a single heartbeat, Alex's entire life changed direction.

Edward didn't even have time to counter. His eyes glazed over as he tensed, an expression of disbelief drifting across his face. He looked down at Alex's blade embedded in his chest and the stain spreading out across his tunic.

"You fool," he gurgled, choking on blood. "My death will change naught. What was before will still be. Listen to Alicia's story and believe it. Do not abandon her, Alexander, for she's a true miracle. Never doubt it. Never...." His gaze shifted past Alex to where Alicia lay, his face twisting into a grimace of pain. "Tell him. Make him...believe. Oh, lass. I'm so sorry, so...."

Edward's eyes filled with tears and one of them fell like a solitary raindrop onto the steel that pinned him. At the same time, his body slumped and his last breath brushed across Alex's face. The blade dipped, and Edward's body crumpled to the floor. Behind them, Alicia let out a cry like that of a wounded animal.

Alex dropped to his knees at Edward's side, shaking and weak. Dear God, he'd just killed a man he'd known since childhood. A dear and trusted friend, or so he'd believed. Never had he felt so abandoned, nor suffered such anguish. Alicia's endless sobs continued behind him.

Where did I fail her? How could I be so easily replaced in her heart and in her bed? Did I ever matter to her at all?

Raw emotion rattled his words. "Would that this wretched stone could turn back time and tell me all that was to come."

Alicia's voice caught on a sob. "You would not have left me?"

He shook his head. "I would not have married you. I shall forever curse the day we met."

She made a desolate sound, a bleak cry that threatened to crack the hardened shell of his conscience. "Alexander, please. There are things to be said."

"I'll hear no more of your lies, woman." His nostrils

flared with the smell of blood as he leaned over and pulled the pale lids across Edward's sightless eyes. "Your lover is dead, as is my love for you."

Nay, my love lives yet. I shall love you always. Always.

"I beg you, husband, look at me." she whispered, her hands tugging at his tunic. "For Edward's sake, let me explain."

For Edward's sake?

He pushed a fingertip against the nauseating throb in his temple. "For my sake, Alicia, take your lies and get out. God knows, I cannot bear to look upon you."

"Please."

"Go." He closed his eyes. "Just...go."

"Then I'm left with but one choice." A soft sigh drifted through the air. "'Tis perhaps as well, since I'm beyond weary of it all. Forgive me, my love. Our life together will never be what I prayed for."

Alex flinched as if struck and lashed out a toneless response. "Don't waste your words. Edward can't hear you anymore."

He heard a sound behind him, like that of a soft struggle followed by a sharp gasp. He assumed she had risen, making ready to leave. Moments later there came a light touch to his knee where it met the floor, a sensation of moisture seeping through to his skin, sticky and warm. He glanced down and saw blood snaking a thin line around him.

But it was not Edward's, and it was not his.

Alex turned, and what he saw emptied his mind of all other thoughts.

Alicia sat against the foot of the bed, eyes closed, bloodied dagger lying in her lap, a hand clutched to her stomach. The front of her kirtle clung to her, the thin fabric plastered to her slender waist by a dark and ominous stain.

"Oh, dear God in Heaven." He set his sword aside and crawled to her, a sickening thought dragging itself across his tortured mind. "Alicia, why? You would rather die than be without Edward? You love him that much?"

A small frown settled on her brow as her eyes fluttered open, their depths now clear and as green as a forest pool. "I love you, Alexander. Hold me. Please."

He could not refuse her, nor could he stop the tears as he gathered her in his arms.

"Yet you choose to go to Edward."

"Not...Edward." She reached blindly for his hand, and he gave it. "'Tis for her I give my life. You might cast me aside, but not her, for none of this is her doing. In my death, I bequeath the responsibility to you."

"Her? Of whom do you speak? What responsibility? What are you telling me?"

"We have a child, Alex," she said, squeezing his hand. "A daughter, born this spring. You'll find her at Creake Abbey. Please take care of her. Give me your word. Her name is Emma."

"A child?" Alex's exhausted mind fumbled with the meaning of her words. "You have a child?"

A sob broke free from her. "She doesn't thrive. She's so weak, so sickly. 'Tis you she needs, to be raised as yours, free of shame, to be loved and protected. Swear you'll do it. Let me hear you say it. Please let me hear it."

"Christ, Alicia. Raise Fitzhugh's child? Nay, I will not. How can you ask such a thing of me?"

She stiffened in his arms, panic in her eyes. "Alexander, please. She'll die without you, I know it. I beg of you, don't abandon her. Please give me your word."

He hoped she might confess her sins, show some regret, ask his forgiveness for her betrayal as she lay dying in his arms. In return, he would then admit that he loved her, that he would always love her. In absolving Alicia, he might begin to absolve himself, perhaps find a way toward a future without her.

But her deathbed confession only announced the existence of a sickly child, born from an illicit affair and hidden away in some abbey. Instead of his absolution, she asked for his promise to raise the child as his own, to become the guardian of another man's bastard. With her final breath she bestowed upon her husband a final insult, one that left him faithless and empty. And for that, he despised her.

Yet in the midst of death, sitting in a pool of her blood, surrounded by the smouldering wreckage of his marriage, he gave Alicia what she wanted. He gave her his word.

"Very well," he said. "I'll take care of the child. Be at peace, Alicia."

"A miracle child," she whispered, and closed her eyes for the last time.

~o~

Although sixteen years had passed, the memories of that terrible morning had not faded. Every detail remained intact and dragging them out had been an exercise in self-flagellation for Alex, old scars ripped open, emotions rubbed raw.

Emma hurt too. He sensed pain in the stiffness of her body and heard it in the occasional muffled sob. She had not spoken throughout the telling, nor had her hand moved from where it rested on the sword. Alex had accepted her offer of protection, moved by her sweet gesture. The stone was no threat to her. He could fend off the worst of the reflections for them both, if need be. Still,

Emma's ability to quell the stone's power impressed him.

"Take your hand from the hilt." He brushed his lips across her hair. "The jewel is quiet now."

She sighed and tucked her hand into the blanket. It worried Alex that she had not yet spoken. He looked out across the moonlit sands and took a deep breath of cool salt air.

"Let's walk a little, *a ghràidh*. Stretch our legs before we head home." He slid from the horse's back and lifted Emma down, looping her arm through his as they set out.

She spoke at last, quietly and without accusation. "Why did you lie about her? About them?"

An easy one to answer.

"You looked up from your breakfast one morning and surprised me by asking where your mother was." Alex shook his head at the memory. "You were only four years old, so young and innocent. I could not bring myself to tell you the way of it, so I made up a story. I turned your mother into Edward's wife and Edward into a hero. 'Twas easy to nurture the lie after that, give it substance, make it real. But I knew one day the truth would surface."

He tucked the blanket around Emma's shoulders, concerned at the way she trembled against him, sensing her anguish.

"'Tis not the cold that causes me to shiver, *Cùra*."

"I know. I'm so sorry, little one."

"Mama died that I might live." Emma hiccupped with a sob. "She must have loved me very much."

Aye, and Alex understood the depth of Alicia's love, for would he not also give his life to save Emma? In responding to her, he answered his own silent question.

"Of that I have no doubt, sweetheart."

"Argante accused you falsely."

Alex sighed. "Not exactly. I readily admitted killing Edward. People merely assumed I was also responsible for your mother's death. She was not the first adulterous wife to die at the hands of an angry husband. Believe me, Emma, 'twas not a banner I carried with any pride."

"Then why did you?" Emma asked. "Why would you choose to carry a guilt that was not yours?"

"Because in taking her own life..." he paused, the image of Alicia's lifeless body still fresh in his mind, "...your mother lost the right to a consecrated burial. I could not bear the thought of her lying in some unmarked grave, so I hid the truth of her passing."

"Dear God." Emma's hand tightened on his arm. "So where does Mama rest?"

"In the grounds of Creake Abbey."

"Do you think God forgave her sins?"

"Aye, I'm sure of it. Have no fear. Your mother is among the blessed."

"I shall pray for her soul anyway. And Ed...my father? Where is he?"

"He rests at his family's holdings, near Canterbury."

The call of a shorebird echoed through the darkness, a shrill greeting followed by a similar response from another of its kind. Alex looked to the east, where a soft glow lit the sky behind the hills.

"'Twill be daylight soon," he said, lifting Emma onto the horse. "We should head back. You need to rest."

He pulled himself up behind her and turned the horse inland.

"*Cùra?*"

"Aye."

"Do you really believe Mama betrayed you?"

He'd been expecting the question, but his heart clenched upon hearing it. He gave her the answer he knew she did not wish to hear.

"Aye, I believe it. Do I not hold the proof in my arms?"

He heard her sigh, saw her face lift to the stars.

"A miracle child," she whispered.

"They both said so."

"But why a miracle? I am but a bastard, born sickly and weak."

Alex shrugged. "No doubt you were their miracle." Merciful God, how that truth hurt. Emma should have been his, born from a woman he adored, from a love he'd believed to be pure and true.

"Then why did they not leave and take me with them? Why did they hide me in the abbey, yet act so freely and without shame in your home? It doesn't make sense."

Emma's words slotted into Alex's mind like a key into a lock, but he had no desire to open it.

"Where would they have gone?" he reasoned. "Edward's family blamed Alicia for everything, including Edward's death. And you were left in the abbey because you were sick, needing special care. As to the behaviour in my home, I cannot comment, other than to say they perhaps considered themselves beyond reproach, beyond judgement."

The edge of the forest loomed ahead, darkness still trapped between the naked branches. Moonlight glinted on frost-bitten earth and cast blue-black shapes across the forest floor. As they approached the tree line, a sudden yet vague sense of foreboding arose within Alex. He squinted into the gloom, senses sharpening like steel on a whetstone.

A faint odour drifted into his nostrils, sickly sweet, like a rotting corpse. It lingered for a brief moment and then disappeared. His ears strained, listening for the slightest sound, anything alien, out of place. An owl hooted from the treetops, while in the distance the yip of a fox echoed around the valley. Both were songs of the night, familiar and non-threatening. Alex relaxed a little.

"I remember her." Emma's voice managed to snatch a small part of his attention.

"Who?" Alex's eyes continued to scan left and right, relieved to see nothing but empty shadows.

"Mama."

Surprised at her response, he turned away from his vigil. "That's not possible. You were only a few weeks old when she died."

"Aye, but I remember her."

"I think not. Perhaps you dreamed of her, created a memory in your mind."

"'Twas no dream. She was holding me, weeping over me. I saw her. She had green eyes like mine. I even sensed her fear."

He had no desire to argue. "You're exhausted, child. Try to sleep a little."

She squirmed, letting out a sigh. "You're not hearing me, *Cùra*."

"I hear you well, but you must consider what you're saying." Aware of Emma's growing agitation, Alex kept his voice gentle. The lass had been through so much. Little wonder her nerves were raw, her mind playing tricks. "You cannot possibly hold memories of your mother, as much as you might wish it. You were but a tiny babe when I took you from the abbey."

Emma nodded. "I know." She turned and buried her face in his cloak, her body shaking with silent sobs.

"Ach," Alex stroked her hair, his heart troubled by her distress. "You're beyond weary, my wee lass. You have learned much this night, and harsh truths they were too. But your mother was right. You are indeed a miracle, a special child. I knew it the first time I saw you."

Emma turned to look at him, her skin pale in the moonlight, her eyes large and soft with tears. "Then why did you leave me?"

Alex frowned. "Leave you?"

"At the abbey. The first time you came to see me, you left me there. Why, *Cùra*? I screamed for you as you walked away. You must have heard me, yet you didn't return. You had no intention of raising me, did you? So what made you come back? Was it guilt that changed your mind?"

An arrow to his heart might have landed softer. He reined in the horse with a violent tug, his head reeling with her words. "How can you know this?" His voice rasped across the tightness in his throat. "How?"

"Because I remember you, just as I remember Mama. I remember seeing your face, your eyes. I was..." she touched her fingers to his cheek, "...soothed by your presence. Why did you leave me? Why?"

Christ have mercy, who is this child I have raised? How can she know these things?

Had she been his, her veins running hot with the blood of the ancients, he might have expected such gifts, nurtured them.

Had she been his.

"*Cùra*, tell me the truth. Please."

He took a deep breath and met her gaze. What he had to say could not be delivered gently, at least, not at first.

"I cannot begin to know how you came by it, but the memory you hold is correct. I told your mother only what she wanted to hear, to give her peace, but I had no real intention of raising you. Why would I? You weren't mine. The truth is, I went to the abbey the first time out of sheer curiosity. I wanted to see Alicia's miracle, the sickly infant born from another man's seed." He paused, aware of the pain in Emma's eyes. "Aye, you were crying when I got to the crib. A tiny wee thing you were, with a pathetic wail. But you quieted when you saw me, reached up and tried to touch my face. I'll admit I was surprised by your reaction. Christ knows, I wanted to feel something for you, sympathy or guilt, yet I felt only resentment and anger."

"So you left me." Her voice shook.

"Aye, I left you, determined not to return. I heard your screams even as I got on my horse and rode like the devil. But I couldn't escape. You followed me, Emma."

Emma's eyes widened. "Followed you?"

"And captured me. Haunted me. I couldn't get your bonny wee face out of my mind." A sigh shuddered from him. "I was wallowing in sorrow and anger, bitterly tired of life. I had the stone, but the cursed thing is no blessing when the heart is heavy. I needed another reason to live, something to pull me to my feet each day and urge me forward. I needed hope. You gave that to me."

A tear rolled down Emma's cheek. "'Tis what you did for me at Thurston."

Alex nodded and glanced up at the sky. "Life draws circles around us, lass."

"But I have no memory of you returning to the abbey, to fetch me."

"I returned two days later, certain of my decision, yet doubting it too. 'Tis incredible how frightening a wee scrawny bairn can be. I had no idea how to care for you at first and I was so afraid you might die. But you thrived and grew like a weed." He tapped the end of her nose with his fingertip. "Since I did not have a wet-nurse for you, I improvised. You sucked on boiled linen cloths soaked in goat's milk and ate poached eggs mashed with butter. I brought you to Cumbria to raise you quietly. I thought we'd be safe here." He frowned, his eyes scanning the shadows surrounding them. "I was wrong."

"You couldn't know Argante would find us." Emma lifted her head and placed a kiss on his cheek. "I know it was very difficult for you, *Cùra*, but I thank you for telling me everything."

Everything? Not quite. What remained, though, was surely no truth but heresy. To tell it would serve no purpose.

"Aye, 'twas difficult, but it needed to be said, and out of tragedy came a blessing." Alex touched his hand to his chest. "You're my child in here, Emma. You'll always be in my heart."

He glanced around again and, sensing no threat, urged his horse forward.

~o~

Argante held his hand up in front of his face, squinting through his one good eye as the sound of the horse's hooves faded into the distance.

"You're losing your touch, Mathanach." He slurped, gulping spittle, frowning at the way his hand blended into the backdrop of the forest. "Emma's on my side now. She did this to me. Sshh, you stupid fuck. He'll hear you. Ears like a fucking fox. Did you see her? I told you she'd come back." He shuffled off through the woods, following the same path as Alex. "Bring her to me tonight, Iain. You know where to find me. And take a bath, will you? You smell like a corpse."

Chapter 27

The Cumbrian forest had changed with the passing of summer. Now the trees stood naked upon a carpet of dank, rotting leaves, adorned only with ribbons of sunlight that fell through the exposed branches. Brambles, their thorns bared like teeth, twisted in thick, impenetrable tangles along the edge of the path. The air was cool and damp, heavy with the smell of decay. This stark woodland was no longer a place one would expect to find forest faeries.

Stephen thought back to the day Emma had stepped into the sunlit dell and saved his life. He smiled to himself, a smile that sank beneath a wave of grief when he thought about what had occurred since. Her life had been dismantled, her innocence plundered, her world torn apart. If she had not been out hunting that day, or if he had died from his wounds, probably none of this –

"Cease your lamenting, young knight." Keir's voice interrupted Stephen's reflections. "It serves no purpose, nor will it change what has happened. You're willing and ready to stand by her. That says much about you. There are many who would not have made the same choice."

"I can do naught else." Stephen pressed a fist to his heart. "She's in here."

"Aye, I know." Keir smiled and nodded down the path. "We're almost there. Remember, Stephen. Do not speak of our visit to Creake Abbey until prompted to do so."

Before Stephen could respond, a shadow swept across the face of the sun, cutting through the dappled light, fleeting as an arrow. He squinted up through the branches, shading his eyes to see a crow circling above them. The bird cawed and disappeared over the treetops. Stephen smiled to himself. It was good to be back.

"We made good time." He looked ahead to the

clearing, excitement twisting beneath his ribs at the thought of seeing Emma.

"Little wonder, lad. You all but set the road alight with your pace." Keir leaned forward and patted his horse's lathered neck. "'Tis a miracle these poor beasts are still upright."

The path widened as it left the trees, opening out to where Alex's house stood in its peaceful glade. No castle, this, with its simple wooden walls and thatched roof. Stephen guessed the entire house would fit a dozen times into Thurston's bailey with room to spare, yet he drew a deep contented breath, overcome by a feeling of being home at last.

Emma was here and he belonged with her.

Alex stood in the doorway of the barn watching their approach, sword in hand, wearing only to a thin shirt and britches despite the cold. Finn appeared at his side a moment later, also holding a sword and similarly dressed.

"Weapons drawn in welcome, my lords?" Stephen slid from the saddle, relishing the stretch in his legs as he grasped Alex's hand. "I swear we present no threat, Alex. Or should I say Caleb? Your appearance has changed somewhat since our last meeting."

Alex laughed. "I was teaching this old man some of the finer points of swordplay. Ach, but it warms my heart to see you, Stephen. And you, my lord Keir. You had a good journey, I trust?"

"Old man?" Finn sputtered. "I can still – "

"The journey was but a blur," said Keir, ignoring Finn and throwing an amused glance at Stephen. "With a herd of weary horses left in our wake. How many changes, lad? Four in two days?"

"Aye." Stephen gestured toward the house. "How's Emma? Did you tell her I was on my way?"

Alex shook his head. "Nay, she's unaware."

"The wee *chailín* is convinced you'll want naught more to do with her," said Finn, "and refuses to believe otherwise."

Stephen frowned. "She should know I'd never abandon her."

"'Tis only because of the child she carries." Finn expression softened. "That's why she left Thurston in such a hurry." "Aye, I know." Stephen sighed. "Thank you, Finn, for bringing her safely home."

Finn shrugged and sheathed his sword. "'Twas a privilege and honour to be her guardian for a few days. She's a brave wee lass."

Alex patted Stephen's shoulder. "I thank God you're here, lad. Go to her. We'll see to the horses."

The familiar smell of the cottage wrapped around him like a warm blanket. Althena looked up from a pot on the hearth, her eyes growing soft as she crossed herself. "Stephen! Praise Mary and all the saints, you're returned." She wiped her hands on her apron and went to him, stepping into his embrace. "'Tis just the medicine Emma needs."

"Althena." Only then did he remember why Alex had left Thurston. "How are you? I heard what happened."

"I'm well healed, thank you." Her fingers flew to a spot on her head. "Alex saved my life."

"May God be praised and may Argante be rotting somewhere."

"Amen to that, although I fear he's still at large."

"If so, we'll hunt him down." Stephen gestured toward Emma's bedroom door. "She's sleeping?"

"Aye, but go to her anyway. I've no doubt you're in her dreams."

The door gave a gentle squeak as it opened to the familiar room, bathed in the dusky light of late afternoon. The small figure on the bed didn't move. Stephen tightened his jaw against a surge of emotion. Being careful not to make a noise, he unbuckled his sword, dropped his cloak across a chair, closed the door behind him and approached the bedside.

Emma slept curled up in a ball, hands clasped together beneath her chin, lips parted, her chest rising and falling in a slow rhythm.

God's blood, she looks so tiny, so frail.

The sight of her both intoxicated his soul and saddened his heart. He bent and pressed a kiss to her temple.

"I've missed you, sweetheart," he whispered, sitting down at her side, stroking her hair. "So much."

A small furrow creased her brow, although her eyes remained closed.

It took all his willpower to resist lifting her into his arms, to hold her and kiss her. "Emma."

Her frown deepened. Stephen took a long slow breath and stroked invisible fingers across her mind, sensing her grief, aware of his name echoing through her dreams as she searched for him.

He answered her call. "I'm here, my love."

Somewhere, in subconscious depths, the connection they shared renewed itself. Emma's body tensed, and her eyes flew open.

"Stephen?" Surely there had never been a whispered word so full of hope, even though disbelief showed in her face. He cursed himself inwardly for leaving her.

What anguish has she suffered since I left Thurston?

Consumed by a warm rush of love, he smiled at her. "Hello, little faerie."

"Dear God." Her fingers traced a line down his throat. "Do I dream?"

Unable to wait any longer, he lifted her against him. "Nay," he murmured, kissing her forehead. "'Tis no dream. I am returned. By all that is sacred, it feels so good to hold you."

"Then...then I haven't lost you?" She clutched at his shirt, her eyes frantic, searching his face. "You still want me?"

"'Tis I who have been lost without you, little one. And I want you more than anything in this world."

Tears filled her eyes. "But I carry Argante's child."

"I know." He lifted her chin and brushed his lips across hers. "And you also carry my heart."

He kissed her again, his mouth gentle, loving how she pressed against him, sensing her need. Her lips parted beneath his and Stephen's world fell away. He groaned as his body responded, consumed by desire. His hand ran down the length of her, and he frowned through his kiss. How thin she was, like a fragile bird.

"Can you feel how much I want you?" he murmured against her mouth, the warmth of her tears on his cheek. "As God is my witness, you are my life. Wait. Let me get comfortable." He pulled away, settled himself beside her on the bed, and gathered her back into his arms.

Her fingers wound through his. "I've prayed for this moment."

"Ah, sweetheart. When I found out you'd left Thurston, it almost killed me. You must never doubt me again, Emma. Never."

"But I was so frightened, Stephen." She trembled against him. "'Twas Anne who guessed my condition. I had not realised it myself, so consumed was I by all that had happened. I had to pretend the babe was yours, but I knew the truth would come out once you returned. I felt compelled to leave. I couldn't bear the thought of witnessing your rejection of me. *Cùra* had left, so I turned to Finn for help."

The recount of her experience tore at him. "I would never reject you, my love. Thank God for Finn."

"I owe him a great debt."

"As do I. You knew, then, that Caleb was really Alex?"

"Aye. I think I knew it all along."

Stephen smiled. "Me too. But he swore me to secrecy."

"I don't want it, Stephen."

"What?"

"This child. God forgive me, but I do not want it." She squirmed against him. "Don't tell *Cùra*, but I asked Althena to give me something to get rid of it. She refused. She said such herbs are poisonous, and can kill the mother as well."

"Then you mustn't even think of it." He looked down at her belly, which showed no sign of her condition. "I swear we'll get through this, Emma. Besides, 'tis not the child's fault."

"But what if it's evil, like him?"

"And what if it's sweet and kind, like its mother?"

Yet he wondered at her words, wondered how this child might be. *Could I learn to love it? Perhaps not as my own, but in some measure? Why not? Did Alex not love Emma? Aye, but perhaps Alex was her true father.*

"Did you tell your family the truth?"

He heard the sadness in her voice and gave her a gentle squeeze.

"Aye, they know everything."

"Then I expect Anne feels justified in her assessment of me. What did Christophe say? And Bee?"

"Well, now." Stephen plumped up the pillow behind his head and settled back, smiling inwardly. "Let me think. I believe his actual words were, 'Tell Emma she'll always be welcome at Thurston and let us know how she fares'. And Bee? I think she said, 'Please give her my love'."

"You jest."

"I do not."

"Then they cannot know the truth of it, surely, or they would not be so –"

"Understanding?" Stephen finished. He reached into his shirt and handed Emma a wrinkled rolled-up parchment. "'Tis a tad weathered after the journey, but it might explain things a little better."

She sat up, a puzzled expression crossing her face as she took it from him. "What's this?"

"A letter from Anne."

"Oh, nay." She handed it back. "I've no desire to read a chronicle of Anne's insults."

"Do you really think I'd even consider giving you such a document? Read it. I swear you have nothing to fear."

Above them, the tiny window in the attic framed the fiery brilliance of a setting sun. As shadows darkened with the onset of night, Stephen rose to light a candle for Emma to read by.

A while later, the parchment lay open on the bed, the ink marred in places where Emma's tears had fallen. She'd been shocked to read of Anne's nightmare, so similar to her own. She wept at Anne's plea for forgiveness, moved to know that she now held a special place in the prayers of a woman who had previously shown her nothing but contempt.

The transformation, Stephen noticed, began soon after Emma finished reading the letter. The signs were subtle at first; increased confidence in her voice, animated hand gestures as she spoke, the lift of her chin, the straightness in her spine. Best of all though, was the return of a familiar light dancing in her eyes, which gladdened his heart.

With sounds of chatter coming from the kitchen, Emma lowered her voice and told Stephen about the previous night on the shore with Alex, her eyes moist as she repeated the tragic tale of Alicia and Edward's fate.

"I knew he hadn't murdered her," Stephen said, kissing away Emma's tears. "'Tis not in him to do such a thing."

"I fear he didn't tell me everything, though." She sighed. "There's more to the story, I know it."

Aye, much more. Indeed, when she told him about Alex's mysterious visit to Thurston's roof, a chill ran through him. Secretly, he doubted Emma's belief that the visit had been a dream. He suspected it was somehow connected to Francis's story.

At that point, he'd been tempted to speak of the meeting at Creake Abbey, but instead told of his growing connection to the stone, his new-found ability to read minds and the likelihood that he was to be a future Guardian.

Emma sat cross-legged at his side, wide-eyed, listening to his tale. She tilted her head and grinned at him. "A mind-reader? A Guardian? Who is this gifted man I'm to marry?"

He laughed. "You may well ask. Ah! That reminds me, speaking of gifts." He dug into his pocket, pulling out a little black pouch. "When I was in London committing treason, I purchased this. It reminded me of you, my little archer."

Emma gasped at the sight of the chain, so fine and delicate, adorned with a tiny arrowhead.

"'Tis made from the finest Welsh gold," he said,

disturbed by the sudden look of dismay on her face. "Do you not like it?"

"I love it, and I shall treasure it, but it reminds me that I have a confession to make." She turned large soft eyes to his and reached for his hand. " I hope you can forgive me."

Frowning, he sat up. "Forgive you for what, sweetheart?"

"I'm afraid I lost the brooch you gave me. The one that belonged to your mother. It disappeared the night I left Thurston. I searched everywhere, Stephen. It meant so much to me, and I know you loved it too. I'm so sorry."

Stephen smiled. "Is that your confession? If I'd only known, I'd have bought you another brooch as well." He cupped her cheek with his hand. "The catch was always loose, my love. I should have had it repaired. Put it out of your mind. 'Tis no tragedy. Here, allow me. The catch on this is well made. There. Perfect."

Emma fingered the necklace and smiled up at him. "I truly love it. Thank you. Perhaps we can go hunting tomorrow?"

"Of course. If you feel up to it."

A burst of laughter came from the kitchen, and Stephen grinned. "Shall we join them?"

~o~

Time wove around them like a tapestry that evening, the hours filled with pleasant images, each one blending neatly into the next. Even so, Alex sensed an undercurrent. A tapestry could hide a damaged wall, he pondered.

But if you look behind the pretty scenes, the damage is still there.

Althena had retired first, encouraged to do so by Alex,

who saw the weariness in her face. A little later, Stephen carried Emma to bed as she nodded off in his arms. When Stephen returned, the room lapsed into silence and Alex cast an amused glance around the table.

"Will someone speak, for God's sake? I'm curious to know why the air has been thick with unspoken words all evening."

Finn smiled. "Ever the perceptive one, Alexander. Strange, though, how your perception is clouded when it comes to Emma. In fact, I'm not so sure she should be excluded from this conversation."

Stephen straddled his chair. "I agree. This concerns her too. I know you didn't tell her everything last night."

Alex frowned and leaned back. "What is this? A tribunal? If you have questions to ask of me, then please ask them."

"Easy, my friend." Keir reached over and squeezed Alex's shoulder. "'Tis no tribunal. But it does have to do with Emma."

"In what way?"

Keir took a measured breath. "While at Thurston, we all became aware of the strong connection you have to the lass."

Alex shrugged. "Is it so unusual that I should have one? I raised her as my own."

Keir smiled. "We have reason to believe that she is yours."

Alex struggled to keep his voice calm. "You're mistaken, my lord, but I would know the reason for your beliefs."

"That is what we wish to discuss with you." Keir glanced at the others around the table, his expression guarded. "Stephen and I took a little detour on our way back from London. We paid a visit to Creake Abbey and spent some time with Francis. What we learned from him was quite interesting."

Alex sat forward, his heart leaping into a gallop. "Sweet Christ. You went to see my father?"

"Aye. What we witnessed at Thurston led us to think there was something unusual about your connection to Emma, something more than that of a surrogate parent. You never did fully explain what led to the estrangement of your father, nor did Francis ever fully explain his sudden withdrawal from the Circle." Keir glanced at Finn and Stephen. "Not that those things, by themselves, gave us any real concern. But the fact is, Emma continues to demonstrate certain abilities that lead us to believe she may be of a Guardian's blood. If that's true, then we must be involved in her life. Inherited traits are to be nurtured and developed in our children. The visit with your father appears to support our suspicions. He claims the girl is —"

"I know what he claims." Alex rose to his feet, an old familiar anger gnawing at him. "But it is simply that my father was fool enough to believe some heretical nonsense invented by a desperate woman."

"Heretical nonsense?" Keir raised a brow. "Consider, Alexander, the stone you guard, the power it possesses, all that it does. Do you consider those qualities to be heretical nonsense? Nay, I think not. How is it, then, you can so readily dismiss Alicia's claim?"

"Do you truly believe..." Alex ran his hand through his hair, "...that I would be unaware of travelling halfway across the known world, making love to my wife, then returning to my paltry bed in the space of one night? 'Tis folly. An impossibility. Emma is Edward's child. Of that I have no doubt."

"Not so. You're riddled with doubt, my friend." Keir's eyes lit with a soft gleam. "I can see it. 'Tis like a parasite, feeding upon what you think you know. Why is it so difficult to believe Emma is yours? Listen to your instincts for a change. You're a Guardian, a man with knowledge of things beyond most mortal comprehension. So why not consider the possibility that you ascended to another realm of consciousness, that your spirit, your soul, took physical form and conceived a child with a woman you loved? That Emma is, in fact, a miracle child?"

Voices from the past, so recently disturbed, echoed Keir's words.

...for she is a true miracle. Never doubt it.

Alex paced, his turbulent mind latching on to the safety of his denial. "If I agree, for a moment, to consider the possibility that what you say is true, then you must explain the why of it, my lords."

Keir narrowed his eyes. "What do you mean?"

"Why only that one night? If I have - or had - such a gift, why do I not ascend to this...this other realm more often? Why did I not visit Alicia once a week? Or once a month? Why only that one night? My need for my wife did not wane with time. I missed her terribly, and the pain of being apart grew in strength as the months passed. So what was different about that night? Explain it to me, if you can."

"I've wondered about that, and I have a theory." Finn shifted in his chair. "The night you appeared on Thurston's roof, Emma had just learned about the child she carried. You were in Cumbria. Stephen had not yet returned. The lass was lost, alone, and desperate. Without hope." He grimaced. "Truth is, Alex, I believe that Emma had other intentions on the roof that night."

Alex felt a twinge of apprehension. "Other intentions? What do you mean?"

Finn set his lips in a grim line. "I believe she went up there to —"

"Kill myself."

Alex stopped pacing as a collective gasp rattled the

air. All eyes turned to the girl who stood, pale-faced, in the doorway of her room, her gaze fixed on Alex.

"Christ, Emma." Stephen leapt up and went to her.

Alex sighed. "How much of our conversation did you hear, lass?"

Emma shrugged. "Almost all of it, *Cùra*. Why did you not speak of your father before now? You led me to believe he was dead."

He ignored her question, a sudden heaviness beneath his ribs. "Is it true? You meant to end your life that night?"

She shrugged again. "I saw no way forward. No way out. My foot was on the battlement wall when I heard your voice. 'Twas you who saved me. You pulled me back from the edge. But when you disappeared so suddenly, I thought you had merely been a dream, a vision conjured up by my desperate mind." She looked at Finn. "I no longer believe that."

"I never did believe it," said Finn. "I sensed your presence, Alexander. I know you were there that night, and I can only conclude you were there because your child was in despair, without hope. I now believe the same thing happened with Alicia. You told us how much you missed her when you were separated. Do you not think she felt the same? She too was alone, helpless, and desperate for your return. I believe you responded to Alicia's call for help, just as you responded to Emma's. In each case, their despair is what pulled you to their side. You created hope where none existed. You were a light in the darkness."

"Thank God." Stephen dropped a kiss on Emma's head. "Thank God you were there, Alex."

I'm here because you have great need of me.

Alex's heart missed a beat as the words rang out in his mind. His words, he felt certain. But spoken when? And to whom?

His eyes had not left Emma's face. "I still find it...difficult to believe." Yet ancient instincts stirred as he looked at her. Was it his blood in her veins and not Edward's? If so, that would mean –

"Our initial fear was that you had knowledge of this ability and had not spoken of it," said Keir. "But it appears that's not the case. That said, it also appears you have much to consider, Alexander. You have, at least, allowed us to open a door in your mind tonight. Do not be tempted to close it until you've explored what lies within." He rose to his feet and looked at Stephen. "In the meantime, the Circle grows impatient for our report on all that has happened, all our findings."

Stephen frowned. "You're leaving now? In the middle of the night?"

Finn grinned as he stood. "Those words are strangely familiar to me."

Stephen's puzzled expression changed to one of disappointment. "But I was hoping you would help us find Argante. With your skills, we should have no trouble tracking him down."

Keir shook his head. "We hunt neither beast nor man, young knight. Our work here is done for now. We'll return in a week or so, for I suspect you'll be summoned to the Circle." He glanced at Alex and Emma. "And I suspect you won't be the only one."

Alex pushed his sword into the soft earthen floor of the barn and ran his fingers over the silver knot on the hilt. The jewel hidden within responded to his touch, pulsing with a soft blue light that grew in intensity until it cast the shadows aside. He fell to his knees, pulled the hilt against his lips and closed his eyes, trying to balance the weight of his thoughts.

Although Alex sought harmony, the Cumbrian night refused to yield it. Outside, a screech owl challenged the peace with its strange call, answered a moment later by the haunting yip of a red fox. Upon hearing that, the chickens in the barn clucked subdued warnings to one other, and Bart snorted before landing a solid kick against his stall door. Yet Alex found some strange comfort in the sounds. They had a simple clarity, each one easy to identify. Unlike the truth, it seemed.

He heard a soft footfall behind him.

"You still have doubts, *Cùra*." It was not a question. Emma's hand rested on his shoulder as she knelt by his side.

"Aye, little one."

"Why did you not tell me about your father last night? Why did you not tell me what Mama had told him?"

He turned to look at her, expecting to see accusation in her eyes. Instead, he saw only love and concern.

"You overheard your mother's story, Emma. To me, it sounded like the ramblings of a woman desperate to hide the truth. I believed my father betrayed me by taking her side, hiding her in the abbey until you were born."

"Do you still believe that?"

Alex released the hilt of his sword and sat back on his heels, watching the gentle sway of his makeshift cross, thinking that even prayer would bring him no peace that night.

"I'm no longer certain what I believe."

He heard a soft sigh and saw Emma's head droop. "It troubles me that you continue to deny even the possibility of it, *Cùra*. Would you not like to be...I mean, is the thought of being my real father not appealing to you?"

Alex resisted a curious urge to laugh. "Appealing?" He stood and pulled Emma to her feet, keeping her hands clasped between his. "The thought of you sharing my blood could never be simply appealing, Emma. Wonderful, aye. Incredible, certainly. The truth is, my reluctance to be proven your real father has nothing to do with you. It has everything to do with me."

Emma shook her head. "I don't understand."

"Ach, child. Christ knows how much you mean to me. But do you not see? If you're indeed mine, then Alicia did not lie. She didn't betray me. Nor did Edward." The notion hovered over him like a hangman's noose. "If I'm to believe your mother's story, then I must also admit to killing an innocent man. Worse yet, your mother, may God rest her tormented soul, died for naught. That thought alone is enough to sicken me. I find myself trapped between two possibilities, neither one pleasant to consider. The only shining light in each of them is you."

He searched her face, looking for traces of himself or Edward in her appearance. But all he saw was Alicia. She blinked at him, stood on tiptoes, and kissed his cheek.

"I understand. But whatever the truth, you're not alone. We'll face it together. 'Tis what Mama would have wanted. For now, I shall leave you to your prayers, but I should like to talk more tomorrow. Perhaps, by then, God will have given you the answers you seek." She turned to leave, pausing at the threshold. "Just know this, *Cùra*. I have no doubt who I am. None at all." With a smile, she disappeared into the blackness.

Alex groaned and dropped to his knees once more, his father's voice filling his head, as clear as if he stood by his side.

Surely you can feel it, lad? Surely you can see it? 'Tis obvious whose child she is.

Behind him, Bart nickered and kicked at his stall door again. Alex ignored him and touched the hilt of the sword to kill the light. The barn plunged into welcome darkness.

God was not the only one Alex spoke to that night. He reached out with his mind, calling for Alicia beyond the limits of mortality, willing her to speak to him. But the dead, apparently, had nothing to say.

Much later, his body numb with cold, his thoughts dull with fatigue, he struggled to his feet and stumbled back to the cottage. He had gone almost two nights without sleep, he realised. Perhaps things would be clearer once he had rested.

It surprised him to see Stephen sitting at the table, staring into the glowing remains of the fire. He looked up as Alex entered, his eyes drifting to the open door. "Everything alright? I was getting worried, but didn't want to interrupt."

"Aye, I'm fine. Just need some rest. I thought you'd be asleep." Alex closed the door, unbuckled his sword and leaned it against the wall.

There was a moment of silence, a moment in which he heard Stephen's breath catch. The sound was like a cold hand around Alex's heart.

"What is it, lad?"

"Why have you closed the door?" Stephen rose to his feet, his face turning stark white in the candlelight. "Where's Emma?"

Chapter 28

Emma dropped to the ground like a lifeless bird; her head twisted back, blood roping its way along the strands of her hair. For a brief moment, Argante panicked. Had he hit her too hard? Killed her here, outside Mathanach's house? Not what he'd planned.

But no. A small cloud of breath escaped from her parted lips, and her chest rose and fell. *She lives.*

A horse whinnied in the barn, and Argante heard the bang of a hoof against wood. That damn stallion. It always sensed him. He should have cut its throat.

The strange blue light in the barn went out, and he held his breath, watching the doorway, expecting to see Mathanach appear on the threshold. But all fell silent.

Grinning, Argante picked Emma up and heaved her over his shoulder.

"You're mine, Emma," he gurgled, heading toward the trees. "See you soon, Mathanach."

The thought of Alex on his trail kept Argante trudging onward, stopping once in a while to glance behind to see if he was being followed. Although Emma weighed little, her inert body dragged at his muscles and pulled on his limbs as he staggered through the forest.

His body ached and his knees buckled, but he struggled on until he reached open countryside. At the edge of the forest he paused, fatigue forgotten as he hummed a raspy, nondescript tune. He'd waited a long time for this night.

The walls of the keep loomed ahead, a dark shape against the frost-bitten slopes of Black Combe. Argante stepped through the doorway and climbed the stairs to what had, at one time, served as the Great Hall.

Moonlight fell through the small, uncovered windows, drawing silver lines across the begrimed floor and walls. Somewhere up in the cobwebbed rafters a bat squeaked, its leathery wings fluttering in the darkness.

Argante placed Emma on the floor by the fireplace. Many years had passed since the massive hearth had held a fire, but the black scars of flames remained, scorched into the cold grey slate for eternity.

"Romantic, don't you think?" He slurped on a mouthful of saliva. "You always bring out the best in me, Emma. But I'll not be lighting a fire. I'm sure you can understand why."

Drool dripping from his lips, he knelt at Emma's side and pulled some strands of hair from her face. His fingers traced her jawline, tracked down her throat and circled a breast. He pushed his hand inside her dress and rolled her nipple between his fingertips. It responded, hardening beneath his touch.

He groaned, his mind high on intense sexual desire, his thoughts haphazard. "God's balls, you're a sweet wench. Open your eyes, will you? I want you awake when I stick my cock inside you. It will be the last fuck we'll ever have, so we should both enjoy it, n'est-ce pas?"

Emma's eyelids flickered. "Ste...Stephen?"

Argante stood, unfastened his filthy braies, and tossed them aside. "My name is Richard. Have you forgotten me so soon? Who the fuck is Stephen?"

Emma looked up at him and for a heartbeat Argante caught his breath, his twisted mind thrown by the expression of profound pity in her eyes.

"Argante," she whispered. "May God have mercy on your soul."

He blinked, his mind settling back into its dark cradle. "Ah, so you do remember me. Good. Do you remember this?" He kicked her legs apart, waving his erection at her. "Ready and willing, just like your mother. I'll fuck her on one side, and you on the other." The walls echoed with his laughter. "Moonlight, a fireplace and poetry. What more could a lady want?"

"You're insane." Emma tried to sit up. She moaned and touched her fingers to the wound on her head.

"Nay. You're confusing me with Mathanach. He's taken up with that black-haired witch. Where did you go? Did he send you away?"

"You'll not touch me," she murmured. "Not again."

"Aye, I will. And you'll like it." Argante took a knife from his belt, knelt between her legs, and pushed her skirt up around her waist. "I've waited so long for this."

She whimpered as he pressed his groin to hers, supporting himself on his elbows, the knife blade pointed at her breast. "Jesus, wench. God have mercy, you feel so good. A bit skinny, but good."

"Alex will kill you," she cried, her stomach roiling at his foul breath.

"He's tried that once or twice already. " He chuckled, slipping his hand between them to adjust himself. "Besides, I'm already dying. But I had to have you just one last time." Spittle spattered across her face as he coughed. "I shall take my pleasure and then take your life. I want to see Mathanach's face when he sees your sweet little body next to mine. He fucked with me. I fuck with you. Seems fair."

A moment later, his scream echoed around the stark walls as Emma's fingernails raked him, grabbing and ripping the scarred skin covering his closed eye. Blinded by agony, he clutched at his face, blood dripping through his fingers.

Emma struggled out from under him, sobbing as she staggered to her feet. Through a red haze of anger, he grabbed at her ankle and brought her down hard, slashing at her leg with the knife.

"You fucking little bitch. I'm going to cut you to pieces."

He pulled her toward him, and pinned her beneath him, his blade pressed against her throat.

"If you kill me," she gasped, "you'll also kill your child."

Argante watched a bead of blood seep from a cut on Emma's throat, frowning as a drop of his own blood fell and mixed with hers.

"My child?"

"Aye," she panted, her eyes fixed on his face, unwavering. " I carry your seed, Richard."

"Lying whore." But he lifted the blade from her throat, allowing her words to settle into his brain.

"I swear it before God. Your babe grows inside me."

Still pinning her with his legs, he rolled onto his side and studied her body. "You're having my bastard?" His mind pondered the revelation. Spilling his seed had always been a matter of self-indulgence. He'd never cared about the consequences of his selfish pleasures. The point of his blade tracked a line down Emma's sternum and across her abdomen, following the small rise of her belly. Emma tensed visibly and a grin spread across Argante's twisted features. A child. His child. *How perfect. How amusing.*

"Does Mathanach know?"

"Aye," she said. "He does."

"Christ. Then he probably won't be too upset to find you dead. I can't see him bouncing my bastard on his knee."

"You'd kill your own child?"

"I'd never let it grow up with that mangy Scot." Still grinning, he rolled on top of her again, his blood dripping onto her face. "It's going to feel me in a moment, giving it a little nudge. I wonder if it'll recognize its father's cock?"

"You're a demon," Emma cried, pushing at him. "You

belong in hell."

"Where do you think I've been for the past few weeks? Ever since you left me, sweetheart, my life has been shite. I burned for you." He chuckled. "Literally."

Was it his imagination, or had the darkness of the room just lifted? Something buzzed in his brain, a warning, the sense of a presence, and a soldier's instinct emerged from the ruins of his mind.

He grabbed a handful of Emma's hair and sprang to his feet, dragging her with him, ignoring her yelp of pain. His arm wrapped around her throat, pulling her back against him like a shield, the point of the blade aimed at her heart.

The entire room glowed with a soft blue light, growing in strength with each moment, pulsing as if alive.

"What the hell?"

Then he saw him, and his cold skin grew colder yet.

"Remember me, Richard?" Stephen stepped out of the light, his eyes menacingly dark in his pale face.

"Stephen de Montfort." Argante's hold on Emma tightened, his befuddled brain trying to make sense of what he was seeing. "But...you're dead. I saw your grave. I saw..."

Emma choked, gasping for breath, and pulled at his arm. Argante glanced at her, his mind searching for something important, something to do with her. Something she had said.

Got it.

"Stephen." He spat out a large wad of saliva. "You're no ghost. This whore asked for you earlier. So, you're still alive. Living proof that there is, in fact, no God."

"Let her go. You're killing her." Stephen took a step closer.

"You're very perceptive." Argante's mouth twisted as he pushed the knife against Emma's ribs. "And very inconsiderate. You've interrupted a sweet romantic interlude between me and Alicia's bastard. Speaking of bastards, where's that Scottish whoreson? I wouldn't want him to miss out —"

"I'm right behind you, Richard."

A hand grabbed Argante's shoulder and something hit him hard in the small of his back. He dropped the knife, shocked by a strange sensation travelling up through his body, as if someone had lit a fire in his belly and poured ice-cold water around his heart. Then the hand on his shoulder tightened and he jerked backwards, aware of a sickening sound, like a boot being pulled free of mud.

"Fuck, Mathanach, I'm impressed," he blurted, through a mouthful of red bubbles, taking Emma with him as he fell. "I didn't see that coming."

Alex towered over him, the hilt of his sword glowing with the strange blue light, the blade dripping with blood.

My blood, Argante thought.

"By the way, the stone was with me all along," Alex said, patting the hilt. "Just thought you'd like to know that before you die, you bastard. Have a nice time in hell."

Argante spat out a mouthful of blood and grinned at Emma, who still lay breathless at his side. "Mathanach doesn't know it yet," he whispered, staring into the green depths of her eyes as his life left him. "But you're coming with me."

~o~

Emma started hemorrhaging on the way home, a persistent steady flow coupled with sharp bursts of intense pain. Each of her cries struck like a blade in Alex's heart, for he had heard Argante's final words. Even now, they filled him with a sickening dread, a familiar feeling - one he had wondered about several times over the past few weeks.

Argante had been demented, aye, but there was more to it than that. Some unseen power had been at play, consuming the man, shielding him from Alex's sight and senses.

Tracking him to the keep had been easy. Argante left a trail even a two year old could have followed. But why hadn't Alex sensed his presence at the cottage? Why had he not felt Emma's absence? What kind of insidious demon had taken refuge in Argante's soul?

They rode their horses hard. By the time they reached the cottage, the flank of Stephen's horse was wet with a mixture of sweat and Emma's blood. Stephen carried her indoors, his face white and grim as he placed her on the bed. Alex caught the desperate look on Althena's face just before she donned a mask of hope. His guts twisted.

Now the two men waited in silence, the only sound being the crackle of wood in the hearth and the occasional hiss of a candle flame as it devoured the tallow.

Daylight crept through gaps in the shutters, yet neither man rose to open them. Somehow, Alex thought, opening the shutters would be accepting the arrival of this new day.

A day he'd never thought to see.

At last, the bedroom door swung back and Althena appeared on the threshold, her face grey and drawn, her hair damp with sweat. Alex tried not to look at the blood staining her skirts.

Both men stood, Stephen's eyes full of hope, but his face tight with fear as he spoke. "She has lost the child?"

Alex gripped the back of his chair.

Althena nodded. "Aye."

Stephen took a step forward. "And...does she rally?"

There was a pause, a small measure of time in which the terrible truth resided.

"I can't stop the bleeding."

Alex gripped the chair harder, his legs weakening, his heart racing.

Dear God, how can I ever begin to survive this?

"But...but she'll recover." Stephen glanced at Alex as if seeking affirmation and his voice rose in fear. "For Christ's sake, Althena. Tell me she'll recover."

"I'm so sorry," she whispered, a sob catching in her throat. "I can do no more. Go to her, Stephen."

"Nay," Stephen ran a hand through his hair, his voice cracking. "Oh, nay. Sweet Christ. It cannot be." He pushed past Althena and went into the bedroom.

"Forgive me, Alex." Althena shook her head as tears spilled down her cheeks. "I tried everything."

He went to her and drew her close, giving way to his own tears. "Don't blame yourself, my love. None of this is your doing."

"She's asking for you. Go to her. Her time is very near."

In all his life, he'd never felt such terror, such hopelessness. Losing Alicia had almost destroyed him, yet even that could not compare to the hell he now faced. Whether she was of his blood or not, Emma was his child, and he loved her more than anything.

More than life.

And what of Emma's fear? God's teeth. She was but a child of sixteen. What in Heaven's name did a parent say to their dying child? Had such words even been invented? Did such dialogue exist? He hesitated in the doorway, his fingers tightening around the sword's hilt. All at once he became aware of the stone's strange silence, as if it, too, was in utter denial.

Candlelight flickered off the walls and a pile of blood-soaked cloths sat in a bucket by the door. Stephen sat on the bed with Emma in his arms, stroking her hair, kissing her forehead, whispering soft words of love to her. Her skin was white and thin as parchment, her lips circled with a pale blue ring.

She saw Alex and, bless her precious heart, smiled at him.

He went to her, settled himself on the other side of her, and took her hand in his.

"*Cùra*," she murmured. "Don't be afraid."

He realised, then, where to find his words. All he had to do was reach into his heart. "But I am afraid, *a ghràidh*. I'm afraid to face life without you. I love you so much."

She smiled again, but Alex saw the life fading in her eyes. "You'll never be without me," she said. "I'll always be with you. Both of you."

Emma's final breath was a fine, delicate thing. It parted her lips and disappeared like a wisp of wind into the air.

At the same time, images exploded in Alex's mind, as blinding as the sun, overwhelming him with their brilliance. He watched them through a mist of tears, priceless memories of a beautiful child who had enriched his life.

Not once, not even for a moment, had he regretted adopting her. He remembered the exhausting nights he'd heard her cry and risen to feed her, only to be blessed by a toothless smile from a crib, while the rest of the world slept. Watching her grow had been a gift beyond value, beyond measure. He taught her the ways of the forest, guided her through her studies, cherished her innocence, and nurtured her adoration and trust. She had thrived with him, learned from him. And he, in turn, had learned from her. They had shared stories by candlelight and dreams by starlight.

"The stars will never shine as brightly again, little

one," he whispered.

Echoes of her laughter faded away to be replaced by Stephen's quiet sobs, each one wrenched from a shattered heart. The lad still held Emma, rocking her gently, his face buried in her hair. Alex's mind went back in time and saw himself on a bright summer's morning more than sixteen years earlier, when Alicia lay dead in his arms, her life's blood spreading out across the floor.

Alex knew Stephen's life would never be the same.

Through a haze of grief, he looked down at Emma's hand, still resting in his. There was blood under the fingernails. Argante's blood, no doubt. His fingers traced a vein across the back of her hand; a pale, bloodless line where life had flowed only moments before. *How can this be? What purpose does it serve, the death of this innocent child?*

"God, help me."

But it was not God who answered.

The past does not stay in the past. It circles around to greet us as we step into the future. One becomes the other. Thus has it always been.

Alicia's death had been of her own doing. Tragic and painful indeed, but a choice had, nonetheless, been made.

And Emma? Was she given a choice?

Nay. Perhaps she had contemplated taking her life at one time, but in the end her demise had been brought about by the wicked deeds of men. He remembered Argante's final prediction.

...you're coming with me.

Could, then, such an end be preordained? Deemed to be the will of God? Surely not.

So why was he just sitting there?

"Step aside, lad," he said, rising to his feet and drawing his sword.

Stephen lifted his head, his face wet with tears, eyes

bright with anguish. "What?"

"Lay the lass down and step aside. I don't have much time."

Alex felt something brush across his mind and saw shock flit across Stephen's face.

"What...what are you doing, Alex?"

"Have faith, Stephen. Am I not the guardian of a stone that lights the dark and plays havoc with men's weaknesses?" Alex smiled. "But consider for a moment. Would such trivial powers merit the protection of an immortal assembly across sixteen centuries? You're about to learn the real truth of why we exist. I ask only that you stay quiet and still."

"Alex?" Althena's quiet voice wandered into the room. May Christ forgive him, for in his grief he had not considered what his actions would mean for her.

"My love." He held out his hand and she stepped to his side. He kissed her, resting his forehead against hers for a moment. "I pray you will understand."

"Understand what?"

"Why I do what I do. Go and stand with Stephen, lass. Say nothing more for now."

Something akin to fear flared in her eyes, but she did as he asked.

Alex knelt at the side of the bed and placed the sword on Emma's body with the hilt resting on her chest, close to her heart. He wrapped her fingers around the twisted silver knot on the hilt, and then covered them with his own before turning his gaze to her beautiful, lifeless face.

Years of training and mental discipline were brought to bear as Alex connected with the stone. He opened a forbidden door in his mind and, without hesitation, plunged into the depths of the stone's divine power. Like a child startled from sleep, it jumped beneath his hands. He felt its growing awareness, sharing its rapturous desire to connect with that most powerful and eternal force under heaven.

Life itself.

With his guidance, it reached out to embrace the young girl on the bed, caressing Emma's heart and mind, hesitating when it found only emptiness within. The air in the room turned ice cold, clouding Alex's breath. He shivered, fighting a violent surge of anger combined with an overwhelming sense of injustice.

"Then make it right," he whispered, shocked at the stone's intense reaction. "Return that which has been taken away. Give her what we mortals cannot."

The anger subsided but the cold increased. Frost formed along the blade of the sword and travelled across Alex's hands, turning them white. He tightened his hold, ignoring the numbing pain, watching his breath all but solidify upon leaving his lips.

A voice drifted into his mind; one he knew right well.

"You will cease this blasphemy now, Guardian"

"Nay, I will not."

"Remember your sacred vow."

"A vow I do willingly renounce."

"There will be dire consequences."

"I'll face them."

"Then may God have mercy on your soul."

"Amen to that, for He has shown me little of His mercy so far."

A small tendril of shimmering light emerged from Alex's hands, curling like a delicate vine up into the air. Another followed, and another, until several of them danced over Emma's bed. A ball of light emerged from the centre and rose above them, pulsing, becoming brighter with each passing moment.

From the silence came the gentle sound of rushing water, like the enduring flow of a mountain stream, coupled with a soft, rhythmic song, reminiscent of summer rain drumming on the mirrored surface of a pond.

Alex knew he was witness to the stone's interpretation of life. The light represented the sun, and the sounds represented mortal essences, the flow of blood through the veins, the beating of a million hearts.

As the stone's power increased, his frozen hands prickled as if wrapped in thorns, an agonizing sensation that had him gritting his teeth. Then, just as the pain became unbearable, the ball of light exploded around him, blinding him for a moment, filling his veins with a force unlike any he had felt before.

The tendrils of light vanished, silence once again filled the room, and Alex closed the door in his mind. The entire episode had lasted but moments, yet he felt as if he had lived another lifetime. His heart pounded, his lungs snatched air, and his limbs shook. Yet beneath his touch, he felt Emma's skin grow warm. Still, he waited for a sign that she lived, and a sliver of doubt wormed its way into his mind despite his belief in the stone's power.

He rose from his knees, sheathed the sword, and sat on the edge of the bed, studying her. Emma's face had lost its grim pallor. The blue lines had vanished from her mouth and eyelids. Her cheeks were now flushed a soft pink, her lips too.

"God's balls." Stephen's voice shook. "What just happened?"

Alex ran a fingertip along Emma's jaw. Her eyelids flickered and, as he watched, her chest rose and fell.

He swallowed against a sob. "You've got your wee faerie back, Stephen."

Emma opened her eyes and blinked at him. Alex's heart clenched. For a fleeting moment he saw Alicia in those emerald green depths, and Emma's first words did much to affirm his impression.

"Oh, *Cùra*. I must tell you. I had such a wonderful dream. I was with Mama. She told me..." She frowned. "But I thought...am I...is this a dream also? Do I live?"

"Aye, you live." He pulled her into his embrace, his heart both light with relief and heavy with regret. "I've told you this many times, yet I must tell you again. I love you, Emma, and I would do anything for you, willingly. You know that, don't you?"

She looked up at him. "I know it well and I love you too, *Cùra*. Are you alright? Is anything wrong?"

"Nay, little one. Everything's fine. Rest now. It will take a wee while to get your strength back." He kissed her and rose to his feet, turning to Stephen, who stood staring at Emma in white-faced shock. "Close your mouth, lad. Come and sit by her."

The look on Althena's face had not gone unnoticed by Alex. She too was pale, her expression one of disbelief. Yet she watched him, not Emma, and the fear he had seen in her eyes earlier still remained.

Alex knew that in choosing to save one heart, he was about to hurt another. He smiled at her and held out his hand.

"Come with me, lass."

They went into the kitchen, the sounds of Stephen and Emma's quiet conversation behind them.

He gathered her close, breathing in the soft scent of her hair, feeling her heart thudding against him.

"Just know that I love you," he whispered, holding her tighter.

She shivered in his arms. "Why does that sound like goodbye, Alex?"

He did not have time to answer.

The door burst open and a dark mist flowed into the room, like a thick fog birthed by a stormy sea and cast ashore. From it, two figures emerged, each surrounded by a familiar unearthly glow, their eyes lit as if flames burned within.

They stood and studied Alex for a moment. He flinched inwardly at the sadness and disappointment in their expressions.

"Christ, Alexander. What the hell have you done?" Finn gestured toward Emma's room. "Where is she? In there?"

Alex nodded and released Althena. "Aye."

"Does she live?"

He nodded again. "Aye."

Finn strode to the doorway and paused on the threshold. Stephen's excited greeting drifted into the kitchen.

"You should have seen it, Finn," he said. "'Twas a miracle. I've never seen the like before. I don't understand why you would hide such a thing, keep it away from the world as you do. Such magic should be shared, not guarded."

Finn did not answer, but turned back to Alex, his eyes blazing.

"May God forgive you," he said. "Do you know what this means?"

"He knows. I tried to stop him." Keir held out his hand. "Give me the sword, Guardian."

Alex gave a grim smile, unbuckled the sword, and handed it, hilt first, to Keir.

"I regret any disturbance to the Circle," he said. "But I stand by my decision, and would do the same again."

"Disturbance?" Finn let out a harsh laugh and it shocked Alex to see tears shining in the Irish knight's eyes. "'Tis no mere disturbance, but a vile betrayal. Such disregard for our most sacred law has not happened in nigh on a thousand years. You have spit in God's eye and mocked us all. The elders are furious - beyond placating. I swear, if you were to appear before them at this moment, they would ignore your rights and strike you dead where you stand. I'm sorely tempted to do that very thing myself."

"What's going on?" Sword in hand, Stephen appeared in Emma's doorway. "Why are you so angry with him? He saved Emma's life, for God's sake."

Keir spoke. "We must leave now, Alexander. You will come with us willingly or forced. Your choice."

"There'll be no resistance from me," said Alex, his voice calmer than his racing heart.

He felt Althena's hand slip into his. "You're not coming back, are you?" she asked, her voice tearful.

He sighed and raised her fingers to his lips. "Probably not, lass. Please forgive me. Stephen, you must take care of Emma and Althena. Swear it."

Stephen stepped into the room, sword raised. "Wait. I don't understand. Where are they taking you?"

"Lower your blade, lad," Alex said, seeing Keir tense at Stephen's threatening gesture. "None of this is unexpected. I knew what the results of my actions would be."

"What do you mean? What results?" Stephen looked from Alex to Keir. "He used the stone to save Emma's life. What is so wrong about that?"

"Do you not remember what I told you, young knight?" said Keir. "Tis a question of balance. Balance in all things. To interfere with God's will is strictly forbidden. Indeed, that vow is the most sacred of all the vows we take. 'Tis the main reason we exist, to ensure that the balance of life in this world is not defiled through the misuse of the stone, that God's decisions are not usurped. The balance must be maintained."

Stephen snorted. "You presume to know Emma's

death was God's will? Did God tell you that Himself?"

Alex smiled and looked at the ground. The lad had bigger balls than the king's stallion.

Keir scowled. "Be careful, Stephen. You're dealing with a powerful order. Do not question our knowledge in this matter."

"I question what you intend to do with Alex. Or is that a secret as well?"

"Nay, 'tis no secret. There will be a three-day tribunal, during which time Alexander may present his case to the Circle. If he's found to have acted with justifiable reason, his life will be spared. If not, and we find he went against God in giving Emma her life, his own life will be forfeit."

"Surely you jest." Stephen look at Keir aghast. "You would take a man's life for saving that of his child? Who's playing God now?"

Keir's expression softened. "Alexander knew the price to be paid for his actions. The law is quite clear." He gestured toward the door. "We must leave. Do not try to follow us, Stephen. It would be a futile exercise. We'll bring word of Alexander's fate as soon as we can."

"Well, that's very noble of you, my Lord Keir." Stephen's lip curled in scorn. "Tell your fellow Guardians to grow hearts, for Christ's sake. The cold-blooded —"

"Easy, lad. The Guardians have every right to be angry. I bear them no ill will." Alex gestured to Emma's bedroom. "I cannot say goodbye to her a second time. 'Tis enough for me to know she lives again. Take care of her, and speak to no one of this outside of these walls." He turned his gaze to Althena. "Ach, my sweet lass. You melted a part of my heart that had been frozen for sixteen years. Please forgive me for hurting you. I would never —"

Tears fell as she placed her fingers over his lips. "I know, Alex. I know. 'Tis enough for me that I have your love."

Finn's anger shocked Emma. The Irish knight she'd come to trust so well stood in her doorway and looked at her as if she were an aberration. His verbal assault on Alex made no sense either, until she overheard Keir's words and Stephen's angry responses. She hadn't realised, until that moment, exactly what Alex had done to drag her back across the mortal threshold. Stephen's mutterings of 'miracle' barely registered in her clouded mind.

She remembered standing in death's doorway, looking back to see Stephen's tears, an expression of disbelief on his face. All she'd wanted to do in her final moments was comfort her gentle knight, as he had comforted her. She'd felt helpless, even guilty, knowing she had to leave him behind.

Alex? She'd seen true fear in his eyes - an entity she couldn't recall ever seeing there before. It was a fear, she realised, born of bitter familiarity. Alex was well aware of what pain lay ahead for himself and Stephen.

Despite her faith in God, death had frightened Emma. Argante's last words haunted her even as her body weakened and her lungs struggled. What if he awaited her beyond that mysterious portal? What if he stood at the Devil's side, ready to commit his soul with hers to an eternal hell?

But her fears were unfounded, her faltering faith misguided.

For a few incredible moments she'd teetered on the brink of two worlds, one hand resting in Alex's warm grip, the other clasped in cool, gentle fingers as her mother pulled her into eternity.

Mama.

It had been no dream, then.

She swung her legs over the side of the bed and pushed herself up onto shaky legs. "Keir wait, please. I beg of you. You cannot —"

She stopped as a brilliant shard of light pierced her eyes, so brief she wondered if she'd imagined it. Bewildered, she looked down at her bloodstained chemise, her mind all at once engulfed by a cascade of words, as if someone had opened a book, shaken the pages, and tipped all the contents into her head.

She pressed her fingers against her temples. "Stop, please. I can't...I don't understand."

From the kitchen, she heard Stephen curse as the cottage door closed.

"*Cùra*," she whimpered, screwing up her eyes against the turmoil in her head. "Wait. I must speak with you."

She heard Althena's sobs and stumbled over to the doorway. "Stephen, please. You must stop them."

He was at her side in an instant, folding her in his arms. "I'm sorry, little one. He knew. Alex knew what would happen. But they'll not kill him. They can't. I'm sure they'll see reason."

She willed her mind to calm itself. "You're wrong. His life will be forfeit. We must go after him. We must stop this."

"How, pray tell?" Althena sobbed, her face pale and drawn. "Keir warned us not to follow them. We don't even know where they've taken him."

Emma opened her mouth to speak but paused, surprised by the sudden silence in her head.

"I know where they're taking him," she said, scowling at her bloodied clothes. "But I must change before we leave."

She turned to go into her room, but Stephen caught her arm. "Wait, Emma. How can you know that?"

A prickle ran over her skin. "I...I don't know. I mean, I don't know how I know. But I'm certain of it."

"Where are they taking him?" Althena's eyes were

wide with hope. "Where, Emma?"

"The circle." She frowned, still shocked to find herself entertaining knowledge that she had not previously known. "They're taking him to the circle."

Stephen sighed. "Aye, love. But we don't know where the Circle is."

"Nay, not that Circle," she said. "Please trust me, Stephen. I'll return in a few moments."

A mysterious but gentle warmth flooded her heart as she dressed, all but thawing out the chill of fear she'd felt at Alex's departure. Still, she knew fighting for Alex would not be easy. They had to defend his actions, present the Guardians with a worthy reason for her resurrection. Did she dare suggest that her life was worth contradicting God's will? And if they failed, how could she reconcile what Alex had sacrificed for her? They must not fail. They would not fail.

A memory touched her, the gentle voice of a woman dead these sixteen years, a voice she had heard that very morning.

That which you lost lies with my ring, Emma. 'Tis the proof he needs.

"What do you mean, Mama?" she asked. "I don't understand. What ring? Will it help our cause?"

There was no answer.

Emma blinked away hot tears and pulled on a pair of loose britches and a warm tunic, all the while thinking about her mother's words. She lifted her sword from its scabbard and ran her finger along the edges, satisfied with the sharpness as she re-sheathed it and buckled it around her hips. At the same time, a discomforting shadow settled itself around her.

Without hesitation, she unbuckled the sword and placed it on the bed.

"Very well," she whispered, obeying the silent voice

in her head. "If that's what you want. We go unarmed."

Stephen was pacing outside her door. He wrapped her in his arms as she stepped into the kitchen and held her tight.

"In answer to your request, I trust you completely," he said, kissing her forehead. "But tell me how you know of Alex's destination?"

Emma rested her head against his chest, taking comfort in the sound of his heartbeat. "In truth, my love, I cannot say precisely how I know. All at once I find myself aware of many things."

"But can you stop the Guardians, Emma?" Althena asked, her face still pale. "Do you think you can help Alex?"

"I intend to try. We need to convince them that what he did was justified, that somehow my death was not meant to be, but I don't think it will be easy. The Guardians are very angry. More than that, they feel betrayed."

"You sense all that, little faerie?" Stephen ran a thumb across her cheek.

"Aye." She smiled up at him. "I do. 'Tis perplexing, but I feel as if I'm part of them somehow - as if we're linked."

Stephen gave her a strange look. "Perhaps you are. Finn and Keir are already convinced there's something special about you, about your connection to Alex. To be truthful, I agree with them. There's more to this than we know. Perhaps you're even linked to what the Guardians are sworn to protect."

A revelation hovered on the periphery of her mind, a truth she could not quite grasp. A prickle ran across the back of her neck.

"What do you mean?"

He shrugged. "I witnessed a miracle this morning. 'Tis

beyond certain the stone has some kind of unearthly power. Why may we not assume that Alex was unknowingly enabled by that power when he visited your mother? Maybe it became a part of you when you were conceived."

"A part of me?" Emma clutched at Stephen's shirt, for it felt as if the ground moved beneath her. "But I've not sensed anything like this before. Why now?"

Stephen lifted her chin, fixing her with an intense gaze. "Sweetheart, the blessed thing just brought you back from the dead. It connected with you on a level beyond any mortal comprehension. Who knows? Perhaps it –"

"Knew me." Emma's knees buckled, her head swimming as the knowledge settled into her brain.

"Easy, love. You're still weak. " He swung her into his arms and settled her in a chair at the table. "We go nowhere until you eat and drink something."

"I understand so little of this," Althena said, with a sigh. "I know this stone is sacred, that Alex had charge of it, but I had no idea of its true worth. If you're indeed connected to it, what does that mean for Alex? And where is this circle you speak of? Is it far?"

Emma shook her head. "Not too far. And I don't know what any of this means exactly. If only..." Her mother's voice once again echoed through her mind. "That which you lost lies with my ring."

Stephen placed a cup of ale and bread in front of her. "That which who lost, little one?"

"'Tis something I heard when I was...with Mama this morning. She said 'that which you lost lies with my ring'. 'Tis the proof he needs.' But I don't know what she meant. What ring? It doesn't make sense."

Althena sat back, her expression thoughtful. "Alex told me he found a gold chain tucked into your blankets when he took you from the abbey. It had your mother's wedding ring on it. Could that be it?"

"Her wedding ring?" Emma tensed. "*Cùra* gave me a gold ring to wear the night Argante's men came to the house looking for you, Stephen. Remember? I pretended to be your wife, told them you were gravely ill to scare them away."

"'Tis perhaps that same ring, then," said Althena. "In the wee box on Alex's table?"

"Aye, that's the one." Emma's stomach clenched with anticipation. "Maybe there's an inscription on it. Some kind of message."

Stephen stood and held out his hand. "Let's find out."

The three of them went into Alex's room and approached the small wooden table sitting beneath the window. Sun lanced through a small hole in the shutters, forming a circle of light that sat atop the small box.

A sign, thought Emma, then silently chided herself for her fanciful ideas. She looked first at Stephen then at Althena, who nodded. "Open it."

The ring caught the sun's rays as Emma pushed the lid back. A fine delicate thing, it sat atop a piece of folded parchment. Emma picked it up and studied it in the patch of sunlight. It bore no marks, no inscription. Nothing.

She let out a sigh of disappointment.

"Perhaps it's the parchment," Stephen suggested. "Maybe there's a message on that."

Emma knew what the paper was, and shook her head. "'Tis merely a picture of Bart I drew when I was but four summers. I gave it to *Cùra* for his birthday that same year."

Stephen picked up the paper and opened it. "Aye, looks exactly like him." He smiled just as Emma gasped, her fingers closing tight around the ring.

"Sweet Mother of God. It can't be."

"What?" Stephen leaned over her, following her gaze.

"What is it?"

Emma could barely see for the tears filling her eyes. "Look." She reached into the box and pulled out a small gold brooch. "'Tis the brooch you gave me. The one I lost. But how did it get...? Oh, dear God." Dizzy, she leaned against him and his arm went around her. "Emma?"

"This proves it." She placed the brooch in her palm next to the ring. "Mama said 'that which you lost lies with the ring'. *Cùra* was truly with me on the roof at Thurston. The night I lost the brooch. It must have caught in his clothing or...or his cloak. Don't you see? He unknowingly brought it back here with him."

Stephen nodded. "'Twould seem to prove it, aye. I wonder, though, why he denied any memory of his journey to Yorkshire, yet did not question the sudden appearance of a strange piece of jewellery the following day. Did he say anything to you, Althena?"

She shook her head, frowning. "Nay, but I think I might know why. That was the morning Bart returned. Alex had gone outside to check on a noise coming from the barn. I was watching through the gap in the shutters, and knocked the box onto the floor. I picked everything up, including the brooch. As I recall, it was lying under the table. Perhaps it fell there when Alex returned during the night, but I just –"

"Assumed it had fallen from the box." Emma interrupted, her heart racing.

"So Alex never even saw it." Stephen finished. "Mystery solved. But will this be enough to help him?"

"I don't see how. Finn and Keir already believe he was at Thurston. This will only serve to prove that they were right." Emma's mind stumbled on an idea and her fist closed around the jewels. "But it helps me, and so might help him after all. We must go, Stephen."

Chapter 29

The winter sun cast long shadows of the two riders as they circled the wide base of Black Combe. A raw breeze whistled down the slopes, combing the amber coloured bracken and ruffling the grey patches of heather. Emma pulled her cloak tighter, tucking her chin into the woollen folds of her hood.

"We should have delayed our journey until you were more rested, little one." Stephen eyed her with concern. "You do not yet have your strength back."

"Actually, I feel stronger all the time," Emma assured him. " You needn't worry."

"Very well. But if you feel chilled, you must ride with me." Stephen edged his horse closer. "The breeze has a sharp bite."

Emma smiled, her eyes watering with the cold. "'Tis tempting to ride with you, my love, cold or not. For now I'm warm enough. I'll ride with you on the way back, when Alex will have need of my horse."

Stephen offered her a grim smile in return. "You're that confident we'll succeed?"

"I'll do whatever it takes." She glanced up at the sky. "I owe him that much."

"I can't believe I ride unarmed." Stephen patted his hip. "'Tis naked I am, without my sword."

"I know, but we must travel free of weapons or entry to the sacred realm will be denied. We'll be in no danger." She hoped. Truth was, she wasn't certain how the Guardians would react to uninvited visitors, armed or not.

By the time they reined in their horses on the crest of a hill, the sun had already sunk below the horizon and the last remnants of daylight were yielding to the night. The only sound, apart from the whisper of the breeze, was the occasional bleat of a solitary sheep calling out to its flock.

Below them, in the twilight of a small secluded vale,

sat a massive circle of ancient, moss covered stones. Emma's soul stirred, aroused by the mystical echoes of three thousand years.

This was a sacred place.

"They're here," she said, thinking out loud.

"Are you sure, little one?" Stephen murmured, his voice doubtful. "'Tis but an abandoned pagan monument. I see no sign of life."

"That's because you're a mortal." Emma smiled and urged her horse down the hill.

They dismounted and approached the stone circle in silence, ribbons of evening mist swirling about their feet. A black shape, silent and swift, dropped from the sky, wings outstretched. A crow. It settled on one of the stones and let out a ragged caw.

"Now I know Alex is nearby." Stephen squinted into the gathering dusk. "But where? What are we looking for?"

"Do you not hear them?" Emma brushed her fingers across the nearest stone. "Listen."

Stephen opened his mouth to answer, but paused, his eyes widening.

"I hear drums," he said. "Nay. Singing. And...laughter. Or is it weeping? Children's voices. My God, what is this, Emma? Some kind of magic?"

She smiled. "Of sorts. You're hearing the voices of those who have passed before us."

"Voices of the dead?"

"Oh, they're not dead. They're simply elsewhere." Emma glanced around the stones. "As are the Guardians."

"So how do we find them?"

Emma stepped toward a large stone at the north end of the circle. "We've already found them."

Stephen followed her. "Do they know we're here?"

She shook her head. "Nay. At least, I doubt it. They're

not expecting an intrusion. Especially not a mortal one."

She traced her forefinger around a single spiral carved into the stone, following what she knew to be the path of the Celts, a symbolic representation of the journey from outer consciousness to the inner soul.

Below it another much younger pattern had been carved into the granite - a line without end that twisted around to form an intricate knot.

The Gordian knot. The symbol of the Guardians.

She closed her eyes and flattened her palm against it. The pulse deep within the rock matched her heartbeat, and something stirred inside her, a connection stretching across millennia. Her skin prickled. She knew the sacred stone was nearby.

"'Tis the same design as that on the hilt of Alex's sword," Stephen murmured. "He told me about it. 'Twas the knot that could not be undone. The Gordian knot. The great king Alexander sliced it open with his sword."

Emma smiled and slipped her hand in his. "Do you feel it?"

He nodded. "Aye, little faerie. I feel it. A pulse, a heartbeat. 'Tis as if it comes from the earth itself."

"It does." She stood on tiptoes and pressed a kiss to his cheek. "Close your eyes, my love, and do not let go of my hand. Your little faerie is about to share her wings with you."

Emma closed her eyes and took a deep breath, emptying her mind of every thought and belief until she became as a newborn, pure of heart and utterly void of human influence. Then her soul took flight for the second time that day, soaring past mortal barriers, this time seeking not a heavenly realm, but an earthly one.

And, like Heaven, it was a realm invisible to most mortal men.

The ground seemed to fall away. For a brief moment,

Emma felt suspended in mid-air, with nothing but the wind in her face and the warmth of Stephen's hand in hers. The only sounds were their breathing and the deep steady pulse of the earth. Then she felt stone beneath her feet and Stephen's hand squeezing hers.

She opened her eyes and blinked away the darkness.

They were in a massive cavern. A pale light, gentle and soft as a midsummer dawn, emanated from the rugged walls, while the corners were steeped in shadow blacker than a winter's night. Several passageways led off here and there, stretching into darkness, yet Emma felt no fear.

Stephen placed a protective arm around Emma's waist. ""My God," he whispered. "Look at this place."

At the centre of the cavern stood a long rectangular table of black granite, and in the centre of that, an ornately carved golden cross. At its feet lay the sacred sword, free from its scabbard. The stone pulsated a steady blue light, matching the strange beat Emma felt beneath her.

This was not an evil place. On the contrary, she sensed only a benevolent force inhabiting these earthly bowels. Neither she nor Stephen would come to any harm. But would they prevail in their quest?

All at once, she heard a collective gasp echo off the ancient walls, and the familiar sound of a sword being drawn from the scabbard.

Keir flew from the shadows like a bird of prey, the light catching his naked blade as he strode toward them, his expression rigid with shock.

"Do you get the feeling we took them by surprise?" Stephen pulled Emma closer to him.

"Aye," she said. "I do."

"How in God's good name did you find us?" Keir asked, his voice edged with disbelief. "And how the hell did you enter here?"

"That," bellowed another deep, angry voice from the

shadows, "is what I should like to know."

"We are unarmed, my lord," said Emma. "We present no threat to you or your companions."

Keir lowered his blade, a muscle twitching in his jaw. "You will both answer for this intrusion."

Stephen's hand stiffened against Emma's waist. "There's no need to threaten us." He glanced at Emma. "As my lady has already indicated, we stand before you unarmed."

Emma smiled. "We would not have been allowed entry to this realm otherwise. Is that not so, my lord Keir?"

Keir frowned and looked behind him, as if seeking guidance from someone hidden in the shadows.

One by one, human shapes emerged from the darkness, eleven in all, forming a semi-circle around the table. These, Emma knew, were the Guardians, their allusive power infusing the air as they studied their mortal visitors with illuminated eyes. They meted out an impression of wolves stalking their prey, yet Emma felt unafraid and did not balk. Instead, she lifted her chin, pushed her shoulders back, and met their scrutiny head on. Her breath caught as she found and held Finn's gaze, unable to decipher the strange expression on his face. Keir sheathed his sword and moved to stand with him.

Emma's mind caught Stephen's unspoken question. "Aye," she murmured. "This is the Circle."

One of them stepped forward, his long hair white as frost, framing a wizened face, pale in contrast to his dark eyes. His tunic was emblazoned with the outline of a shield, split by a black chevron and graced with the silhouettes of three ravens.

"Who are these intruders? These interlopers?" he demanded, his words rolling around the cavern walls like thunder as he strode toward Emma, who recognized the angry voice as the one she'd heard earlier. "And one of them a mere maid, no less. How can this be? 'Tis a grievance against our order."

Emma stood her ground and inclined her head. "'Tis my honour to meet you, my lord Riderch. We mean no disrespect."

He gasped and stopped mid stride, his eyes widening.

"How do you know me, child?" he asked, his voice now bearing a hint of wonder.

Emma shrugged. "In truth, I cannot say how. But I do know you. You're Lord Riderch, ancient king of the Northmen, a revered elder of the Circle." She looked past him to the men at his back. "I know all of you. Every one."

A movement caught her eye, something off to her left. Another figure, who had been seated in shadow, arose from his seat and stepped into the light. His face was drawn with fatigue, yet it shone with pride and love when he looked at her.

Cùra.

Emma's heart missed a beat, her eyes burning with sudden tears. She let out a small cry and took a step forward, only to be stopped by a firm yet gentle hand.

"You will not approach him," said Riderch. "Not yet. I would know first how you came to be here, how you found us. Only a Guardian would know of this location. Indeed, only a Guardian would know how to enter this sacred place." He glanced at Stephen. "And this one is a mere infant among us, still unaware of all that we are. So you will tell us, young maid, how you know of our secrets. I pray this is not an additional transgression by the man who raised you. Has he betrayed us even further?"

Emma frowned and shook her head.

"Nay, my lord, he has not. Something occurred this morning, soon after I was...resurrected." She saw Riderch tense, his eyes narrowing. "I was visited by a light, brilliant like that of the sun. It brought with it many thousands of words that filled my head like grains of sand, overwhelming me. Since then, my mind has played host to information that was not there before. I cannot tell you why it happened. I only know that it did. Stephen and I came here of our own accord, using knowledge imparted to me by some unknown source." She looked at Alex. "This man has committed no transgression."

Riderch offered her a sad smile, his expression one of regret. "Oh, but he has, child. Alexander has committed the most serious transgression of all. I cannot imagine, therefore, what you hope to gain by this intrusion into our sanctuary."

What she hoped to gain? Had the centuries addled the man's brain?

"My lord Riderch, what I hope to gain by this intrusion is mercy." She looked over at Alex, her throat tight with emotion. "Mercy for the man who is my father."

Riderch shook his head. "'Tis not your place to speak for Alexander, my lady."

"Aye, it is," Emma replied, lifting her chin. "I am born of a Guardian's line, cognisant of the Circle and the laws which govern it. The sacred scrolls state I am entitled to put forth an argument for leniency, even absolution."

"Christ help us. First the lass enters our realm uninvited, and now she's quoting the sacred scrolls. What next?" Riderch's mouth twitched in apparent amusement. "Will you be taking up yon sword to challenge guardianship of the stone?"

"Of course not." Emma gritted her teeth, irritated by the Guardian's mocking tone. "All I ask, my lord, is an opportunity to defend my father's actions."

Riderch's amused expression changed to a grim smile.

"I hear what you ask, child, but as I understand it, Alexander has never acknowledged himself as your rightful sire. You are but his ward, not his blood kin in the true sense."

"But I am his. I know it. I've always known it." Emma glanced at Alex, who was watching her, and then turned her eyes to Finn. "My lord Finn, tell them, please, who I am. Tell them I have the right to speak."

Finn's expression did not change. "I'm no longer sure who you are, my lady."

Emma gasped, bewildered by his cold response. "What...what do you mean? We talked about this. You told me you believed I was Alex's child." She fingered the brooch pinned to her tunic. "Look! I found the brooch. Remember? The one I lost the night we left Yorkshire? It was at the house. *Cùra*...I mean...my father must have brought it back with him, perhaps tangled in his cloak. Don't you see? It proves he was on the roof at Thurston that night. And if he was at Thurston then surely my mother told the truth about –"

"Calm yourself," Riderch said, his voice stern. "I'm displeased by this breach of our sanctuary and the apparent ease with which you achieved it. It only adds to the disturbance within our order. We are still coming to terms with what has happened. Our most sacred law has been broken by a man we trusted - a man we held in the highest esteem. And since your life is the result of his transgression, some Guardians may find your presence here to be...offensive."

"Offensive?" Emma blinked. "I have no wish to offend anyone, my lord."

"No doubt. Still, propriety insists I dispatch you back to mortal ground without delay." Riderch studied her, his eyes flicking briefly to Stephen. "But my instinct, for a reason I've yet to fathom, tells me otherwise. Or perhaps it is my conscience that speaks. In any case, I see no harm in at least considering your request."

At his words, a murmur of what sounded like protest rippled through the Guardians. Riderch raised a hand, and the voices stilled. "So, the Circle will discuss your claim and advise you of our decision; a decision you will abide by without argument. In the meantime, you'll be made comfortable. Keir, please escort the lass to one of the ante-chambers."

Stephen took Emma's hand. "The lady does not go anywhere without me."

"Aye, she does. You'll stay here, lad," Riderch said, frowning at Stephen. "There are things we must ask of you. The lass won't be harmed."

Stephen shook his head. "I think not, my lord. I must go with Emma."

"It's alright, Stephen." Keir stepped forward. "She's in no danger. You have my word."

"Obey Lord Riderch, Emma. You too, lad."

Emma flinched as Alex's voice drifted across the cavern. God save him, he sounded so weary.

"I suggest you listen to him," said Riderch. "It would not be wise to test my patience further."

"Perhaps it would serve us better to do as they say, little one," Stephen murmured, bringing her hand to his lips. "Or at least, serve Alex better."

Emma sighed, troubled by a vague sense of defeat. "Aye, perhaps."

She followed Keir, aware of the scrutiny of the Guardians as she skirted the table. Finn regarded her with a solemn expression and then turned away. Her heart clenched, injured by his obvious snub.

Emma had come to care deeply for the gentle Irish knight. She loved his humour, admired his courage, and would be forever thankful for his chivalry. What, then, had changed? Did he blame her, somehow, for all that had happened?

She paused at his side. "You once said if I had need of you, I had only to speak your name," she whispered. "You lied to me, Finn."

He snapped his gaze back to her, eyes bright with anguish. "Forgive me, but I find that I...I cannot... "

Keir's hand circled her elbow. "Leave him, Emma."

"Nay." She tried to pull her arm free. "I must know why he –"

"Leave him." Keir's voice rose as his grip tightened. "Come with me. This way." He led her down one of the passageways, the darkness diluted as if lit by moonlight.

"I know the way," she retorted without thinking, and Keir turned dark, questioning eyes upon her.

She sighed. "I spoke the truth earlier, my lord. I swear I don't know where this knowledge comes from."

"I'm certain it will be investigated," he said, and steered Emma into a small, dimly lit chamber. "Wait here until one of us comes to fetch you."

"How long might that be?"

Keir shrugged. "I cannot say. A while, I should think. The Guardians, especially the elders, do not hurry their discourse. And we have much to consider."

As do I, she thought, glancing around the sparse chamber.

"Please, Keir, tell me what ails Finn. Why does he deny me?"

Keir gave her a sad smile. "Finn's heart is clashing with his faith. For all his jesting and lighthearted banter, he's a man who holds fast to his beliefs and will not compromise his convictions. Alexander's actions have wounded him greatly. He believes you've been reborn without a God-given soul. His loyalty is torn, his heart broken. I swear I've never seen him so disturbed."

Shock twisted her stomach. "Finn believes me to be without a soul?"

"Nay, not without a soul, but a soul reclaimed without God's blessing. There are several in the Circle who share this belief. Because of it, they may find your presence here to be – "

"Offensive," she murmured, remembering Riderch's words. "Do you share that belief, Keir?"

"Nay, my lady. I don't agree with what Alexander has done, but I don't believe God has condemned you because of it."

His words calmed her a little. Hope would be lost if all the Guardians considered her as Finn did. Still, the loss of his friendship sat heavy on her heart, and she swallowed against a sob as she spoke.

"Will you speak for Alex? Help me to help him?"

"You can't ask that of me, Emma." Keir sighed. "Please understand. Alexander knew full well what he was doing and the consequences of it. Our vows are taken very seriously."

"I know. Forgive me. But do you believe there's at least a chance I can save him?" She watched Keir's face, needing to see a hint of hope. It did not appear.

"You have not yet been given permission to speak for him." He traced his fingers down her cheek. "And since you claim to have knowledge of all that we are, you must already know the answer to your question." He turned to leave, pausing in the doorway. "For what it's worth, my lady, I do believe you to be the daughter of Alexander. May God have mercy on you both."

Emma wiped away an errant tear. Keir was right. She already knew all the answers. Only a miracle would save Alex. Exhausted, she sank onto a fur-draped ledge, dropped her head into her hands, and offered up a desperate prayer.

She lost the fight against fatigue and slipped into sleep. Even there, peace eluded her, her dreams haunted by dark images, their features unclear, their words incomprehensible. Then, out of the midst of her torment, a shadow stepped forward. It was a man, his features blurred but familiar. He spoke, his voice distant as if far away, yet comforting and also familiar.

"*The past is before us but they do not yet see it.*"

"*Who are you?*"

"*You will know me as I know you. Have faith, child.*"

A shadow loomed over her and touched her hair. She screamed and lashed out, only to feel hands grasping her wrists.

"Nay," she cried, struggling against whoever held her. "Let me go."

A pair of arms gathered her up and soft kisses rained down on her face. "Easy, sweetheart. Open your eyes."

This voice she knew too. This voice she loved. "Oh, Stephen. Thank God. I thought...I thought you were –"

"Hush. I know. You were dreaming. You've been asleep for hours."

She tensed in his arms. "Hours? Why didn't someone wake me? Have the Guardians come to a decision? Will they let me speak?"

"I don't know yet, love." He stroked her hair back from her face. "Keir came to fetch you earlier, saw you were asleep and thought you should rest a little longer. They've agreed to let you see Alex."

Emma heard something in his voice. "What is it, Stephen? Is something wrong?"

"You must speak with Alex. He'll tell you more."

A weight settled on her shoulders, one that had not been there before. It slowed her steps as she went to see the man who had chosen to sacrifice his life that she might live.

She found him pacing in a similar chamber to her own. He stopped and looked at her when she appeared in the doorway, love filling his eyes.

"*A ghràidh.*" Surely, Finn was mistaken, for no God-forsaken soul could ever feel as hers did at that moment. She ran to him and threw herself into his arms.

"*M'athair,*" she whispered in the language of their ancestors, listening to the thud of his heart against her ear. "My most beloved father. Do you see the truth now? Do you know who I am? Please say you believe it."

"With all my heart, child. I've been blind and foolish. Please forgive me."

"When did you know? When, *Athair*?"

She felt the caress of a teardrop on her hair.

"Sit with me, daughter, here at my side. There's much to say." He sank onto the furs and she settled herself by him, sharing in his tears as he acknowledged what she was to him. "I shall convince the Circle to pardon you, " she said. "You've done no wrong."

He cocked his head and smiled at her, tucking a strand of loose hair behind her ear. "Look at you. 'Tis such a sight you are. Did you crawl backwards through the brambles to get here?"

The weight on her shoulders lifted a little, eased by Alex's teasing. She smiled back.

"I would crawl backwards through hell to save you, *Athair.*"

Alex took a long deep breath and closed his eyes for a moment. "The very first time I saw you at the abbey."

Emma frowned. "What of it?"

"That's when I knew you were mine. You reached out and, without uttering a word, told me who I was, but in my grief I chose to ignore it. 'Twas easier to blame your poor mother and Edward than to admit I'd made a terrible mistake. What I had done was unbearable, unthinkable, so I convinced myself you were Edward's child, that Alicia had betrayed me in the worst way. A man comes to believe a lie if he lives with it long enough. But truth never dies. It merely waits for the right moment to present itself again. Nor does the passage of time ease the pain of it, little one."

"But Mama understands, *Athair*. She told me she has forgiven you."

Alex sighed. "Do you forgive me, Emma?"

"You know I do. You must tell the Circle your story, tell them how you have borne the weight of your conscience all these years. Tell them you could not bear to lose me, as I intend to tell them I cannot bear to lose you. They'll understand, *Athair*. I know they will."

She nodded at him, trying to encourage his agreement, ignoring the sadness in his eyes and the sudden twinge of pain under her ribs.

He took her hand in his. "I've already spoken with the Circle, Emma. No matter what you plan to tell them, I think you must still prepare yourself."

"Prepare myself for what? How...when did you speak with them? Surely they haven't come to a decision. They've yet to hear me."

"And they will hear you, but do not expect too much from them." He ran his thumb along the back of her hand. "I knew what I was doing when I brought you back from death's grip, *a ghràidh*. I understand and accept the consequences of my actions. I must ask you to do the same."

"I shall never accept them," Emma declared. "Never."

Where was his resolve? His fight? How could he accept defeat so easily? She sat back and studied him, noting the fatigue on his face, the peppering of stubble on his chin, the silver threads winding through his dark hair. She touched her fingers to a vein pulsing in his throat.

"What is it, *Athair*?" she asked. "What has driven you to surrender? Do you believe as the other Guardians do? That in bringing me back you have gone against God's will?"

"Nay," he replied. "My conscience is heavy, but not with my decision to bring you back. I would do the same again."

"Then what is it?"

Alex rose to his feet. " I'm haunted by a truth I refused to see. I accused an innocent man, killed him needlessly, and your mother died because of me. Who can live in peace with such a burden?"

Emma stood and faced him, a flush of anger warming her skin. "A burden? You speak to me of burdens? Then please, allow me to share mine. My mother did not die because of *you.* Nay. My mother sacrificed her life because of *me.* And now, it seems, you wish to do the same. 'Tis surely a truth which claws deeply at my own conscience." Her voice trembled as she placed her hand on his chest, over his heart. "Please tell me my father does not wallow in self-pity. If so, then I reject him and ask that my *Cùra* be returned to me, the Guardian of the stone, the man who raised me. I pray that man is still here, that he'll not abandon us without a fight. If he's weary, he can lean on me and on Stephen. But he can never give up. Not while the stars still shine."

It was as if time paused, waiting to see if Emma's words would have any effect on her father's despondent soul. After a few moments of silence, Alex took a deep breath, blinked away his tears and placed his hand over hers. "Forgive me, little one. I forgot."

Emma frowned. "Forgot?"

"Aye." He smiled and gestured to the rugged ceiling.

"I forgot to look up."

Chapter 30

The soft light in the cavern picked out small crystals embedded in the black granite surface of the table. Emma had an impression of looking down on a reflection of the night sky splashed across a moonlit lake. At the centre stood the gold cross, glowing as if aflame, casting a halo around the sword, which lay with the tip of the blade pointing toward her. The silver hilt was dormant, showing no indication of what lay within. A ruse, Emma knew, since she could feel the soft steady pulse of the sacred stone, like the heartbeat of a sleeping child.

A heavenly child, who had given Emma life after a demon had taken it away.

The Guardians sat in silence, studying her. Earlier, Stephen had insisted he be allowed to stand with her when she faced them. He had challenged their adamant refusal and confronted Keir, who stayed calm, swearing Emma would come to no harm.

"I'm not afraid, Stephen," she assured him as she left his side.

But she was afraid. Her thudding heart said as much. The Guardians were intimidating - steeped in tradition, discipline and ancient wisdom. They had lived long, travelled through time and history united in their quest to manage and control an unearthly artifact. Because she possessed their knowledge, she understood their commitment, their sacrifice, and despite everything, applauded it.

She knew how important their vows were, how strictly they adhered to their laws. And she, better than any other, knew the reasons why. The stone carried a power that could never be allowed to fall into ignorant hands.

The Guardians were not only keepers of the stone, but also protectors of mankind.

Alex's actions had fractured the Circle's unity. They

had trusted him without question and he had betrayed them. She knew their anger was no less profound than their sadness.

Riderch's voice startled her. "We have heard Alexander. He has not denied or tried to excuse his actions, and has confessed to acting with full and complete awareness of the consequences. As decreed in our sacred scrolls, his life is, therefore, forfeit. Unless, of course, you can offer a defence that might counter that judgement."

Emma took a slow breath. "Nay," she said. "I cannot."

A murmur ran around the table and she saw Keir's eyes widen.

"I don't understand." Riderch leaned forward. "If you have no defence to offer, child, then why are you here?"

"I'm here to ask for mercy, my lord, for in trying to defend my father's action, I would also be upholding my right to life. Since some of you believe me to be an abomination - a living blasphemy - upholding that right may further insult your beliefs." She looked at Finn and saw him close his eyes. "So I will not attempt to justify my existence, even though I believe my soul to be as it always was. Nor will I condone what my father did. Indeed, if my life means his death, then I do gladly offer myself in his place."

Riderch sighed. "We expected you to say that, lass. 'Tis a noble gesture, but not one we will consider."

Emma nodded. "As I thought. So all I can do is ask for mercy. Please, my lords, I beg of you. Spare Alexander's life. Cast him from the Circle if you must. Deny him the stone, deny him your friendship, but don't deny him what is left of his mortal time on this earth. My father is a good man, a kind man. His heart is true, his soul pure. He has people who love him, who will mourn him for the rest of their days if you take him —"

A curse echoed off the walls as Finn rose to his feet. He stared at her for a moment, his expression tight with emotion before he turned away and strode from the chamber.

Although he had no way of knowing it, he also took much of Emma's resolve with him.

Did her presence offend him so much that he could not stand to be in the same room with her? And what of the other Guardians who were of like mind? Were her pleas falling on prejudicial ears? Even Keir, she noticed, had lowered his gaze. Despair weighed on her as she struggled to keep from dissolving into tears.

"I beg of you," she gasped, gripping the edge of the table. "Set your opinions of me aside and think of what you do here. You can't kill my fa...Alexander. You can't. He doesn't deserve to die."

A vibration ran through the earth, slight, but unmistakable. Emma frowned and looked at the ground, her attention pulled back to the table as the sword jumped, sliding fully an arm's length across the granite. Then it pivoted on its hilt, turning in a frantic circle, the steel flashing with reflected light from the cross. Moments later it stopped, seemingly halted by an unseen hand, the tip of the blade pointing directly at Riderch.
The hilt, glowing as red as a Blacksmith's forge, clattered against the granite as if something within strained to escape. Emma held her breath, consumed by a sudden surge of incredible energy, her emotions twisting with anger and fear.

A wave of tension, as apparent as a moving shadow, rippled through the Guardians.

"Your request for mercy will be considered," said Riderch rising to his feet, face pale, eyes fixed on the sword. "We will let you know of our decision. Keir, see to the lass. I want her out of here. Now."

Emma followed Keir in stunned silence, her mind a tangle of emotions. She made it as far as the passageway before the strange sensations vanished, leaving behind a dark sense of dread. Unwilling to face Alex or Stephen, she leant against the wall, dropped her head in her hands and wept.

"Don't despair, my lady," Keir whispered, placing a hand on her shoulder. "'Tis not over yet."

"But it is, my lord," she answered, feeling chilled to her core. "I've failed, I know it. Did you see Finn's response? He hates me, and how many more of the Guardians feel the same? I sensed their reaction, the tension they shared. My pleas were wasted, resented even."

"Nay, little one. As Riderch said, your pleas will be considered, and I can tell you they will be considered without bias. As for Finn's response, you misunderstood. None of the Guardians are capable of hate, Finn least of all. I told you, he's conflicted, his conscience is in turmoil. He left only because he could not bear to see your torment." Keir gave a wry smile. "And our reaction was because of the way you connected with the stone. It was very impressive, considering it was surrounded by eleven of us. You breached our defences with apparent ease. That's why Riderch wanted you out of there. You felt its power, didn't you? Did you know what you were doing?"

Emma pressed her fingers to her temples, rubbing at a slight throb of pain. "Aye, I felt it, but I believe you're mistaken. I didn't connect with the stone. The stone connected with me."

"At last." Stephen went to Emma's side when she stepped through the doorway. He embraced her with the warmth of his lips and a gentle touch of his mind. She knew he sensed her fear.

"Stephen," she whispered, finding some comfort in speaking his name.

Alex, who had been sitting on the fur-covered ledge, rose to his feet.

"Good, you're returned. Come and sit by me, little one. There are things that must be said."

"Keir assures me the Guardians will consider my plea," Emma told him. "But my heart is heavy, for I fear I've failed you, *Athair*."

Alex smiled, sat down again, and patted the space next to him. "You haven't failed me, *a ghràidh*. Not in this, nor anything else. Sit, please. You too, Stephen."

Weary beyond words, Emma flopped down and rested her head against Alex's shoulder, looping her arm through his. She leaned into his warmth, breathed his scent, and absorbed every measure of his essence, sickened by thoughts of losing him.

"Perhaps they will simply deny you the stone and send you home with us," she said.

"Perhaps," he murmured. "But in case they do not –"

"They must." She kissed his cheek, fighting tears. "They must."

"But in case they do not," Alex repeated, slipping his arm around her, "there are things I would ask of you."

"What things?" Stephen asked, settling himself beside Emma. "What do you want us to do?"

"First of all, lad, I want you to continue training with the Circle." Alex leaned forward to look at Stephen. "Riderch tells me you refuse to cooperate unless they show leniency toward me. Such threats serve no purpose. I want you to reconsider, no matter the outcome of this tribunal. 'Tis a special gift you have and it must not be wasted. Keir is willing to spend time with you in my place, if necessary."

Stephen gave him a look of disbelief. "You surely jest. If they do carry out this...this merciless punishment, they can't expect me to continue as if nothing has happened."

Alex shook his head. "I bear the Circle no ill will, and neither should you. They abide by the ancient laws and rightly so. I expect nothing less from them, which is why my fate cannot be allowed to influence your destiny. It would do me a great honour if you took Guardianship of the stone. You should not turn away from it, young knight. It gave Emma back to you."

Stephen sighed. "My prayer is to see the stone resting at your side once more, Alex. But I shall think on what you say."

"Good. Remember, the Guardians do not act out of malice," said Alex. "There's not one among them who takes pleasure in these proceedings against me."

"Perhaps not, but a law should not be so rigid as to deny any hope of mercy," Emma murmured, shivering at a sudden image of her father dying by the sword. Of course, she knew the ritual, knew the blade promised a swift death. But it was a bitter promise, bereft of any comfort.

"Should my life be forfeit, there's something else I would ask of you. I want you to visit my father. He must be informed of what has happened. Tell him...tell him he was right about Alicia and about Emma." Alex pressed his lips to Emma's hair. "Tell him I'm deeply sorry for doubting him, and that I never stopped loving him."

Stephen nodded. "Of course."

Emma closed her eyes against a fresh burn of tears. "My beloved father," she whispered, snuggling against his chest to listen to his heart. "Please keep faith. We're not yet defeated."

How long had they been in this strange realm, she

wondered? She couldn't be sure, for there was nothing to indicate the passing of day and night. They had snatched at sleep here and there, shared simple meals with little cheer. Time had no real meaning for the Guardians, but for Emma it was like a hidden wound, bleeding away the hours until Alex's judgement. Nothing could stem the dreadful flow.

Later, when she looked up to see Keir in the doorway, something twisted inside her and a prickle of anxiety ran across her skin. Alex rose to his feet and she reached for his hand, stepping close to his side.

"If you're afraid, child," he murmured, lifting her fingers to his lips, "you should stay here."

"Are you afraid?" she asked, searching his face for any sign of fear, knowing even a hint of it would push her to her knees. Her strength was at the mercy of his.

He shook his head, his expression calm. "Not at all."

"The Circle awaits," said Keir, his voice quiet, his gaze fixed on Alex.

Emma squeezed his hand. "I'm staying with you, *Athair*."

A hush descended as they arrived in the main chamber. The light was subdued, shimmering across the cavern walls like moonlight on water. The Guardians were seated, the sword resting next to the cross as before. Keir bade Emma and Stephen wait at the edge of the shadows while Alex took his place at the foot of the table.

They wasted no time. Riderch stood, his expression impassive, although his voice faltered when he spoke.

"The Circle deliberated long and hard before arriving at its final decision. It has been, to say the least, a most...distressing process. Indeed, this is the closest we've ever come to a breakdown in our order."

He paused, his jaw clenched. Emma heard the vibration of silver on granite as the stone reacted to his obvious battle with emotion. She looked around the table, seeking clues in the faces of the Guardians, but each had their eyes focused on the sword, their expressions unreadable. Her fingers dug into Stephen's arm as Riderch continued.

"But we were reminded that the law must be reasoned free of passion. We cannot allow our passion, or the passion of others, to blur the truth. And the truth persists. The power we so fiercely guard has been abused. God's will has been usurped and the balance of life and death disturbed. The ancient writings are quite clear in their demand for retribution. He who uses the stone's power to restore life to a departed soul will forfeit his own. Alexander has confessed and offered no defence. Therefore, we are left with no choice but to pass a judgement of death upon –"

"Nay!" Emma cried, clutching at Stephen, her legs buckling. "Tell me, in the name of God and all His saints, how this can be right? He's my father. You can't kill him. Please, just...just let me take him home. We'll live out the rest of our days in peace and never bother you again, nor speak of the stone to anyone. I swear it upon my life. Please let him go. Dear God, I beg of you, please."

Stephen folded his arms around Emma and spat out his disgust at Riderch. "'Tis a merciless decision."

Riderch sighed. "Believe me, we share your distress, but the law is clear. Alexander knows and accepts it."

"Your laws are too harsh." Emma's stomach lurched as she fought a wave of dizziness. "My father doesn't deserve to die. You can't take him from me."

Riderch's gaze snapped to the table as the sword rattled, bumping against the cross. He nodded to one of the Guardians, who reached across and grasped the hilt.

"Stephen." Alex's voice was hoarse with emotion. "Get the lass out of here."

"Nay, I shall not leave you, *Athair*." Emma coughed on a sob and tried to free herself from Stephen's arms. "I shall not leave here unless you're with me, warm and well at my side. Let me go to him, Stephen, please."

He looked at Alex. "I'll not force her to leave you," he said, releasing her.

Half blinded by tears, she started around the table toward her father, but Riderch stepped into her path.

"Please stop this, my lady," he said, not unkindly, taking hold of her arm. "It will not change anything. The decision has been made."

"Decision?" Fury replaced fear as she turned to face the Guardians. "There was only ever one decision lurking in your wretched minds. Most of you, I am certain, never even considered an alternative. You judge me to be without a God-given soul, but it is your souls which lack God's blessing, for they are as cold as the granite before you and as equally unyielding."

A voice drifted out of the shadows. "The wee lass makes some very valid points. Take your hands off her, Guardian."

Emma caught her breath as a vague memory stirred from its resting place.

Dear God, she knew that voice. It had spoken to her in the distant past and more recently...where? In her dreams? Was she dreaming now?

Nay, she was not, for the shadows moved aside and a man stepped forward. He was tall, with an aged but handsome face and strange opaque eyes that watched her from below a thick mass of white curls. Beneath his fur-lined cloak, she saw a golden lion emblazoned across his black tunic. In contrast to his fine clothes, a crude wooden cross hung from his belt, as did a string of worn wooden prayer beads.

Emma had seen him before. But where?

Without exception, the Guardians rose to their feet, a collective murmur of shock filling the air.

"Did you not hear me, Riderch?" he demanded, a soft Highland lilt edging his words. "We are avowed to protect the weak, not bully them. If there's a single bruise anywhere on her skin, you'll answer for it."

The weak? Still furious, Emma pushed herself away from Riderch and faced the visitor.

"I am not weak, sir," she said, glaring at him, trying to figure out why he was so familiar.

The man's lips twitched with the beginnings of a smile. "Ach, 'tis true you're strong of heart like your father, but you're still a scrawny wee bairn, even after all these years. Did you not feed her properly, Alexander? Come here, child. Stand at my side so I might see you better. These eyes of mine do not work as well as they once did."

That voice.

"The past is before us but they do not see it...have faith, child."

She touched her fingers to her temple. "I've heard you in my dreams. But how...?"

He nodded, smiling as if he had a secret to tell.

The memory surfaced from the depths and Emma's heart clenched. She saw him as a younger man with only hints of silver in his curls, his eyes not yet clouded by time. He was leaning over her crib, crooning to her, his gentle voice mixing with her feeble cries. And she saw her mother, weeping in his arms.

"Mama," she murmured, stepping over to his side. "You knew Mama."

A slight frown settled on his face. "Aye, I knew your mother well, may God rest her soul. I never thought I'd look into her beautiful eyes again, yet here I am looking into them. You're exactly as I remember her, and it gladdens my heart to see you." He looked at Alex, his expression softening. "And I know your father. It gladdens my heart to see him too, although it has been many years since we've spoken."

"But who are you?" Emma peered up at him. "How do you know me?"

"I was with your mother the day you were born, little one. My name is Francis Mathanach." He touched his fingers to her cheek. "I'm your grandfather."

"My...?"

She spun round, seeking affirmation from Alex. He gave a slight nod, his face etched with emotion. At the same time something sparked in her mind, startling her with its truth. She turned back to Francis, her heart racing.

"It's you, isn't it? In my dreams and in my thoughts? All that I know, the sacred knowledge. It came from you, didn't it?"

"Aye, I shared our secrets with you," he replied, throwing a defiant glance at the Guardians. "I knew how swiftly the Circle would respond to your father's actions. I needed something to delay their judgement until I arrived. You did well, child."

Emma shook her head, fear for her father's life surfacing anew. "But I've failed, my lord. You heard them. It's too late."

"I think not. And please, call me 'grandfather'." He smiled and tugged on a strand of her hair. " Or '*Seanair*' if you'd like me to truly spoil you."

Riderch cleared his throat. "Your return to our order can only be deemed an honour, Francis, although it's regretful you're here under such sad circumstances. But the lass is correct. A judgement has been made."

Francis shrugged. "I intend to challenge it."

"There's nothing to challenge," Riderch replied.

"Alexander has confessed."

"Christ, Riderch. I'm not here to dispute what he did." Francis cast his gaze around the Circle. "I'm here to open your eyes to the injustice of your decision, for you're all blind to the truth."

"Which is?" Keir asked. "None of us desire Alexander's death. If you can give us a valid reason to stay his execution, 'twould be an answer to my prayers."

A murmur of agreement wandered around the table.

"How did you know to come here?" Alex asked. "How did you know what I had done?"

Francis paused as if choosing the manner of his response, emotion evident in the deep rise and fall of his chest. Emma understood his reaction and blinked back tears. She knew he was about to speak to his son for the first time in over sixteen years.

"As you well know, Alexander, the bond between parent and child is a powerful thing," he said at last. "Especially when forged by a love which knows no boundaries. I never told you this, but I knew the moment Alicia died. I heard your soul's lament, felt your pain and wept for your suffering. Four days ago, while immersed in prayer, I heard it again. Only this time it was worse. This time I knew the blow was a fatal one for your spirit, inflicted by that most unjust of all fates; the death of a child. I knew Emma had died because I felt..." His voice faltered and his hand drifted to the cross hanging from his belt. "I felt the absolute surrender of your faith. And I understood it, my son. Believe me, I understood it completely, for I also know what it is to lose a child."

Emma slipping her hand into his, swallowing against a lump in her throat. He squeezed her fingers and gave her a smile.

"Besides, I carried yon sword at my side for many years," he continued, gesturing to the table. "The link to the stone is still with me, so I knew you'd used its power to bring her back, and I willingly confess to offering up a hearty prayer of thanks." He turned to the Circle. "Resurrecting this child was not an affront. It was an atonement. I pray I can make you understand that."

"There's naught I want more than to understand why Alexander thought it was right to do what he did." The gentle Irish voice echoed across the chamber. "God knows, I'm beyond weary of questioning my own beliefs."

Emma's head snapped up as Finn spoke. He was watching her, his expression wrought with misery. A twinge of sorrow fluttered beneath her ribs and she lowered her eyes, reluctant to see the sadness in his. Francis squeezed her hand again.

"I know what some of you believe about the wee lass," he said. "So, as someone who has spent sixteen years in God's service, let me tell you this. For the past four days, I've shared Emma's thoughts and walked in her dreams. I've felt her pain, her fear, and her courage. I'm aware of all the torment she's endured, before and since her resurrection. But above all this, I've been conscious of the love she has for those fortunate enough to share her life. My granddaughter is utterly selfless. I have no doubt about the purity of her soul, nor the strength of her spirit."

"I agree the lass has spirit," said Riderch. "But she shouldn't be here, Francis. The balance has been disturbed. There must be a reckoning."

"A reckoning," Francis repeated, his lips thinning into a hard line. "Aye, a reckoning indeed."

Hope fluttered in Emma's heart. She looked at her father and dared to imagine that they might yet endure. He met her gaze, and gave a slight shrug. Francis released Emma's hand and started pacing.

"How old are you, Riderch?" he asked.

Riderch frowned. "Why do you ask?"

"I would like you to consider your own situation before you make another claim that my granddaughter should not be here."

"Oh nay, my friend. You cannot make that comparison. Our longevity comes from years of exposure to the stone's power, but if one of us should die, then so be it."

Francis stopped pacing and regarded Riderch with a steady gaze. "Nonetheless, you must concede that the stone's influence releases us from mortal bonds."

"Aye, I'll grant you that, but the influence is residual. We are not deliberately going against God's will. If this is the basis of your argument, Francis, I fear you're wasting your breath."

"Nay. I merely resent your belief that my granddaughter should not be here when most of you have already spent several lifetimes on this earth. How dare you suggest she's undeserving of life! You misjudge my son and misjudge his child. Aye, and the real culprit is among us, yet you have ignored its part in this saga, other than to watch it dance on the table whenever the wee lass speaks."

Riderch's eyes narrowed as they flicked to the sword. "The real culprit?"

Francis nodded, an impassioned breath tearing from his lungs. He studied Alex for a few moments before shifting his gaze to Emma. She shivered under his scrutiny - not from fear - but from the intensity of the emotion she saw in his eyes.

"Legends in the making," he murmured, as if thinking out loud. "'Tis both tragic and beautiful, the story of their lives, a story still unfolding."

Francis turned to face the Guardians, straightened his spine, and lifted his chin.

"You ask for a reckoning. Very well. Let us tally up and see who owes what to whom. As you know, Alexander took possession of the stone with the Circle's full approval, but against my better judgement. I felt he needed more time, more training. He proved me wrong. From the start, his own powers meshed with what lies within that wretched hilt. Perhaps that's why he learned to control the stone so quickly. They each share an unearthly magic. I wonder, though, if he might have rejected the honoured role of Guardian had he known the price to be exacted."

He stepped toward the table and stroked his fingers across the smooth black surface. The sword's hilt took on a soft glow.

"It demands much, this stone that fell from the sky. Its power invades a man's soul, steals his heart, plunders his mind."

He snatched a deep breath and looked at Alexander.

"God knows, it has taken so much more from my son. It stole the life of his wife and his best friend. It kidnapped and raped his child and came close to killing the woman he now loves. It even tried to kill his horse. You must concede that none of these things would have occurred had Alex not vowed to safeguard mankind against a celestial beast we can never fully tame. Are you keeping score, Riderch? Are you, Finn? Is your perception of balance changing at all?"

Riderch shifted on his feet and looked at the ground.

Torn by the expression of utter pain on her father's face, Emma let out a sob. The sword rattled as Francis turned to her and parted with a soft curse. "Forgive me, little one. This will not be easy, but I must —"

"Wait." Stephen stepped out of the shadows, went to Emma's side and pulled her into the refuge of his arms.

"Thank you," she whispered, shivering as she leaned

into his warmth.

Stephen nodded to Francis. "Pray continue, my lord."

Francis returned the nod and faced the Guardians again. "My son loved his wife beyond measure, yet he watched her die even though the power to bring her back lay well within his reach. He kept faith and held true to his vow, but it tore open a wound that to this day has never healed. Seeking solace, he took the child and disappeared into this northern wilderness where they could live in relative peace."

Francis paused and looked briefly at Emma.

"But it didn't last. Strange to think Alexander held such power in his hands, yet he failed to protect that most precious of his possessions. In truth, the stone was the catalyst in the desecration of Emma's innocence, for it was the stone that brought Argante to these hills. The results of his vicious assault and slander hammered a wedge between father and child. Something precious was lost, or at least damaged forever. Yet it would appear, at least on the surface, that Alexander remained strong and kept his faith. Indeed, he asked for your help, and you gave it. You allowed him to use the shield so he could watch over Emma while she was in Yorkshire. But evil intervened again in the shape of Argante. I'm sure I don't need to remind you what pulled him back to Cumbria. Are you beginning to see a pattern here?"

He let out a deep breath, bowed his head, and rested both hands, palms down, on the table. Emma blinked away tears and looked at the Guardians. Several had their heads bowed too, as if in prayer. The rest were watching Francis with obvious intensity.

"Perhaps you should rest, my lord," said Keir, his voice soft. "No doubt your journey was arduous. I warrant we all wish to hear you out, but if you're fatigued, we can wait until such time –"

"Nay. This will be finished today, and soon." He straightened. "It was around this time that a miracle took place high up on the roof of Thurston. Although he has no memory of it, Alex appeared to Emma and pulled her back from the jagged edge of her life. Perhaps the stone enabled him to go to his child, or perhaps the unique bond they share inspired it. In any case, Finn brought the wee lass safely home to Cumbria with Argante's seed growing in her belly. But again Alexander failed to protect her. Argante captured her with no —"

"Nay," Emma cried, for she had seen Alex's head drop in a gesture of despair. "Please, *Seanair*, stop. You're torturing him. My father has never failed me. Never. There was evil magic at work. Argante had changed somehow, become something other than human. He blended into the forest as a leaf might rest unnoticed on the ground, his presence hidden from us all. It was not my father's fault. It was not."

"Ask your father if he believes he failed you," said Francis, his expression hard. "'Tis his conscience which tortures him, lass, not I. I warned you this would not be easy."

He turned back to the Circle.

"I saw Argante's face in Emma's dreams. 'Twas indeed a countenance from hell, something vile and utterly evil. The bastard meant to kill her and himself. He wanted Alexander to find their lifeless bodies side by side. What on this earth, I wonder, could motivate one man to harbour such hatred for another? Even as he died, Argante threatened to take Emma across the eternal threshold with him. Ponder that threat, if you will."

A shadow of pain crossed his face.

"The little lass bled to death. 'Twas neither a swift nor merciful end to her young life. She died in Stephen's arms, holding her father's hand. The last thing she saw...was...ah, Christ help me...I cannot..."

Emma fought to speak over the lump in her throat as she continued for her grandfather. "The last thing I saw was fear in my father's eyes," she said. "He said he was afraid to lose me, because he loved me so much. I...I promised I would always be with him just before I –"

"The past does not stay in the past," Francis interrupted, his eyes on Emma. "It circles around to greet us as we step into the future. I once told my son he was blind to the truth. It took Emma's death for him to admit that she was truly his. He also realised what her death would mean for that young knight at her side, so he used the stone and brought the wee lass back. Nay, he took her back, and it was a selfless act, since he knew his life would be forfeit. You speak of balance? Ach, I feel the scales are tipped well in favour of that damned stone at the moment."

He lifted the wooden cross to his lips and kissed it.

"My sight is not what it was, but I still see miracles. Aye, there's one standing right over there with her mother's bonny eyes and her father's courageous heart. 'Tis a blessed wee soul she is, born of the stone and resurrected by it. Who knows what power she possesses? 'Twould be a sin to injure such a precious spirit."

Francis closed his eyes for a moment, his fingers playing along the string of worn wooden prayer beads hanging from his belt.

"My son confessed to breaking our most sacred law, but his action was not one of malice, nor was it intended to do harm. He was not seeking to demonstrate his power over a weaker soul, nor attempting to assert his strength against God's will. When Emma died, Alexander couldn't see beyond the next moment. Is it any wonder? Grief blinded him to everything other than his sorrow. Consider what had already been ripped from him before that terrible morning, then ask yourselves if you could suffer as he did without casting the stone aside and relinquishing your vows."

He gave a grim smile.

"But despite all these sacrifices, it seems my son has not yet given us enough of himself. Nay. There is one more thing you demand from him, that being his own precious life. Just like all the other lives he has lost, it will be surrendered in the name of this celestial relic we protect. If you choose to dispatch his soul, you will set an example and create a future for this sacred Circle of which I want no part, for it is not God's will that Alexander must die. It is yours and yours entirely, and may God forgive you for it. Aye, I've completed the reckoning, my lords, and I find there is indeed a debt to be paid. The problem is, you're demanding it from the one who is owed. Be certain, then, your decision is justified, for no punishment is as final as death."

He gestured toward Alex, his voice harsh. "Go and stand with your father, Emma. You go with her, Stephen."

Emma jumped at the ferocity of his command.

"I would not wish to get on the wrong side of your grandfather," Stephen murmured as they crossed to where Alex stood,

"*Athair*," she whispered, looping her arm through Alex's. "Your father is magnificent."

"Aye, little one, he is." Alex smiled. "I'd forgotten."

Beneath their feet, the earth rumbled with a slow steady beat, while the rocky walls gave off a gentle light which, Emma thought, belied the tension in the atmosphere. No one spoke. Even the sword lay silent at the foot of the golden cross. All eyes were on Francis, who stood poised like a great bird, surveying the Guardians with a dark expression.

"There will be no further discussion," he said at last,

raising his chin. "The Circle's decision must be immediate and unanimous. So, if anyone still believes Alexander's life is forfeit according to the sacred scrolls, you must take up the sword and finish him now. No one will stand in your way."

Ice-cold shock chilled Emma's skin as she stepped forward. "Oh, nay, *Seanair*. You cannot –"

"Be silent, child, or I shall have you removed from the chamber," Francis snapped, glaring at her with such ferocity that she shrank back to stand at Alex's side.

For a few moments, no one moved. Emma's breathing slowed, as did the rapid thud of her heart. Then she saw a hand reach across the black granite, grasp the hilt of the sword, and lift it from the table. The Guardian raised the blade in front of him and looked over at Alex.

Finn.

No one spoke as the Irish knight made his way around the table, his expression determined, his dark eyes glittering. Emma shivered and felt Stephen tense at her side.

"Easy, young knight," Alex muttered. "Do nothing."

Finn stopped an arm's length away, the sword resting in his right hand. Emma saw the hilt glowing beneath his fingers.

"Not you, Finn," she whispered. "Please. Don't hurt him."

Finn pressed his lips to the glowing silver hilt and ran a fingertip along the blade. Then his gaze locked with hers. "'Twill be painless, *mo chailín*, I promise."

"Jesus Christ, Finn," Stephen muttered, wrapping an arm around Emma. "Think about this."

"I've thought of naught else for four days," he said, flipping the sword over and presenting the hilt to Alex. "I believe this belongs to you, my Lord Mathanach."

Chapter 31

Snow was falling on Black Combe, large feather-like flakes that swirled and danced in the wind as they tumbled from fat winter clouds. The ancient stones challenged the ghostly deluge like a circle of dark sentinels, guarding their secrets as they had for several millennia.

Emma filled her lungs with brisk morning air, blinked snow from her lashes and set heels to her horse, keeping stride with the three other riders.

Soon the giant monoliths disappeared behind a curtain of white. Above the riders, a crow cut a determined path through the air, silent and watchful, following their trail across the bleak countryside.

"Are you warm enough, little one?"

Emma glanced at Stephen and nodded. "The cold cannot touch me today. I'm protected by a warm shield of happiness."

Stephen laughed. "Aye, I see it reflected in your smile."

"Thank God for my grandfather."

"And Finn. What a gesture. I was sure he meant to strike Alex down where he stood."

"So was I." Emma smothered a sigh and twisted her fingers through the coarse mane of her horse. Stephen had unwittingly found a weak spot in her shield of happiness.

Despite his noble salute to Alex, Finn continued to maintain a level of aloofness toward Emma and it saddened her.

"Why does he behave so?" she'd asked Keir as she was preparing to leave. "Does he still resent me?"

"Far from it." Keir smiled. "He has much to say, but will only come to you when the time is right. You'll see. In the meantime, go with God, my lady."

They left the magical realm different to the way they found it. As a result of Francis's argument, the Circle had agreed to revisit some of the ancient laws. They acknowledged the stone's power was far-reaching and often unpredictable. It was not only the stone which merited protection, but the welfare of the Guardians themselves.

The Guardians.

Emma looked ahead to where Alex and Francis rode side-by-side, tears of pride stinging her eyes. To think she was descended from these men and carried their blood in her veins. A prickle ran across her scalp at the thought of such a heritage. There was still so much to learn, so much to discover. The stone that sat at her father's side held more than the mysteries of the stars; it held the key to her very life, her existence. Even now she felt the tangible connection, knowing it had always been there, cloaked in familiarity.

A child, after all, had no cause to question its fingers and toes. Such was Emma's bond with the strange jewel in the sword. Only recently had she recognized the miracle of it.

She remained immersed in similar thoughts until they reached the quiet of the forest. Here, where bare branches cut the wind, snow floated down unmolested. Only the soft fall of horses' hooves disturbed the peace, a disparity that pulled her from the depths of thought. Content to be almost home, she held out her hand and watched snowflakes settle on her fingers.

"Beautiful," she murmured as the delicate shapes melted against the warmth of her skin.

"Aye." Stephen reached across, wrapped his fingers around hers and brought the palm of her hand to his mouth. "Beautiful indeed."

"'Twas just over there where I found you." She gestured through the trees. "It seems so long ago now."

"Much has happened since." Stephen sighed. "But not

a day goes by that I don't thank God for sending you to me. When I saw you standing there, my little forest faerie, I knew I was both found and lost at the same time."

"Is that so?" Emma wrinkled her nose at him. "As I recall, you alluded to not having enough blood left for an arousal. Such insolence. You're fortunate I didn't leave you to your fate."

"I can't believe I said that." He grinned. "I was obviously delirious. I only have to look at you to –"

"We can hear every word you say." Francis twisted around in his saddle and gave them a stern look. "And we have heard enough."

Stephen grimaced. "Apologies, my lord."

"Aye, well, the sooner you two marry, the better, I think." He turned back, but not before Emma saw the smile tugging at his lips.

"I agree," Stephen replied, his eyes on Emma. "Wholeheartedly."

They reined in their horses at the edge of the clearing and looked down at the house. It was a peaceful scene, belying any indication of the drama that had so recently unfolded there. Smoke spiralled up from the chimney, the smell of woodsmoke pungent in the air. Around the clearing, chickens fluffed their feathers against the cold and scratched for meagre pickings in the snow-covered earth. The crow, which had stayed with them the entire journey, settled itself on the roof of the barn and gave a loud caw. Its raucous announcement was followed by a familiar whinny from the barn and the loud bang of a hoof against wood.

"Welcome to our home, my lord Father," said Alex. "This is where I raised Emma."

"Hmm. 'Tis very...quaint," Francis replied, arching a brow. "And I can't believe you still have that damn horse."

Alex chuckled. "A wondrous beast he is, impervious even to the Devil's malice."

In an apparent response to Bart's clamour, the cottage door flew open and Althena stepped out, tossing back her long dark hair and pulling a shawl around her shoulders. She looked over at them, hands flying to her face as she dropped to her knees, her cry of relief echoing through the trees.

"Ach, my poor wee lass," Alex murmured and urged his horse forward.

Emma started to follow, but Francis reached over and grabbed her reins.

"Nay," he said. "Not yet."

Alex rode to where Althena knelt, slid from the saddle and lifted her from the ground. He wrapped his cloak around her, drawing her close. Although they could not hear his words, the soothing inflection of his voice was quite plain. She clung to him, her sobs carrying through the bitter air.

"God forgive me," said Emma, swallowing against the thickness in her throat. "I forgot how she must have suffered these past days all alone, wondering if he still lived."

"I'm sure she's been on Alexander's mind too," Francis observed. "He loves her very much."

"I pray he'll find some peace now," said Stephen.

Emma exchanged a knowing glance with Francis, who smiled.

"I believe that day is coming, lad," he said, spurring his horse forward. "And right soon."

~o~

It was a night of quiet celebration beneath the cozy

thatched roof. Candles burned, logs crackled, ale flowed and stew bubbled in a pot over the fire.

Alex sat at the table, his arm around Althena. Occasionally, she closed her eyes and rested her head against his shoulder. She had lost weight, and her face, though lit with obvious relief, bore shadows of fatigue. Alex had all but spoon-fed her two bowls of stew until she protested, laughing, that she would burst if she ate one more mouthful.

Francis sat across from them, leaning back in his chair, thumbs hooked through his belt, a contented flush upon his cheeks. Emma sat on a warm sheepskin next to the fire, enfolded in Stephen's arms.

"I'm so happy to be home," she said, savouring the warmth and security of Stephen's embrace.

"As am I," he murmured, trailing kisses across her hair.

"I'll admit the place has charm." Francis glanced around the room. "But you need more space, Alexander. Perhaps this arrangement worked for you and Emma, but your little family has grown."

Emma sat up. "Well, I love it here and would not want to live elsewhere."

"Then I suppose I shall have to consider enlarging our little cottage." Alex pressed a kiss to Althena's cheek. "Would you approve of such a plan, my lady?"

Althena nodded, her eyes bright. "As long as I'm at your side, Alexander. 'Tis all I need."

"'Tis a blessing to have you there, bonny lass. I'm a fortunate man. And what of you, Father? Will you stay be staying with us as well?"

"I should like to, at least for a while. Riderch asked for my help re-writing some of our laws and I was happy to accept." He winked at Emma. "I wish to spend time with my great-grandchildren when they arrive. 'Tis a new beginning for us all, I feel."

Alex sat back, his expression hardening. "Aye, and that said, I intend to tear down the old keep. I've no desire to live in its evil shadow."

Francis frowned. "It doesn't belong to you."

"It sits on crown land, so I'll need permission from Henry." Alex grinned. "I'll get Finn to persuade him."

"'Tis a fitting tomb for Argante." Stephen pulled Emma back against his chest. "I hope the rats have feasted well."

Emma shivered. "How did he become so evil?"

"Argante was always evil," said Alex. "Though at the end he was utterly deranged. I don't know what devilish power possessed him."

"He was filled with hate," said Francis. "The stone responds to strong emotion, good or bad. I suspect it affected Argante somehow."

"Yet I wonder if we should not hold some measure of pity for him," said Emma. "His was such a desolate soul."

"Pity?" Stephen spat in the fire. "After what he did? Never. Hell is too good for the likes of that bastard."

"I agree with you, young knight." Alex sighed. "I've no regrets about killing Argante. I only wish I'd acted sooner. Things would have been very different."

"You have more than made restitution for anything you did or did not do." Francis leaned forward. "Stop torturing yourself. The past has been met and dealt with."

Not entirely.

Emma saw the skin tighten around her father's eyes. Francis saw it too, and exchanged glances with her.

"Well, I feel like some fresh air," he said, pushing his chair back. "I wonder if my granddaughter might give me a tour of my son's extensive property. I should go and pat Bart on the nose as well."

Emma giggled and rose to her feet. "It would be my

great honour, *Seanair*. Since the property is so extensive, I should warn you the tour might take some time."

He grinned. "Will we need horses?"

Alex laughed. "Enough of your mockery. Don't stay out there too long. 'Tis a bitter night."

"The next full moon?" Francis asked as the cottage door closed behind them.

Emma looked up at the clouds. "Aye. About seven days, I should think."

"I pray for a clear night," he said, following her gaze.

"As do I, although it matters not. Rain, snow or storm, that was the night agreed upon. I doubt there'll be another chance."

~o~

Francis's prayer was answered. Seven days later saw a night cold and clear. A full moon hung overhead, carpeting the frozen earth with silver light. The ground crunched beneath their feet and their breath clouded around their heads. Emma's stomach fluttered with anticipation.

"You said you wished to discuss something with me, daughter," said Alex, "yet you've said little since we left the house. What's on your mind?"

She sighed, nudged by a sense of guilt for misleading him. "You are, *Athair*."

"Me? Why? Is something wrong?"

"Nay, nothing is wrong. There's something I want to show you."

"What is it?"

"You'll have to wait and see."

"Hmm. A mystery." He rested a hand on her shoulder. "Do I merit a clue perhaps?"

She shook her head. "Nay. No clues. We'll be there

soon enough."

He fell silent, but Emma sensed his eyes on her. Finally, he spoke,

"You're as skittish as a spring hare. Tell me why. What is it you fear?"

"I don't fear anything," she replied, steering Alex onto a darker, more narrow track, trying desperately to cover the tremble of emotion in her voice.

"This trail leads to the sacred oak." Alex squinted into the woods ahead of them. "Is that our destination?"

"Your destination." She stopped at the edge of the path. "Not mine. I shall wait here until you return."

"What?" He tilted his head, moonlight reflecting in the silver flecks of his eyes. "I don't understand. What's going on? Why can't you come with me?"

"Because I haven't been invited." Emma looked up through the leafless trees to where the stars shimmered. "You must go alone."

He shook his head and glanced around him. "And leave you here unprotected? I think not, little one."

"I'm not unprotected." She smiled and patted her sword. "I swear to you, I'm in no danger."

"Then tell me what this is about." His jaw firmed. "Or we'll still be standing here when the sun rises."

Emma ran her fingers over the stubble on his chin. "This is about you, my precious *Cùra*, my beloved father. It is about your past and your future. I cannot...nay, I will not say more than that. We'll have much to discuss on the way home. For now, please don't fear for me. I'll be quite safe, I promise. There's magic at work in the forest tonight. Do you not feel it?"

Eyes narrowing, Alex studied her for a moment. "What awaits me in that quiet glade? Will you tell me that?"

Not what, but who.

"I will not."

"As I thought." He looked to the moonlit trail ahead. "Very well, against my better judgement, I shall play along with this mysterious venture of yours. But, daughter, if you're not here when I return..."

Emma smiled, stood on tiptoes, and pressed a kiss to his cheek. "Trust me, *Athair*."

With a mumbled curse and a soft shake of his head, he stepped into the night's dark cloak, leaving her alone. Nothing disturbed the crisp, cold air save the pale clouds of her breath. The wild creatures were still, the woods silent, yet behind the peaceful facade Emma felt the stirring of an unearthly realm.

A perfect night for miracles.

As if to sustain her thought, a voice she had longed to hear carried from the shadows.

"What does await him in that quiet glade?"

A sudden rush of relief forced a sob into Emma's throat. "Peace of mind, I hope."

"Then I pray he finds it."

"Have you found it, Finn?"

"Not yet."

He stepped into the moonlight, his skin glowing and eyes afire.

Emma's voice wavered. "Why does it elude you?"

"Because I ignored my heart and wronged someone I love." He looked off in the direction Alex had taken. "At the time of their greatest need, I betrayed their trust. It troubles me immeasurably."

She followed his gaze, a twinge of pain twisting beneath her ribs. "My father bears you no grudge. You know that."

"Aye, but I'm not talking about your father." Finn turned back to her, his expression taut with anguish. "I was crippled by my beliefs, Emma. Bound by them. They held me captive and I couldn't free myself, even though my heart demanded release. I heard your cry for help and ignored it. I failed you and went back on my word. I deserve nothing less than your anger and scorn, but I desire your forgiveness."

He touched her cheek. "Why do you weep, little one? What compels these tears of yours? Are they for your father, or for me? Please say they're for me. Say you still care for a foolish Irish knight. Lie, if you must. Please, *mo chailín*, tell me I haven't lost your respect, that you might one day trust me again, and –"

"Stop." Emma wrapped her fingers around his. "My tears are compelled by happiness, Finn. Keir told me you were conflicted, explained how you suffered. I was afraid too - afraid I'd lost your friendship, something I value very much. Of course I forgive you, willingly and with my whole heart. Truth is, I can't tell you how pleased I am to see you."

He exhaled and kissed the back of her hand. "*Pie Jesú*. I cannot tell you how pleased I am to hear it, my lady."

"We must put the past aside." She gestured down the path. "As I hope my father will do after this night. Will you wait with me? Until he returns?"

"Of course." He tapped a finger to his temple. "Francis told me you'd be alone out here. I know I have to prove it to you, but I renew my vow to be at your side whenever you have need of me."

"Then I'm blessed, my lord," she said, looping her arm through his. "So, now we're friends again, will you please come to the wedding? We're to be married a week tomorrow at the local church. I know Stephen will want you there, and I certainly do."

Finn scratched his head. "Well, now, that all depends."

Emma frowned. "On what?"

"On how refined a celebration it will be."

"How refined?" She shook her head. "I don't understand."

"Ach, *mo chailín*. The cold night air is numbing your brain. I shall attend your marriage to Lord Stephen De Montfort under one condition."

"Which is?"

"That you promise me a full night of drinking and fighting."

Beneath a canopy of stars, the Cumbrian forest echoed with laughter.

Chapter 32

The oak was a tangled silhouette against the sky, its naked branches laden with a fine coat of moonlit frost. Alex paused at the edge of the clearing, his eyes scanning the perimeter. Nothing moved, yet something intangible infused the cold air and tingled on his skin. More from habit than readiness, he fingered the hilt of his sword and approached the ancient tree.

He looked down at the broken pieces of granite lying among the twisted roots, a testament to the tree's victorious struggle to survive. Then he lifted his eyes to the heavens and eternity.

"What now, Emma?" he murmured.

A whisper brushed against his ear. "Alexander."

Dear God. Did he dream? Had a wandering spell cast itself upon him? This was, after all, a magical place, a place of spirits. Maybe he'd imagined it. Maybe it was only a wisp of wind through the trees.

He held his breath.

"Alexander. Turn around."

He must have died, he thought. How else would he hear the precious voice of a departed soul speaking so softly in the night? But could a dead man weep? If not, then why were his cheeks warm with tears? And could a dead man still feel the beat of a lifeless heart? Surely not. Yet he felt a solid thud against his ribs. He looked at his hands and clenched his fingers, seeking proof of his awareness, of his essence. As if to reassure him, the stone at his side trembled within its silver chamber. Bewildered, he turned toward the sound of the voice, not yet trusting his senses.

A sound escaped from deep inside him, a cry of disbelief and anguish. Sixteen years vanished, gone in an instant, absorbed by the beauty of her face and the love in her eyes. Her entire form was opaque, shimmering like moonlight on water. But there was no doubt.

None at all.

"Alicia." Afraid she was just an illusion, he traced his fingers along the ghostly line of her cheek. His skin tingled. "Ach, Alicia. I've missed you, lass. So much."

Aye, the dead did cry, for he saw the glimmer of tears in her emerald eyes.

"I've missed you too, my love." The sound of her voice was like music to him.

"But...how can this be? What is this miracle?"

She smiled. "A miracle among miracles, prompted by a recent visit from our precious child. Oh, Alex, such a wonder she is. I knew you would teach her well and raise her to be strong and pure of heart. You didn't fail me."

Alex shook his head, his chest heaving with a sob. "Oh, but I did. I did fail you, and in the worst way. I doubted you, called you a whore. A whore! You, my wife, whom I loved above all others, and love still. It sickens me to think of what I did. May God forgive me, I killed Edward for naught and you died because of me. Aye, may God forgive me, for I can never forgive myself."

"Hush, Alex. You must not hold blame for any of it." Her light faltered and faded for a moment before glowing bright again. Alex gasped and reached for her.

"Nay, don't go," he said, his heart clenching in panic. "Please. Not yet."

"'Tis the spirit world which pulls me. I don't have much time, so you must listen and believe. I bear you no ill, nor does Edward. I need you to forgive yourself, for the sake of my soul and yours. I need you to let go of your guilt." A ghostly tear fell as she caressed his cheek. "My beloved husband, I've waited so long for this night. My spirit could never reach you before. Your mind was closed, your heart filled with anger. I could do nothing until you believed the miracle of Emma's conception and accepted the truth."

"I do accept it." Alex sighed. "I confess I knew it all along, but it was easy to deny a memory I never possessed."

She studied him for a moment. "Close your eyes, Alexander."

"Nay. I want to look at you."

"Trust me. Close them, my love."

It was her farewell gift. He watched the years fall away, turning back like the pages in a book. She gave him her memories of that miraculous night. How could he ever have forgotten? He'd soothed her despair, kissed away her tears and tasted the sweetness of her skin. They had shared a love without boundaries, unhindered by time or distance. His body had joined with hers, each of them needing and wanting. And a child had been conceived. A miracle child.

An unshed tear escaped through his lashes and rolled down his cheek.

"Now you will always remember," she said, her voice fading into eternity. "I love you. Go in peace, Alexander."

He opened his eyes.

The shadows shifted and a shaft of moonlight tumbled through the branches to land on a piece of shattered boulder. Alex nodded, understanding. At last he was free to move on without the burden of remorse and regret.

Aye, little one. There is, indeed, magic at work in the forest tonight.

"Thank you, *a ghràidh*," he whispered, and looked up at the stars.

A warm surge of energy leapt from the stone and wrapped around his heart.

It was time to go home.

~ THE END ~

Thank you for reading! I do hope you enjoyed The Cast Of The Stone. I would appreciate you taking the time to leave a review on Amazon.

I would love to hear from you with comments about the book! You are welcome to email me at allwrite@rogers.com

Made in the USA
Charleston, SC
19 December 2014